Ghost Sex

Ghost Lovers – Book Three

SALLY SWANSON

DEDICATION

To all of my friends and readers,
your encouragement and resounding support
make the Ghost Lovers series possible.

And to my family,
your patience and unconditional love
fill my life with special moments.

Thank you all.

ACKNOWLEDGMENTS

Cover art: Eros by Dan Houston
http://www.architecturalwalldecor.com/home

Cover design: Andrew Swanson

CHAPTER 1

A frosty grip squeezed the inside of Fara Trotter's throat until she couldn't breathe. Inch by inch, the morbid chill spread, and the numbness crept into her fingers. She didn't notice her cellphone slipping until it smacked the top of her foot, but the phone didn't matter, not right now. She pressed her eyes closed and then reopened them, blinking twice before daring to look toward the curb.

Guy was gone.

A tinny voice echoed between her shoes. Off-balance, she swooped up her cell and accidentally hit the speaker button.

"Fara!" J.C. Calderon's shouts echoed from the phone with enough volume to carry across the church's small portico. "What's going on? What's wrong? Fara! I knew we should have postponed the shoot in Naples until I could leave Puerto-"

She started talking over him. "I just saw a ghost."

Immediately, he fell silent.

She fixed the phone while bracing her body in the corner where the wrought-iron fence met the building. The solid wall made her feel more stable, and she leaned her head against the weathered stones. Words as rough as the hewn bricks scratched through her throat. "A ghost. I saw a ghost."

Even with the church blocking some of the wind, the steady Mediterranean breeze pushed against her cropped hair. With a rough hand, she ran her fingers through the spiked angles.

"Dios mío, not again." He whispered. "How do you know it's a ghost?"

She forced out the truth while trying not to remember. "I saw Guy Carver die."

He didn't reply, but the tension emanating across the phone line spoke volumes. She wanted to shout how she didn't kill him, but in a way, she did. That incident verified the curse she carried beyond a shadow of a doubt. And now, J.C. was next. Loving Fara was a form of suicide.

Sick tension lifted from her stomach. The fiery memories of Guy's death were too raw to relive. Taking a short series of sharp breaths, she sought her inner Zen.

She didn't want to go through anything paranormal. Her plan was to get in and get out, just like the missions she used to run, and seeing Guy's ghost instantly filled her mind of those bygone days. Why Guy, and why here of all places?

Thankfully Father Dominic, her assigned escort from the Roman Catholic Diocese, beckoned from the doorway and distracted her from the awkward silence. "The church just reopened. I've got to go. I'll call when I get back to the rental house and tell you what I found out about the ghost bride. Chow." She hung up before her co-producer could even take a breath. Immediately she turned off her phone and shoved it through the small opening at the top of her backpack without releasing the drawstring.

Inside the venerable church, golden light drifted from lofty windows, casting slanted shadows. Half of the roman arches glowed while darkness masked the other side. A few short months ago, she would have equated the symbolic division as good versus evil, but now the scene struck her differently. Darkness crept slowly across someone's life and in the end engulfed all, yet some souls remained mired in the transition. Only some were trapped. Others refused to continue into the next plane. Regardless of their circumstances, they were all damned until someone showed them the way.

More rapidly than what seemed reasonable within the normal passage of time, the distinct shadow crept across the central aisle and stretched to touch her arm. An unmistakable sense of cool serenity flooded her awareness. She closed her eyes, absorbing the tranquility. As a girl, she loved bright sunshine, but now darkness gave her comfort. It was where she hid all of her pain and sorrow, including the memories of Guy.

Why would his ghost appear here of all places? He died in Baltimore.

Just that one thought recalled the buried details, replaying the vivid scene in her mind. Even though they only needed to go a few blocks from their apartment, Guy insisted on driving. She left him waiting in the car while she ran into the liquor store. Just after her fingers rounded the tall bottle of vodka, the car exploded. The incendiary blast left no intact remains, but Fara held a memorial service anyway. She invited his family from Alabama, but either they didn't receive the notice or they didn't care enough to attend the service. The small and quiet ceremony didn't have a color guard or twenty-one gun salute. CIA didn't get the regalia; they were invisible, especially in death.

She took one long stare over her shoulder almost expecting to see Guy athletically striding through the heavy doors then gamboling down the stairs. A residual ghost repeated the same events over and over again whenever the circumstances aligned just right. J.C. had taught her that.

Maybe she was just mistaken. Guy was of Italian descent, and a lot of Italian men specialized in Frank Sinatra chic. Quite honestly, she didn't get a good look at him before he pulled down the classic Ray-Bans, yet her intuition resonated on a deeper, intimate level. They were more than lovers, more than friends. They were partners to the bitter end.

The priest touched her arm, and she opened her eyes with a shock since she didn't realize she closed them. His softly spoken Italian was even more reverent inside the sanctuary. "You see, this church is recognizable right away from its four stone columns, but now only three still bear the bronzed skulls." He motioned toward the closest sets of bones with a gnarled hand nearly as grave from age. "They are shiny from the caresses of the devout. Believers in the power of the dead have conferred upon Purgatorio ad Arco the nick-name of Cap'e Muorto."

"Skulls? This is the church of skulls." Her senses were clearing, and she recognized the Byzantine architecture surrounding the rows of simple wooden chairs. Centuries ago, the area would have been open, and the parishioners stood or knelt on the hard floor throughout the mass. "That's why the Cult of the Dead meets here?"

"I don't think you understand, Signora Trotter. Here in Naples, more so than any other place, the living and the dead have a relationship, a devotion to each other." He extended his hand again, guiding her into the light. "During the terrible bloodshed of the war, many lost their lives far away from their families, so their loved ones adopted the remains of another who had died long ago. The devout believed if they helped a soul in purgatory cross into heaven through homage and prayer, the grateful spirit would guide their lost loved one to the gates of heaven. Now in less stressful times, the living asks the dead to bless them with favors in this world."

"Let's see if I'm understanding this right," Italian was one of the many languages Fara spoke fluently. Even though the priest had a heavy Venetian accent, her confusion wasn't a language barrier, rather a new way of thinking about death, a subject in which she was an expert. "Let's say I helped a soul or two ascend to heaven, then it's possible for one of my deceased love ones to pass through the gates of St. Peter?"

"Signora Trotter, do you believe?"

She didn't answer and approached the marble altar. Genuflecting upon one knee, she crossed her torso and bowed her head toward the larger than life painting of souls ascending to heaven, then added a silent prayer.

Guy was a trained assassin, but he was a good man and didn't deserve to be damned to wander throughout eternity. Maybe that was it, why he appeared here. Perhaps her assistance to the ghosts in Puerto Rico earned enough supernatural brownie points to help him find salvation.

As if able to overhear her soulful monologue, Father Dominic waited until her thoughts ceased to touch her shoulder. She followed him around the gilded front wall and past sumptuously ornate red velvet chairs sitting on a raised dais. A small chamber behind the main altar was noticeably cooler, nearly incased in marble. Dark and rough in comparison, a sturdy wooden slab leaned against the wall, and the priest unlatched a shin-high wooden gate.

The steep stairway descended between narrow off-white walls. At the base of the stairs, a black metal gate stood open.

Unlike the corroded gates in Puerto Rico's Fort San Cristobal, this wrought iron was pristine; even though, this edifice had to be at least two hundred years older than the fort. She touched the metal, expecting layers of thickly encrusted paint. Rather, the metal was smooth. Either this had been recently replaced or preserved. She shook her head. Any metal this close to the coast would corrode. Nothing would stop that chemical process.

As she examined the gate, the air grew thicker and heavy to breathe. She knew it would be stale, but this was different, a combination of dampness and decay found only in places where the dead gathered. And then she noticed something else, not quite a scent, rather an impression. She closed her eyes and concentrated on expanding her aura, which in turn fine-tuned her inner perception.

"Mrs. Trotter?" His voice jerked her back to the physical world. "This is a place of power. Many find it difficult to cross the threshold. If you want to go back-"

Without any further delay, she passed through the tangible barrier into the hypogeum, and the impression of the amassed dead slid around her body, engulfing her in an invisible embrace. Static charged over her skin, lifting the fine hair on her arms.

The ancient sanctuary stretched below them. She glanced back up the short stairway and then down into the lower chamber again. The depth perspective was wrong. The crypt's vaulted ceilings seemed far too tall to be below the church, like fitting the Empire State Building inside of a bottle. Her fingers curled lightly upon the protective railing, and she glanced down, easily thirty, maybe even forty feet. Without points of reference, it was hard to determine.

Naples was an ancient seaport, dating back to the cradle of human civilization. As one culture fell, another grew on top if its remains. Compressed layers preserved bygone eras in haunting clarity. This was a prime example.

He waved toward the dramatically-peaked arches. "Everything in this place belongs to the Cult of the Dead. In the seventeenth century, plague killed nearly half of the city. Paupers and aristocrats alike met within these walls, joined by the desire to pray for loved ones lost, which didn't discriminate between rich or poor. As many as sixty masses a day were observed for the lost souls to ascend from purgatory. Come, signora, this way."

He led her deeper into the labyrinth of chambers, where several altars and tiered crypts segmented the uneasy tomb. Skulls stared in eternal vigilance, propped up in manmade displays, boasting the bizarre and macabre at the same time.

Posted against white tile walls were photographs of the loved ones who sought salvation or perhaps photos of those who provided the prayers. A few tintypes of people in Victorian-era clothes stood alongside Polaroids which were next to ink-jet prints on regular bond paper. Moisture trapped behind cheap plastic frames made the digital colors bloom, like a photographic embellishment of holy light. She searched the faces hoping to see men who looked like Guy, but not one was a good match, not like the man in the church's courtyard.

Again, the priest waved with a reverent twist of his wrist, "Beyond the long catacomb for the aristocracy are larger rooms meant for burials of people of lower social rank, but all buried here had been believers. Yet over time, the tombs were sealed and long forgotten until the Second World War. As Axis and Allies alike swept across the land, Neapolitans sought refuge underground and rediscovered the nameless graves. The Cult of the Dead continued until 1980 in spite of the fact that they received no support from religious authorities. Rather, the Church ardently opposed the practices as heresy and eventually closed the underground. In 1992, the local cultural association, Incontri Napoletani, intervened. One of our most devout families supports the facility in exchange for personal benedictions."

"That young woman?" So rattled by seeing Guy, Fara had forgotten about the beautiful blond who preceded him out of the church to an awaiting limousine.

"Aleri Caravaggio, the daughter of Donna Elena Caravaggio who is the most powerful woman in the city."

"Why does she come here?"

"This way, I show you." He touched her elbow and led her deeper into the crypt where more elaborate shrines with candles and flowers honored the polished remains. Rosaries draped the edges of tiled crypts along with statues of the Holy Mother and others of winged angels interspersed with haloed saints.

Fara turned, and her breath caught in amazement. The processional leading up to this particular crypt overflowed with fresh and silk flowers, crucifixes, rosaries, and statues. Front and center were two skulls in a rectangular boxy shrine. The one on the right wore a bridal veil. "That's the ghost bride."

"The faithful call her Lucia. She married and only a few days later lost her life. Young women come to her to pray for assistance in finding a good husband. Signorita Caravaggio comes to pray almost every day."

The striking woman was youthful, no older than twenty. When she stepped from the church, the breeze caught her golden hair, and the late afternoon added a glow of radiant fire. The unbound lengths tumbled down her back like a satin waterfall. In all her life, Fara had never seen a woman as lovely. "With her being beautiful and rich, I don't think she would have any trouble finding a husband."

The old man waved a bent finger. "Not every husband is a good husband."

"I understand that." While staring at Lucia's skull, Fara's memories drifted back to her own short marriage. She and Jason only had three weeks before he shipped out for his last tour in Afghanistan. It seemed so long ago when she buried him in Arlington National Cemetery, but in truth, it was less than three months. In the weeks that followed, her life changed. She encountered ghosts who were all very real. An ocean of bizarre experiences separated her current life from the past, at least until she saw Guy. Just that one glimpse opened the floodgates to those turbulent years she wanted to forget.

"Signora Trotter, kneel and pray. If you believe, you feel the power." The priest backed away from the altar where three white candles were still burning from Aleri Caravaggio's offering. His movement stirred the flames, and trickles of wax let loose, streaming down the sides to form a communal puddle in the center. The wax continued to flow until the three circles touched to form the shape of a clover inside the triangle. Just beyond the trinity stood a brass candlestick pitted with age, strangely dark amongst the light.

The dancing flames reached inside Fara and drew out the frustration of her flight arriving late, the hysterics of the terrified realtor, and then finding the church closed to the public for a private service. Even her short fight with J.C. about his grandmother quit simmering inside of her and drained into the ambient power of the crypt.

While watching the candles, her pounding headache cleared, and she realized how others interpreted the tranquil, almost hypnotic effect as divine. Perhaps it was. After the experiences in Puerto Rico, she knew there was more between heaven and hell than just the souls of man. Inexplicable forces manipulated the living and the dead, of that she had no doubt. There was power here in the catacombs, either infused or preserved by the Cult of the Dead. Regardless, the force was tangible, what some might call magic.

Skirting the tiny table filled with offerings, she carefully reached past the candles. Two skulls sat side by side with a silly, dollar-store figurine of a cherubic angel between them. The jaws were missing, and empty holes lined the upper mouth where teeth had once been. Her fingers encountered the slope of the skull's forehead just under the edge of the lacy veil.

Brilliant colors lanced her mind, transforming into visions of women in long dresses and men in silken pantaloons. Music drifted, at first lightly with the tones of a flute and mandolin then the rich notes of a harpsichord joined the chorus. In perfect unison, the men lifted the women in a swirling array. From a raised platform, she watched a raven-haired beauty toss her head back for the full light of the candle-lit chandeliers to highlight her classic features.

A singular flare of anger sizzled throughout her awareness. Intrigued by the out of place rush, she wondered who the girl was. At first she looked like Vivian Dufrense, the ghost she helped in Puerto Rico, but instead of vibrant green eyes, this woman's were dark, nearly black, under even darker brows if that was possible, with pale white skin so fair she looked like Snow White.

Fragile. Delicate. Virginal.

With a swirl, the ladies switched partners, and the smile Snow White gave to the next man was not innocent. If the two were not yet lovers, they soon would be. She curtsied toward the tall and equally saturnine gentleman with a soft twinkling in her eyes. Each toss of her head, caress of her hand, and blink of her lashes exuded sensuality. At the end of the song, he dropped his head and briefly passed his lips over her ear to which she radiantly smiled.

"Signora Trotter?" Her name echoed softly within her head, bringing her back to the present. The priest softly continued, "We started late, and you see, the church closes at dusk. No one, guest or member alike, is allowed in the catacombs at night. Spirits do not rest when observed. We must go, but may return tomorrow."

Fara didn't argue. For some strange reason, she believed him.

CHAPTER 2

The limo eased away from the curb, and Gaetano Caravaggio touched the window as if the physical sensation would help him make sense of seeing Faradahl Alecto standing in front of his church. The woman looked like Fara, but he couldn't be certain unless he saw her eyes. Fara's were greener than a cat's eyes, yet rarer, more like polished emeralds. They glimmered with an inner power so intriguing Gae sometimes lost track of his thoughts and had to catch himself. The only time he gave himself completely over to her mesmerizing power was while making love.

A slight smile relaxed his pursed lips. Unlike other women who kept their eyes closed during sex, Fara's distinctive eyes would glaze with passion and then spark when she climaxed. At that most intimate moment, he could reach inside her otherwise impenetrable shield and see her true self. Fara was tender and loving, and when her eyes softened with pleasure, he knew with absolute certainty she was the woman for him.

The rest of her body was even more amazing. Statues of Venus had nothing on Fara. Her form was a dichotomy of hard and soft, angular and curved, built to drive men mad with desire. And like the mythical sirens who lured men to their deaths just off the coast of Naples, she had a magically lyrical voice, especially when she sang. Time itself waited for the final lingering tones to drift before advancing once more.

Their favorite Thursday night date was going to the karaoke bar. He would sign her name on the list at least every fifth slot and select the most provocative songs in the music catalog. Each one, every note and tone, carried her love for him. Even if she never said it, he knew she loved him.

As she became absorbed in the lyrics, he would watch the other men react to the sultry sound. Her lyrical power reached inside a man and made him mad with passion. More than once,

Gae got into a parking lot fight over a man wanting to get a little too close to her. He enjoyed a good fist fight almost as much as the bewitching command of her voice, and she knew it, allowing him to bust a few punches before taking him home to bed.

The only doubt he had about this woman being Fara was her hair. After she left the Army, she swore never to have short hair again. Just moments before he triggered the bomb in his car, he watched her walking into the corner liquor store, and her magnificent hair caught the afternoon light, blazing the dark sable mane with streaks of burnished gold. That was over four years ago, and by this time those glorious lengths would drape her waist if she stayed true to her plan.

How could he doubt that? She was the one person who always followed a plan. Since his return to Italy, he dated countless women, and no one was as determined or as rational. Fara was mouth-watering sexy and down to earth, brilliant and methodical, yet fabulously creative and spontaneous at just the right moments. Fara took the most intricate conundrums and unraveled them into the finest details. She always said the obvious was rarely the truth.

Inhaling deeply, he tried to think past the obvious. So many tourists visited Purgatorio ad Arco from all over the world. Fara had been born in Egypt, and an American couple adopted her as a newborn. Perhaps she had a sister or a cousin who just happened to be visiting Naples. It was possible, but it was too much of a coincidence to be probable.

The second thought fled immediately, but his blood chilled. He wasn't a superstitious man or spiritual for that matter and internally scoffed for even thinking about Fara being dead and her ghost was haunting him. Once a person was dead, that was it, the end. He had killed enough to know nothing happened at the moment of death. No mystical mist or cloud of energy ever rose from the deceased. They definitely didn't continue on as ghosts. If so, twenty-two men and four women would be making his life a living hell.

Though discounting the souls of strangers was easier than his own father, who devoutly believed, enough to bankroll the Incontri Napoletani and reconvene the Cult of the Dead. No one other than the powerful don would have been able to convince the cardinal. Gae wasn't sure what it cost, but in the end, his father was sure he had bought his personal stairway to heaven.

Gae scoffed at himself again. Lazarus Caravaggio was enough of a control freak to come back from the dead to keep running the family business, especially with the modernizations. Aunt Elena wanted things done her way, yet she kept lecturing him on assuming his family duty. He wished his father would reappear and tell her to back off, but no such luck. His father was dead, buried, gone. No ghosts roamed amongst the living, including Fara's ghost, regardless of what his family and the Cult of the Dead professed.

The third option regarding Fara was the most likely. He knew better than anyone the only permanent way to leave the Agency was death. Although they had government benefits, very few made it to retirement age. Joseph Daily promised his assistance would remain confidential, and the $50,000 Gaetano paid him had sealed their bargain. Four long years passed since they faked Guy Carver's death. If the CIA discovered he was alive, they would send their most trusted agent to put him into the ground for real, and they knew Fara could get close to him.

God, what was he thinking? Fara wasn't an assassin. She would kill if she had to, but her specialties were infiltration and interrogation. Many times, she didn't even have to resort to physical persuasions. Her sultry voice compelled men to tell her their most closely guarded secrets.

He prided himself on being able to read people, and the startled look on the woman's face held genuine surprise and disbelief. Hell, she even dropped her phone. Those reactions didn't fit with Fara's behavior. She was an ice queen when it came to business. If it had been her and she was here to kill him, he would have been dead the moment he walked out of the church. She definitely had a clear shot and would have put a bullet in his brain. Clearly, that woman wasn't here to kill him.

One side of his mouth tried to smile while the other side frowned. If Fara ever discovered he faked his death, she would want to kill him. He heard she held a small memorial service, and it ate him up inside. Still, he couldn't tell her. He couldn't tell anyone who knew him as Guy Carver.

He sighed again and leaned into the plush leather seat. The agony of leaving her had finally faded, and now the stabbing pain in his chest was back, full throttle, charging through him like hellfire. The worst part of dying was losing the only woman he had ever loved.

Luigi Corelli shoved his shoulder. "You coming to the club tonight? It's karaoke night."

Gae didn't answer but turned to stare out the window, shielding his eyes from the late afternoon with a forearm. The limo picked up speed heading toward the Posillipo rise. Houses blurred into a colorful array punctuated with light and shadows as if a modern artist splashed paint onto a canvas. After rounding the hilly bend, the roadway narrowed, bound by hill and sea, then a thin sandy crescent met an expanse of hazy blue. Even though he grew up here, every time he saw the coast, the beauty amazed him, but today he couldn't focus on such things.

"What's up with you man?" Luigi waved a hand in front of his face.

"Can't you see something happened?" Aleri had a similar lyrical tone and cadence to her voice, soft yet strong, inviting while intimidating. It would take a strong yet sensitive man to love her. Someone who was good to the core because if any man mistreated her, Gae would enjoy exacting the punishment. If any man did what he had done to Fara, he would kill him.

His heart flip-flopped once more, second guessing if Daily had been right. Gae wanted to tell her and take her with him. He nodded to himself while almost hearing Daily's voice inside his head. If Fara had disappeared too, he would have never gotten away with it. The key was her truly mourning him. God, was it worth it?

When he didn't reply, Aleri continued, "Who was that woman?"

"A ghost from my past coming to haunt me." He rubbed his face, and the five o'clock shadow scratched over his palm.

His cousin eased his hand away and held it gently. "Mama will insist you stay for the séance tonight. You can find out more about your ghost then."

Their distant cousins, Luigi and his brother Mario, groaned in tandem, having been coerced into sitting through some of Aunt Elena's séances. She'd been trying to contact Lazarus Caravaggio every Friday night for the past four years.

"You know she expects you to." Aleri raised the back of his hand to her smooth cheek.

"I don't need a séance. Once we get home, I'm doing some research on the internet." Every waking hour, some part of him had wondered what had become of Fara, but at the same time, he didn't want to know.

The house of Caravaggio was secluded, inset into a cliff which overlooked the bay. Along with the rugged terrain, security gates and cameras kept the complex secure. Gae waited for their driver to stop before he extended his hand to his younger cousin. Even though they were on their own property and in front of their own home, they still waited for the hired muscle to ensure the way was clear.

Aleri used the moment alone to squeeze his hand. "You know many women go to Lucia and pray for you to propose."

"So I've been told, yet those women are asking for a good husband. I'm not the man for them." He led her across the concrete drive and up the front steps. The ground on either side of the entry looked barren since the gardener cut down the tall juniper bushes at his aunt's request. Aunt Elena was being overly cautious since the assassination of his father.

Aleri stopped on the rectangular landing. "You're too hard on yourself. You're a good man, Gaetano. It's just you gave your heart away to someone in your past. By the look on your face, I assume it was the woman at Cap'e Muorto. She was striking. Even though I only looked at her briefly, I noticed she had the most startling eyes…"

"What?!" He spun around and grabbed her thin shoulders. "What color were they?"

The butler opened the door and stepped back, waiting patiently alongside the door.

Her sassy smile meant trouble, and she cocked her head to the side, grinning with alacrity. "I'll only tell you if you promise to attend the séance tonight."

"Alright, I promise to be there."

"And participate?"

He bit back the urge to shake her. "Yes, I'll do whatever it is you want. What color were her eyes?"

With that smile still perched on her cheery lips, she hurried into the foyer as if propelled by the sudden gust of wind. The waning afternoon glowed, drifting through the glass ceiling panels. The angular light tumbled within the churning storm clouds, casting a hesitant orange glow upon the white marble floor.

"Come on Aleri, tell me." He lunged forward and snagged her arm just as she was stepping up onto the staircase.

Turning, she stared with a drilling intensity. "What's her name?"

"I don't even know if that was her, but I will know without a doubt if you tell me her eyes-."

She cut him off. "Her name."

His hands curled into fists, and like a petulant child, he stomped one glossy leather shoe. "Faradahl Alecto."

"The news reporter?" His aunt's voice was suddenly behind him, and he spun around.

"What?" Both Gae and Aleri answered in unison.

"Faradahl Alecto was a reporter for CCN in Afghanistan. I admired her strength to be a woman working in such a male-dominated part of the world. She was in the heart of the fighting, the worst of the worst, Baghran and Kabul especially."

During the political unrest in Egypt, they were offered an undercover assignment to assassinate Hosni Mubarak, and Fara adamantly refused. Since she didn't know who her parents were, she wouldn't kill anyone who could potentially be family. No one else ever got the right to refuse an assignment. "She would have never gone to the sandbox."

Aleri offered, "Perhaps that was a different woman."

"I doubt there is more than one woman named Faradahl Alecto." Aunt Elena shrugged. "She had the most incredible voice. Just made you want to believe every word she said. She was CCN's lead foreign reporter, on almost every night, at least until she was abducted."

"What?" He felt the blood drain from his face and pool in the lowest chamber of his heart. Although he tried to control his voice, the words sputtered out of his mouth. "Who abducted her?"

"You know," Aunt Elena wagged a finger at him, "if you paid attention to the news, you would find out a number of interesting facts and events that happen in the world. It's been four years since we got you out of that mess with the CIA. Hiding from the world isn't the same as hiding out. Your alter ego died, not you, Nipote. I promised your father…"

"I know. Alright, I know what I promised. What I don't know is what happened to Faradahl Alecto?"

"It was all over the news at the time," she pursed her lips and tapped a fingertip to the rounded edge, a habit of hers while in deep thought, "at least two years ago. The Taliban accused her of being a spy. There was international outrage, even the UN got involved. A covert unit rescued her, but not before the Taliban tortured her for several days. The subsequent reports never said if she recovered. You know how they cover breaking news but don't revisit the story to say how it all turned out in the end. The last broadcast said she was in critical condition and in need of several complicated surgeries. After that, who knows."

"So she could have been a ghost?" Aleri's smile was too bright for the topic. "I'm not the only one who can see ghosts. Soon you will become a believer too."

Aunt Elena turned, boxing Gae out with her body. "Did you have a good visit with Lucia?"

"Aleri, what color were her eyes? Or the deal's off," he pressed forward, "forever."

"Nipote, how did you know Faradahl Alecto?" His aunt's eyes widened with apparent realization. "So, the Taliban was right. She was a spy. You knew her at the Agency."

"Yeah, I knew her." His heart squeezed tighter in his chest.

His cousin looked at him with an intensity few women had as if she could reach in and touch his innermost feelings. "Her eyes were as green as young leaves on a pomegranate tree."

"Shit." He looked wildly around the foyer. "Now she knows I'm alive."

"But is she alive? That's the question." Aleri laughed until she met his blistering gaze.

"I'm going to find out." He charged up the stairs three at a time.

CHAPTER 3

The house stood alone on a corner. Under the peaked tile roof, dark and narrow windows stared upon equally narrow streets. Parked cars crowded the curb except in front of this lonely old house. The isolation tugged at Fara's senses. She had a knack for finding things, and something in that house needed her.

"You don't want to stay there." The cab driver's Italian growled from one too many cigarettes, including the one smoldering from the corner of his mouth. "There're stories."

"Like what?" She braced a forearm nonchalantly on the front seat.

"Listen to old, Renzo. It looks at you with il malocchio."

The evil eye. Fara chuckled, low and throaty, which most men called lusty. She shot a quick glance, and Renzo hadn't reacted to her inadvertent come-on. Good, she didn't want to be misconstrued. She was in a solid relationship. Oh, she and J.C. had their moments, but then they had their moments. Hot and steamy. Stormy and compelling. Lustful and entertaining. Life with someone didn't get much better than that. J.C. was the right man for her, a good man.

She missed him!

They'd only been apart for a day, and most of that was the transatlantic flight. She shook her head, hoping to dislodge the needy feeling. She'd never felt that way with any of the other men in her life.

Something shifted across the windows and pulled back her attention. She stifled asking Renzo if he'd seen it. Clearly, it had to be a shadow of a bird. "I don't scare easily. Ghosts are my business."

The middle-aged cabby hadn't taken his eyes off from the house. "You psychic?"

"No," she replied slowly, not wanting to stir up local curiosity. "I produce a TV show about ghosts. Look, I

20

appreciate your concern, but I can take care of myself. There's nothing in that house that can be worse than what I've already experienced. Believe me. I'm prepared for anything."

"You won't last one night. The dead aren't quiet..." Grumbling the rest of the sentence, Renzo reluctantly left the cab and shuffled around the back to open her door. One at a time, she peeled the backs of her bare legs off from the vinyl seat cover and stepped out onto the uneven pavement.

The late afternoon was getting darker by the second. Clouds amassed over the water, and then shifted with the breeze, tearing into ragged bands. An errant current slipped past her bare legs, sliding up the curve of her calf. The sensation continued to climb up her inner thigh and then shivered up her spine.

If this place really was haunted, perhaps the show's executive producer would let her change the storyline. Robert Hartz owed her big time for saving his life, but haunted houses were passé when compared to the Cult of the Dead guarding a skeletal bride. That combination would make for good TV whether the ghosts were real or not, and she didn't need the ghosts to be real to make a steamy reenactment of a romantic tragedy.

"Get in, get out." Surprised she spoke out loud, she swung the backpack over her left shoulder and simultaneously depressed the gate's latch, pushing against the metal bars. With a persistent shove, the uneasy spring groaned.

Out of the corner of her eye, the cab pulled away, and the boys edged closer. With a wicked little smile, she let go of the metal. They jumped at the resounding bang.

She took two steps toward the porch and then something compelled her to look up. Like fingers interlacing, the jumbled clouds knit together to obscure the sun. The resulting shadow passed overhead, and the roof appeared to lean toward her.

Standing motionless, she stared at the house, not afraid, but alert. When nothing else happened, she brushed off the effect and pulled the single key from her pocket. Before inserting it into the lock, she glanced over her shoulder and winked at the boys who were staring through the bars of the gate. They didn't move or acknowledge her in any way.

What was up with the locals and this house?

Earlier that day, Fara had called the rental agent after her flight arrived, just as they prearranged. The woman seemed rational when they met at the airport. She drove slowly and chatted while Fara caught glimpses of the coastline, edged with rough rocks. No wonder that cruise ship sank when it came in too close to shore, but that was north of here, on the other side of Rome.

During the walk through, Fara didn't have time to notice the house because the realtor was a real piece of work. The military's shrink would have loved delving into the Italian's psyche. This woman's nerves made Don Knotts appear stable. She had rushed Fara from room to room, opening each door then stepping back. Not once did she look inside. She bypassed one door entirely, claiming it was a locked storeroom, but according to the apparent layout of the house, that room had the best view of Mount Vesuvius and the coastline. It should have been the master suite.

The house was spacious and in reasonably okay shape for an old rental overlooking the beach. Oddly, it was less than the daily price of the hotel she almost booked. The entire crew would stay under one roof, but she was on her own for the next seven days. Without the distraction of J.C.'s ardent libido, she would get some real work done.

Shit! She thought about him again. That man had become an addiction.

With her backpack still balanced on the single shoulder, she turned the knob, swinging open the heavy wooden door. The ominous creak was so cliché. The scrape of rusty hinges grated upon every nervous system the same way, except for Fara's; to her it was a squeaky door, nothing more.

The interior of the enormous open foyer was dark and cool, but not serene like the church. A transitory feeling hung in the stale air. She sensed something anticipatory, expectant, even depressed, but not evil. True malevolence was easy to detect, and this didn't convey enmity or spite. She extended her palms, sensing the air. If something was here, the ghost wanted to remain hidden, and that was just fine.

Her suitcases were still in the front hall where she put them when she did the walk-through, and she left them there once again. Flipping on the lights, she ignored the ground floor and took each step of the magnificent staircase slowly, grazing her hand along the aged banister. The polished wood slipped under her skin, cool and smooth. The texture reminded her of the ghost bride's skull in the catacombs. She lifted her fingers and slid the tips over the edge of her thumb. The vision of the couples dancing clung to the inside of her mind, yet now she felt as if she had missed something transient and more profound than what she saw on the surface, there for only a moment. The heavens rumbled with approaching thunder, and the edge of the sensation slipped away.

All of the upstairs doors were closed. Aged fixtures hanging from the ceiling cast a hazy glow over the worn runner carpeting the center of the abnormally wide hallway. Mismatched tables and a discarded straight-backed chair sat upon scarred hardwoods in the space rimming the faded carpet.

She opened the first door. It was decent, but clearly not the master bedroom. Leaving it open, she continued to the next bedroom and found a reverse layout, neat and practical. A faint scent of furniture polish clung to the stale air. The next door on the side with an ocean view was the eternally locked room, the one without a key, as if that mattered. A devious smile curled the edges of her lips.

The backpack landed on the floor with a clank, and she rummaged through the assortment of what she considered personal necessities. No one other than Guy, or maybe J.C., would understand the odd assortment. Absently, she swung the handcuffs on a crook in her finger then shuffled them out of the way. They always came in handy when least expected, like when she cuffed the hotel detective to the bed. He might have lived had he stayed in her room. She shrugged, no way of knowing, at least she didn't have sex with him. J.C. was all the man she needed.

In a lot of ways, he reminded her of Guy, similar build and muscular tone. Even their shoulder-length hair had comparable body and softness, at least until the hellfire burned J.C.'s hair down to his scalp. He wore comfortable clothes, loose fitting cotton shorts and faded t-shirts. As long as she had known Guy, every day he could have done a full photo shoot for *GQ*. Even when he dressed down, he had style, just like the man at the church.

Finally, her fingers encountered the short zippered pouch. It always had a way of going straight to the bottom of the bag, just like keys in a purse. Even in the dim light, the silvery utensils glittered. A single fingertip rotated on the needle-fine tip while she imagined how digging into someone's back molar would cause the truth to rise.

She blinked then squeezed her eyes closed. The shrink had warned her how repressed memories would rise unexpectedly. "God, why now?"

Something moved, just outside her direct line of vision. While she was still looking toward the staircase, a flash of lightning pulsed through the open doorways of the first two bedrooms with a rumble of thunder not far behind. If the first movement had been lightning, she would have heard the resulting sound. So logically, something else had to cause the movement. Perhaps the reluctant ghost hoped on distracting her, yet she didn't feel anything otherworldly.

Since the sequence of events in Puerto Rico, Fara had refined her sense for the paranormal, not purposefully, but it was there just the same. She was the only one in this slumberous old house.

She pulled out two of the picks and inserted them into the old-fashioned keyhole, but she could pick a lock this simple with an old-fashioned hairpin. While holding the first spindle in position, she rotated the ninety-degree pick counterclockwise. The click of the tumbler was loud and pronounced, just like she knew it would be.

A sharp clap of thunder resonated, growling like an animal issuing a warning. Shrugging off the effect of not seeing the preceding lightning, she turned the pitted brass knob and opened the door.

The next flash lit the enormous bank of windows. Soft sheers hung limply yet were still remarkably white. The window jams were little more than aged shards of splintered wood. The flaking paint had more substance than the rotten strips.

The toes of her high-heeled sandals touched the slightly raised bevel of the wooden threshold, and just inches away, a massive layer of dust covered the wooden floor. It reminded her of the first snow of the season before footprints and car sludge turned the pristine into something gray and ugly. Pristine wasn't quite the right comparison to this neglected room, yet the layers of dust laid just as undisturbed.

If she walked inside, she would leave tracks, but who would know? The realtor wouldn't investigate, and not even the best cleaning crew would want to tackle this nightmare.

After weighing curiosity against the intangible negatives of being caught snooping, Fara drew in a deep breath and stepped forward. The moment her body crossed the threshold, the lightning and boom hit simultaneously, knocking the power out. Her battle-tested nerves didn't even flinch. It was a minor inconvenience, nothing more.

The curtains wafted, and a faint scent of ozone freshened the air. Sliding the penlight from her skirt pocket, she clicked it on, and more out of training than rational need, she swung the beam into every corner and over the fusty bed.

As if responding to her scrutiny, the air stilled, becoming oppressively heavy and difficult to breathe. Her senses tingled, and aching loneliness charged into her, of love and want being forever denied. Despair fed despondency. It was something tangible, as real as the canopied bed or armoire. Someone was here.

Charging forward without a care about leaving tracks, she opened the armoire, checking for an intruder. Yet if someone was in the room, wouldn't he have disturbed the dust?

Her revolving contemplations ceased when she noticed the dress from the vision, the dress the beautiful Snow White wore at the Renaissance ball. Carefully Fara's fingers reached toward the velvet and silk. No more than the very tips of her fingertips encountered the fabric, but even with that minimal contact, the dress shattered, unraveling on a cellular level into a moldy heap.

With a puff, a cloud of dust swirled, launching its way into the air. She covered her mouth to stifle a cough yet stayed trained on the vision. Like an animated corkscrew, the dust-devil continued coiling toward the windows. With a rush of a transient breeze, the mirage swung radically and then dissipated at the old-fashioned vanity.

The layered dust concealed the true color of the wood. The design reminded her of something from the art-deco era, but this was much, much older. The central expanse of the vanity was broad yet narrow, still covered with randomly tossed baubles and jars. An opera monocle leaned against a little porcelain pot; its connected chain snaked under the masking grime.

Nestled in the back left corner, an aged brass mirror had oxidized. The dark brownish-green added to the illusion of curiously textured bark. Five twisted roots coiled upwards to form the pedestal. Its branches held a circular mirror, small according to today's standards, but back then, all of these items were luxurious. The silvering had tarnished into obscurity, leaving the surface streaked with uneven swirls of a leaden paisley gone mad.

In the opposite corner, an oil lamp still held fluid in its clear glass base. On a whim, she lifted the glass shade and chimney. The wick appeared in order. She even thumped it with the back of her fingernail to be sure and then sniffed the air for the telltale scent of kerosene. The strong scent was heavy but not sharp. This had to be from an age before petroleum, perhaps whale oil. That was probably why the wick remained preserved.

Carefully, she walked backwards within her own tracks to fish the lighter out of her bag. Before reentering the room, she squatted next to the doorway and examined the spoor. The prints cut into the aged residue about a half-inch deep.

In that short time, the thunderous clouds had descended, blanketing the outer windows so thickly the vapor seeped through the aged frames. An eerie silence descended with the cloud, gripping the world in an enshrouded fist; the only sound was her own practiced breath coursing slowly in through her nose and out through her mouth. The room continued to thicken with the heavy vapor, coalescing yet without true definition.

Fara hated fog. She almost was killed while playing cat and mouse with a mark in the fog. She pushed the memory down and another rebounded with just as much strength and resiliency. Purgatory would be like this, filled with an endless gray void. Perhaps with more good deeds, she'd escape the empty fate. She helped free Vivian and Felipe. She would certainly determine a way to help Guy. She saved J.C. and Rob. Yet deep down, those were insignificant compared to her former transgressions.

She boldly stepped back into the vaulted past, and the fog swirled and licked her ankles, physically guiding her toward the vanity. Her heart skipped when the flame caught the wick immediately. The unique jumping glow illuminated only the immediate space yet provided enough diffuse light to define the swirls in the dust the rogue whirlwind cleared.

Oh my God! There were words.

… lp me leave 164 …

The message was still under a fine powdery layer, like someone wrote a secret message with a fingertip only to be revealed by a light dusting of powder, and this particular secret message lasted for ages.

While covering her nose and mouth with her shirt, she wafted more of the sooty layers, "…elp me leave 1643." The last number was a different script than the rest, with a curved curlicue at the bottom edge. The oddity of the words finally struck her. They were in English!

She blew harder toward the left. The heavy grit lifted then fell rapidly but didn't reveal any more of the message. Her stupidity struck her. This wasn't dust; it was ash.

Mount Vesuvius was a prominent landmark only five miles or so southeast of Naples and was the only volcano to erupt on the European mainland in the past 100 years. Fara closed her eyes and focused. There was something associated with an eruption of Vesuvius and World War II. While remembering seventh grade geography, she swept an index finger along the upper curve and felt the texture of the powdery dust. Definitely ash.

It must have leaked through the windows and settled sometime in the 1940's around the time the Allies claimed this part of the coast. But that logic didn't yield the entire story. This room was older, centuries older than that.

The lady's trinkets would more accurately provide a verifiable date. Some unknown power grabbed her hand, drawing it directly toward the tallest object. The flesh of her fingers tingled before they encountered the intricate design of the perfume bottle. It was front and center, as if this was the last item its owner ever touched. The arched lid rose above the other objects like a veritable Mount Vesuvius, but in reality, the vial was only about six inches tall and created out of a bright yellow metal. She weighed it in her outreached palm. It felt like solid gold.

The filigree design was more than intricate. The spectacular artistry of sculpted vines interconnected with raised flowers, some with five and others with six petals. Four inset oval bevels revealed the inner glass core. But what caught Fara's attention was the spectacular lid, of half-arches rising on a queen's crown. Tall and majestic, the glass stopper fit so perfectly the contents were still liquid in a glorious shade of amber, glowing with energy. Hypnotically, she rolled the vial across her open palm.

Treating it tenderly, Fara used the gentlest pressure, but the delicate stopper remained sealed against the ravages of time. Grabbing the bottle with her left hand, she twisted yet still the seal was vacuum-tight. With the back of her fingernail, she thumped the stopper, at each juncture of a half-arch, all the way around, and then pulled. With each attempt, she added more force until finally she pulled with all of her might. The willful seal broke with a resonating smack.

A delightful scent drifted, like perfume, but with a hint of hidden spice, making it more masculine than feminine. She had smelt the scent before but couldn't quite place it. Holding the vial with two fingers on the upper rim, she rocked the tiny decanter, swirling the liquid again, this time in front of the lamp. The deep golden mass was still vital, not gummy or evaporated with just a sticky lining upon the inner bottle. This time she replaced the stopper and then rocked the decanter far enough for the oil to touch the glass lid. She rubbed the sticky liquid between her finger and thumb. The scent grew from the chemical reaction with her skin, heating almost uncomfortably, but it didn't burn. She sniffed her fingers and then drew in a deep inhalation of the enchanting scent. The scent filled her head, creeping through her senses like tendrils of smoke, warming her memories.

* * * *

Incense burned on the mantle, drifting through the chilly air. She and Guy were inside their apartment, huddled naked in front of the roaring fire. The table-top Christmas tree stood in front of the window whose curtains were pulled back, and they watched the enormous snowflakes falling lazily through the night sky.

A carol rounded through her head, and then she allowed the words to fill the room, "...The world in solemn stillness lay, to hear the angels sing..."

"You sing like an angel." Nuzzling her gently, he inhaled through her hair and then blew a gentle whisper of breath over her ear and neck. When she shivered, he chuckled in that deep and sexy way, winding sensually into her inner core. "Are you cold?"

"With where your hands are, you know my body temperature even better than I do."

He slipped his fingers from her and scooted back. "Then yes, I think you're cold."

Bristling, she turned, but Guy was no longer there. He peeked around the kitchen doorjamb. "I want you to close your eyes." His voice resonated, once again sliding into that deep place within her.

"Hmm, with you I don't know if that's such a good thing."

"You don't trust me?" Although he tried to sound offended, playfulness coated the words. Guy didn't let her see this side of his personality often. His smile lit the sparkle in his eyes. Normally cold and calculating, those delicious amber eyes were warm pools of fiery decadence.

"I trust you more than anyone."

"Prove it to me. Close your eyes."

A smile crept to her lips, and her tongue lazily glided along the upper edge while contemplating the pros and cons. With all of her senses in overdrive, she did as he asked. She heard his heels make contact with the carpeted floor and the soft hush of bare feet rocking along the carpet. She felt him standing behind her, and then he knelt, descending silently like dusk rather than a six-foot wall of muscle.

Something excessively soft brushed her left shoulder, even softer than his hair which often brushed her face and shoulders when they made love. The light tingling then swept over her nipple, drawing it even tighter. The skimming continued randomly, left and right, arm and leg, along the flat planes of her stomach, over her smooth back until every exposed inch had experienced the lush softness.

"Umm," she hummed as she dropped her head back and arched her torso toward the ceiling, silently requesting more.

"Wait, don't move."

Movement rustled toward the table, and then she heard the unique whoosh and click of a cellphone camera. "That won't be posted on the internet, will it?"

"You know me better than that. Whenever we're not together, I'll keep this with me to remind me of you." His voice dropped deeper as melancholy brushed his words just as softly as he had brushed her flesh. "Now sit up, but keep your eyes closed."

A luxurious weight slipped over her shoulders, thick silk, and then soft fur brushed the sides of her neck. He lifted the upper edge until fur caressed her forehead. "Okay, look at me."

Fara opened her eyes, and the camera clicked again. Her smile grew as she beheld horizontal silver and gray bands aligning at the front in decorative points.

"Oh Guy. It's chinchilla. You shouldn't have." Hopping to her feet, she hurried to the hall mirror.

"I hope you're not one of those animal-rights activists." He followed, standing behind her.

"With my reputation?" She spun around, and the arms of the coat swung with a life of their own. "It's incredible. Stunning and magnificent."

"That's what I thought, yet it still doesn't compare with you." He inhaled deeply. "I love you Fara."

She was never at a loss for words, but she couldn't answer. Guy's declaration sent a shocking thrill through her, all the way to her toes. He had never mentioned love, not ever; although, their relationship had progressed in that direction. They were living together, yet both of them were well aware love was a luxury neither of them could afford. No man ever survived loving her, but if anyone could, it would be Guy. He was even more lethal than she would ever be.

He waited in anticipatory silence and then whispered, "Shh, no need to say anything. Now come with me." He led her back to the fireplace. With an artful sweep like a matador cape, he swung the coat from her shoulders and spread it over the carpet in front of the hearth. With an outstretched hand, he claimed hers and knelt in front of the fire. With a finger, he raised her chin.

The flames cast a fiery radiance across his formidable features and danced in his eyes, making them glow like pools of liquid gold. In the fine lines at the corners of his eyes, she saw his disappointment, but with a lazy smile, he positioned her lips to receive his kiss. That deep part of her recognized it instantly for what it truly was; Guy was claiming her for his own. Despite her well-fortified sense of self-control, she trembled.

His erection grew instantly, pressing its heat against her abdomen, and the familiar craving jumped inside of her, licking her with internal fire just as much as the flames warmed her skin. She wrapped her arms about his neck and kissed him, pouring everything she couldn't articulate into the embrace.

* * * *

The scent of the perfume drifted and along with the recollection of both joy and sorrow, for that was their last Christmas together. Just after the spring thaw, Guy was gone.

Fara stared at the bottle still clutched within her hand, wondering how the liquid called forth such a tender and poignant moment, where beauty and pain collided into one. She never told Guy she loved him, part out of wanting to protect him and mostly trying to preserve herself. It was most painful regret of her life.

She owed it to Guy to help him. In Puerto Rico, she had rescued two trapped souls at nearly the cost of her life. If the Cult of the Dead's beliefs were true, she could leverage that spiritual goodwill to negotiate his release from purgatory.

No longer worried about leaving spoor in the dust, she walked boldly across the floor to the open door. With a lingering touch, she felt the intricate contours of the antique vial fill her hand. The amber liquid glowed as it crossed the threshold.

CHAPTER 4

Instead of brilliant orange hues, sunset sickened to a brief pallid green, and then night ruled the sky. Powerful gusts of wind propelled sheets of rain into the glass panels of the conservatory. At this time of year, storms blew through with the prevalent ocean breeze. They were just a part of life on the coast, part of nature's rhythm. Gae actually enjoyed them. Storms whitewashed the land, leaving a cleansed feeling in their wake. Nature's renewal. He wanted to embrace the storm and let it wash away his past mistakes.

His aunt reminded him daily of how he needed to move on with his life, and seeing Fara's likeness in front of the church instantly reminded him of what he had left behind. In retrospect he should have told her, but at the time, he didn't trust anyone, not even her. Only his old boss knew, and now Joe Daily's silence was ensured. Gae found the obituary in the Post's archives. The CIA mastermind died two years ago, which added another layer to this mystery involving Fara's appearance. Why here? Why now?

His search revealed several significant details, but he had to dig for the information. Faradahl Alecto didn't have a Facebook page with a "love me" wall of photos. An agent would never go public, but even after she supposedly left the Agency, she retained that same heightened privacy. It wasn't easy following her path from Afghanistan to Germany to North Carolina, but his diligence prevailed. He had never doubted her feelings for him until he found a marriage license. Last August, she married Lieutenant Jason Derrimore Trotter. The fact soldier-boy died didn't lessen the sting; Fara had replaced Guy Carver with someone else to love. Now he wondered if all of his anguish for leaving her had been for nothing, but inside of his soul, he still loved her and hated himself for it.

The rain suddenly intensified and washed up the panes of tinted glass, and debris flew within the gale-force winds. The tall and slender palm trees lining both sides of the driveway lashed back and forth. He continued to stare blankly until the water sliding on the glass obscured everything. Mother Nature was crying for his sins.

The pervasive scent of frankincense drifted in hazy tendrils from the incense burner on the mantle of the lit fireplace. They didn't have occasion to have a fire frequently, but his aunt suggested it would add to the ambiance for the séance. His father used to light it periodically to dry the air in the conservatory, saying it helped preserve their library of medieval literature. Gae glanced over his shoulder at the massive wooden bookcases. Really, he should donate the books to Incontri Napoletani for real preservation, but he didn't have the heart to part with what his father considered their greatest treasure.

"Nipote," Aunt Elena called from the round table consuming the center of the room. "Signora Lucedio is ready. Please, come join us."

Reluctantly, he sat in the vacant chair.

Aleri placed her palm within his and gently squeezed. "See it's a good night. The spirits are restless."

"I've felt their presence all day." Signora Lucedio shifted her unnerving gaze from Gae to Aleri. "What time did you leave Cap'e Muorto? Was it late afternoon around 5:00?"

"Sì," Aleri answered brightly.

"And a woman from a foreign land was waiting there."

"Sì," The girl's voice quivered hesitantly and eyes widened.

"I've seen her in a vision. Souls stir in her wake." Signora Lucedio looked directly at Gae, locking her black eyes onto his. "She is of the living yet knows the dead. You know this woman."

"So she wasn't a ghost?" Aleri didn't mute her apparent disappointment.

"Is she a believer?" Her mother turned to the psychic.

"She walks the edge between worlds. She's dangerous." Other than an overly dramatic voice, Signora Lucedio didn't go in for dramatic silk scarves or gypsy coins. She looked like a middle-aged Italian woman, slightly overweight with hair died a dusky red. She had a teacher's sternness to her face, one that would make even an innocent child squirm under the scrutiny from twenty paces away. That disapproving heaviness poured from her in almost tangible waves.

Gae hadn't been innocent for far too many years; that she knew without having to be psychic. He acknowledged her with a slight nod.

The woman replied in kind, and her dangling earrings swung. She wagged a red-tipped fingernail toward him, visually adding to the effect. "This woman marches the trail of death." The psychic inhaled slowly and labored with an even lengthier exhale. "Dalal treads the path of the Sirens with the same lonely fate." Her head drooped toward her chest and eyes closed. "Spirits come."

Dalal? Gae wondered if it was a new nickname for Faradahl? "Why has she come here?"

His aunt's close friend didn't answer. Her form continued to relax into a trance until she appeared asleep. A whisper, ever so soft, drifted from her lips. "Don Lazarus is coming. Finally, he is reaching out to you, for now is the time."

The fire fluttered in the hearth, and the storm paused with its own transitory anticipation. Gae reluctantly continued holding hands at the table, but he would prefer to leave. Tingles pricked the back of his neck and drifted down his back. Something about this wasn't right.

It wasn't his first séance, yet this was the first when something tangible was in the air, more than the edgy power of the storm pushing its way overland. Swirling patterns swept across the glass, like fingers trying to encounter a breach to come inside. More and more came, pulsing within waves of rain and power. Although the water had to eventually slide down the glass, the energy permeated the panes. The momentum paused, as if to enjoy its triumph while recoiling its strength, until once more it pulsed forward.

"Close your eyes and focus." The psychic's voice resonated, flowing within the dynamic waves. "Repeat with me, Lazarus Caravaggio, we call upon you."

The interior of the room grew heavy and expectant, and the air was so thick with power it was hard to breathe. Filling like a glass from the bottom up, the tension gathered until the world felt like it would crack under the strain.

"Lazarus Caravaggio, we call upon you. Lazarus Caravaggio, we call upon you. Lazarus Caravaggio, we call upon you." Combining into a single voice, the chanting rose, and with each verse, the power level in the room upped by another degree.

Gae didn't join in, so his eyes were wide open when he saw the image of a man staring at him through the window, floating easily forty feet above ground level. Passively the figure waited for someone to acknowledge his presence. Gae fought the urge to leave the circle; anywhere was better than being where he was. Still, he didn't think he could let go, not even if he wanted to. Unnatural power flowed from one clasped hand to the other, drawing and feeding the maelstrom. Like electricity finding passage through a circuit, the flow continued, more internally than externally, connected to what was manifesting inside the room.

Tendrils of the heavy gale trembled, and a flash lit the sky, outlining the unmistakable shape of a man. Large hands reached out and pressed palms against the glass. Gae hoped it wasn't his father, for hopeless despair poured through the room, tainting the spinning energy with despondency.

Quick as a lash of a whip, an invisible hand reached into Gae and found the secret place where he concealed all of his remorse and regret. He strained internally against the invasion, but the touch used his own strength against him. Riding the inner power, it unlocked his soul, and the faces of those he had killed poured forth, forming out of the ethereal foggy mist and joining in a grisly dance macabre. All of the specters' eyes were foggy orbs swirling with sightless vision. The chill they brought continued to wash over the room in wave after endless wave. Suddenly, all activity stopped, but the energy did not dissipate. The power shimmered inside the room expectantly waiting for a command.

"He is here." Signora Lucedio's voice cackled with glee. "Don Lazarus is among us. Speak. Speak through me."

Fire lit inside Gae's body, searing with blistering white light. The sensation grew into a burning force, hotter than the inside of the sun. His heart clenched in his chest. With his next breath, the condensed heat exploded outward.

The scent of his father's favorite pipe clung to the air, and Gae felt safe and at peace. His father was a strict and harsh man to everyone except Gae. He truly loved him as much as a father could love a son, yet Gae would never become the man his father wanted him to be.

Words resonated inside his head, more so than hearing, they were just there, "You are the head of the family now, and your time is at hand. Seek out your heart's desire and make amends. Use her strength. Only together will you focus the power for them to be free."

A book flew off from the shelf at the far end of the room. Another then another followed, lashing in direct retaliation to the reenergized storm. Lightning strikes hit as each book struck the glass wall in turn, and one at a time the ghostly visions disappeared until only the first man remained, and he pointed at Gae. As white as one of Jupiter's legendary thunderbolts, a line of power shot from his finger and hit Gae in the chest.

At that same moment, a shrill scream pierced the expectant silence, and Aleri collapsed face down onto the table.

CHAPTER 5

Heavy velvet, the color of the deep sea, surrounded the huge canopied bed. The fabric wafted, adding the illusion of waves. Fara sat perfectly still in the center of the white sheets, as if perched on a tiny raft floating upon the endless ocean. The rumpled velvet bedspread bunched at the foot of the bed, and its lighter blue complimented the drapes. Where vertical met horizontal was a drifting horizon, a midnight sky above cresting waves. Fara's silk nightie clung to her moist body heat, tight yet not restrictive. The lighter gray silk completed the color palate. All four shades from white to ocean blue had to be on a sample card at a paint store.

The motion had awakened her, drawing all senses alert. In the logical root of her mind, she knew all of the windows were closed and locked as were the doors. Ever vigilant, she would never leave something as simple as that untended. Even her bedroom door was bolted from the inside. There was no central air conditioning or heat to cause air currents. So what could be triggering the movement?

All was quiet, almost too quiet, which made the rapid beat of her heart resound loudly in her ears. Taking a deep breath, she let it out slowly, focusing.

Mount Vesuvius was considered active, and volcanoes were in areas of tectonic activity, where the crust of the earth collided along faults. Tremors, some barely perceptible, would jiggle the land. Of course, that had to be it.

The physical explanation was plausible and rational, but she was trying too hard to convince herself to accept plausible and rational as truth. The obvious was rarely the truth.

With a soft flow, the drapes moved again, yet overall stillness prevailed. Like an insect flicking antennae to sense the air, Fara's intangible sense flowed, not from a single point, but a force emanating from her aura. She visualized golden vitality flowing, curling, and curving along the still air as if they were tendrils of gilded smoke.

Something on the other side of physical consciousness shifted closer, edging forward and slipping back cautiously, like a small fish along a predatory reef testing the waters. Each time it emerged a wave pulsed into this world. Psychic tremors were not physically verifiable in most circumstances, but Fara didn't doubt what she sensed. The preternatural distortion intensified, and with one final sharp thrust, the fine membrane between the worlds of perception burst. Something or someone emerged.

More from instinct than tangible need, her hand shot under the silken sheets and grasped the knife hidden under the pillow. Without looking, her skillful fingers drew the silver blade in one smooth motion. She would have preferred her Browning, but traveling with a handgun sucked even with a governmental ID, but as a civie was next to impossible. But that didn't matter now. She felt the weight in her hand, balancing it within her grip.

The knife had been a gift from Guy, who definitely wasn't a flowers and candy sort of man, yet he had been so shy and cautious while waiting for her response. His eyes grew wide and then met her smile with one of his own. She had never received such a thoughtful gift, which also came with lessons on how to use it to her best advantage. The tip of the blade became an extension of her hand, and with that same tip of honed steel, she spread the blue draped waves. The room's papered walls were blue and silver with shadows dancing within the hypnotic print. Swirling, the pattern came to life, drifting in ethereal waves.

The aural power she had sent out came back with a scorching hunger and edgy need like a desert wind, beading a heady sweat, both inside her blood and along her skin. The unusual caress mellowed until it glided sensually along the edge of her jaw, sliding heat and power in its touching wake.

She had met demons and angels charged with more power than a human being could hold. Though at times, entities tried to mask their capacity, but even hidden, each held a signature feel. Powerful spirits could easily leap from one plane of existence to the next while an average ghost took time to dissolve from the spiritual plane and manifest in the physical. With a slow exhale, she sent the heated rush back into the room to the presence who waited for the growing tension to accumulate enough power to materialize.

Using the tip of the knife, she parted the drapes wider. Taking a quick breath, she peeked out and expected, or more so hoped, nothing would be in the room with her. Unlike other ghost shows where the researchers turned around to find nothing, a vaporous apparition stood near the windows bathed in something drifting between fog and shadow.

Surreal light from the late-rising moon hazily wandered through the windows, and when the hoary glow contacted the ghostly presence, radiance shimmered, adding or perhaps even magnifying its luminosity. Like a finely cut diamond, the silver aura glimmered, absorbing the ambient power. With another preternatural pulse, the glow expanded into a vaporous bubble, and all light bent toward it. Even the meager reflection from Fara's polished blade visibly bowed in its direction. The sense of motion returned, and the world contracted, finally connecting the entity with this world.

The broad line of shoulders and narrow hips were unmistakably masculine. Losing no time, he was intent upon his purpose and leaned forward to grasp the telescope. A ripple of muscle skimmed under the loose-fitting white shirt, and delicate lace cuffs flowed with the motion, falling back to expose long-fingers, powerful yet delicate. He tipped the device downward and rotated the eyepiece. Shoulder-length waves of unruly dark curls obscured his features. In the glimmering moonlight, radiance lit every wave of the lazy curls, adding brilliant silver highlights to the dark sable lengths. Combined with the emanating glow, he looked like the mythical god Apollo, yet she knew who this was. Like something out of a nightmare just before jerking awake, the sensation of falling tugged dizzily at her mind, but this was no dream.

"Oh dear God," Fara closed her eyes tightly while whispering the breathy prayer.

Trembling energy broke over her skin, different this time, like a cool wind from the grave, and touched her central core of power where all of the too painful to remember memories amassed. During the day she denied their existence, but at night when darkness crept into every shadow, the foul became real as it was now. A rational person would be afraid, but when the terrible images of what she had done resurfaced, she realized she was the scariest thing in the room.

Her fist clenched tighter around the hilt of the knife, not that she expected to use it, but it gave her a concrete hold on reality. She squeezed it twice more, moving her fingers up along the grip until they bumped into the shoulder-notch, fitting perfectly against the first knuckle of her index finger. The knife was real, and she was definitely awake.

Testing her control, she focused, and the rush of her golden energy swirled. Her own glittering maelstrom reached out, suffusing the room with her essence. Again, the energy curved toward the manifestation.

The masculine body stared intently at something earthbound, and she wondered what would be so damned important to expend such power to come into this world. With the angle of his body, it was impossible not to look at how perfectly his ass rounded out the seat of his pants. The tense fabric clung to his muscular thighs like cellophane.

Something in her body reacted instinctively, tightening down low. The suppressed need to see him, hold him just once more overcame all reason. She was trembling, and the pulse ran down the back of her throat, nearly choking her. She gasped and realized it wasn't her pulse she was feeling, rather his.

"Why are you here Guy?" Her voice resonated, hazily rolling within those same surreal energy waves. "What are you up to?"

Tension pulled between his shoulder blades, and his breath came out in a sharp hiss. The apparition drew away from the eyepiece but didn't turn completely. Hair hid his features, and her breath caught with the thought of what might remain of his perfect face. Her heart constricted, not knowing what she would do if he turned to her and was burned or scarred beyond recognition.

No other man was as sinfully flawless in life. Perfectly balanced, his brows and nose framed eyes, glowing with an inner light. All he needed to do was look at a woman, and she would melt. Fara had fallen victim too many times to count. His sensual lips parted like curtains of brushed velvet and revealed impeccably white teeth, naturally aligned. Guy's smile was more than just esthetically pleasing; it would light a golden fire in his eyes, one she never thought she would see it again. The horrible explosion had scarred her memories, and she had forced all of them, the good and bad alike, into that hollow of her soul.

With a quick dip of his head, he swept back the locks of hair and turned to face her. Her trepidation instantly dissolved into the masculine perfection of the shimmering image. On an even deeper level, she warmed. Despite whatever tragedies were met in death, there was hope for each soul to find ultimate beauty, regardless of what happened to their earthly form.

He studied her as if he was looking upon a stranger and didn't speak. The dead were mute, usually. Only the very powerful retained their humanity. The longer souls roamed, the less likely they were able to comprehend. Like straight out of Homer's Iliad, the earthbound dead really did forget who and what they were. They were abandoned, doomed to repeat events, skipping back and back again like a scratched vinyl record until someone intervened to show them the way.

He approached the bed, and his bare feet made no sound, moving too smoothly as if something other than his legs propelled him forward. His features shimmered with the otherworldly connection. The angular face was as she remembered with a square jaw and prominent cheekbones. Handsomely beautiful, but no longer perfect. In death, his features were darker and hollowed, which some would call haunted.

Regardless of the change, he was clearly the man she had loved all those years ago. She had lied to herself, burying away the emotion because the loss hurt to the point of blistering her heart. She had said he didn't matter. That she hadn't really loved him. It was great sex and nothing more. Neither of them had any expectation that they had a future together. Lie, lie, lie, and more lies. She was a master of twisting a lie until it resembled truth, but not anymore. How could she continue to lie to herself when the man she had loved stood before her?

Despite her well-fortified barrier of self-control, a single tear escaped and carved a hot and slow path down her cheek. As if the tear was a zipper, it opened a long and thin line down her inner barrier. Like a force too long under pressure, her self-control poured out, leaving her barren and vulnerable.

Stopping next to the bed, he untied the small string at the softly ruffled throat of his shirt. A wicked smile thinned the edges of his closed lips, and naughty little thoughts played over his features, private things one only dared to think at the darkest hour of the night.

A focused wave rolled over her, shivering through her like a tiny orgasm. She knew what he wanted, yet still she had to ask, "What are you doing?"

He spread the laces on the old-fashioned shirt, exposing skin the color of the winter moon. His nipples were tight circles, just a shade darker than his skin, also pale with death. With a gentle tug, he pulled the shirt out of his pants and eased it over his head. Dark curls clung tightly to the ashen skin, a stark contrast, yet in a very masculine way they complimented each other. The curly outline formed the shape of an arrow, and her eyes followed the path of dark curls to where they disappeared in a single line under his waistband. The memory of how she ran her fingers along the playful curls made her want to do it again.

Innately, her body responded, acutely remembering their nights of heady passion. He was a caring and compassionate lover. In each intimate caresses, he allowed tenderness to flow, but over the course of their foreplay, desperate lust would overtake them both. They enjoyed sharing their bodies and encouraged creative interplay. Once after a Halloween party, they played pirate and princess. Perhaps that was his favorite memory, and he recalled those details to help her identify him.

The opening in the bed curtains was still balanced upon the tip of her knife. He crawled through the gap and passed within centimeters of the blade. He didn't notice or didn't care. The dead didn't worry about dying; it was the ultimate "been there and done that" cliché.

Scooting, Fara made room. The drapery released, skimming over the tip of the blade, and ripped into the heavy silence. While keeping her eyes trained upon him, she kept moving back until she felt the pillow softly press against the small of her back. She leaned into the downy softness while slipping the knife into its hidden sheath as she had done a thousand times. The simple act brought with it a fleeting feeling of normalcy.

Balanced upon his knees, he fingered the lacings of old-fashioned britches and slid those long, straight fingers within the tight confines between fabric and flesh, peeling the cloth away from his body. He was standing hard and erect like carved alabaster, while his chest rose and fell with pronounced breaths. The contract clashed within reality, yet the uneasiness only filled her with increased determination.

Unabridged desire shimmered over his skin, filling the enclosed space with wavy ethereal light. He leaned forward until his energy tingled, and gooseflesh rose on her exposed skin. Her nipples drew tight, rising to hardened peaks under the fine layer of grayish blue silk. The touch of ancient perfume between her breasts was thick and heady, changing and morphing within the sexual tension, challenging covetous pheromones to rise. The perceptible forces met and mingled. Conflicting yet complimentary tides of life and death filled the space between their bodies with heady anticipation, heating and brusquely chilling at the same time.

She was afraid to touch him, yet her hand reached out, encountering what should have been flesh. The glow crept upon her skin, carrying an electrical vibration, yet there was no real substance. True to her initial observation, a marble statue of the god Apollo could not have been more masculine or beautiful. Guy was just as ideal but not solid in any way. Compared to the other ghosts she had encountered, his vivid amber eyes were real, not swirling orbs of purgatory. But what did that truly mean? Was his soul trapped or just waiting? Waiting for what? When she discovered the answers, she would know how to help him find eternal peace.

"Mi amore," his breathy Italian was fluid, propelled by something other than breath. He slid the britches further down his corded thighs. "To behold you once again is an eternal fantasy, one I prayed would come true."

"But how is this possible? Why are you here?" More questions wanted to continue, but his power poured over her, rippling with a shudder.

He brushed those gloriously sensual lips with the tip of his index finger. As if that simple touch switched on more voltage, the shimmering electrical glow brightened until she had to close her eyes against the glare.

Wanting to see his physical perfection, she opened her eyes. The energy coalesced, and he became tangible. The stinging light faded, and only a hoary glow alighted his bare flesh, sparkling with power. She raised her hand to his shoulder. The radiant hum still covered his skin, yet he was solid and as real as any man in this world. Yearning need to touch him one last time overcame any shadowy hesitancies.

Guy was here. Fara was here. At least for tonight, their worlds were no longer apart.

Suddenly, he fell forward, catching himself with his arms. Knowing he was a ghost only added to the allure, and forbidden temptation overcame reason. She kissed his chest, shoulders, and neck. It was flesh, yet at the same time, it wasn't. The heated vigor formed a skin-like barrier, and her tongue tasted the power. At every point of contact, the power encasing his skin shimmered into her, connecting with something too deep for words. Soul to soul, they were at last one.

Forcefully, his hands cupped her head. He stared into her eyes, and flames flickered within their depths. She felt the darkly erotic press of his erection against her abdomen only a moment before he forced a bruising kiss into her lips. Allowing insanity to reign, she kissed him back with teeth and tongue, swaying with the blinding force. At times, they both liked it rough, and the potency flared inside of her like a caress stroking from the inside out. The pleasure shimmered, caressing her in ways she had never even imagined were possible.

Leaving her mouth wanting more, he kissed her face, and then his lips and tongue brushed the hollow of her cheek, depositing icy hot energy in their wake. The caresses continued over the hard line of her jaw and down her neck, adding playful nips along the way, enough to heighten the senses yet not break the skin. Her blood rushed just under the surface, and she physically felt it pulsing against his lips, as if that too was an energy of his to call and command. Arching into the embrace, she offered all she could give and demanding all he had.

His shoulder-length hair caressed her skin, soft as silk. The extremes of rough and smooth set her inner senses ablaze. The ache between her legs grew, desiring the same extremes of pleasure. Just how would that irreconcilable hot and cold feel upon her most intimate flesh?

With the spiking urgency, his kisses grew and hands cupped her head once more. She had loved the way Guy ran his fingers through her hair while massaging and kneading her scalp. This just wasn't the same. Her hair had been a source of pride, and to some degree, comfort until the demonic hellfire burned the thick lengths almost to her scalp, but he didn't seem to care.

Her fingers brushed his bare chest, playing over hardened nipples. As if surprised by the intimate gesture, his body jolted. The heated rush played over his skin, adding a frost-like glimmer of color, not alive, yet not dead, definitely not dead. Strong hands splayed across her waist, and then slid higher, drawing up the silk of her nightie along the way. Upon reaching the swelling rises of her breasts, his hands slipped under the fabric, squeezing them with broad strokes. Urgency grew until her nipples were clasped between fingers and thumbs, rolling the peaks. Releasing them with a definitive pull, he stared at her bare breasts, and when he met her gaze, those glorious flames blazed like a feral lion's eyes.

Tightening with need, his body shifted, and his muscular weight pressed her into the down mattress. Line for line, curve for curve, his body molded to hers. Releasing a lingering hum, she spread her legs, making space for him to be as close as a man and woman could be. Her inner thighs drifted over his hips, reaching higher to caress his waist. Her calf muscles graced the curves of his rounded ass while her fingers lowered over his back, sliding along the muscular chords with rhythmic intensity.

Sharing the tempo, his lips and tongue nipped at her neck, sliding into the dip above her clavicle. His tongue licked the heated flesh and with each broad sweep glided lower. Grasping the spaghetti straps with his teeth each in turn, he eased the silk from her shoulders until it bunched like a shedding skin along her ribs.

Fara held her breath when his lips curved over the feminine rise. Balancing upon his elbows, his hands cupped both breasts, and he pressed his face to the line of cleavage, inhaling deeply. Drinking in the scent of the perfume, his body grew firmer and hardened achingly between her thighs.

The inner battle between the longing for more foreplay and the physical need to feel him within her raged. She wanted his teeth and tongue to do all of the nibbles and licks in the way only Guy could do, and yet the need to feel his naked flesh inside of her ached so badly. Just the thought of being with him one last time made her moist with need, and her hips naturally arched toward him. He aligned with the unspoken invitation, and fitting against her perfectly, continued the motion, inch for long aching inch.

His member grew so hard and full until it stretched her inner confines. Raising her head, she stared past those alabaster abs and watched the velvety smoothness slide in and out of her. His hips were careful and slow.

Tenderness and a touch of triumph played within his serious expression. His skin glowed more brightly from the intimacy, and the resulting ethereal tingle was not of the earthly world. Never before had Fara felt a man quiver within her, at least not like this. During the empty nights of solitude, she enjoyed a party of one with the assistance of her vibrator. This was more than vibration, more than a hardened man. Each stroke thrust urgency saturated with energy, exploring areas neither had found on their own. Like a plug connecting into an electrical outlet, the current flowed. He plunged inside of her, harder and faster. Each tingling rush curled down to her toes, taking her with him into a different realm, a higher plane of existence.

Breathlessly, she screamed, twisting underneath him, until she dominated the rhythm of their erotic dance. Her nails clawed his chest while her body took what she wanted, what she needed. Wanting to experience him to her deepest core, she lifted her calves, and one at a time, he moved his arms to position them upon his shoulders.

As if still understanding her on a molecular level, he matched her challenging need, thrusting harder, plunging his hardened shaft to the hilt, and she accepted each invasion openly while encouraging more. Each full contact exploded with that amazing energy, brilliant and luminous, as if he was truly an ancient god.

With her legs still perched on his shoulders, he lowered his body toward her, pinning her down into the bed until she could barely breathe. While maintaining the nearly impossible rhythm, his teeth sank into her earlobe and then bit her neck. Brilliant pain exploded within the tangible energy. Basking in the shimmering lust, Fara was willing to give him anything. His tongue swept in an arch, and suddenly those teeth sank into her shoulder, hard enough to break the skin.

Just like the stories of the undead, he suckled upon her pulsing flesh, drawing her ever deeper into the abandoned lust. The pleasurable pain wavered on the edge of orgasm, drawing even more than her body would otherwise offer. The power was there, just under the skin, beating in her veins. The surge made his long hair flare around his face like a small wind. She felt his need, and it wasn't just for sex. He needed to touch her life, her humanity to keep a grip upon his own. He was warming himself with her physical body, gathering her warmth and life to him to fill the dark stillness of death with a burning wash of life.

With a final suckling smack, he licked the crimson blood from his lips before diving back upon her mouth, but the taste was there. The sweet metallic allure was heavy and in some perverted way decadent, like sadistic candy. Savoring that powerful taste of life's very essence, she basked in the power dancing over her skin, prickling like fine needles. The thick taste heightened the erotic combination of pleasure and pain, sending her screaming toward the emotional horizon.

"Let me feel your power." A caged growl moaned deep within his throat.

By that command, her orgasm burst, alighting every cell within her body with licking flame, burning a path all the way down to her soul. She was breathing so hard she couldn't think, only feel wave after glorious wave of her own pleasure. Unlike a normal climax, this one kept growing, kept surging in breaking swells. His well-timed thrusts anticipated the next and then the next, drawing yet one more from her already sated body. Through that orgasmic fire, her energy flowed, oscillating between extremes of hot and cold, life and death. Her screams broke through the night, raspy and hoarse. Again, he held her at the edge of continuing ecstasy, encouraging each eruption of passion to build into another.

Fara's body was bursting with sexual fervor, and the once unending hunger flowed from her and into the world, she couldn't stop. The craving appetite, the ache, the urge, the lust, the unending mourning, all of those deeply seeded forces came to the surface and erupted through her orgasmic delight. Although blinded by the fury, she kept her eyes open, enjoying each glimpse of his face held in deepest concentration.

Harder and faster wasn't possible, and yet he continued growing and heating, perhaps even absorbing her throws of passion. A hoarse sound preceded a change, short thrusts held him deeply within her, and only then did he join her with a climax as mighty as a supernova, exploding with all of lust's ultimate power. His strangled shout echoed throughout time itself. The world went white, and she was suspended in it, consumed by it. She was floating in perfect bliss.

Slowly, very gently and quietly, the brilliance faded until she felt her body. Saturated with endorphins, her heart beat sluggishly and head was dizzy. She finally closed her eyes to feel every last ride of each softening wave. Power continued to roll through her and over her, each lessening a minute degree until her heartbeat finally steadied. The need to wrap herself in the afterglow and snuggle against him was strong. Still simmering, basking in delight, she lazily raised an arm to run her fingernails down his back, but her hand passed through empty air.

"Guy?" She bolted up to sit all alone on the giant bed and pressed a hand to her abdomen. The shimmer of his energy was still within her.

"Guy!" Panic filled her voice, and regret seared through her. She had lost him again and still hadn't told him the truth of what she had been carrying inside of her since his death. *I love you* remained poised upon her lips.

Flinging aside the bed curtain, she reached for the lamp on the small table and switched it on. The energy-efficient bulb glowed in a cool shade of greenish-white light. As her eyes adjusted, she now realized the curtains around the bed were red. Her heart suddenly fluttered out of beat. She swept a hand to clutch at her chest and grabbed the front of her sweat-soaked Army t-shirt. Thinking back, she didn't even own a silk teddy.

Brusquely, she jumped to her feet and started across the room decorated in warm shades of reds and russets like the sun at dusk. There wasn't any swirling patterned wallpaper, no telescope by the windows. She tried the bedroom door. It was still locked. Twisting the key, she swung it open and nearly ran down the hallway to flick on the light switch by the staircase.

Drawn by an unseen tide, she gravitated toward the door of the abandoned room yet had to pause before turning the handle. A nagging suspicion knew what she was not mentally prepared to find. Her hand clutched the knob and twisted it firmly, swinging open the door, fully expecting to catch Guy standing in the room.

No one was there. The musty chamber was just as empty and just as lonely.

There wasn't a switch for electric light, so Fara jogged back to her room and snatched the flashlight off the bedside table. The beam jerked while she ran back. She wasn't sure what she had expected to see, but certainly not this. The room was exactly like she had found it hours ago. Pristine in its own way. Not even the floor bore any tracks where she had walked earlier that same day. Time had rewound itself.

Barefooted, she strode into the room, and the sooty dust curled around her toes. Swinging down the beam of light, she clearly saw her new tracks, definite outlines of bare heels, curved arches, and toes. She swung the beam onto the wallpaper and recognized the swirling pattern. Hastily, she rubbed a palm over the textured print to reveal a faded yet still blue rendition of what she had seen when Guy approached the bed. Rushing to the large covered bed, she flicked back the drapes. The fine line where the sharp-edged dagger tore the fabric was there. Under a pound of dust, the bedspread was in the lighter hue of blue. She thrust her hand under the pillow and encountered a dagger. Turning the jeweled encrusted sheath in her hands, she withdrew the blade and felt the weight of it. Even her forefinger met the shoulder notch perfectly, as if this had always been hers.

She turned. There, right where she remembered was the telescope angled toward an earthbound point. With her heart leaping, she rushed over and leaned forward. The change in the angle of her body pulsed in her shoulder. She pinched the neck of her t-shirt and pulled it back. The flashlight was at an awkward angle, casting more shadows than light, but it was enough. Two distinct rows of teeth marks outlined the rounded ball of her shoulder.

Not wanting to process, she peered through the eyepiece without jarring the telescope's alignment. An ancient building stood on a prominent point of the coastline. Waves breaking against the rocks enshrouded the palace in misty shadows. Just then, the moon broke through the pendulous clouds, and an otherworldly glow lit the scene. The Mediterranean's churning waves caught the light, and silver streaks swirled with the final remnants of the storm's power. Crashing into the promontory, they foamed and flooded the Roman arches under the impressive mansion. Carrying the moonlight within the supports, the glow disappeared into hidden recesses, consumed by the protected darkness. Shadows shifted, and she felt something waiting, staring back at her with curious regard. The psychic caress was similar to Guy's ghost while in his transitory form. Did he retreat to that castle?

Thinking of him was enough to tighten her body. She had never been a touchy-feely woman, except with him. Guy knew exactly how to stroke her and embraced every inch of her body. No other lover had been so creative. Tonight's performance was more traditional, yet original at the same time. In Puerto Rico, she had given her body over as a vessel for a ghost to experience physical love, but that wasn't the same, not even close.

His orgasm bathed her with a protoplasmic blast. The sensation was like a star exploding within each living cell. The blinding rush was so extreme her body still hummed with the energy. It was like a caffeine high with a chaser of a dozen or so energy drinks.

This latest brush of energy was pale in comparison, similar in ethereal texture but not in intensity. The true power might be more, brushing her with just a taste to lure her into complacency, masking itself as something it was not. She knew the danger of taking anything on face value. Layered complexities could hide true power, delighting in playful deceptions.

CHAPTER 6

Aunt Elena's séances were dull family gatherings around the antique table, specifically designed to commune with the dead. After enduring the weekly sessions, Gae used whatever excuse to be absent from the hand-holding enclave. Every Friday night at 10:09, the day and time of his father's death, Signora Lucedio would claim spirits were stirring and feign a trance.

The most enjoyable part of the night was watching the expressions of the pseudo-psychic. At times she looked euphoric, but mostly her facial muscles constricted until she had a sour face, adding depth and definition of the age lines extending from the corners of her mouth and eyes. But that remote entertainment was repetitious; week after week was exactly the same. The cruel and unusual punishment would soon be over once Signora Lucedio sucked in the final sour grimace without forging a supernatural connection. Then, Aunt Elena would speculate on why the spirits wouldn't speak. He knew she wanted to place the blame on him for being a nonbeliever, but she never said that out loud. His aunt was many things, but never ungracious.

Most of the time, the subject detoured to finding an appropriate husband for Aleri. Once that topic was exhausted, they would all turn upon him, like wolves falling upon a lone stag. He'd endured the established diatribe on how being the patriarch came with responsibilities, as if he could ever forget. He faked his own death to return to Italy ahead of his intended schedule without the woman he loved. There was no way to forget, and he tried in every way possible. He couldn't even remember how many women he slept with since then. He didn't want to know. None of them compared to Fara.

Tonight, he would have preferred the traditional Friday séance blasé. He still wasn't quite sure what the hell happened. Never in his life had he seen anything so bizarre and macabre, not even in the catacombs of the Cult of the Dead. But this had happened, only a few hours ago, right here in his house.

Even though he tried not to think about it, his father's voice kept tumbling in his mind, and he was the only one who heard him. Practical to the core, he assumed the recording had to have come from Signora Lucedio, yet he heard Don Lazarus Caravaggio's voice more within his mind rather than physically. No one else had heard him.

Even though his father didn't mention anyone by name, there was no other woman with whom he had to make amends, well maybe there were more, but not to the same extent. He had wronged Fara and would have to own up to his actions.

His father was always big on quoting destiny, and he constantly said destiny was waiting for him. It wasn't a shattering secret. Everyone who was present, even Signora Lucedio, had heard him speak of it. If she was to craft a message from the beyond as a hoax, it would be an appropriate phrase.

He was back to his original conundrum. He was the only one who heard it; no one else received that particular message. Although Gae wanted the incident to be a con of some kind, he had that feeling in his gut.

Fara was the one who helped him focus his instincts. She had some sixth sense to her, always knowing where to aim a full second before he did, yet he was faster than all of the other agents in their class, which put her into a class by herself. She not only knew where the target was going to be, she hit the heart with the first shot. Any direction and height, even swinging or swirling effigies, she was dead on but didn't like being a shooter. In her own sadistic way, she preferred manipulating and intimidating a victim. She said a quick kill wasn't a challenge and being trigger happy lost information. A mark had to be kept alive and able to speak to get the most out of them. Although Gae was a born assassin, he didn't have the stomach for Fara's specialties, which she tended to savor, yet the woman was damned clever and could get most men to talk without having to spill a drop of blood.

"Lady Dracula," he murmured out loud, but it didn't help him in the least to resolve his problem.

Although his father's phrase to seek out his heart's desire was pretty vague, there was only one love for him in this world, and he had to base all of that upon a lie about who he was and where he was from. Hell, most of the story he told her came from the movie *Sweet Home Alabama*. He had seen bits and pieces one night when he couldn't sleep and was too lazy to get up for the remote. He assumed Fara would never discover the coincidences because she hated going to a movie theater and rarely watched TV. Now she was supposedly working for a tawdry ghost show reenacting tragic love stories. How strange was that?

Not nearly as strange as the voice telling him to focus their power for them to be free. Who the hell was the them? He didn't give a rat's ass for anyone beyond his family, and of course Fara. Now even the possibility of mending the damage he caused her seemed beyond hope. The only personal truth he ever told her was about being in love with her, and that was the one thing she didn't seem to believe.

Guilt built inside his chest, and he blew out a long breath trying to release the tension. He would take anger and hate, fear and envy before subjecting himself to guilt or regret. No, in many ways regret was worse. Guilt was an emotion one earned out of action while regret was more subversive since it was based upon inaction. He felt guilt from lying to her and regret for not telling her why Guy Carver had to die.

Before he realized it, his hand swept into his pocket and pulled out his old cellphone. The photo of Fara at Christmas was incredible. Her alert breasts peaked toward the ceiling while her hair flowed like a glimmering dark chocolate waterfall in the glowing firelight. The alignment of the background flames seemed to grow out of her body, like an aura of energy exploding into the unsuspecting world. She had an inner power, of that he had no doubt. Whenever she climaxed, he had no hope of holding himself back. One night, he had run through an entire box of condoms and still never seemed to have enough of her.

His chest ached, and he absently rubbed the spot. His father was right; it was time to make amends. Even if Fara was able to put him behind her, he hadn't been able to do the same. He needed to find out once and for all if they had a future together in order to move on with his life. He had to find her and explain. If she was here to kill him, at least then he would be put out of his misery.

Stopping by the edge of the fireplace, he stared absently at the glowing coals amidst the mound of ash. All of the wood had burned with the exception of a few smoldering chunks. The gray waste filled the space under the wrought-iron grate and barely cast any light into the room, but he didn't turn on a lamp. He didn't want to disturb whatever remnants of the psychic episode remained. Something was still here, not his father, but something. Closing his eyes, he focused like Fara had taught him. So many people talk about a third eye, but she described it as empowering his aura by opening his solar plexus and feeding it energy from the core of his body. Half the time he wasn't even sure what she was talking about, and it wasn't a language barrier. His English was better than most Americans. Her concepts were just that complex.

From the tender spot in the center of his chest, he visualized the heat coalescing, building into a coal of its own, and then he let the energy flow. It inched forward, hesitantly at first, flicking at the supernatural residue coating his world. Using the flow of power to guide him, he stepped slowly toward the circular table. Four clawed feet stretched from a pedestal formed in the shape of a lion's head. Its menacing jaws stood open, and the pale glow from the coals added shadowy reliefs.

The table's flat surface depicted gladiators in heavy masks slaying lions. The design incorporated an authentic gladius inset into the wood. A tablecloth covered the scene, so thick with gold embroidery the threads appeared to be made of metal. Gleaming wasn't quite the right word, nor was shimmering. The final orange smoldering hues from the fireplace highlighted the otherworldly energy still clinging to the fabric.

Gae sat in the chair he had occupied only hours earlier and stared at the night through the glass panels. The faces of the damned were no longer there, but he would see them for all eternity, trapped by his final blow into a prison constructed of their own sins. He was an enforcer, meting out justice to those who wouldn't receive it otherwise, murderers, thieves, rapists, and other felons whose sins tainted the essence of life. On some level, he should feel regret or at least remorse for having killed them, but he felt nothing, not even in his dreams. One who kills on a regular basis should at least have nightmares, but instead, those sweat-drenched dreams all included Fara. On the night before he saw her at the church, she had been the in the car when it exploded, not him. He took another cleansing breath. She could exact her revenge. If she wanted him dead, he wouldn't stop her.

His hands scooted over the tablecloth, feeling the texture under his palms, half-heartedly willing the power to rise once again. It wasn't like him to be hesitant, but whatever force descended upon them caused Aleri to collapse and hit his chest with enough force to stop his heart. Although he quickly recovered, she laid motionless, comatose. Once the doctor arrived, Gae and Aunt Elena waited in the hall for hours. Hesitantly, the middle-aged man declared Aleri was physically well, just unconscious without apparent cause.

The news filled Gae with such loathing he excused himself to return to the conservatory. He didn't know why. Nothing made sense. He dropped his head onto his hands, bending his upper body until it laid upon the table. The scent of incense still lingered in the cloth, and it reminded him of Fara. Withdrawing the phone, he set it on the table in front of him. It was almost an antique, an old flip style. Of course, his daily phone had a touch screen and internet, but nothing would make him get rid of this phone or this picture. They both held her essence and helped him connect to that moment in time when life was better than good.

If it hadn't been for some lucky hit man's chip shot, his father would still be alive, and none of this would have happened. Gae would have worked through the term of his CIA contract and married Fara after explaining who he was and why he had an alternate identity. She would have understood.

Anger and frustration poured into his system, swirling into a foaming emotional cocktail. Pushing away from the table in a jerking lunge, he swung around to stare into the eyes of the portrait over the fireplace. The Caravaggio men bore a strong family resemblance, especially in the jawline and defined brows, yet their most striking feature was piercing amber eyes. For his whole life, he hated looking his father in the eyes, as if the great Lazarus knew exactly what he was thinking. Now when he looked in a mirror, his father's face stared back at him. Each sin Gae ever committed caused one of those deep-set lines. No amount of candles or investment in the Incontri Napoletani would change that. If he believed in one piece, he had to believe the entire package. If there was such a thing as an afterlife, Gae was on an express ride to hell.

Pulling himself away from the startling likeness, he headed toward the glass wall overlooking the sea. The storm had passed, yet a few odd drops of water still clung to the windows, strange how they could hang there while others had streamed down the glass or evaporated into the heavy night air. It was sort of like the irony of life. Some events streamed while others stuck, and at any given time, he never knew the how or why of it all.

He shook his head trying to fling the memories away from him as easily as a dog shakes water out of its fur. Logic, not mysticism, provided order in the natural world. Regardless of how tempting it was to relax his firm hold upon reality, he refused. The living ruled his world not the dead. Corpses rotted, and skeletons crumbled. They all returned to the earth, each in their own time.

Although indisputable logic made perfect sense, the situation didn't, and the occurrence definitely wasn't imagined. During the medium's trance, all of the women had been so absorbed in the chant none of them noticed the books fly across the room, and the physical proof laid scattered across the floor. Patiently, he gathered the tomes, and after smoothing the bindings, placed them on the table. He even searched under the burgundy wingback chairs just in case one slid under the upholstered set, but he only found the scent of his father's pipe tobacco still clinging to the fabric.

Just when he got to his feet, he noticed one final book nearly torn from its binding, and his stomach sank wondering what his father would have thought about that. The single copy stood on end, and the pages softly rustled with an imperceptible draft.

His heart beat loudly in his ears. Slowly he snuck up on it, almost expecting the book to disappear before he was able to touch it. He rubbed a finger over the gilded letters on the spine. This volume definitely wasn't the oldest or the rarest. His father added this one to the collection more out of idle curiosity of a local family who died out centuries ago. *The Court of Anna Carafa, a Historical Narrative* by Mrs. Horace Roscoe St. John, published in London, 1872. He read the author's note:

> *Certain portions of the narrative contained in the present volume are so strongly tinged with the appearance of romance, that a doubt might naturally arise as to their authenticity. The entire record is, however, strictly based upon the testimony afforded by the works of the standard historians of Italy, together with those of the numerous chroniclers, whose pages tell the fortune of noble Italian families…*

Gae skipped forward, leafing through the pages, not exactly sure what he was looking for until he saw mention of the Syren's Palace. The thought drew his eyes to the coastline, and at that same moment, the reluctant moon broke free of the clouds and cast a hoary glow over the world. The exterior brightness made the interior of the room dim, as if it wanted to hide in obscurity.

He turned on the lamp and settled into the chair at the table, sorting the volumes by date. This had to be coincidence. He read one after another, starting with the oldest first. Those were handwritten in an archaic style of Italian, like Chaucer was to Old English. As hard as he tried, he wasn't able to understand the flow of the artistry, except the references to the house built on the point of the Posillipo rise.

He continued reading, skipping four hundred years and then a century, then two. In *Leggende Napolitane*, Signora Matilde Serao described the palace as he remembered, "*The only thing you can smell under its vaults is the sea. Its high, wide, glassless windows look like soulless eyes.*"

Gae hadn't been to the old palace since he was a teenager. It was a popular make out spot. The first time he had ever touched a girl's breasts had been after he whispered the lonely rumors about Anna Carafa. She cuddled close as the waves foamed against the rocks. The wind slipping through the foundational arches complimented the whispering surf with whimpering implores. And just like Signora Serao described, the scent of the sea was strong and somehow tainted with the endless wash of time.

The power of a ghost story wasn't the story itself, but how it was told. The rumors about Anna Carafa killing her husband's niece for falling in love with Anna's lover had been popular folklore for centuries. The strange thing was every book sitting on the table in front of him confirmed a different aspect of the story, adding individual pieces until the simple ghost story seemed not only plausible but also historically factual.

Dragonetto Bonifacio originally built the palazzo in the Sixteenth Century. The stories of men being seduced and then tossed to their deaths into the sea started in that era, and then the Ravaschieri family took over the stronghold. Gae would have to ask his aunt, but if he remembered correctly, they had a distant yet shared heritage with that family from Genoa. In 1571 Luigi Carafa di Stigliano purchased the palace. His final living relative, Anna Carafa, inherited the property along with his hoarded fortune.

She was an exceptional beauty, but all personal accounts conveyed a vain and unhappy woman who expected everyone to bow to her excessive whims. When her lover, Gaetano di Casapesenna betrayed her, Anna went into a rage, and at that same time her niece, Mercede de las Torres, disappeared. One account said the eighteen-year-old fled to a nunnery, but when Gaetano searched for her, he could find no trace of his beloved. Refusing to go back to Anna, the man escaped the city by joining the army and died shortly thereafter in battle, a military version of suicide by cop.

Gae set aside that last book and rubbed his eyes. When he looked up, dawn tinged the sandbars at low tide, adding a pink hue to the wet sands. The waves slipped in and out, rhythmically, one overlapping the other. Since his return to Naples, every day of his life was just like the waves, one slipping over the other, not exactly the same, but close enough not to notice the subtle differences. Each lost day brought him closer to death with nothing to show he had lived.

Feeling the need seeping from the marrow of his bones, he strode into the garage, past the black Lincoln, and the little blue Peugeot that Luigi and Mario tooled around in while out on their own. His father's collection included a 2002 Lamborghini Diablo and a 2006 Ferrari Enzo, but Gae still preferred the freedom of his Ducati 1098 or MV Augusta F4. With a definitive lunge, he grabbed the Ducati's keys off the rack on the wall. Even though the Ducati was bright yellow, it was still less flashy than the Augusta. He found his motorcycle helmet and leather jacket in the back storage area and walked the bike out to the driveway.

Defiance stretched within his resolve like a creature clawing its way out after being caged far too long. He hadn't gone for a ride on his bike in over two years. Not that he didn't want to, but his aunt was adamant. Since his father's murder, a hazy gauze of protection smothered his life. He was the last male heir of his long-standing bloodline. Just like the Carafas, families had come and gone throughout history, but that wasn't the core issue. If he died without a male heir, their control in the region would crumble. Even if Aleri married a strong man who could continue the family business, others would come and challenge their territory. When a shift in power structure happened, innocent people died in the crossfire. He didn't need more blood staining his soul.

Above and beyond the influence of the government or the church, his family had ruled the streets and defended the peace in Naples for over two hundred years. Even World War II didn't wrest the power from the new don's grasp. His father was younger than Gae was now when he collected the townspeople into the hidden catacombs, ensuring he scavenged enough food and clean water for thousands. After surviving the blistering eruption of Mount Vesuvius and the ravages of war, Lazarus Caravaggio invested the family's fortune into rebuilding the city.

When Gae joined the CIA, he told his father the reason was to hone his skills, but he needed to break away from the old ways. With the turn of the 21st Century, a new generation of business owners wanted to modernize their protection to electronic surveillance and alarms, rather than relying on muscle to keep them safe. His father wouldn't hear of it, but now as the new patriarch, Gae implemented and modernized. As the head of an official security business, he wasn't an enforcer; when needed, his employees did the dirty work. In the last four years, he issued contracts twice, and both times the assholes deserved the bullets.

The family did things the local police couldn't, at least not without being tied up in trials for years. He and the chief of police had an agreement, which they both abided. Each used their influence to uphold the law to its truest interpretation.

Gae's experience with the CIA did fine tune his abilities, but not in the way he originally imagined. It was Fara, not the Agency, who taught him how to focus his inner instinct. At first, he thought her lessons smacked of Obi Wan teaching young Skywalker. She opened up something inside of himself and taught him how to feel on another plane, not only the force of ambient energy floating through the world, but something even deeper and at times more elusive. She taught him how to love.

Playfully, he nicknamed her Lady Dracula, and the name stuck like a good nickname did. Any other woman would have hated it, but not Fara. She knew she was lethal, and he loved her for that too. She was the only woman he had ever met who understood the challenges he faced. Unfortunately, he was never able to share the truth with her of the future burden he carried. He had meant to tell her but never got around to it, and then it was too late.

Just like the growing dawn, the memory of their first date glowed in vivid detail. He had two categories for women, cling-ons and gemites, and Fara didn't fit either of them. A cling-on flaunted her femininity, clutching his arm and leaning in to show off creamy breasts and softly rounded shoulders. Fara had curves in all the right places, but never flaunted. He couldn't really have called her cool or aloof because she was attentive, to both him and the National Gallery exhibit.

She had worn a blood-red dress and matching stilettos, making her almost as tall as he was, yet she was petite, and in many ways delicate. Even with the tall heels, she was graceful, gliding through the displays. Although she didn't seem to notice, every man noticed her. Some blatantly stared until their wife or girlfriend elbowed them into behaving. Instead of Fara draping herself on Gae, he made sure to be within touching distance of her, holding her hand or putting an arm about her waist, not out of the desire to protect her, because she could do that herself. He wanted every other man in the vicinity to know she was with him. Until that day, he never felt the bite of jealousy, but he never wanted a woman as much as he wanted her.

The traveling exhibition recreated the rooms of a Romanesque villa with artifacts discovered in the ruins of Pompeii. The twisted body casts of the victims didn't unnerve her, not like some of the squealing airheads ahead of them. Fara waited patiently for her turn to edge closer to the exhibit and read how archeologists poured plaster into the hollows within the hardened ash.

Gae's second category, the gemites, would have focused just on the bulky golden bracelets and other gems and coins encased in glass displays, but she didn't coo over them either.

While at dinner, Fara stared at her fork, twisting it in her fingers, and then proceeded to analyze how in every display case, silver spoons were part of the families' prized possessions. The larger and heavier the spoons, the wealthier the family was. She then added her observation over the lack of forks. He had never thought about that simple piece of daily life. Poseidon carried the trident, and gladiators used fork-like spears, known as fuscinas, in the arena. She was the first person in his life to question why the Roman's didn't eat with forks, and he found it remarkably insightful.

Upon leaving the restaurant, men in passing vehicles slowed down to look at her. She was attractive, but there was something else, something beyond description, which made Faradahl Alecto mouthwatering sexy. Gae didn't want their date to be over, but being like one of those hounds was worse. He wanted her so desperately yet wasn't quite sure how to ask her to go home with him. For the first time since he was a teenage boy, he was unsure of himself with a woman.

She drew him toward the parking lot and held onto his arm softly, her fingers heating his flesh as if the sleeve of his jacket didn't exist. This was a different kind of hold upon him, drawing him in closer and closer, as if he lost where he ended and she began. When they reached the car, she stopped, and with a dominant twist, pushed him against the BMW's door, abruptly but not too harshly, just enough to get his undivided attention.

Her voice was low and sultry, barely more than a provocative whisper, "While I was in Russia, I picked up a brand of vodka not available in the states." In the moonlight, her green eyes looked silver and twinkled mischievously. She ran her tongue along the curve of her lower lip. "Care to come with me and give it a taste?"

The sound of her voice still resonated in some part of his heart or mind, maybe even inside of his soul. From that night on, they were lovers, stealing every chance to be together, but it still wasn't enough. A few weeks later, he asked her to move in, a big step for them both, but something never felt so right.

And he ruined it.

His heart twisted, and he was back, standing in his driveway, staring straight at Palazzo Donn'Anna. Something tangible was in the air. He had to go there and go alone.

With an easy swing reminding him of carefree days, he straddled the yellow motorcycle and adjusted his helmet. He even opened the gate with the remote in his pocket before starting the Ducati. The familiar rev of the sweet motor made him feel better inside, like getting a lost piece of himself back. Before anyone could try to stop him, Gae fled through the gates.

CHAPTER 7

J.C. Calderon faced the humid embodiment of pure Caribbean heat and closed the sliding door quickly to keep the AC from escaping. This week he started paying his grandmother's bills and never realized what electricity cost. His grandparents' house was tiny, barely larger than his own apartment in Miami, but the bill was over $600 a month. At first, he thought the amount was a mistake and called PREPA, the government-run power company. He discovered the $600 bill was the lowest of the year. When he questioned Abuela, all she said is that his grandfather liked a cool house.

That wasn't the only thing Eduardo Calderon liked.

Despite the heat, he shivered. The conflict ate him a little piece at a time. He thought he had loved his grandfather, but now... now? If Fara hadn't been there to save him, he would be - shit he didn't even want to imagine what he'd be doing. If she hadn't risked her life, he would one day be brainwashing his own son or grandson to do Maboya's bidding after breeding with a nice Taíno girl his grandfather handpicked.

Even though the momentous horror of it was over, the real battle had just begun. Eduardo Calderon and the five other men who were Maboya's human servants were all sucked straight to hell. There were no bodies, no evidence, nothing. The cops didn't even know how the missing men had been connected. Since J.C. was the only one left, he had to talk to the San Juan cops and the Feds, since Puerto Rico was a U.S. territory. After spending hours in the interrogation room, they let J.C. go, yet the next day a man and a woman in dark suits came knocking.

Steeling himself to their questions, he rehearsed answers in his head, but this couple asked questions about Fara, not the missing men. What was even weirder was the man was blind. Not that J.C. had anything against blind people, but he didn't think they became FBI.

65

He took a hearty drag on the cigarette and watched the paper burn in the final glow of dusk. He had started smoking because his grandfather smoked. With a sudden breath, his eyes widened, and he flicked the damn thing into a puddle left over from the late afternoon rain. The butt let up a final sizzle and was gone. Shoving his hand into his t-shirt breast pocket, he withdrew the pack and held it upside down. His fingers squeezed, twisted, and ground until tobacco rained over his bare feet. The sweet and lingering scent filled the air.

He inhaled three deep breaths before summoning enough courage to call Fara, again. He'd called so many times he knew after the sixth ring there was a two-beat pause before voicemail picked up. His heart fell a notch with each ring. She didn't forget to call him. She never forgot any fucking little detail. That was in her genetics, as if she was hard-wired with a perfect memory. Just after the sixth tone, he took a breath and braced himself for yet another embarrassing display. "Hi Fara, it's me again. I don't want to sound like a paranoid new boyfriend, but I'm genuinely worried about you. If anything just text me and let me know you're okay. Okay?"

He hit the red button and then bellowed his frustration into the night, scaring the chirruping Coqui frogs into temporary silence. He jumped when his phone went off to Cheap Trick's, *I Want You To Want Me,* the custom ring tone he set just for her.

"Hi, where are you? Are you okay?" He answered a little too quickly and knew he sounded pitifully desperate.

"Hi J.C." Her thin chuckle smoothed over the connection and climbed on up inside of him. God she had a great voice. The rush was a better high than smoking some island weed, and after the day he had, an herbal high was tempting.

"Thank God you're alright. You said you'd call over twelve hours ago." His voice was edgy and rough, but at this point, he didn't care.

"A storm came in, and I didn't have any reception on the cell or internet. Even the power was knocked out for hours." Her voice was even and so matter-of-fact, he instantly believed her. "When I woke up, the phone was still out. I didn't know service was restored until I got your call just now."

He paused. "You okay?"

"Of course, why wouldn't I be?"

"Because I've been doing research on that house you rented, and when I finally got to sleep I had this crazy dream. Did anything happen last night?" He waited for her to respond and heard the sound of a motorcycle and squeal of tires. Her drawn out pauses infuriated him. He shouted her name, but it did no good. Jesus, he was paranoid.

"Hey sorry about that." The tempo of her words had nearly doubled.

"What happened?"

"This crazy man on a tricked out Ducati swerved around a car but didn't realize it was waiting on a moped. Damn, I thought for sure there was going to be a wreck right in front of me. The dude had the best reflexes I've seen in ages. Amazing…fucking amazing." A slice of a laugh slid over the phone line. "We've had some pretty amazing dreams. Did we do anything in your dream we haven't done before?"

"I thought you weren't listening."

"I'm pretty observant."

Now, it was his turn to laugh, and he relaxed just a bit, slipping down until his head rested against the back of the chair. "It wasn't that kind of dream, but I wish it was. You were lost in an underground labyrinth, and I kept trying to find you. Every time I got close enough, you would drift away like a wisp of smoke." He swallowed, gathering his courage. "I feel like I'm going to lose you."

"J.C." She took a deep breath and held it for a couple of seconds, "You're not going to lose me. It's just this is the first time we've been apart since we became lovers."

"Don't do anything stupid, please."

"Listen, nothing's going to happen to me, to you, or to us." A truck laid on its horn. "Damn! Another close one. A blue Peugeot just cut off a delivery truck."

"Where the fuck are you?"

The ambient sound muffled; she had to have cupped the phone. "At an espresso bar not far from the coast. I'm getting some breakfast and then will do more research. I have a hunch and am following it to this old palace gone condo."

"Did you see her yesterday?"

She paused a little too long again. "See who?"

"The Ghost Bride."

"Yeah, but I didn't have much time and need to go back later today. The Cult of the Dead sort of worship her. There's this one blond chick who's a regular down there. The priest told me she comes to ask Lucia for help on finding a good husband."

"Who's Lucia?"

"That's what the Cult of the Dead named the Ghost Bride. They call her Lucia, but no one really knows who she was for real. They even have this crazy neon sign with that name hanging on the wall. The whole place is a historian's nightmare. There're seventeenth century crypts decorated with modern photos and dollar-store crap."

"If I was seeking guidance on finding the love of my life that's definitely where I would go." He smirked. "So what did Lucia tell you?"

"To hang around a moldy, old Caribbean fort and seduce a man named Juan Carlos."

His hearty laugh discharged the last of the awkwardness clinging inside his chest. "Just be careful."

"Aren't I always?"

"No way." He ran his hand through his hair. "You're reckless and daring." And dear God, he loved her for it.

"But I'm still careful."

"I'll give you calculating, but not careful." His phone clicked, and he checked the incoming call. Not again. "Fara, the Feds have been by."

"Just stick to the pieces of truth as we laid them out, and you'll be fine."

With a touch, he sent it to voicemail. "It's not me they're interested in."

Her voice stilled. "What did they want?"

"They were asking about you." He was on his feet and strode across the tiny patio. "Stuff like how long we've worked for *Ghost Lovers*, how well do I know you, did you go off on your own or did we stay together in the fort. Sounds like they suspect you of something."

"Hmm, what did you tell them?"

He stopped pacing. "That's all you have to say?"

"What else am I supposed to say?" She inhaled a sharp breath. "J.C., we shouldn't continue this conversation over cell phones."

"You really were a spy, weren't you?"

"I'm just cautious." Her voice had gone very flat. "What did you tell them?"

"I answered their questions truthfully, just as you recommended. I told them Rob introduced us as coworkers, and we visited the fort to write and then produce the episode on the Pink Lady." He stalked back toward the sliding glass door.

"Good. The truth always works." The line got that feeling of emptiness once again. A few moments later, she said, "J.C., I've got to go. I'll call later."

A deeper emptiness echoed across the line. Still he stared at the phone, while all of the words he wanted to tell her clogged his throat until he couldn't even breathe. He looked down at the tobacco still clinging damply to his feet. Shit, he wanted a cigarette.

Immediately his phone rang again from the same 202 area code. The Feds must have put the call into an instant redial queue. Instead of trying to stall, J.C. sat down and braced for another round of interrogation.

CHAPTER 8

Where that girl on the moped had come from, Gae didn't know, but at least he didn't wreck his bike. Adrenaline pumped through him, and he savored the high. The heady rush filled his head, which was now in a different place. Something about going fast and then nearly dying were perfect catalysts to find his inner Zen, what Fara called a moment of clarity.

Only a couple of blocks after the near accident, he left the Ducati parked on the side of the road, almost directly under a blue circular sign with the international swipe across it in red and a picture of a tow truck under it. All of the cops knew his bike, and if they didn't, they would learn. Aunt Elena kept repeating he had to assert himself. Well today was the day.

Behind him, he heard traffic but didn't pay much attention to the unending stream of vehicles in every shape and size. Without looking, he could tell what went by from the zippy hum of a moped to the deep rumble of delivery trucks. The sound of morning rush hour was normal, wonderfully normal. He hadn't been out on the street in months and especially not alone.

Although Luigi and Mario were okay to hang out with, Gae had reached his personal limit. If he of all people couldn't protect himself, then he was in trouble. He understood the brothers protecting Aleri. She was a perfect target, unending sweetness in a mixed up and crazy world, a girl who could star in her own fairy tale.

When he left the house she was still lying motionless in her bed like Sleeping Beauty, and the heavy nagging in his gut crept back. The back of his neck prickled, and he glanced over his shoulder.

Nothing was there.

What really happened during that damned séance? In many ways he didn't want to know, but avoiding the truth hadn't worked out too well. If he had just told Fara –

Shit! He couldn't keep second guessing the decision. He just had to deal with the consequences if he was able to find her again. Naples wasn't a huge city, nothing like Rome or even Baltimore, but he knew all too well if someone wanted to stay hidden, it wasn't that difficult.

The opening to the palazzo was now fenced and gated. He personally knew the developer who had renovated some of the old palace into condos and should have gotten a key from him. With one hand, he grabbed the squared bars and rattled the main gate to the residential entrance.

His hand slipped into his jacket and withdrew a thin wrap. Picking a lock wasn't hard; it was all about angles and using the right tools. Regular household locks like this one had a simple tumbler system, but the motion took precise skill which was nothing like the movies portrayed. A woman using a bent hairpin might have worked on one of those old keyhole-style locks, but not today's deadbolts. At least, he couldn't imagine how, but if there was a way to make something like that work, Fara would be able to do it. She was the one who had taught him this trick.

He dropped his head and closed his eyes. Every time when she jumped to mind, guilt chilled his blood. Shit, he had to stop thinking about her, but she was everywhere, in everything.

The tip of the 90 degree pick made contact and demanded his full attention, and with meticulous accuracy, he turned the inner spindle. He held it in position and inserted the second pick. Although traffic was moving past the gated entry at a steady pace, morning rush hour was slow enough for someone to wonder what he was doing. The elbow in the road headed away from him, and he blocked that angle with his body. The second pick connected with the tumbler, and with a final twist of his wrist, the lock clicked open.

Confidently, he passed through the gate and shut it behind him, enough to where it appeared closed. The deadbolt had a dual lock, and on his way out, he didn't want to have to pick it while facing traffic.

As with most inner courtyards, decorative plants lined the sides of the stone path. Low groundcover grew closest to the crushed rocks. The gangly flowers were in the back. The blooms seemed too heavy for the spindly stalks and leaned in the direction of the prevalent breeze. The only species he recognized by name were those bluish-purple irises with thin swatches of yellow striping each petal. All of the others were just flowers. Tiny yellow petals covered some plants, while others had spires of orange growing at defiant angles from dense green bushes. Fara probably knew each of them by not only their common florist's name but also whatever long Latin-sounding official name they had. She'd have taken the time to smell the flowers and run her nimble fingers along the velvety petals. Her fingers used to caress his face in the same way.

Again, the thought of her made him stop. Until yesterday, he never realized how often she popped to mind. She had touched or affected everything in his life, including sex. No other woman felt like her, and unfortunately, while in the act of making love, those memories were top of mind. Regardless of how beautiful the woman was or how adept of a lover, she had no hope of being Fara.

Underfoot, the crushed path curved with the contours of the rocky escarpment, but instead of following the final turn toward the apartments, he continued straight toward the massive arches supporting the palazzo.

Just as if he had stepped off the end of a diving board, he was instantly in water. The indigenous plants covered the ankle-deep pool. The slushy mix of more water than dirt squished under his Salvatore Ferragamo boots. Instantly, the fine leather absorbed the mucky liquid, and as quickly as two steps later, they sucked and swooshed depending upon whether he was placing or lifting his foot. If he had been following anyone, it would have been dangerous. Today it was just damned irritating, and his $800 boots were ruined.

So focused on where he was walking, he had forgotten momentarily on why he was here until the ground solidified into a hard, rocky mass. Surprised by his inattentiveness, he glanced up, and Palazzo Donn'Anna rose taller than a mountain.

He remained motionless in the shadow of the giant building, feet firmly planted shoulder-width apart, but the feeling of motion continued, leaning the structure with a sigh toward him, as if the gentle yet steady breeze bent the stone palace as easily as the irises. Clearly, he rationalized the distortion had to be from the lack of sleep or from reading all of those books. The optical illusion wasn't real, couldn't be real, yet a shiver crept up his spine a vertebra at a time, arching his back as his eyes slid up the empty windows all the way to the top. He didn't remember which book said, "…the dark windows stared across the sea like hollow, soulless eyes. Always watching. Always aware, yet blind to the modern world…" The shock of saying the quote out loud surprised him.

In immediate response, a woman's giggling laugh grew and then quickly slipped away with the breeze, but somehow the sound changed the physical dynamics of this place or more appropriately this time. He could see the palace for what it had been, when this magnificent place called only the richest and most influential to its gate. Where he was standing had been a boat dock, and colorful paper lanterns lined the coast, guiding the licentious to the privileged decadence of Anna Carafa's infamous parties. He blinked, and the imagery disappeared.

The steady breeze continued off the water. The sun was now high in the morning sky. The omnipresent sound of traffic still trembled in the distance. Those daily events were all part of the real world, but just underneath the normalcy, something else was there, waiting for him under the pilings.

A sigh of an artic breath slithered through the barren support arches, as smoothly and easily as a venomous snake sliding through tall grass. Even though the air around him was undisturbed, he felt it coming. His eyes stared intently along the tunnels formed out of the long rows of archways, but he knew his eyes couldn't perceive what was there. Eyes perceived light, and whatever was under the palazzo didn't belong in the light. The curving shapes were dark silhouettes clinging to perpetual shadows. Daylight didn't venture into those hidden depths.

Ambient sounds drifted further and further away until all he could hear was the sliding hush of whatever approached. His breath passed over dry lips, which he absently licked with the edge of his tongue. The chapped texture was real, yet he felt trapped in an irrational nightmare. As if he was really asleep, he couldn't move, couldn't wake out of this skewed reality. Trying to get a grip, Gae blew out a quick breath, and it misted into fog. The artic shiver arrived.

He hadn't shaved since yesterday morning, and the current physically touched him, like how a woman would slide her hand over a man's cheek to feel the rub of rough stubble. He shivered, but not malevolently. The contact was more of a caress than a warning, as if breathy fingers discerned his appearance. Standing his ground, he held his breath until the unseen hands drifted over his jawline and down his shoulders. Inhaling a shaky breath didn't really help. The chilled fingertips passed over his torso then along the front of his jeans. It was a woman's touch fondling him under the denim, as sure and probing as real fingers. He tried not to react, but his body betrayed him, growing firmer within the confines of his jeans.

With another burbling laugh, the entity dissipated, and he envisioned the snaking chill sliding back into the deepest shadows. The physical manifestation might have gone but not its power. The laden force ebbed and flowed with the now noisy waves crashing into the bulkhead, as if the elements condensed and fed energy upon this point of the earth. From miles up and down the coast, this point collected and condensed ambient power.

Perhaps that was why Dragonetto Bonifacio originally built his palace here. In the fifteenth century, the man controlled most of the western coastline. According to the books, the earliest documented atrocities were of Queen Joan luring young fishermen to a night of passion then throwing them off her balcony and into the sea. Did her actions initiate the damage, or did the place taint and corrupt the living into committing such atrocities?

While contemplating ways to research earlier histories associated with Posillipo, unease itched inside of him, again like a caged animal clawing for release. He clapped his hands over his eyes and then grasped handfuls of his hair, tugging at the roots. Standing like that, he stared up at the empty windows, with images of the ghost stories flinching through his mind until he couldn't stand it any longer. His need for another adrenaline fix pushed him through the outer arch.

Immediately, he sensed the change, but of what he wasn't really sure. The texture of the world just felt distorted, as if everything he had ever held *en veritas* skewed.

Inside the ruins, the massive structure held more than physical weight. Over hundreds of years, perhaps longer than even a millennia, psychic impressions of strong emotions soaked into the stone foundations, staining the place with corrupt residue. He practiced what Fara had taught him on focusing his internal awareness, but nothing had ever been this clear or intense. The incident during the séance bared his soul to the phenomena, and now he didn't know how to turn it off. He could feel each and every distortion shiver down his spine when he walked over a contaminated spot. In some places where the trauma was acutely defined, the resonance was strong enough to see faint images. Pale figures materialized and dissipated as if they too were controlled by some ebb and flow of a cross-dimensional tide.

He assumed the older a place was the longer it was able to absorb abnormalities, and these wet, hollow chambers were thick with shiver places. He stopped and fought the urge to wrap his arms around his torso. Where he was standing was one of those places, a pit where psychic energy collected. His body tingled with icy heat prickling over his skin. He focused on the tangible surf pounding the natural bulkhead and felt the physical vibration rumbling through the rock foundation, but the paranormal vibration was even more pronounced.

His head grew light, and he steadied himself with a hand against one of the old pillars. The beat of his heart thudded in his temples, and a hush whispered, almost a woman's voice yet not quite. The sound drifted and then came back. The second time she spoke clearly, right against his ear, "Come, come play with me."

Other than her ruffling laugh, true silence reigned. Not even the relentless surf vibrated into the rocks. The world had stopped.

He wondered if death felt like that, like being in a bubble of nothingness, unable to acknowledge the world spinning under him.

A shot pierced the bubble of sheltered silence, and the echo continued through and between the columns. If it hadn't been for the chunk of pillar chipping from the impact, he wouldn't have been able to discern the line of fire. Pressing his back to the column, he withdrew his Beretta and took two sharp, short breaths. Staying low, he darted in the opposite direction and pulled up behind the next archway in the diagonal sequence. Out of the corner of his eye, he caught movement and aimed.

A second shot chipped the back of that pillar, and the other person ducked behind it, crouching low. Even with short hair, there was no mistaking Faradahl Alecto. With a muscular lunge, she leapt forward.

Instantly, they were moving in the same direction, back toward the gated entrance. Gae ran faster than she did and closed the distance a pillar at a time until they were separated by about twenty feet. Apparently sensing his approach, she looked at him and shock stunned her features, freezing her green eyes into horrified pools. So startled, she rose about halfway until the next bullet whizzed past.

"Shit!" She hunkered back down and cast him a quizzical sidelong stare. All she had was a blade in her hand, the knife he had given her, and his heart picked up a beat. She still carried it with her after all these years.

She motioned toward the far side of the palazzo, silently asking who was shooting at them, and he shrugged a reply. He motioned with the pistol toward the path and held up three fingers. Exactly on the unspoken count of three, she ran, and he covered her with four shots in a fan array and then took off in a dead run. He caught up and hurried her through the gate when a final shot rang through the complex. Hastily he tossed the helmet from the seat, and without a word, she swung onto the motorcycle.

At a frantic pace, Gae weaved through cars and trucks, running signal lights and forcing the cross traffic to squeal to a halt. He didn't even slow down when he reached the turn-off, racing up the hillside while taking the hairpin turns with precision. She clung to his back with her head tucked low against his body. She was the only woman who had perfect balance while riding on the bike. She was the only perfect woman he had ever met.

CHAPTER 9

Fara kept her face hidden behind the shoulder of Guy's leather jacket. She'd ridden on the back of his motorcycle enough times to learn without a helmet anything in the air was a projectile. She wasn't about to be picking bug guts out of her teeth this morning, but even bug guts would be preferable over bullets. Nearly two years had passed since she'd been shot at, and each time a bullet whizzed past her head, she hoped it would be the last. Leave it to Guy's ghost to involve her in a psychic version of the shoot-out at the O.K. Corral.

The bike started to climb the hillside. She automatically squeezed with her thighs to keep from sliding back, but this much physical contact didn't make any sense. Between her tensed thighs, the vibration of the bike hummed. Only Guy knew how horny she got while riding on his bike; sometimes they would go for a quick ride as part of extended foreplay. Was he planning on seducing her again, now, during the day?

But this manifestation felt different than Guy's ghost had felt last night, even after he achieved full form. Even the manifestations in Puerto Rico had a separate sense to them, something other worldly. The man driving the Ducati wasn't ethereal real; he felt earthly real. His breath expanded and contracted his ribs. His hair fluttered against the side of her cheek and smelt of the sea and just a hint of his favorite Brioni cologne. Those were tangible.

The questions raging through her mind distorted, as if reality had suddenly skewed. Did she die and now was in limbo with Guy?

She didn't think so.

Did anything else happen?

Just to be sure, she started running through the timeline of her morning. She ate breakfast while on the phone with J.C. who told her the Feds were asking about her. They probably assumed she mentally snapped and killed the men in Puerto Rico. Could they be the ones shooting at her?

He leaned into a hairpin turn, and she balanced with him, relaxing her left arm while tightening with her right. She heard of physical ghostly manifestations, but nothing this extreme. Under the supple leather, the shoulder holster and the bulk of the Berretta were on his right since he was a lefty. Guy always had a gun on him. That wasn't the strange part; she would expect even in purgatory he would still have a gun in some shape or form. After what she had experienced, nothing would surprise her in that regard. The dead had to be resourceful.

But a motorcycle? And not any bike, a Ducati 1098, the same one she saw almost wreck earlier that morning. The realization lit her mind and caused her head to rise just enough for the edge of the wind to strike her face. The man with the extreme reflexes was Guy.

Oh shit! She was back to where she started. How in the hell was this possible?

The pitch of the motor's whine lessened, and he shoved a hand into his pocket. His thumb pressed a remote imprinted with fingerprint technology, and the unmarked gate swung open. At a steady roll, they eased past the intercom/keypad unit on the edge of the drive. Even though he drove slowly, this was all too fast and wild to make sense.

He stopped in front of a multi-level mansion, made more from glass than solid walls, but she had to halt her architectural appreciation when a large man with a drawn 357 came lumbering out the front door, followed by a woman who was seriously shorter but not any less ominous with a nine millimeter in hand. Her face was as red and round as a ripe beefsteak tomato. Her mouth was clearly yelling at them, but the hum of the motorcycle drowned her out. As soon as Guy cut the ignition, the scolding came through full throttle.

"… To protect you. All the thanks I get is to see you take off this morning, and on that motorcycle. I've told you never to-" She broke off the rant when Fara swung off the bike.

Fara made sure she stuck the landing; even though, one of her heels had broken while she was running out from under

Palazzo Donn'Anna. Despite that wobbly distortion, the pavement was solid under her feet and felt normal. Right now normal was just peachy.

During the woman's diatribe, more men flooded through the open double doors, and each bore arms. Suddenly eight gun barrels, large and small, were pointing at Fara. She had sheathed her knife and tossed it into her backpack during the straightaway Guy had taken along the coast. If she went for the knife, they would assume she had a gun. Getting shot at again this morning wasn't on her to-do list, and at this range, they wouldn't miss, at least not all of them.

A sudden burst of adrenaline flooded her mind and helped assemble her priorities. Live first ... worry about Guy's ghost second.

"That's the woman from yesterday, outside of Cap'e Muorto." The big man's beard was close cut yet hid most of his face, but Fara could still see the shock wash over his expression.

"Where the hell am I?" She shouted over the cacophony of raised voices. They stopped and stared. She didn't shout quite as loudly the second time, but her voice carried in the sudden silence, resonating off of the mansion's glass façade. "What the fuck is going on?"

Guy swung off the bike and stood within three feet of her. He swept a hand through his hair, pulling the windblown tangles out of his eyes, revealing fine creases edging toward his temples. A full day's growth of dark stubble hid the angular contours of jaw line, but in the light of day, his face didn't appear nearly as hollowed or dark. He shoved his hands into the pockets of his jeans which caused the jacket to gape across his chest, and his eyes actually twinkled when he smiled at her. "Hello Fara."

"What are you doing?" Out of the corner of her eye, she noticed an insect on her shoulder, something similar to a love bug. She eyed it warily and brushed it off. Without a doubt that was real. "What's going on?"

He tipped his head, and an odd slip of the breeze caught his wavy hair, almost blowing it into his face, but not quite. "Aren't you surprised to see me?"

All of the armed guards had taken up positions near the front stairs, a neat and professional array poised for an assault. There was no fucking way for her to keep an eye on everyone at once. If they shot her, then they shot her. Resigned, she sighed and turned back to Guy. "I saw you yesterday."

The line grew between his brows. Most people formed a number 11 when they furrowed their brows, but his worry line formed a single 1, just slightly off center. "And you recognized me?"

Wanting to keep things as simple as possible, she decided being vague would probably yield the same response. "You know I did."

He took a step back, and she moved forward, to which Guy held out a palm. "Fara, stop. I've got to figure this out."

The synchronous clicks of safeties being flicked off held her mid-step, and all eight barrels were pointed at her and only her. Maybe they couldn't see him?

"You need to figure what out?" She wanted to grab him and shake him, but physical contact might not be the best thing in front of witnesses. "Where am I, and what's going on?"

"Tell all of us Nieto, what's going on?" The large woman broke ranks and approached. "Who is this woman?"

Fara now saw the nine millimeter was a Smith and Wesson M&P, ten-round, low profile carry, with a real nice black Melonite finish. Under other circumstances, she would have complimented the woman on her choice of gun, but not today.

"You of all people should recognize her." Guy retorted sharply.

She stopped, staring at Fara's face. "Oh dear God, it's Faradahl Alecto. I watched you on CCN every day. What happened to your hair?"

Fara wanted to comb her fingers through the brushy spikes but stalled the urge. How her hair looked was way down the priority list. Slowly she turned her gaze from the robust woman to Guy.

Her stomach clenched as the incongruent pieces added up in her head. The systemic rise of adrenaline continued to heat her blood, degree by smoldering degree. Cautiously, she walked up to him and shoved his shoulder, none too gently. She could barely breathe, yet "You're alive" passed through her lips.

The nod was just enough to cause his precariously perched hair to fall into his eyes. "Yeah."

Her heart skipped a beat, hitting the inside of her ribs as it palpitated out of sync. "You're alive?"

He tossed his chin back defiantly. "Did you think a ghost was driving a Ducati?"

She knew how her face grew cold with abject horror, and it had that chilled tingle right now. Swallowing past the lump in her throat, she tried to recover, "Ghosts can have style."

"Ghosts?" His slightly lopsided smile drew out the shallow dimple in his left cheek, exactly as she remembered. "You thought I was a ghost?"

"I saw you die." She had seen him die. She leapt over massive pieces of twisted metal and chipped plastic rubble, but little remained of Guy's body other than chunks of smoldering flesh. "You're not dead?"

His face drained of color. "Why do you keep saying that? Why is it so hard to believe? I'm standing right in front of you."

Her stomach flip-flopped, and she felt as if she was going to hurl. If he was truly alive, then who'd she have sex with last night?

"You're not dead." Her voice warbled just as her knees began to buckle.

"Fara!" He lunged to catch her, but what he caught was her fist square up against the side of his jaw. Off-guard, the force made him stumble and then fall down to his knees.

"Shit! Shit! Shit!" She stomped in a small circle, flexing and spreading the fingers of the hand the Taliban had broken. "You're not dead?!"

"Stop saying that." Hopping to his feet in a liquid movement that was so very Guy Carver, he wiggled his jaw back and forth a couple of times.

"Then what the hell happened in Baltimore?" She wanted to hit him again and keep on hitting him until he was good and truly dead. When he stepped close enough she let loose again, this time with a left jab to his chest, just inside of the holster. She heard the air hiss out of the side of his swelling lip.

"Fuck Fara! Would you stop hitting me?"

"No!" She swung again, but this time he dodged.

"You can still pack a punch." His smile was more than a little askew, and he rubbed his right pectoral muscle. "The car exploded, but I didn't die. I parked over a rigged manhole cover, went down, and triggered the blast."

"You son of a bitch! You let me think for the past four years that you had been blown to bits. I picked up chunks … chunks of what I thought was your flesh."

"I had a side of beef under the back seat." His face remained neutral, unchanging, which only added to her need to explode.

"I trusted you." She struggled to control her anger and keep her expression blank. "Why the fuck would you do that to me?"

He continued the neutral scrutiny as if this was a game of chicken. Ain't no chicken being served tonight. She didn't move, not even to blink because if she did tears would spring to her eyes. She wouldn't cry in front of him, not now, not ever!

Guy Carver wasn't dead. The man she saw at the church was real. Her thoughts spun through the new variables, trying to make sense of it all, but there was just too much information, too much baggage. She had cried over his casket in which she had placed the remains of a side of beef!

With his left hand poised to go for his gun, he smirked, "I never thought you would be petty, but I guess I was wrong."

"Petty? You purposefully let me think you were dead. That's just, just…" Reprehensible, disgraceful, inexcusable, none of those held enough impact. "You're a fucking asshole!"

"Sometimes," he smiled that lazy and seductive grin. It used to melt her, but not now. Not today. Not ever again. Alive or dead, Guy Carver would never touch her again.

"Yeah, at least we can agree on that. How could you do that to me? I thought…" Pushing his declaration of love out of her mind, she had to clear her throat to continue. "It was all a lie. Everything we had together was a lie. Fuck," the breath puffed out of her lungs, and she looked down. She couldn't bear to look at him, but appearing meek was worse. Summoning up a dose of courage, she raised her gaze. "Were you ever planning on letting me know?"

When terrible pain happened, it aged the eyes first. His amber eyes bore the weight of ages, but it wasn't enough, not for what he put her through. "I couldn't, at least not until I was sure you weren't working for the Agency."

"Well, *Ghost Lovers* is about as far away as it gets." She snipped.

His lips pulled into a thin line. "So you ran scared."

"I ran, but not scared." The words were hard to force out of her throat, so hard and cold they bit into her inner darkness. "I couldn't bring myself to go home to our apartment, to walk the same streets, to go to the same stores. I took Daily's offer because I didn't give a damn anymore."

"Shit," muttered under his breath. "He's the one who talked you into the sandbox?" Turning, he stomped a few steps away and then faced her again. "Fuck!" The exclamation echoed across the driveway.

"He was your inside man, wasn't he? I should have guessed. It had fishy written all over it. You put the beamer in the shop just two days before it happened. I thought Georgie set you up."

Guy remained motionless. She hated the way he could become so still it was like he was the fucking dead, and that thought made her cringe inside. She had fucked the dead. Not the ghost of a dead lover, but a ghost. She didn't even know who he was other than he looked a hell of a lot like Guy. It was more than she could deal with right now, and she tucked that away to agonize over later.

"After seeing you at the church, I did some research." He had the audacity to edge indignation into his voice. "Georgie's place got torched on the anniversary of our first date. You do it?"

"Oh I wanted to, but I didn't have any proof to go after him. I always had to have proof before *I* killed someone." She bit back just enough for the words to gain full meaning and gleefully saw him wince just a little, but it was still enough. "I guess Joe didn't want any loose ends."

He cautiously stepped forward, back into her reach. "You really went to the sandbox to get away from me?"

Her eyes narrowed, sensing more in the change of his inflection than he could possibly realize was there. "It bugs you, doesn't it?"

"The Taliban abducted you." He swallowed so hard, his larynx bobbed. "You were tortured."

She barely breathed out the word, "Yeah."

"It's my fucking fault."

"Yeah." Nodding, she left it at that and strode toward the gate with as much grace as she could muster with one broken heel. After two lopsided steps, she bent sideways from the waist as to not flash anyone the lace panties under her skirt and pulled the straps from each ankle, none too gently.

Turning in a final violent protest, she threw the shoes one at a time. He dodged the broken one, but she had anticipated the cut to the left, so the second hit him squarely in the groin, pointy heel first. She wished it had been the knife he had given her. That would have been appropriate; she couldn't get busted for killing a dead man. With manic and violent images of how she would kill him flipping through her mind, she continued down the drive.

"Wait!" The red-faced woman called out after her, and the gate started to close.

A hitch inside of Fara told her this was one of those life changing moments. If she all out sprinted, she could make the gate, about twenty meters away, mostly downhill, but with one more second of hesitation, escape would not be an option. She waited for that second, but the why evaded her conscious mind. Turning, she looked the woman straight in her hazel eyes. The sun was nearly overhead, but Fara squinted rather than shielding the glare.

"On TV, I could tell you had green eyes. I just never expected them to be so, so stunning. In this light they shine like emeralds." Suddenly, the woman smiled, and her whole face changed from the furious killer tomato to calm and even gracious. "You deserve to understand why this happened. Please come inside and have a drink while we explain."

Biting the edge of her lip, Fara wondered where this new semblance of normalcy was going. Being suckered into a line of bullshit wouldn't improve things, not at all. But at this point, what would?

"Gaetano had to do what he did." Continuing in a calm voice, she reached out, trying to touch Fara's arm.

"Gaetano?" She was an expert in evasion and half-stepped, half-jumped to the side. "Your name is now Gaetano?"

The woman continued. "His name has always been Gaetano Fidel Caravaggio."

Guy's face had lost the icy neutrality. He actually looked sheepish. Never in her life had she seen him look contrite or meek, especially not sheepish. "Come inside Fara, and I'll explain. It does have a rational explanation."

"Rational? You lied to me about who you were, where you were from, even how you died. Shit Guy. It was all a lie, and now you expect an explanation will make all of that just go away?" She evaded again when he tried to take hold of her arm. "You come back from the dead and say it was rational?"

"Just hear him out. Come inside, out of the sun." The woman smiled warmly. "I am Elena Caravaggio, and this is our home. No harm will come to you. You have my word on that." With an almost nondescript wave of her hand, all of the guns lowered and holstered simultaneously. If everything else hadn't been so totally fucked up, that would have looked strange. Unfortunately, it seemed the most reasonable thing that happened all day.

The armed men remained in position, like a muscled receiving line, except they didn't greet her as she walked past them. Each seemed to size her up, and she did the same. One-on-one she would probably be able to take them, but not all of them together, or even back-to-back. Her workouts had been sporadic, and she wasn't nearly as honed as she used to be. Silently she vowed if she lived through this day, she would reinitiate her daily exercise regimen.

Elena entered the house first. Guy motioned for Fara to go in second, but she wouldn't trust him, not at her back. She crossed her arms and shook her head while defiantly standing on bare feet with frosted pink toenails. The only way she was going in before him was if he picked her up and carried her inside, and good luck with that. She wanted a reason to beat the shit out of him. That was the only thing that could possibly make her feel better at the moment.

Waiting just as defiantly, Guy didn't move until his aunt ordered him into the foyer. He finally sighed and stepped around Fara.

After checking the armed men who were flanking her in neutral stances, Fara passed through the doors. The seven guards followed her, taking positions automatically at key doorways inside the house, as if this was a familiar drill.

The interior was open and breezy with a deep foyer. Waves of sunshine poured through the peaked glass ceiling. Mature palm trees grew out of ocher pots and lined the straight staircase against the right wall. At the landing, the metal banister continued to the left. An additional third floor was visible above that. She didn't see a staircase leading up to that level, but she did see an armed man standing near the far edge of second floor railing. The balding man next to him was beading sweat. He appeared unarmed and uncomfortably out of place.

"Come into the conservatory." Elena motioned to the long room on the right.

Fara paused before entering. Her personal shields were full-on, bolstered by anger and wariness, yet even through the emotional blockade, she could still sense something otherworldly in this place. Unless she opened herself to the energy, she wouldn't be able to tell whether it was residual or active. At this point, safeguarding herself was more important than adding anything else to her current inventory of weird.

The room was longer than wide. This doorway was the only apparent entrance, yet it wouldn't surprise her if there was a secret panel either behind one of the bookcases or even through the floor.

She willed her feet to go forward, focusing on her metaphysical shields in order to step into the potent room. Outside of the windows, the ground fell away sharply. When she and Guy drove up, she hadn't noticed the cliff, only the rounded end of the drive. No wonder the road didn't continue.

Massive panes of glass with a greenish hue formed the wall facing the angular coastline. The view was magnificent, but she ignored it for now and clicked a close-cut fingernail against the glass panel. At least 50 mm thick, it had to be level F79 or greater. This could take multiple shots from a submachine gun, probably had an H bullet-resistance glazing. This wasn't only a house; it was a *Better Homes and Gardens'* bunker.

Without commenting, she turned around and faced the room, keeping the safety-glass at her back. It was easier to judge the length of the opposite wall than by the glistening glass panels whose seams were nearly transparent. Each bookcase was about six-feet wide, built-ins. Four were on either side of an equally wide fireplace. That single wall was about fifty-feet long by twelve feet high, and in the breezy hollow above the highest shelf was a collection of ancient Roman pottery, spotlighted by recessed key lighting.

Not much impressed her these days, but how anyone would have that many books outside of a library was incredible. Not paperbacks, but real leather-bound books. She couldn't see them closely enough to gauge accurately, but from just their spines, they appeared to be incredibly old. A stack of about ten sat on the massive table in the center of the room. Some of those looked to be hand-bound with parchment yellowed from age. She wasn't an antiquarian book dealer, but on one stakeout of an eccentric older woman, Fara spent plenty of time in her private library while waiting for her to return to her home in Prague.

A wistful sigh trembled through Fara, but she didn't let it show. That was her last solo assignment before partnering with Guy. The Agency preferred to send couples into tourist destinations. They blended in better than a single man or woman just hanging out in a hotel lobby or on the proverbial street corner. While it lasted the work was good, and the locations were even better with him at her side.

Her eyes darted across the room, and thankfully, he wasn't looking at her. She approached the table, noticing the name

Carafa was on almost every book. Fara slipped the topmost off from the stack and smoothly slid it inside of her backpack hanging from her left arm. She didn't know why exactly, but an inner instinct just told her to do it.

She glanced across the room once more. Guy and Elena were at the bar, speaking in hushed voices while pouring drinks from crystal decanters. She assumed the clear liquid was vodka, because Guy knew she hated gin. Glancing at her watch, 11:20 was a little too early for spirits, but after the morning she had, she was tempted. Of course, she'd refuse. Water out of a sealed bottle was the only acceptable choice.

As the adrenaline dissipated into a lulling downer, she continued her assessment. The fireplace was a work of art, magnificently sculpted with lions clawing up marbled slabs. Even the andirons were made with large lion faces with snarling maws, jet black in comparison to the white marble, yet just as pristine.

Apparently, they had a fire in the hearth; the scent of sooty ash added a sharpness to the air. There was something extra in the lingering scent, something also burnt but different. Fabric held scents so much better than the air. She was tempted to sniff the tablecloth for a clue. She moved a little closer, but before lifting a corner of the cloth, she noticed the likeness in the portrait over the mantle.

"He was my brother-in-law, Don Lazarus Anton Caravaggio." Elena approached with two glasses. "When he died, Gaetano had to come home and assume his place."

"No thank you." While waving off the drink, she watched Guy out of the corner of her eye, and his gaze swung from the painting to her.

"I told you she would only drink a bottle of water." He smiled, and the timid shyness was gone. Vintage Guy looked at her and extended a bottle of water. "It's sealed."

"Thank you." When she reached for it, he didn't let go right away, and their fingers brushed. Her feelings braced, not allowing his touch to permeate her defenses. "So Don Lazarus was your father?" Originally, he had told her his father's name was Larry.

He nodded. "He ran the family business, and I couldn't leave the Agency to come and do this. They had to think I was dead or else they would ask me to leverage the power of the family to their will." He inhaled as if wanting to continue.

Elena motioned toward him. "When Gaetano saw you yesterday, he thought perhaps the Agency discovered the deception and sent you to kill him."

The door violently banged open, and the young blond woman Fara had seen at the church stood in the center of the doorway. The woman's disheveled hair hung in her face, hiding her expression but not her eyes. The tiny beads of darkness shone through the mass like black diamonds. She pointed directly at Fara, "Harlot! Out of my house!"

CHAPTER 10

"Aleri!" Both Gae and Aunt Elena exclaimed in unison.

But Aleri didn't acknowledge either of them. Taking another step forward, she intensified her repellent gaze set upon Fara. "Vengeance is mine."

The coarse churl grated within Gae's gut. Never in his life had he heard such venomous hatred, especially never from Aleri. The fetid sound shocked him to the point of inaction. He couldn't process. All of his training and experience suddenly failed him.

"Revenge is sweet." With a high-pitched laugh, she tipped her head, and her hair fell back with the motion. His cousin's face contorted, distorting and mutating her features until another face stared at him, only momentary, but long enough for Gae to know. The visage was familiar, but in his current state of mental disarray, he couldn't place it.

"Purgatorial wreathed serpents, only their everlasting power shall slake my thirst." She thrust out her hands and stared at the outstretched palms. Throwing them toward the ceiling, she cast another blood-curdling scream, piercing the heavy air.

As if the motion created a conduit, negative energy flooded the room, and he could almost see the putrescence emanating from Aleri. The melodious power his cousin held in her voice was now twisted and malevolent, perhaps even embodying the very essence of evil. The thought crept through him, and the fine hairs raised on the back of his neck. As he gaped, her eyes darkened like poisoned honey until all of the irises transformed into a deep, dark blue.

Doctor Palermo appeared in the doorway. "Donna Caravaggio, when Aleri awoke, she didn't appear to be this," pausing, his hands waved in quick circles, "in this state of unrest. Even without having gone to the window, she knew you had a guest and insisted on greeting her."

The doctor approached Aleri cautiously from the doorway. Reacting to an unspoken cue, Aunt Elena reached for Aleri's arms. When they touched, the girl screamed again. "Don't let her touch you, Gaetano. You are mine. You belong to me."

While Aunt Elena struggled with restraining Aleri, she beseeched the hesitant doctor who had grown paler and looked as if he was going to be sick. "What's wrong with her?"

Contorting, Aleri shrieked, and Aunt Elena screamed over her to be heard. "Do something!"

Gae wasn't sure what to do, but when Aleri pulled one arm away from her mother and struck her, he lunged forward and gathered his cousin's hands into his own, smoothly rubbing the backs in large circles with his thumbs. He stared at her hands, not able to bring himself to look at her distorted visage. "Aleri, I love you, and you will never lose me. Fara isn't here to hurt me or you. Here, let me help you back to bed. You're not well and need to rest."

She quit struggling and self-control seeped back into her countenance. Sliding her hands softly away from his, she smoothed her palms over his cheeks. "I love you, Gaetano."

A thin yet still icy thread shivered up his spine, reminding him of the manifestation at Palazzo Donn'Anna. Aleri's hands were chilled, and her fingers smoothed over his face and then down onto his shoulders, just like that … that … He couldn't even bring himself to think the word ghost, yet it was just there. A ghost had groped him, and now his cousin's hands were following the same path. Before they slipped any lower, he grabbed her wrists.

Using the motion as momentum, she pressed her body against his and kissed him. Not a simple peck on the lips. Her lips smoothed seductively over his mouth. Shocked, he gasped, and she forced her tongue inside his mouth, suckling erotically.

Illogically, he instantly grew hard within his jeans and hated himself for it, especially when she ground her mound against his erection. He tried to force her off from him gently, but her strength belied her delicate frame. Finally, he had to use all of his power to push her away. "Stop!"

She tipped back her head and let out a drifting laugh, lifting and falling in half-toned notes, and the chilling similarity struck him again.

After fleeing with Fara, he had forgotten about his brush with the unexplained, but now there was no denying something was happening. First his father's ghost, then a ghost under Anna Carafa's palace, and now his poor little cousin was acting insane, no, not insane, possessed.

The doctor grasped Aleri's arms just above the elbows and stretched them behind her, yet even with the distorted line of her body, she still leaned in toward Gae and whispered, "Come, come play with me."

He felt his eyes grow wide, and the chill in his spine crept through his nervous system, gripping his heart with cold fingers. He couldn't think, and in some small way, he didn't want to think about what was happening.

"Help me get her to her room. I have a sedative in my bag." Sweat ran in rivulets down the tension lines on the older man's face.

So focused on Aleri, he didn't see his aunt motion for the guards, but Anton and Mario were suddenly there. Someone counted to three. Anton hooked his arms under Aleri's shoulders, and Mario lifted her feet.

"Gaetano!" She screamed over and over again, stretching her outstretched fingers toward him. Kicking with the strength of someone three times her size, she flailed her legs, trying to break free.

He wanted to help Aleri, but whatever that thing was he couldn't, wouldn't play a role in its macabre plan. Still wincing at each of her grating implores, he followed them up the staircase and across the landing to the last room on the left. He stood in the hall, reluctant to follow them inside the door. His chest was tight, aching in the overly sensitive spot, and from that damaged place, he felt it. That abnormal something was in there, waiting inside the room, and it needed him for something.

"Gaetano," Aleri whimpered exhaustedly in almost her normal voice.

"She acts better when you're near. Come inside Nieto!" Tears ran down his aunt's face leaving vertical tracks of melted mascara. "Please! Gaetano!"

He took that final step.

He had been in Aleri's room more times than he could count, yet now it was different. The air was too thin to breathe, like the atmospheric pressure wasn't at sea-level, rather at 10,000 feet, and it was nearly as cold. Whenever he went skiing, the height made his head light to the point where it was difficult to direct his own thoughts. That same mind-numbing lightness filled her room, and although he fought internally, his thoughts drifted back to Palazzo Donn'Anna, the Syren's Palace. The same chill clung to this space. Whatever had been there had followed him home. He ordered his revolving thoughts to stop there. This started before he went to the Posillipo rise. It started at the damned séance. What had happened?

Constant threads of suffering pleaded to let her go. Although he didn't want to, the proverbial train wreck compelled his eyes. Aunt Elena tied her daughter's wrists the bedposts while the body guards struggled each with a leg. Aleri had been in decent shape for a thin wisp of a girl. They would work out in the basement gym, and at her best, she leg pressed fifty pounds. Mario weighed four times as much and Anton was even bulkier than that. How could she be so unnaturally strong?

The doctor's bag stood open on the small bedside table, and he removed a syringe and a small pharmaceutical vile. His hands shook while drawing down the clear liquid. Even while releasing the air bubbles, more than a standard thin line of fluid escaped through the needle.

Gae remembered the doctor having the steadiest hands. Palermo had done such a good job with the knife wound on his back, no one except Fara had ever noticed the scar.

The needle stood poised in the doctor's hand and lowered toward Aleri's flesh. Flinching, he spun away from the sight.

Heavy drapes darkened the room. Aleri loved the light and rarely closed the drapes, even at night. He opened them with a swish of both wrists. Brightness streamed across the bed, and Aleri screamed, flying into another fit, making the bedposts groan under the strain. It had to be an optical illusion, but the sunlight made her look even paler, an off-shade of ghostly white. Small particles danced millimeters above her skin, glittering like motes of dust.

Not believing his eyes, he shook his head and looked again. The swirling patterns primarily encircled her face, distorting the features between two likenesses, similar in appearance, yet distinct. The face just above Aleri's face turned toward him only slightly; however, it was enough for him to see the second set of lips pull into a thin smile. Again, the familiarity tugged within him. He should know that haughty face, that arrogant expression under high arching brows. He had seen it before. But where?

Disgusted by his own weakness, he couldn't stand the double vision any longer. Just as he went to pull the drapes closed, the blue Peugeot pulled through the gate with Luigi at the wheel, and Signora Lucedio was with him. This too struck him as odd, but right now nothing felt right. Again, just like on the mountain, his brain struggled to process, and he felt physically ill. His stomach fell even further when Fara passed through the now closing gate on his Ducati. He dropped his head and pressed his forehead to the window. The warmth of the glass felt good, better than he could possibly describe.

"Nieto, close the drapes." His aunt shouted over Aleri's unintelligible, hellish sounds sputtering from twisted lips. She held her daughter's bound hand as the tranquilizer started working, and the room fell into a hesitantly expectant hush.

The swish of the drapery rings skidding on the rod was omnipresent. The room returned to darkness. Aleri opened her eyes, staring directly at him. The two faces had merged into one, and the look she gave him wasn't her own. A seductive smile grew, and she arched her hips in invitation. Her thrashing had forced the loose covers over the edges of the four-poster, and he focused on the design of the twisted post nearest him. She'd seen the unique bedroom suite in an antique shop in Rome. At that time it struck him how her fingers caressed the carved wood delicately, lovingly like an older and experienced woman would stroke a man.

The door opened. Signora Lucedio stepped into the room confidently, even triumphantly. Either she didn't feel the malignancy or was impervious to the effects. An edgy and smug smile creased her lips. She inhaled deeply, and the temperature in the room plummeted.

Puffing up with the jolt, something about her was different. Even in the dusky light, her skin was firmer, and the pale red hair grew vibrant. If he didn't know better, he would say her very aura glowed with rejuvenation.

"Oh Magdalene, thank God you're here!" Tears tumbled from his aunt's eyes in huge drops, nearly washing away the remnants of the mascara streaks. "It's Aleri. We don't know what's the matter with her."

His senses were in overdrive, tingling warning throughout every nerve. This was wrong, very wrong. He pushed away from the window and approached the foot of the bed. His fingers wrapped around the carved bedpost while he tried to verbalize his aching suspicions. Refusing to look at Aleri, he focused solely on Magdalene. "Signora, we should go downstairs and discuss what happened at the séance."

"What do you think happened at the séance?" Her hazel eyes were brighter, glowing with power.

"I don't know. That's why we need to determine what's happened. Aunt Elena, why don't we all go downstairs?" He motioned toward the door, where freedom from the oppressive energy awaited him. "Let's go discuss what's happening here."

"I don't think that would be wise." The psychic said, laying a hand onto the shoulder of Aunt Elena.

"I don't think that would be wise." Aunt Elena repeated.

Fire sizzled in his veins, pushing out his own doubts. "This is her fault. Don't listen to her." The turbulent frenzy picked up tempo, making him want to scream with frustration. Controlling his tone, he spoke through gritted teeth. "What did you do to Aleri?"

"Me?" Signora Lucedio's eyes twinkled with red highlights encircling dilated pupils. "Elena, it appears Gaetano is overwrought and should leave. His presence is disruptive at this juncture. His presence is disturbing Aleri."

"His presence is disturbing Aleri." His aunt perfectly mimicked the tone and cadence.

"We need to stay here at Aleri's side." The woman's fingers slid to the back of Aunt Elena's neck, and she faded, aging ever so slightly.

His guts twisted with uncontrollable foreboding. He would never be able to explain his actions, but it was still better than letting that woman lay her hands on his family. He released all of his churning energy into a single pouncing move and separated the red-eyed bitch from his aunt, landing on top of her on the hard tile floor.

The woman didn't even shriek. In a move faster than the eye could follow, she laid her hands onto his face. The energy physically drained from his body. He struggled to move, and focusing on a single hand, he slapped away that bond.

From behind, a massive hand closed around his shoulder. Fingers dug under his clavicle and lifted him to his feet. He swung, and his fist connected directly against Luigi's chest. He might as well had hit a frozen side of beef.

"Wait, I want him to watch." The woman now appeared twenty years younger and rose from the floor with agile grace. "Aleri, look at me sweetheart. Yes, let's make you feel better."

The woman glowed until she radiated light like a captured star. She inhaled again, making the room frigid, and then she blew all of that energy into Aleri.

His cousin's body reacted, trimming and filling, morphing into a similar yet different woman. Features took shape, and the countenance of the shimmer he had seen in the sunlight sank into Aleri. Time stood still while the molding sharpened Aleri's cheekbones and lengthened her nose.

Now he remembered. In the front of one of those books, that same face was in a portrait of Anna Carafa.

He may have failed Aleri for the moment, but maybe there was hope. He had to find Fara. She was the only person who might know what to do; that was if she believed him. Throwing an elbow directly into Luigi's solar plexus and a second blow into his throat, Gae bolted for the door.

CHAPTER 11

Tremors shook within Fara's core. Since she saw Guy in front of Cap'e Muorto, all of those carefully sealed memories seeped from the dark spot hidden within her soul. Now they churned inside of her, along with the new pain of Guy's deception. Her internal balance was off, and the steady vibration of the Ducati's motor only made things worse. The external and the internal shudders were out of sync, exponentially amplifying the combined effect.

A sickening clench tore through Fara's stomach and forced her to stop on the side of the road. Like something out of a horror movie, the sickness propelled out of her body with a force not of this world.

A few shaky breaths later, she felt steadier and cleansed her mouth with a baby wipe from the tiny travel pack she carried in her backpack. She hadn't been physically ill in years. The last time had been from tequila shots at the karaoke bar, and even though it was the good stuff, the alcohol was way too much for her.

Shit! It was another Guy memory.

The urge welled up again, except nothing was left in her stomach. Doing something between breathing and heaving, she leaned back against the rocky hillside and chastised herself for not taking the damned bottle of water. But when the opportunity arose to escape, she had to move quickly, and to her surprise, nary a guard tried to stop her. Only the man in the blue Peugeot said something as she zipped past him just before the gate closed. Oddly, she thought that was the same man she had seen earlier that morning following Guy. He had been far enough ahead of her to have parked on the back side of the palazzo and been shooting at ... at...

Fara focused. That made no sense. Why would one of Guy's men be the shooter?

Guy's men?

The five W's of journalism kept pounding questions inside of her skull along with the omnipresent jackhammer of a post-vomiting headache.

Who was Gaetano Caravaggio, really?

The man Fara had known intimately for over two years wasn't even real. Since the end of their relationship, she set her standard for all other men by his actions and intelligence, even his looks. Now she saw the flaws in her logic, but then it made perfect sense. If a man whose childhood home was a trailer outside of Birmingham had such cosmopolitan grace, every man could achieve the same refined style and elegant taste. Instead, her homespun hero was old money from an even older family. Maybe he didn't think she was good enough for him to take home. She was a convenient and willing sex partner, whom he used and then discarded in order to return home to his family.

What was his family?

Both he and his aunt referred to the family like the word meant more than what it would to most people. They had a cadre of armed guards, armed servants, and lived in a home made out of the same type of impervious glass as the Pope mobile. They also were the patrons of the Incontri Napoletani, home base for the Cult of the Dead.

Gae was a dark soul. She always knew that, but dark wasn't necessarily evil. It was just dark, twisting between black and white extremes. Fara swayed back and forth over that line every day of her life, and lately, the distinction was even more blurry. Her true self slept just under the surface, staring out of her own eyes like a blurry reflection from a calm pool of water. That was where the joy of slaughter resided. The place where her sadistic lust to plunge her hands into hot blood waited for her. She thought those days were over, but they would never be over. Seeing Guy made her acknowledge there was never an end. The primitive urge existed inside every human, weak or strong, embedded in human DNA. She couldn't condemn Guy for being what he was because in truth the dark was part of her true self, and even his cousin, Aleri.

When Fara first saw Aleri coming out of the church, she appeared perfectly normal. Well maybe not normal. She was perfect, like a fairytale princess, beautifully poised, impeccably groomed, and exquisitely dressed. Yet, every fairytale had something bad happen to the heroine. The Beast took Belle prisoner. The bad fairy cursed Aurora to prick her finger on a spindle. Cinderella was a slave to her vain stepmother and stepsisters. The evil queen foisted a poisoned apple onto Snow White.

Snow White? Fara dropped her head into her hands as she remembered the vision of the dark-haired beauty. Who was that woman? Where was all of this heading?

All she wanted to do was shoot an episode for a cable TV show. It shouldn't be this difficult. Maybe she should just head back to the house and write the entire episode, just make it up and not go back to the catacombs until the day of the shooting. But that stupid house had issues too.

Her stomach flip-flopped again at the memory. She had sex with a ghost.

Ghost sex!

The internal disorder rang in her ears, repeating the phrase. Ghost sex. Ghost sex. Ghost sex. Who'd have thought ghost sex could leave the body so rattled?

It certainly didn't occur to her at the time. What was she thinking, especially when she had a really decent man, one with a warm pulse, who said he loved her?

She believed in J.C. She trusted him, and trust was always in short supply. He was real, and she knew all of the skeletons, well demons, in his proverbial closet. Life wouldn't be easy. Emotionally, he was high-maintenance, but she couldn't blame him for being wired. When life settled down into a normal rhythm, so would he. She wished he was here, and then reconsidered. First, she had to find the shooter before anyone else was in the line of fire. She couldn't bear it if J.C. took a bullet intended for her.

Why was she being shot at?

She hadn't done anything, not lately anyway, and those disappearances in Puerto Rico weren't her fault. At least two more would have died if she hadn't intervened.

Even the Feds would talk to her before just assassinating her, wouldn't they?

If she was the target, the rental house would be under surveillance. Maybe that would be the best way to determine what to do. Go by the house and see if it was being watched. If she stopped in town and bought a helmet and some jeans, she could approach closely enough to get a good look at anyone in the vicinity.

But if she stayed on the bright yellow Ducati for too long, the cops would pick her up. No one showing the firepower Guy's family had would be on the right side of the law. If they were what was obvious, they had the cops in their pocket. Would Guy really call the cops on her?

Why wouldn't he? He lied to her about everything else, and she had trusted him. Her heart fell as if freshly stabbed and twisted again. Trust was something she gave to very few people, and it never meant anything to him.

She never meant anything to him.

The one truth she held above all others was he had loved her. When the Taliban had her strapped to that damned table, she silently repeated, if she died she would at least join Guy. Sudden tears sprung to her eyes, and she swiped at them with the back of her hand.

Dear God, how could she have been so gullible? She failed to follow her own mantra - the obvious was rarely the truth. So what was obvious now?

Fact one, Guy was alive.

Fact two, he was tied to organized crime and quite possibly the head of a mafia family.

Fact three, someone wanted to kill one or both of them.

With each point, she ticked her nail against a scrubby dandelion stalk and watched the white seeds drift.

The headache started to clear, and she put herself mentally back under the palazzo. The second shot hit her column. The first sounded like a ricochet, but perhaps the shooter aimed for

Guy first and shot at her only once she moved. Until that time, the shooter didn't know she was even there. All of those hired guns at his house weren't there for decoration. The obvious conclusion was the shooter was after Guy, but the too obvious was rarely the truth.

Which left the Feds.

She pulled out her phone and listened to J.C.'s phone ring ten times before rolling into voicemail. "Hey J.C. I wanted to get those names from you, of the people who've been talking to you about me." She couldn't say too much in case her phone number was tapped, but email or text would have an even higher probability of being detected. "Give me a call. I'm headed back to the crypt this afternoon to do some cut-away shots and check light balances. If I don't pick up, it means I don't have a signal, so leave me a message."

She almost hung up, but a single, bright ray of hope fluttered inside her inner turbulence. Since Guy was alive, maybe she wasn't cursed after all. As an afterthought, she whispered reverently, "I love you and miss you."

A patrol car eased past her but didn't stop. If she didn't get out of here right now, she might not have a second chance. She got to one knee and gave a last push. Black pulsing waves passed behind her eyes. Standing on slightly bent knees, she balanced and let the dizziness sway over her. That she could handle, but the nausea was once again on edge. Her inner sense felt off, just like her stomach; the breakfast had to have been bad. Had someone tried to poison her?

Her phone rang, and her heart sprung to life, doing a little flip-flop inside of her chest. "Hi J.C."

Instead of his mild tenor, a much older man spoke to her in Italian. "Signora Trotter, I have been waiting at Cap'e Muorto. Are you coming?"

Fara glanced at her watch, surprised it was already 1:10. "Yes, of course Father. I have one stop and will be there in less than fifteen minutes.

CHAPTER 12

The interior of the church was as empty as Gae's soul. He called out, and his voice shot across the structure designed to amplify the spoken word. A priest quietly closed the rectory door, and upon recognizing Gae, bowed reverently. He knew it was a sign of respect, but the carry-over from feudalism irritated the hell out of him, especially today. The elderly man scuttled toward him.

"Don Caravaggio, we were not expecting you." A quizzical look rounded Father Rugo's dense brows. "La Signorita is not with you?"

"No, not today." Gae tried to smile, but he felt something closer to a grimace tug at his tense expression. "Secure all entrances to the complex. I do not wish to be disturbed."

"There is an American woman in the crypt with Father Dominic." He said it more as an apology than a fact. "She has the Cardinal's permission to record a television program."

"Fara Trotter," his tension immediately amplified. As soon as she had shown up, all hell broke loose, literally. "That's why I'm here. I don't want to be interrupted, not by anyone. Do you understand? No one enters the church."

"Of course," the priest's hands trembled, and then he bowed once again, this time even more humbly.

Knowing Father Rugo would follow his order, he proceeded immediately. Since his return to Naples, he couldn't remember coming to Purgatorio ad Arco without Aleri at his side. Why would he? He didn't believe any of that Cult of the Dead mumbo jumbo bullshit. Even with the day's weird events, logically something else had to be the cause.

Mass hypnosis?

Fara was good, but not that good. She worked wonders with the siren quality to her voice, but only on men. If she was the cause why would Aleri... He couldn't even bring himself to think it, but he gave up believing this was all just a nightmare over an hour ago.

Although nothing at this point would soothe his discord, the sound of the latch lowering onto the metal doors added a sense of security, and after getting shot at, that at least was something. Fara probably knew something about the gunman too. Damn it to hell, he wanted, no, he needed to assert control over his life, and that centered around a single person, the woman who had bewitched his mind over four years ago.

The entrance to the crypt stood open as did the lower metal gate. Quickly he trotted down the steps but stopped abruptly when he encountered the same energy he had felt in Aleri's room. Whatever it was, he wasn't about to let it intimidate him. Inhaling as if he was going to dive underwater, he charged into the invisible disturbance, down the staircase, and into the aged underground with its nearly endless labyrinth of crypts.

The lights were on, yet darkness lingered in shadowy corners, as if that was where the abnormal coalesced. He braced himself against the gathering pressure, just like when he went scuba diving, but he wasn't that far underground. The pressure had to be inside his head rather than real, and the more he concentrated, each murky step became heavier than the last.

Part of him wanted to confront Fara, and a deeper element wanted to beg her forgiveness. That conflict licked his inner anger, making him almost ill. Even if her voice hadn't been echoing from deep within the crypt, he sensed where she was. A part of him was tuned into her, feeling her on a deeper level than mere senses imparted. He envisioned her kneeling in front of Lucia, whom Fara called the ghost bride.

He'd grown up hearing the story of Lucia's brief marriage but never quite understood why women thought she had some kind of magical prowess, especially upon learning the legend. Women should want more than Lucia's few weeks of bliss. He could almost hear Aleri chiding him, saying in her sweet voice how a few weeks of true love was better than never finding love at all. Aleri. His expression twisted again along with the knot in his heart. He loved his cousin more than life itself, yet Fara owned a part of his soul.

"Fara!" He charged into the decorated crypt where candles burned on the miniature altar. His former partner relaxed against the far wall, reviewing an image on the palm-sized camcorder.

"Father, would you mind blowing out the candles?" She spoke as if she hadn't even heard him.

Now was not the time for her to ignore him!

The priest didn't move except for his eyes shifting from Gae to Fara and then back.

Barely controlling himself, Gae strode the final two steps until he was within striking distance and pointed at the priest with his hand cocked in the shape of a gun. "Out! Get out now."

Father Dominic clasped his hands and squeezed until his knuckles turned white. "Don Caravaggio, this is unexpected. Father Rugo said…"

"I have permission to be here." Fara spat out heatedly.

"Not you." He pointed in her direction. "You're staying right where you are until I have some answers." His gaze swung once again to the priest.

The old man cast a pained look in her direction. "Signora Trotter?"

"It's all right Father." She set down the camera on the far edge of the altar, facing the skulls. "Gaetano Caravaggio and I met earlier today." Her voice was flat, meting out the words as evenly as a metronome. "Go ahead. I'll be fine."

"Signora, this is most unex…"

"Get out!" Gae whirled around and squeezed his hand into a fist. "And lock the gate." Forcing his hand to relax, he patted his pocket, and feeling the bulky cell phone, his broiling anger mellowed. Normally he kept the old phone on his bedside table, but since he saw Fara at the church, he felt compelled to keep it with him. "Lock the gate behind you … please." He patted his pocket again and dropped his voice to a more reasonable tone. "I have my keys."

"My allegiance is yours, my Don. Your will shall be done." The old man muttered within a brief bow.

Fara's demanding eyes shot up to meet his, and her lips pressed together, forming a tight line. "Why did you do that? Why are you here?" Her succinct voice grew even shorter, clipping the single syllables, definitely nothing like the smooth siren flow that compelled him to do whatever she asked of him.

"I need to talk to you," he lowered his voice, "without being overheard."

"Okay talk." She swung a leg over the edge of the tiled crypt and leaned into the slab more than actually sitting. Crossing her arms tightly boosted her defiant pose. What she probably didn't realize was she also boosted the upper curve of her breasts. The creamy mounds rounded above the scooped neckline of her shirt. That part of his body with a mind of its own decided this was a perfect time to become acutely aware of each and every breath she took.

In his voluntary thoughts, questions spun inside of his mind so quickly he couldn't really seem to focus on a single one of them, and then his involuntary mind took control. All he could see was her. Her eyes were green fire, brilliant, beautiful, and even more dangerous than what he remembered. A thought passed over those eyes, darkening them into a bewitching shade of Tibetan jade. Another dose of adrenaline lit his body, humming with the need for action, yet he remained motionless, waiting and watching to see what she was going to do.

The metal gate clanged shut in the distance, and her intense gaze shot toward the sound. "For wanting to talk, you're quite the chatterbox." Not making eye contact with him, she looked toward the camera, and the edge of her brow furrowed. Her profile was exactly as he remembered. On any other woman's face, her nose would have appeared large, but the shape complimented the rest of the angular contours of her cheeks and chin, stunning and very feminine.

Retreating backwards, he moved around the freestanding crypt and propped himself on the edge across from her. Swallowing his frustration, he found a blank tone within himself. "What's happening?"

She slowly shook her head with an equally blank face.

"Shit Fara, you know what's happening here."

"What?" She raised both of her hands and shrugged. "This is it. To produce the *Ghost Lovers* episode on Lucia. As soon as the show is over, I'm outta here."

He shook his head, not buying it. "Why would you get shot at for that?"

Her smile caught him off guard. "I thought the shooter was aiming for you."

Gae hated how her answers always produced more questions in his mind. The too familiar frustration welled up inside of him again, and despite the careful regulation, his voice tensed. "*Ghost Lovers* is a cover, isn't it?"

"No." She sighed warily.

"Tell me the truth!" His hand tightened on his pocket.

Her eyes followed the motion, but she was still way too cool to read. "I did. *Ghost Lovers* is just a job."

"Fuck!" His fists grew tight again. "Fara, you're going to answer me or…"

"Or what?" She smiled again, and her arms spread as widely as her challenging grin. "Go ahead and kill me. I know you were behind it."

"Behind what?" All of the heat in his veins instantly chilled, stirring his anger, lust, and fear into jumble of confusion. "I don't want to kill you."

"Nice acting but coy doesn't become you, and it's insulting to me. With what you did in Baltimore, you owe me at least the truth. The shooter was your own man, the one in the blue Peugeot. It was a clever touch for him to miss you first and then aim for me."

"Fara, I don't want to kill you." He repeated, more out of need to say something while his mind processed. Luigi was driving the Peugeot and arrived back home with Signora Lucedio.

Luigi?

"I found out your secret identity, and now you need to ensure I don't talk. I understand why you want me dead. You keep fingering the gun in your pocket. So just do it already, but at least be man enough to pull the trigger yourself." Her features tightened but not her voice.

He quit breathing while numbness consumed him. Dear God, not Luigi! But if so, what about his older brother, Mario? They were the only two men Gae trusted. The foundations of his world shook, crumbling the last vestiges of his hold on truth. He turned back to Fara and imagined the same look was on his face right now that he had seen on hers when she discovered he was alive. Betrayal cut sharper and deeper than any blade ever could. "Are you sure? Luigi was there?"

Her eyes narrowed, studying him for a few seconds too long. "All of the pieces add up."

The place in his soul where he went when he killed called to him. After he pulled the trigger, he would stay cold and numb for days, safe in his self-imposed refuge. "Go on."

"Go on? Did that fake explosion in front of Zimmer's rattle your brains? You're smarter than this." With a huff, she turned, and reaching to full extension, grabbed the bottle of water next to the candles. The flames danced from the disturbance, and the jumping light animated across the pair of skulls. "Okay. Let's say I believe you had nothing to do with the shooter. Then, why are you here? Your bike is safe; I parked it across from the police station."

"I know. I have trackers on all the vehicles." The idea lit his mind. No one else knew he had practiced on their vehicles before offering the service to clients. He could review the vehicle movement logs for the day. He would be able to know if Luigi was there for a fact, rather than conjecture. Finally, a fucking ray of hope on the blackest day of his life.

"Okay." The normal smoothness of her voice returned. "Let's move on to option number three. Why are you here?"

"What's wrong with my cousin?" His voice dropped low, to a near whisper. The inevitable chill edged into the depths of his heart by just thinking about the sudden change. "Tell me what you know about what's happening to Aleri."

"No." She set the plastic bottle down with a hollow thud.

He sucked in a breath with her name balanced on his tensed lips. "Fara!"

"No!" The word rang off from the smooth surfaces and would have echoed if Fara hadn't immediately lit into him. "I don't owe you anything, and I have enough problems of my own. If you didn't arrange the shooting, now I'm back to square one. Shit." She slipped off the edge of the crypt and started piling her things into the open backpack.

"I'm not letting you slip out on this one. Aleri is the sweetest person on the face of this earth. She's an angel, a goddess, and now, now?" His hands started sweeping into circles which mirrored his thoughts.

"Kissing cousins." She had the gall to pause, and glancing over her shoulder, blew him a kiss! "If that's legal here, why not go for it. She's pretty, and apparently *really* likes you, in that familiar sort of-"

With one swift hand, he caught her by the throat. His fingers itched, wanting to squeeze, but he knew once he started, he wouldn't be able to stop. Forced words edged through gritted teeth. "She's a sister to me."

Strangling someone was one of the most intimate ways to kill. He had only done it once and remembered how his hands started to ache long before the last heartbeat coursed through the carotid artery. Under his thumb, he felt Fara's pulse, strong and steady. She didn't fight or even struggle. She closed her eyes and tilted her head back to expose her throat.

"Fuck!" He threw her toward the ground, and she knocked over the candles. "What's happened to you? The Fara I knew was a hellcat and wouldn't take shit. You would have filleted anyone who touched you like that." When she didn't answer, he panted while his mind circled back to his original problem. "What going on here Fara? I need to know. Aleri's mixed up in it."

She swallowed and then her gaze narrowed, beaming directly into his with green fire. "First, tell me why you had to fake your death to disappear? I still don't understand. Was your father the Godfather or something? And now are you?"

Gae's breath caught, no one ever dared called his father that. "No, it wasn't like the movie, not at all."

"Oh, I see. You are the good guys, like Batman, a vigilante group created to protect the poor from costumed villains."

Knowing her jab was tit for tat, he grit his teeth and let it go. "He provided security and stability in a country ravaged by war." He balanced the flat of his palm on the white tile between them. "He worked in tandem with the police and made sure the streets stayed safe."

"For a price." She spat back. "And if they didn't pay, you were the ones those same citizens needed protection from. I think that's called extortion."

"It's the conclusion most people jump to, but it's not like that. At least not since my father assumed control over the area, and I definitely haven't done that." He stood and stormed across the room. When she didn't move, he turned back and closed the distance until he stood directly in front of her. "I run a legitimate security business, with surveillance cameras and armed guards."

"Your guards just do extra services on the side."

He nodded only once. "When needed."

"Dear God, you go from being one of the good guys to, to, the mafia?" She shrugged.

He lifted her hand and touched the reddened knuckles delicately, surprised when she didn't immediately pull away. "We were never the good guys."

"Maybe not, but we had a purpose." She tugged, but his fingers sensed her intention and closed tightly. The feel of holding her hand was exquisite torture, conjuring so many memories of better times.

"And so do we." He lifted her hand to his lips.

Jerking away from him, she twisted in a feline motion, dropping into a low crouch alongside the crypt. She grew perfectly still, as alert as a predatory animal sensing danger. Then he heard it too. Even though someone wanted to remain very quiet, the metal gate still scraped ever so slightly, disturbing the air with tiny ripples of sound.

Within those discordant waves, the air grew heavy, and the malevolence he had felt earlier steadily rose in intensity. The stench of it clung to the crypt, as if the decayed bodies had somehow become gooey again. Shadows shifted, and a rush lit his awareness. Every sense screamed inside of him. He pulled his gun and pointed it in the same direction as Fara's gaze. Slowly, step over step, he rounded the crypt and approached her.

Up onto her feet with an agile hop, she lunged to grab her pack and then grabbed his gun arm, spinning him toward the recesses of the hypogeum.

He hated anyone touching him while he was aiming, and this time anger flared brightly. He was actually glad for it, preferring to feel mind-boggling anger over the insipid weakness of fear. Leaning into her frame, he kept his voice low. "I'm not running away."

Her whisper breathed against his ear, "Brute force won't stop what's in motion. It will consume," her eyes darted toward the doorway. Instantly the ambient heat seeped away, leaving a chill to which every hair reacted. "Let's go, now."

The deep, venomous quality of her tone told him more than her words, and he had enough wherewithal not to argue. Perhaps she felt the evil too. God, of course she did. Fara always sensed everything before anyone else. It was what made her so effective and indispensable to the Agency. There was no way in hell they would have let her go. Although he didn't sense her lying to him, there was more, so much more to discover as to what she was doing with *Ghost Lovers.*

Hand in hand, they ran deeper into the crypt, twisting their way through adjacent rooms until they reached the limits of the electric lights. Determining they were far enough away to be relatively safe, Gae stopped. Pressing Fara against the wall, he kept a hand on her shoulder and leaned around the corner. Somewhere in his gut, he hated himself for running away. Perhaps he could leave her here and sneak back to get close enough to hear what was happening.

Fara took a half-step away from him, and squatting down, started to rummage in her backpack. Any other woman would make noise when even trying to produce a tube of lipstick out of a purse, but she silently produced something that looked strangely enough like lipstick. Perplexed, he shrugged. With her thumb over the end, she clicked on the tiny flashlight and then immediately turned it off.

Although a flashlight would be handy, he knew where they were. As a boy, he had explored nearly endless passages through the macabre crypts more times than he could remember. The front section claimed by the Cult of the Dead was a mere fraction of the overall series of catacombs. Right now, he and Fara were in the chamber where the recently deceased would be drained of fluids, a simpler form of preservation than the Egyptians' mummification, but effective. Some long-forgotten, desiccated bodies still remained upright in the curved hollows, just on the edge of the impenetrable darkness. He couldn't see them but knew they were there nonetheless.

Ribbons of abhorrence tangibly floated in the air along with sounds emanating from Lucia's shrine. The two elements were distinctive, yet intertwined, carrying the schizophrenic emotions of both glee and enmity. The murmur of voices was so thick it was like an ocean, charging and crashing, then waning once more. He was close enough to hear the rambling sounds, but too far to understand the words. Someone laughed, high and bright, like a hand rising from the noise, just to be swallowed back again and lost. The similarities with his unnatural encounter under the palazzo intensified his awareness. A shiver climbed his spine, and the skin on the back of his neck crawled.

"Gaetano?" Aleri called clearly. "Where are you?"

He jerked innately toward the melodious tone, but Fara stopped him with a hand pressed against his chest. She tapped his shoulder twice, but quickly negated that with a sideways sweep, and then tapped four times.

There were four people. Four? Was Mario in this too? Gae could possibly understand Luigi, who carried a belligerent chip on his shoulder of being the poor relations, but his brother was a good man and a true friend. Right now, there were no true friends, except his Berretta. His fingers curled around the pistol's textured grip. Squeezing his gun made his pulse slow, clearing his head enough to think.

"Gaetano," Aleri's voice demanded. "I know you're here, and I need you so badly. Please, come to me. Come, come play with me."

Fara jerked him back behind the wall before he even realized he was moving.

"Gaetano!" The bitterness crackled down the tunnels, sizzling the close air with negative energy.

Fara wrapped her arm around his waist and started moving, drawing him deeper into the long-forgotten burial chambers. The flashlight clicked, but she kept her thumb over the end to shield the light. Her flesh glowed red around the nail, outlining bone. Focusing on the fleshy glow, he followed her, but Aleri crept into his mind. Once again, each step became heavier than the last. He felt as if he was on a leash, stretching the tether as tautly as it would go, and upon reaching the end, he would snap back to her regardless of what he did to avoid it.

Thankfully, Fara seemed unaffected. Whenever he thought of her, he became stronger, and his mind briefly cleared. She started to turn toward a dead-end, but he swung his hand around her waist, this time leading her forward.

"Gaetano" slithered down the tunnels, echoing at least three times with the increasing distance. Still, the pull on him was so strong. Struggling internally against the unseen force, he buried his face in the line of Fara's spine.

Immediately she stiffened. The flesh between her shoulders was hard and taut under his cheek. The tension in her body grew until it was palpable. He didn't know what was wrong, but right now, nothing could be right. His hands touched her arms tentatively at first, then he hugged her to him. The closeness felt so true and real, yet still something else was off, something that had nothing to do with their current situation.

"Gaetano" snapped closer, striking him as tangibly as a whip.

A shudder ran through his back, making him want to turn and run to Aleri. His breath came in a long gasp. "What's happening to me?"

"Shh." Swiveling, Fara whispered directly in his ear. "Is there another exit?"

He used their old code and tapped twice on the front of her shoulder for yes, but then he leaned into her, breathing heavily, as another domineering wave tugged him with the manipulative undertow. "I have to go back and discover what they're doing to Aleri."

Fara shook her head no, and her cheek brushed his as warm breath coursed along his ear. "I left the camera running as evidence in case you killed me."

That snapped him back, fully into the moment. "You really thought-" Her fingertip pressed to his lips, and an erotic rush lit through him. His mind and body filled with the close temptation.

"If I can sense them, they can sense me. We're too close." She grabbed his chin and turned his face to within inches of hers. "Is there another exit?"

His internal struggle played a challenging tug of war. "I'm not leaving."

"That's not your cousin. It's just a trick to get their hands on you." She tensed, looking over her shoulder to stare into the impenetrable darkness. "We've got to go."

The core of trust still existed deeper than his conscious mind. Reluctantly, he continued, leading her into areas where no one had been in years, probably since he was here twenty years ago against his father's wishes.

Cobwebs heavy with dust draped the archways, and the air was just as thick. Each step of progress challenged the tiny penlight, and the darkness was winning. Ahead of them was obscure, but behind them was even blacker, as if all of the energy was being sucked out of the air. There was no other way to describe it other than a giant abnormality was consuming the essence of this place. His essence included, drifting back into the trap, one cell at a time, with the same irrefutable attraction as a black hole in space gathering all nearby matter.

He stopped to catch his bearings, and using the moment, she pulled out a bottle of water. In the stiff silence, he heard her swallowing. Suddenly, his throat felt gritty. "Would you share?"

On the surface, the phrase was innocent enough; however, it was their secret code for wanting sex. At a restaurant or in a crowded room, they used to say that to each other when they were thinking about finding a place to be together.

Her muscles froze. "I can't."

"Can't or won't?" His voice warbled, and although he hated sounding so needy, he truly needed her now more than ever.

"I threw up after leaving your house. I think it was something I ate for breakfast, but on the safe side, you shouldn't drink after me." She reached her hand into the pack and extended an unopened bottle. "Here."

While wondering whether her excuse was real or if she was putting him off, he accepted the offer. Although the water was room temperature, the wetness eased the brittle feeling in his throat, while his other thirst wouldn't be slaked so easily.

Her breath hitched as if she was going to say something and then thought better of it. She clicked off the flashlight.

Total darkness changed nothing physically. The catacomb's walls and archways were there. Plague victims reclined on the slabs. Yet, the lack of sight made the imagination actively conjure other bits and pieces of reality. Purposefully, he calmed his charging pulse and focused, urging his other senses to life.

He heard her screw on the top of her bottle and the hush of the drawstring cord on the backpack as it tightened. His inner urges insisted he fire off questions about her life, and at the same time, filled him with miserable doubt. She had gotten married. Married! He had a hard enough time wondering how to ask her to move in with him, never mind marriage; although, the idea had crossed his mind several times. Shit, he should have had the balls to ask her back when he held her undivided attention. A woman as sexy and voracious as Fara wouldn't stay unattached for long.

A bolt of pure enmity crackled down the corridor. The malevolence was coming, as tangible and real as any living entity. Immediately, Fara grabbed him, tugging him forward through the black obscurity, bumping and feeling their way. In the next chamber, she flicked on the light for less than a second, and then shoved him into a meager gap where fresh air hadn't ventured in a thousand years.

The walls were no longer upright. The upper slabs had fallen toward each other forming a peak just a few inches over his head. On either side, layered in long rows, skeletal remains laid in prostrate poses, seemingly sleeping for all eternity. Fara shoved him deeper into the dusty webs and followed, again wedging him as deeply as possible in the gap between the broken walls. Pinned on three sides, a trace of panic fluttered adrenaline into his system. The closeness sucked in, as if the slabs would continue to fall, crushing them under the massive weight.

The air was so thick with dust it was hard to breathe. The tightness in his lungs burned; still he knew better than to cough. It was so dark there was nothing to see, yet he couldn't keep his eyes closed. Every time he blinked, stringy webs grabbed his lashes and snagged on the stubble of his beard. Sticking out his lower lip, he blew upwards, but the clinging strands remained in place. Before he could try it again, Fara shoved her elbow into his ribs and pushed, compressing his arms against his sides.

The crackling shiver flickered closer. Even nestled behind Fara, he felt the burst of negative energy. Every instinct told him to push her out and run like the devil. The broken wall leading to the aqueduct was only two, maybe three chambers away. As a boy, he had looked through the hole but didn't venture down into the flowing water. Not that he was afraid. He just wasn't sure he would be able to climb back up, and if the son of Don Caravaggio went missing, the city would begin an all-out manhunt. If something like that happened, he would have lost his privileges forever.

The icy cold flickered more frequently and with greater intensity. The hair on his body bristled. Fara shivered, and he felt the ripple flow through her body. Adrenaline charged his system, but his mind diverted to other thoughts. Her body pressed even closer, enough for him to feel her breathing deepen into long and silent inhalations. There was barely enough room for them both, slightly overlapping, his shoulder over hers. By some odd chance, they were facing opposite directions, with his gun arm lodged against the back wall. His right hand was against her hip, which rounded under his touch. The sensation of the spider webs faded as her luscious heat filled the space, pushing away the icy chill. She was always warm to the touch, but this was almost feverish. Perhaps she really was ill.

A trickle of power flowed, like he was close to a live wire, just hot enough to shimmer current into the air, but that was impossible. There wasn't electricity this deep into the tomb. He tipped his head to ask her if she felt it too and then realized it was Fara. Her power took form around them, filling the enclosed space.

Normally he was never at a loss, but this was something he couldn't accurately describe. It was like a warm, soundless hum. He had heard whispers of special agents, who learned how to manipulate more than just minds, but Fara hadn't been in that program, at least not when he knew her.

Even protected behind her psychic shielding, he felt the iniquity approaching. Through the narrow slit in the wall, just past her chin, the darkness shifted. The entire area was pitch black, but this was even darker than that, obscuring the absence of light with its abnormal presence. He pressed closer, leaning into Fara while straining his eyes. Pitchy shadows silhouetted her profile, flowing in frigid waves.

Vigorously, the frequency of the heat surrounding them increased, fighting back the cold and winning degree by degree. The energy formed a physical shield at the end of the nook, just past Fara's chin and shoulder, as if an overlay of herself shimmered in front of her actual body.

He didn't understand what he was seeing through the narrow gap between the crumbling walls. The world was suddenly cast into reverse, like night vision. Tendrils of shade drifted forward and then flowed back, blown by an unseen breeze. Perhaps the thing had been human once, but now the malevolence distorted the form, more akin to a paranormal jellyfish floating in a dead sea. The wraith continued forward and then drifted back, propelled by some unseen tide.

He held his breath, not wanting anything to give away their position, and yet the primitive instinct to run fed his muscles. Knowing not to move wasn't enough when his body was in overdrive. Sucking on the inside of his bottom lip, he bit down hard enough to break the skin. Still, the edge of pain couldn't keep him focused. The adrenaline demanded release, heightening his senses.

The heat surrounding him carried Fara's scent. Not only that, her pheromones danced in the energy. Suddenly, everything became perfectly clear, and it had nothing to do with bolting out into the open.

She sucked in a struggling breath, and he pushed his right hand between the rough wall and her waist. His fingers were spread, and the contact filled him. He remained motionless, waiting for her to react. She didn't even seem to notice, yet he did. His touch connected them, and the heat from her body tingled, beading sweat over his palm. The sensation crept into his nervous system. Closing his eyes, he allowed it to dominate him. Only Fara belonged inside of his world.

Long moments later, the final tendril drifted forward, slithering deeper into the labyrinth. As it moved on, the sickening tension in the air eased. Slowly, not more than a molecule at a time, she relaxed, and in direct relation, the shield of energy relaxed too. She nearly melted into his side and would have fallen if the close walls were any further apart.

He started to ask, "What…"

Her hush was barely more than a breath, yet the air passed from her lips within an inch of his own. Impulsively, he stretched his neck to fill that minor distance and brushed his lips across hers. She had nowhere to go, no way to move away from him. She couldn't even admonish him with a sound.

Knowing he had her trapped made him smile. Knowing she couldn't see him smile made it grow into a full-blown grin. He wanted to reach out and cup her face, showering it with rapid kisses. He wanted to share everything he had with her, right here, right now. He was suddenly rock hard.

Stiffening, Fara leaned toward the opening, giving him an advantage to shift his straining erection against her hip. Her heat radiated, but this time he defined the electrical charge as sexual. In the close proximity, he could almost smell her readiness. Fara, more than any other woman, was a sexual goddess, so wet and willing at any time of the day or night, and in a startling variety of locations. On assignment in the Yucatan, they explored the ruins of Cobá for a militant rebel, and while standing at the top of a recently excavated Pyramid of the Painter, they had the most exotic and erotic experience of his life under the pale crescent moon. Definitely nicer than the dusty catacombs of the Cult of the Dead, yet it would be an interesting addition to their repertoire.

Standing next to her in the ageless dust, he closed and spread his fingers, rubbing her abdomen. Her sudden shock shifted her body just far enough for him to lower his hand and cup the mound within her jeans. The remnants of the electrical heat resided here. He felt her tingling through the denim.

She pushed her hips forward, trapping his hand against the wall. True, it kept him from moving his hand, but it also increased the pressure of his fingers upon her. There would be hell to pay when they finally got out alive, so he decided to make every second count and pulsed his middle finger against her rhythmically.

Her head fell back against the dust enshrouded wall, and he heard her swallow before whimpering, "Stop."

He brushed his nose along the edge of her jaw toward her exposed ear. Honestly, he preferred her hair long. Yet short hair had some advantages, and this was one of them. While inhaling the scent of her skin, his tongue flicked to her earlobe. She shivered, and then he added teeth to the nibbling assault.

"It will come back." The sound of her voice was too soft and pale to be even thought of as a whisper, but the underlying tone held a current of pure Fara.

"Shh," the sound curled on the end of his tongue. Straining to the fullest extension of his neck, he drew her earlobe into his mouth. A silent moan escaped her, and then he felt her resistance falter. The tempo of her breathing increased, and her pulse sped under his lips upon her neck. Her back arched, forcing his hand harder into the rock wall. Under other circumstances, the scraped knuckles would have been painful, but his fingers were pinched so tightly he felt the initial quiver of her orgasm start under his touch.

The air chilled, and the unnatural force shivered across the opening of their hiding place.

"Gaetano, come, come play with me." Innately, he bumped against Fara as every nerve impulse within his body screamed to follow the voice.

CHAPTER 13

Instantly, Fara froze, bracing against Guy's motion while the initial orgasmic ripples flowed through her nervous system. She wanted to cry out. She wanted to beat Guy to a pulp. But right now, what she wanted didn't matter. A personal shield took a lot of power and stamina, and she held the first longer than ever before. It was as if someone or something had aided her, doubling a power unto her own.

This time, the interrupted orgasm emitted its own power, and though she had never attempted to control and channel an orgasm, now would be a dandy time to start. She slowed her mind and gathered the internal force into the kernel directly in the core of her being. On command, it pulsed to life, and the cloaking shimmer returned. Instead of being diminished, it was brighter and more vibrant than the first.

Through the energy, atoms sparkled like dust motes in a beam of light. The negative relief of the image was more startling this time as the entity's face paused less than a foot away from Fara's nose, sniffling in her direction. Even with the decay of time and the toll of bitter damage from whatever had condemned this soul, the entity had once been a human female. Now more akin to a night shade, the creature opened her mouth and flicked a sinuous tongue into the air. Each snake-like strike almost reached the fragile shield and made Fara's heart skip out of rhythm, bounding in her chest. She wanted to close her eyes and concentrate on the shield, yet the need to know her adversary was stronger.

Her eyes focused and became more accustomed to the fluctuating image. Tendrils of long hair flowed in all directions as if floating in the sea, undulating around the creature in an abstract pattern. At the center of the Medusa-like mass, the woman's face was one smooth plane of pale, nearly translucent skin, without rises for a nose, lips, or brows. The flow of gray tightened into an abnormally long neck, like the stalk a plant rather than a human throat. The creature continuously gulped, causing the larynx to bob up and down. The chest didn't expand and contract with breath, so perhaps similar to the gills on a fish, the throat drew in breath.

A lace collar extended down from the base of that gasping throat. The wraith's clothes draped her from shoulder to floor. The fabric was dark, barely discernible, except for its decoration. Exceptionally bright in contrast, strips of white ermine arced over her shoulders. Pearls draped the bodice in low sweeps down to the pinched waist. The wraith's dress was essentially from the same period as the gown in the armoire back at the rental house, and Fara's thoughts strayed to the image of the dark-haired beauty. With the loss of concentration, the shield wavered.

Recognition dawned across the creature's expression, and a growling hiss emanated.

Fara reengaged her focus, hoping the entity didn't have time to discern Guy's presence.

The wraith simply waited outside of the shielded barrier, continuing to flicker its tongue while the throat abnormally bobbed.

The drain of reengaging the psychic shield made Fara's head lighten dizzily. She couldn't continue the stalemate forever. Drawing upon the final ripples of energy still pulsing against Guy's fingers, she drew it upward and blew through parted lips, so gently and easily even a candle wouldn't have flickered.

The wayward soul's tongue flickered rapidly, tasting the air.

"Go on your way. I am not the one you want." Fara infused her best mindful wile in between and through the words. Her vocal prowess had never worked on women, or on the dead, but now would be an ideal time for that to change.

Seemingly satisfied, the condemned spirit turned back toward Lucia's shrine. Fara didn't take her eyes off the creature until the last flowing tendril of snaking hair twisted from view.

Although she should have felt elated, she was physically weak and morally weaker. For over four years, she wanted one last kiss along with the opportunity to tell Guy Carver she loved him.

Now, she didn't know if she could. This wasn't the time or place to discuss their former relationship, but she couldn't keep from thinking about their lustful desire to find the strangest and most unusual places to have sex. The hypogeum was about as strange as they would ever find, and the need to feel his living heat inside of her one final time was omnipresent.

With her eyes closed, memories flashed through her, sensual and heated remembrances of their most unique locales. The open sailboat adrift in Watergate harbor lulled lazily on the calm water until their motion caused the halyards to clank against the metal mast. The 9th hole on Paso Doble's golf course made her feel like a sexual nymph in the glittering moonlight, and then there was Mexico. The usual Mayan sacrifice called for blood, but instead they offered the vitality of consecutive orgasms. Now, they were in a crypt where the dead had lain for centuries. What did they demand in payment for disturbing their rest?

She wanted to admonish Guy for any number of errant rules his disappearance had broken, but what was worse was the embodiment of regrets. Oh dear God, his lower hand had plucked at her aching clitoris like a bass guitar, and her challenging need had betrayed her.

With the tip of her tongue, she licked his flavor from her lips. Even this late in the day, his mouth faintly tasted of toothpaste. He brushed after every meal, even while in the field. Apparently, that hadn't changed. Neither had his ability to ignite her innermost desires. But so many other elements of her life had changed since he had died.

Suddenly resurrected, was he willing to assume their former relationship, or was he just toying with her for old time's sake?

The air lightened, and the chill dissipated by several degrees. Glad to focus on their physical situation, her sideways scoot released his hold. With the residual energy still shuddering inside of her, she peered into the contours of the passageways. After scanning with every vestige she could summon, she didn't sense the creature and then took her hand off from Guy's shoulder, allowing him to ease out of the confined space.

Once free, he drew his gun. She wanted to tell him it wouldn't do any good, but she knew better than anyone how just the weight of the pistol was comforting. She didn't have any other type of comfort to give. Especially not as guilt crept through those same internal channels that only minutes before were rapturous. She loved J.C., but somewhere deep within her inner depths, she had always loved Guy. Nothing she had with anyone else replaced her special feeling just for him.

"Which way?" She didn't want to lean so closely to his body, but being overheard would have been worse.

His fingers rounded both of her arms. She stiffened against the potential kiss, but he only leaned in to whisper, "Follow me."

Holding her hand, Guy led her deeper into the burial chambers. She kept repeating the turns in her head just in case they had to return the way they came. Even with her startling memory, the distortions in the darkness and odd localized energies made her lose track.

At the far corner of the next chamber, the stone shelves had collapsed and knocked out a chunk of wall. Without asking, he took the flashlight from her and stooped to look under the triangular gap. Even the meager glow of the penlight showed too much. The decay of mismatched body parts was beyond gross, as if the cobwebs had absorbed the flesh and formed shadowy veils over fragile bones.

As soon as they entered this narrow chamber, she felt a current of energy, barely detectible. It roused something deep within her gut, disturbing her inner awareness. While Guy cleared their point of escape, the energy disturbance grew, humming deeply within her, reaching the most sensitive spot inside of her awareness as if it knew her.

Instantly her psychic defenses engaged. Spinning to face the source of something incredibly powerful, she realized it was different, somehow familiar, definitely not malevolent like what they had encountered only minutes ago. She closed her eyes, blocking the standard visual input which the brain used to filter reality, and let her mind reach. This energy signature was female and familiar. Fara held up her hands like an Evangelical minister and felt the air. Just under her skin, tangible pulses tingled. Using the intensity to guide her, she crossed the narrow room.

An image formed. These were the remains of Snow White.

The sounds of Guy's soft footsteps followed her. "What are you doing?"

"There's something with us." She held out her fingers and wiggled them. "Here, let me see that." She shone the beam into the upper crypt on the left.

This side of the room was still intact. If these burial chambers had been decorated, the tokens had deteriorated over the centuries. The bones felt old, much older than the spaces in the adjacent rooms, probably plague victims from the Middle Ages.

She rose up onto her toes to see across the highest point. The power radiated as tangibly as the sun, yet the glow wasn't apparent to the eye. The skeleton rotated suddenly, jaw gaping as if the absent tendons held onto the cranium by sheer will alone. The empty sockets reflected the light for just a second, filling with energy as if the soul still held onto this body.

Unsteady, Fara didn't stare too long at those supposed eyes. Ambient power wavered through the ground in long undulating strokes. An audible clunk, from the spine disengaging from the cranium, preceded the skull falling from the ledge. Not thinking about the consequences, Fara dropped the flashlight, dove forward, and caught the grayed skull in both hands.

"Shit! What the hell are you doing?"

The upper teeth were loose but still in place, relatively large and well-formed. She wasn't an expert in anthropology, yet she knew the condition of teeth told a great deal about the life of a human being. Snow White ate a balanced diet and had some sort of oral hygiene, indicating a high social rank.

Guy reached out.

Stronger than a magnet, the skull nearly flew from Fara's hands toward him. The closer Guy was the stronger it pulled. The power continued to spiral, stronger and stronger. Purposefully, she avoided gripping the eye sockets because the being was inside, still using this body. While clinging to the temporal curve, her fingers encountered a crack in the skull. Suddenly, she had that knowing chill surge up inside of her, and instinctively, she tucked it against her torso and turned her back toward Guy. "No, don't touch it."

"Why not?"

"I don't know, just..." spreading her fingertips over the smooth contours of the sloping forehead, she stroked it absently. Something about it boosted her awareness. The overlap of physical sight and psychic impression was disorienting, like wearing 3-D glasses outdoors. Colors shifted, and the overlay of the physical objects undulated at skewed angles. The psychic sight penetrated the physical walls, and she saw distinct patterns of life energy, bodiless souls, tens of thousands waiting for release. The power here collected the dead and didn't allow them to leave, exactly opposite from what the Cult of the Dead professed. Instead of the souls ascending from purgatory, this place was purgatory.

Realizing she could see them, the souls swarmed closer, looking at her as curiously as she regarded them. They were beautiful, like oblong bubbles of ethereal light. Then suddenly they fled like scared fish along a coral reef. Some hid near their former bodies, while others fled to dark recesses.

The wraith was coming back.

Enhanced with this second sight, Fara perceived the clear outlines of the feminine putrescence. She had been beautiful and stately, yet dark at her inner core. That darkness not only approached; it fed as it came, inhaling the unlucky souls who didn't hide well enough to escape detection.

Taking a step closer to the chamber's opening, she whispered harshly to Guy. "Get out of here!" When he hesitated, she snapped, "No questions. Go! Now!"

Thankfully, he listened. With minimal resistance, he slid feet first and then wormed the rest of his body through the meager opening in the broken wall. A slosh of falling into water faintly echoed when the entity's chill suffused the room.

Of its own accord, the skull twisted in Fara's hands and faced the creature. The empty eye sockets filled with white-hot, burning light. She tried to release it, yet the flesh of her hands seemed fused to the sloping contours. A brilliant burst discharged in an explosion of white.

Fara was falling, falling through an endless expanse. She couldn't breathe. There was no air, only endless white light.

CHAPTER 14

J.C. had never been good at lying. He had run through countless variations of the events at San Cristobal, and each sounded as lame as the last. Angels and demons, ghosts and human minions, hell, the truth was more fanciful than any lie. The Feds wouldn't believe him, no one would, and he was out of options. The agents would be at grandmother's house in Bayamon any minute. Swallowing the hard lump in his throat, he decided. He would be a man and own up to the truth, letting the consequences fall.

The doorbell rang with a stinging sharpness, biting him to the core.

He took one last look around him; his last moment as a free man. The small house was always the same, except Adele Calderon was usually in the kitchen with the small countertop TV moaning with telenovelas. Thankfully, she had listened to him, and about thirty minutes ago, he drove her to Rio Hondo Mall. The parking lot for K-Mart was right behind their back fence, but it took over fifteen minutes to get through three traffic lights by car. He hoped she would have someone to call to pick her up after he was carted off to jail.

What would she think if he just disappeared like his grandfather?

J.C. didn't know if her heart could take another shock like that, or worse yet, she would be left all alone in the world. His grandfather paid all the bills and had everything in his name. Of course, he kept over a cool million in insurance, but he was just missing, not officially dead. Without his monthly income, Abuela would starve.

The bell rang again, and this time he forced his feet to move. With each step, his will increased, resigned to his fate. What happened in the dungeon of Fort San Cristobal wasn't his fault, but it certainly wasn't Fara's responsibility. If someone had to take the blame, it should fall on his shoulders.

Be a man. Be a man, repeated inside his head. He had to suck it up and be a man.

His fingers curled around the doorknob. The metal was as hot as the Puerto Rican afternoon. Taking a deep breath, he opened the heavy steel door and blinked as the woman's hand stopped in its approach yet still fell forward in a knocking motion, nearly hitting him in the chin.

She pulled back with conviction. "Juan Carlos Calderon?"

He looked between the federal agents, both in conservative dark suits, probably the same ones they wore yesterday. Certainly, they had to recognize him. Well, maybe not the blind hombre, but the woman appeared to have all of her faculties. "We met yesterday."

"Since Special Agent Finius can't see you, he needs to hear you identify yourself for reporting purposes." She motioned toward the blind man, and her plastic badge wagged. Her name was Chrystal, Chrystal Delphae.

J.C. stared at the woman's plain fingernails and thought of how nicely Fara kept her hands with a bright manicure. This woman was blond and stout, nothing like the exotic temptress who was his girlfriend. His girlfriend! God, it was just his luck to find the woman of his dreams right before he had to do life in prison for murders he didn't commit.

"I am Juan Carlos Calderon, J.C." He stepped aside and opened the door wider.

The blind man entered first, swinging his white-tipped cane, and in the crowded room, every swing bumped into something. He tapped the leg of the armchair. Apparently sensing the difference in the sound of the thump, he felt the back with spread fingers, and moved forward, sitting down precisely in the center of the cushion.

Agent Delphae closed the door behind her and then headed to the sofa.

J.C. remained by the door. For only a fleeting second, he thought about running. But where would he go? In Scotland, Lily Sloan would be able-

No! He stopped himself before the crazy thought took root. He had to own up to what happened. If he ran, they would go after Fara. "Would you like something cool to drink?"

Keeping her eyes set to his every move, Agent Delphae shook her head no. "Mr. Calderon, are you aware of what celestial occurrence happened on the night of March 20th?"

It was the worst day of his life, one he would never be able to forget. "Abib's New Moon."

The only sign of interest was a slight tip of her head. "Why don't you have a seat?" She continued in a disinterested monotone, like a waitress at a cheap all-night diner. Her plastic ID badge with a holographic seal was more official looking than an oval nametag with a name pressed out on a label machine. Flo came to mind, but J.C. had never met a waitress named Flo.

The room was small, and the only other chair was on the far side of the coffee table. It had a small round pillow with petite gathers around the blue rosette center. His grandfather liked holding the pillow in his lap, stroking the pleated folds with the tips of his fingers.

He stared at the chair, not wanting to sit there, but sitting next to Agent Delphae would be worse. He didn't know whether it was more appropriate for him to step over the woman's legs, or the blind man's legs and cane. He decided the blind man was the least risky and just as J.C. lifted his foot, the man scooted out of the way.

"How did you-?" J.C. broke off, not knowing how to phrase the question without sounding insensitive.

"I have a keen sense of hearing. More developed and with a broader range than most humans." Agent Finius said the word *humans* as if he didn't count himself as one.

"So I see." Oh shit! J.C. winced at his blunder. "I mean I noticed."

The man's face lit with a smile. "No worries Mr. Calderon. I'm not easily offended. I was born without sight, so I have learned to adapt."

Removing the pillow with the minimal amount of contact possible, J.C. set it onto the beige tile floor and sat down. Neither of the agents said anything, so he waited. The silence grew heavier until he just couldn't stand it any longer. "I told you everything I knew yesterday. I'm not sure how I can help you."

"Tell us about the Cult of the Dead." The woman didn't blink. Her cold eyes drilled into him, the shade of deep ice, but it was more than just the color. They sent an uncomfortable chill along with the piercing gaze, as if it was made out of ice, no something even colder.

He opened his mouth, ready to answer about San Cristobal, but then he did a double-take. "The Cult of the Dead?"

"In Naples," she paused again, and the pattern of her voice reminded him of Fara with pauses filled with unspoken influence, "under Purgatorio ad Arco."

Agent Finius continued. "Your co-producer, Fara Trotter, is in Naples, isn't she?"

"Yeah," he scratched the mosquito bite on his arm while trying to think ahead of them, but he had no idea where their line of questioning was heading. "Fara went as scheduled. I stayed behind to help my grandmother get settled without my grandfather's assistance."

"He's not coming back?" The blind man spoke with the same calculated rhythm. Perhaps all federal agents had a class in speech patterns.

Was his grandfather coming back? Shit, he hoped not. The very thought bore into his soul. The truth left his mouth slowly. "I don't know. I don't know where he went, exactly."

"Mr. Calderon," Agent Finius replied. "We know what happened at the Fort. We know about the followers of Maboya and Eduardo Calderon's involvement."

His throat tightened. "Then can you tell me where he went?"

"No," Agent Delphae added with a harsh dryness, "Fara Trotter saved you. How did she do that Mr. Calderon?"

He nearly melted and was glad he was already sitting in the chair. "I have no fucking clue, Agent Delphae."

"Special Agent Delphae," she corrected. "What happened to her in Afghanistan?" Her tone barely lifted at the end of the sentence to indicate a question. Clearly, she knew the answer.

"She was abducted and tortured." He winced at the memory of the heavy scars lacing down Fara's back.

"Fara Trotter was part of a special program." She continued.

He had to concentrate to get the image out of his mind. "Like what?"

Her tone went even flatter. "I'm sorry, but I'm not allowed to share those details with you."

"Look lady, you're the one who brought it up." J.C. shifted, almost reaching for the damned pillow, but caught himself.

Her partner cleared his throat. "Did you ever see Mrs. Trotter do anything out of the ordinary?"

"There's nothing ordinary about Fara." Not wanting to meet her drilling stare any longer, J.C. shifted his focus to the blind man. "You're going to have to be more specific."

"Did she ever tell you to do something you didn't want to do but couldn't keep from doing anyway?" His voice swayed with the words, sashaying along like some smooth verbal dance.

"You're talking about her Jedi voice thing." He almost added, like you're doing, but decided better of it.

The woman scooted forward and interlaced her fingers between the knees of her pantsuit. "We don't use cliché movie characters to describe special abilities, Mr. Calderon. Its name is audio hypnotic induction."

His twisted smile grew into a grin. "The Jedi thing is a lot easier to remember."

Special Agent Finius chuckled softly. Setting his cane next to his chair, he shrugged out of his sport coat. J.C. didn't know how he was able to keep it on this long. The house was cool, not cold. The man had to be sweating, but not a drop of perspiration darkened his blue dress shirt. Just by the sense of touch, he folded the jacket at the shoulders and doubled it over the arm of the chair. His identification badge dangled. It was upside down, but for the first time, J.C. really took a good look at it.

Special Agent
Warren Theodore Finius
F.P.I.

"Wait a minute." He tipped his head just to be sure the central letter was a P and not a B. "You're not FBI?"

Delphae answer crisply. "We never said we were."

"Then what the hell are you? You introduced yourselves as-"

Her tone continued, "Special agents, which we are."

J.C. nearly rose. "There's no FPI?"

"You sound very sure of yourself." The overwhelming feeling the blind man was looking at him made J.C. very uncomfortable.

"I'm not the smartest man alive, but I'm pretty sure FBI doesn't have a P in it."

Finius chuckled, and the sound rolled around the room. "Federal Paranormal Investigations. FPI is a little known branch of the CIA."

With a humph, Delphae propped an elbow on the back of the couch. The gap in her suit jacket gaped just enough to reveal a curve of pale, white breast. "That stands for Central Intelligence Agency. You probably heard of that one."

He resisted the urge to flick her off and kept his hands clasped in his lap. "Yeah, so has anyone who owns a TV. Okay, you're like a real version of agents Skully and Mulder. So what do you want with me?"

"Your cooperation." Delphae answered all too neatly. "We have a potential hazard in the public domain."

Tightening his expression, J.C. put on his bad-ass face he used on the streets of Miami. "You're talking about Fara."

"Yes, Mr. Calderon. Faradahl Alecto Trotter." The woman balanced her fingertips together, lifting them as she crossed her left leg over her right. For the first time, she broke her steely gaze and looked at her hands. "Where is she?"

"That's a trick question. You already know she's in Naples." Out of the blue, a blend of a marijuana high and drunken buzz flickered through his brain. To shake off the effects of the rush, he rose from the chair and circled around it, holding onto the wooden trim. He tried to think of what game they were playing, especially since he didn't know the rules, but it was hard to think, as if someone else was inside his head doing it for him.

"Was in Naples." With a huff, she stood as well, once again staring at him with unblinking intensity. "Where is she now?"

The invisible fingers massaging his brain stopped, and his grip relaxed. "I spoke to her late last night. Well there it was morning. She was having breakfast at a roadside café. Someone nearly had a car wreck at the intersection."

Delphae glumly nodded. "We know about the call."

"Is that the last you heard from her?" Finius moved the dark glasses down the bridge of his nose, and his pale, nearly colorless eyes stared straight at J.C. Other than the lack of pigment, they looked normal.

"It's the last time we talked. She called me a few hours ago and left a message. I had just gotten up to the window at the DMV. I had to help my grandmother get a driver's license."

"What did her message say?" Delphae fired off the question without taking a breath.

Finius didn't even give him a chance to answer. "Do you still have it on your phone?"

"No." He felt the heightened energy sizzle, making the humid air come to life.

Delphae rose to her feet with a sudden hop. "The call was only twelve seconds in duration, untraceable. Did she say anything out of the ordinary?"

His lopsided grin grew, but he wasn't about to share how Fara said she loved him and missed him. "She didn't sound like herself."

"Was she distressed?" She added a slight wheedle to her words.

"Distressed? No." This time he was prepared, and the mind trick didn't numb his brain. He kept his cool. "What the fuck is going on?"

"She went off grid." The blind man interjected and stood, taking a step toward J.C. without the aid of his cane.

He took a step back. "What do you mean by off-grid?"

"Finius, what are you doing?" The woman tensed for action, and the ambient energy shivered. In an automatic reaction, J.C.'s abs tightened as if preparing for a sucker punch.

"Every person who receives FPI training has a chip implanted under the hairline for tracking purposes. It's tied into the body's energy grid, unique to each individual. The grid uses the body's internal power to emit signals. The sub-frequency is under the range of normal hearing, so it can be transmitted undetected." Agent Finius took another step forward and rounded the end of the coffee table.

"How did you do that?" A chill swept up J.C., and he edged one step back, closer to the patio door. If they attacked him, he would break for the fence and sprint to the mall. He knew his changes were slim to none, but at least it was still a plan. Fara always said to make a plan.

Finius smiled broadly and removed his black wraparound sunglasses completely, folding and then tucking them into his shirt pocket. "My eyes have an unique flaw, Mr. Calderon. I can't perceive natural sunlight. However, in areas where psychic energy has coalesced, I see echoes of the physical world through the metaphysical one. Your grandfather, Eduardo Calderon, preferred sitting in the chair that you just vacated. He had a powerful aura, and such power takes time to dissipate. Psychic trauma will also stain an area, which is how I saw Faradahl save your life and the life of Robert Hartz, your boss with *Ghost Lovers*. The visual climax will repeat over and over again until all of the accumulated energy disperses."

"Like a residual haunting," he murmured.

"Some call it that." Agent Delphae shot her partner a rueful look.

Either Finius didn't notice or didn't care; hell, the hombre was blind after all, well, technically. "I have never witnessed someone channel energy with that much intensity. The resonance will remain in the dungeon of Fort San Cristobal for years to come. Some call the channeling a thoughtform, where the imagined, once visualized, becomes real."

Delphae clipped, "I don't think it's wise to go into such detail-"

"Normally," he cut her off. "This one is an exception. Remember, you do not see what I perceive, regardless of how hard you try. We need him. You said that yourself."

"Why would I want to help you? I'm having enough difficulty getting my own shit back together." J.C. softly added, "Why me?"

"Let me continue to explain." Finius waved off his partner's snort of derision. "To influence the minds and wills of others is not easy. Some never master audio hypnotic induction even after years of diligent training. Taking that to the next level to use a thoughtform to draw upon the great universal and abundant power of light to heal or protect is theoretically possible, yet exceptionally rare. In fact, this is the first documented case. Someone would have to integrate the resonance key of earthbound ambient energy and channel it in a specialized thoughtform. Once that someone mastered the power, he or she could use the energy for good or evil."

J.C. wanted to say, like duh, but he just spread his palms in a duh shrug. "The force versus the dark side."

"That is one way to visualize it, if you must." Delphae snipped.

"I can see the remnants of decades of manipulation in this house, yet currently you are unstained. From the time you were a child, your mind has been manipulated, right there." He motioned to his grandfather's chair. "None of those negative thoughtforms your grandfather inflicted upon you remain upon your person, which is highly unique. Actually, yours is the first case I've ever witnessed. In the dungeon, Faradahl channeled all of that derision, all of the negative energy into the vortex, leaving your soul cleansed and rejuvenated, and you're unharmed.   I have never seen anyone facilitate such a transmutation through the power of light." He smiled.

"Faradahl Alecto Trotter is more powerful than anyone on record." She looked at her watch and tapped the crystal face twice.

"Which is why we must find her." Finius concluded.

"I still don't understand why I…"

Delphae quipped. "You are tuned into her light."

J.C. was amazed when she didn't add the word stupid to the end of her sentence, but her tone certainly said it. That snapped him back into the current reality.   No amount of verbal description could possibly explain how Fara controlled the vortex, transmutation of light, or whatever the hell it was. Here, he thought they wouldn't believe him, and now he was the one who was having trouble believing. "And you need my help."

"Your relationship with Faradahl resonates on an unique wavelength." Finius' fingers felt the air above J.C.'s shoulder and fluffed in tiny circles as if brushing away pieces of lint. "Her light shields you, even now. Such a unique color." He continued down J.C.'s left arm until his hand hovered over his emerald ring. "It's green. Normally psychic light is yellow, red, or blue."

The man stopped speaking, but J.C. knew what he would have said. The connection had something to do with his ring. Fara wore the matching stone, and the two rings were joined metaphysically.

"Never seen her equal, you mean. No one has ever left the grid." Delphae took a single step closer and picked up the blue pillow as if it was a challenge. For a second she was perfectly still, and then a shudder raked her body. Her face lost what little color it had, and she shivered again.

"Is Fara dead?" J.C. sucked in a hurried breath, and his right hand clasped over his ring. The humming resonance was there ever since they sort of inherited the matching wedding rings from the ghosts of Felipe and Vivian Cordova.

"We don't think so. When a tagged individual dies, the chip emits a final signal, a beacon which leads us to the body. That hasn't happened." The blind man reached out and took the pillow from the other agent's hands, setting it down onto the chair where it normally stayed. "She just disappeared, and our assignment is to find her."

J.C.'s stomach clenched until he felt sick while the details raced through his mind. "Like I said, she's in Naples. Not Naples Florida. She's in Naples-"

"Italy. Yes, we know where she was." If words could cut, hers would be icy blades of steel. "Under the church in the catacombs of the Cult of the Dead."

He threw his hands up into the air and then realized he had seen his grandfather do that same motion thousands of times.

His jaw snapped shut, and he crossed his arms tightly. "Then why are you looking for her here?"

They both stopped and faced him. In unison, they replied, "You are our link to her. The closer you are to her the brighter the connection will become."

"You're going to use me like some metaphysical blood hound?" He ran his hand through his hair, tugging with mounting frustration. "Did you think of calling her?" He pulled the phone from his pocket.

With glazed anticipation, both agents waited while the call rang for the sixth time and rolled into voicemail. Agent Finius grinned a sideways smirk as if validated. "Mr. Calderon, we need you to come with us to Naples. Mrs. Trotter is an enigma, a special individual who's immensely powerful-"

"And dangerous." Delphae's face held the exact opposite expression, about as sour and contrite as anyone J.C. had ever seen, changing his initial impression of how she appeared to be the sweet girl next door. Anyone knocking on her door would be mental. "Will you come with us willingly?"

He didn't say anything because he didn't know what to say. Fara was an enigma, and she was dangerous. In fact, she was the most dangerous person he had ever met, and after working for the news in Miami for all those years, that was something. Yet, as they mentioned, she wasn't evil. Powerful. Beautiful. Fara was his woman, and she was in trouble.

J.C. stared at his phone, willing it to ring, and jumped when it did. His heart fell when he saw his grandmother's number. He swallowed hard, and yet the tightness in his throat only grew more pronounced. "I have one condition."

Finius didn't hesitate. "Name what you want, and we will take care..."

J.C. couldn't hear the end of Finius's sentence over his partner's growl of frustration.

CHAPTER 15

Gae's eyes stung like a son of a bitch, yet he swallowed his curses, not willing to give up his position. Fara must have had a weapon light with a high intensity discharge, at least five thousand lumens of brilliant white light, which meant only one thing. *Ghost Lovers* was a cover for covert work. No civie, not even ex-ops, carried such sophisticated tech for incidental use.

She had lied to him.

He couldn't blame her. If the situation were reversed, he wouldn't trust him either. Nothing would have injured her more than what he had done to her. She would never trust him again, but he had to try. He leaned forward and felt his body tense, primed and ready to catch her as she dropped through the hole in the wall. He had a long list of mistakes to make up for, and being here for her was one small step toward atonement.

Slightly offset luminous white rings in the form of the oval opening moved wherever he looked, as if ghostly eyes stared back at him out of the nothingness. Because of it, he couldn't see a damn thing. Logically, the wall had to be about a meter to his left. His arm stretched, and his wet shirt constricted. With a low grumble, he pulled it off and discarded it into the moving water still flowing from an inland source for over two thousand years.

He eased his fingers into the jelly-like scum covering the old bricks, tracking them across the mortar. Oddly enough, the line of the stonework was off, not level, at least not what he thought was level. Letting go of the wall, he assessed his position, rocking slightly to perfect his balance. He was standing upright, squarely upon both feet. The footing was slightly graded at a downward slope to his left, but not enough to throw off his inner balance by much.

Brushing off more of the slimy growth, he tracked his fingertips over the surface. The bricks were aligned in a regular pattern, just not in the way he had expected. The rows were diagonals with bricks set in diamond shapes rather than squares. He felt row after row and marveled at the Roman's ingenious engineering. The very shape would translate any earth tremors through a waveform and not crack the bricks. That was how the aqueduct remained whole and functional after eons of earthquakes and volcanic eruptions. They turned the bricks. Simplistic genius.

Following the pattern, he stretched higher, and at the very edge of his reach, the surface was dry. Where the original grouting had worn away from the smooth stones, he worked the fingers of his left hand into the crack. Swinging his body for momentum, his right hand reached higher. Working his way from crack to worn space, he steadily moved upward in a spider-like crawl until he reached the joint where the arched ceiling began, and finally the toes of his boots found dry purchase.

The exercise wasn't strenuous, but his heart still thumped loudly in his chest. Other than the steady gurgle of the water flowing below him, it was the only atypical noise. Fara was silent, either knocked-out or taken. His heartbeat quickened even more, and a fresh blend of adrenaline pulsed through his veins.

On the third sweep with his right foot, he bumped the left edge of the opening and scuttled over the ancient bricks. Leaning to the furthest stretch of his precarious balance, he peered inside. The tomb was dark, except for the residual circles of light which still burrowed every place he looked.

"Fara?" He whispered hoarsely, and then swallowed while waiting for a reply. Had he just given up his position to the wraith?

Closing his useless eyes, he focused his other senses. A hushed moan, slightly more than a breath, reached his ears.

"Fara, you okay?"

An uncharacteristic groan permeated the space, echoing through the dark silence.

"Shit!" muttered under his breath. He reached through the hole and spread his fingers, grasping for something solid to leverage his body. He didn't even want to imagine what it was.

Waving his hand with a sweeping motion, several miscellaneous body parts shifted out of the way. Thankfully, he felt the edge of the broken slab and curled his fingers around the jagged yet solid surface.

Worming his way up into the chamber was actually easier than forcing his way out since his body was stretched to full extension, and his chest and abdomen were slick with the gelatinous slime from the tunnel. He scooted, worming his way forward. Then something grabbed him, near the waist. Instinctual force made him twist, and a belt loop ripped but didn't completely give. A growl of frustration rose to his lips, and he swallowed the sound. Rocking as far as he could onto his right side, he unbuttoned the fly and worked the belt loop off from an errant piece of stone. With one shove, he was finally through. He didn't waste time to take a breath. Instantly, he was rolling into the open and up onto his feet.

"Who's there? Where am I?" The low voice asked first in Spanish and then repeated the questions in Italian.

"Quiet," he replied flatly in Italian while straining to hear if anything was near, yet the chamber felt strangely empty, devoid of the chilled menace and the oppressive energy. The uncomfortable tightness in his chest released. Pretty certain they were alone, he asked, "What happened?"

"Where am I?" Panic infused her trembling voice, raising the volume with each word. "Who are you?"

Shit, she was shell-shocked. Localizing the sounds, he treaded silently across the narrow chamber, at least until he stepped on the flashlight she had dropped. With a crunch, it switched on. Her ear-rattling screech carried with a thousand echoes. If anyone was still in Lucia's chamber, they would definitely be on their way.

"Fara, shut up." Swooping down, he picked up the penlight. Smudges clung to the left side of her face; she had to have fallen and maybe hit her head. She was dazed, yet otherwise appeared unharmed. He extended his hand. "Come-on, we've got to get out of here. You go down first."

Her fists clenched and arms drew into her chest, hefting the upper edge of her bosom into view. Those wide eyes slid over his chest, as if seeing him for the first time.

"Damn it Fara, just do it!" When she didn't immediately obey him, he lifted her from her feet and shoved laterally in the direction of the hole. The fine hairs on the back of his neck lifted when the tingle crept up his spine. "Jesus, they're coming. Go through the God-damn hole!" This time she didn't argue and wriggled through the crack. A shrill screech preceded a flailing splash.

His muscles jerked toward the opening, and then with a second thought, he twisted to grab her gear. Fara kept a small arsenal with her at any given time, better be prepared. The skull she'd been holding slid off the backpack and rattled hollowly onto the hard floor. Seizing it in a quick sweep, he thrust it through the small opening in the top of her backpack.

The chill in the air deepened, and shuffling steps approached. It didn't sound the same as when the wraith had followed them. Actually, he didn't remember hearing steps at all.

He tied off the string and thrust the backpack through the hole ahead of him. It hit the water only a second ahead of his body. He entered without causing a ripple, but his feet slipped out from under him when they hit the slimy bottom, dunking him under the cool surface. Gaining his footing, he waited while crouching next to the wall.

Silent minutes passed like hours. Gae ventured a step. Nothing happened. He gazed up where he knew the break in the wall should be. Nothing was there.

"Where are you?" Whispering cautiously, he shone the light down and then up the aqueduct. The thin, yet powerful, beam arced over her back. She was facing the opposite wall, working her way against the mild current, going uphill.

What the hell? Fara would know to go downstream unless it was impassible. He swung the light down the tunnel. He didn't see an obstruction. Casting another cautious glance both up and down the tunnel, the closest exit had to be downstream.

"You're going the wrong way," he spoke just loud enough for the sound to carry but not too loud to echo.

Turning toward his voice, she stopped and raised a hand to shield her eyes. "What is that strange light?" An unusual hesitancy lisped through her voice.

"I thought you did it. It wasn't a light grenade?" Leaning forward, he swept his arms through the water until his fingers encountered her backpack. Now filled with water, it was one heavy mother. Holding it upside down, he clamped his hand over the small opening, pouring out the accumulated water. "You okay?"

Remaining where she was, she cowered against the wall.

"Tell me what happened." He switched to English, her native language.

She shook her head no.

He took a step toward her, and she retreated by the same distance. When he stopped, she stopped too. Fara had never backed down in her life, at least not the Fara he remembered. Either the Taliban did a total number on her or whatever happened in the chamber rattled her. Maybe it was a combination of both. Although that seemed plausible, it didn't quite fit. She looked the same, a serious expression surrounding piercing green eyes. But now, she was like a wet cat caught out in a storm, all wide-eyed and wary.

He tried to shake off the sensation, but again, the brittle edge prodded his inner senses sending warnings throughout his system. He decided to continue to speak in English and push for more details. "What happened? What caused that bright light?"

"Your words are unknown to me." She replied in an odd Italian dialect, slurring her r's with a whispery thin lisp. "What language are you speaking?"

That caught him off guard, sending his nerves on the offensive. He stopped, his mind spinning into a new line of questioning in Italian, "What language do you prefer?" When they lived together, Fara spoke over twenty languages and was able to localize dialects to sound as if she was from a particular region. She picked up languages like some women collected shoes. What was she up to?

"We are in Italy, are we not?" A full dose of arrogance laced through her accented Italian. "Are you abducting me for ransom?"

Again, he paused. "No, you know better than that."

Grabbing her throat in a single hand, she gasped as if preparing to scream, yet the closely knit words were almost silent. "You're an assassin."

"I thought that was settled. I didn't try to kill you." The bright white rings from the burst had faded completely, leaving her perfect face staring back at him. Still, something was different; she looked at him like a stranger.

This had to be a prank. "Quit yanking my chain." He forced a smile.

She gazed around her and motioned toward the current. "Is it underwater?"

"What?"

"The chain."

"No," he approached slowly. She didn't remember him. She didn't remember anything. "Look, I'm not here to hurt you. I'm rescuing you. Don't you recognize me?"

"I ... I can't ... There was a sudden light. My vision is improving with each passing moment, yet my eyes are clouded. Detail escapes me. Nary it hath not dulled my sense of hearing, for even the tone of your voice is foreign. If you be truly my rescuer, then be good enough to add your name."

"Gae," when she didn't reply, he added, "Gaetano."

"Gaetano," his name poured from her with a sigh of relief. "Did you see the light too?"

"I saw it."

Her emerald eyes glanced up and down the tunnel, and then faced him. "We're underground. Do you know a way out?"

"Yes, I think so, but you'll have to trust me." He extended a hand toward her.

Without hesitating, she slipped her hand into his, and her chilled fingers tightened. "I trust you to lead me out of this foreign place."

Although something still felt inherently out of balance, he wasn't going to pass up this opportunity. He had never heard of light causing amnesia, but this could work to his advantage. What if he could get Fara to fall in love with him all over again?

Sliding his arm around her, they continued forward following the steady decline. About a kilometer downstream, the flooring leveled, and the depth of the water increased to his thighs. The principle chute led off to the right, but an errant branch blocked the flow.

Gae thought back upon the stories his father told him. Men had to maintain the aqueduct, cleaning debris from the channels. Along the tunnel's upper walls the original Roman designers built access points and handholds near potential bottlenecks to facilitate clearing the system. The Romans' design used a natural gravitational flow, which would mean all this water would eventually flow into the sea. Right now, he was hoping for a better alternative; they were at least five kilometers from the coast.

At the juncture of each branching tunnel, he examined the handholds where two walls met and rapped his knuckles against the wall. The stone was tufa, formed from compressed layers of volcanic flows, and it was as durable today as it was a thousand years ago. He left Fara holding the flashlight and climbed up the recessed divots.

The city had grown over the top of the forgotten waterway, sealing off the exit. Still, at every juncture, he tried each historic access point, climbing to the top. Fara waited for him with the fading penlight in her hand, a single star in a vast, dark universe. The similarity was profound. She was the spark of hope in his bleak existence.

He reached the top of the next connection. Feeling his way, his finger located the warped edges of an ancient trap door, and his heart leapt. He searched every square inch, but couldn't locate a latch. Using as much leverage as he could muster from his precarious perch, he pushed against the wood, might as well have been stone, just like all the others. Disappointed yet not defeated, he climbed down and returned to Fara's side. She didn't ask. Hell, she didn't need to.

He extended his open palm. "Can I have the flashlight?"

She looked at it oddly and then extended it to him.

In the opposite corner, he climbed up the second set of grips. As he rose, he heard something. Music! Even the bad singing didn't faze him. He placed his hand against the rough wood and felt the vibration of the driving beat.

Taking the flashlight from his pocket, he shone it on the door. The plywood was worn but not nearly as old as the wooden slab on the other side. The end closest to the wall had thin streaks of rust, apparently from recessed hinges.

He threw his shoulder into the trapdoor, and the resulting crack echoed. He doubted anyone heard the sound over the pounding karaoke, especially since the singer went for volume over talent. Gae opened the broken hatch and poked his head through the opening.

"Stop right there. This establishment is protected by Caravaggio Security."

Elation made him fling the door completely open. Even with the noise, he heard the safety click off the trigger. "Antonio, it's me."

"What the hell? Don Caravaggio, where did you come from?"

Antonio Malloba was slight of build, but wiry in a fight. Never with him, of course, but he had seen the man leverage a drunk or two out of the bar.

Gae clapped the outreached hand and used the man's grip to gain his feet. "Jesus, I'm glad to see you." He didn't hear Antonio's next question, so focused on his task. "Do you have some rope? A friend of mine is still down in the aqueduct."

A coil of rope was in the far corner and looked as if it had been there about as long as the trapdoor. He thought about just throwing it down as is, but decided to tie a loop into the end. In a way, he was surprised he needed to; Fara climbed better than he did and should have been up into the storeroom already.

"I'm sending down a rope," he called into the echoing cavern, and then turned to Antonio. "Would you give me a hand?"

He rubbed his filthy hands on his thighs before grabbing the rough coil. He felt movement on the other end.

He leaned over the opening and shouted into the darkness. "Did you remember your backpack?"

"The bag with the large handles?" Her voice echoed hollowly.

"Yeah, the bag." He swallowed his mounting frustration. "Put the loop of the rope under your shoulders and then slip the backpack on. Let me know when you're ready."

"Gaetano, I rely upon your protection and place my confidence in your charge." Her voice slipped up through the darkness. If he hadn't known Fara was down there, he would have thought it a different person.

"I won't let you down." He pulled and felt her weight swing on the end of the rope. Even if she was still trying to get back at him, she wouldn't have put herself at risk doing it. Especially with her amazing agility, scaling the wall would have been simple, but instead, she let him pull her up. Even Aleri would have had enough common sense to use her feet to scale the wall and use the rope as a failsafe.

Aleri! His heart flopped. He hadn't even thought about his cousin, not once. Guilt sliced through him, but he had to stay focused. Listening to the karaoke singer, he timed his pull of the rope with the beat. He asked Antonio in a similar rhythm, "Seen Luigi tonight?"

"Not yet, but it's still early. Only about 9:00."

They'd been down there for over six hours. With one more heft, the men pulled Fara into view. Her hands clutched the rope with knuckles whitened with fear. She rose through the hole in the floor and relief poured over her features. He thought about chastising her, yet there was gratitude and devotion in those eyes. He had never seen her so totally relieved, meek and contrite. She was even shivering.

He turned to Antonio. "I'll give you a month of free monitoring if you help us out of here undetected." He looked down at his own filthy bare chest. "We'll need some clothes."

The man took off his leather coat, and Gae motioned to Fara. The tips of her fingers barely extended from the sleeves. Her face was pale, and now that the raw emotions quit playing in her eyes, they appeared darkly hollowed, a mere shadow of her former self.

"If you zip up, from a distance people might think you're Antonio. The zipper." He pointed to the front of the jacket. With a huffed out breath to help maintain control, he stepped over to her. "Jesus Fara, what's going on with you?"

She remained silent. Antonio returned with an old hoody, probably something out of the lost and found. Gae pulled it over his head and hunched down into the fleece. No one would recognize them. They were up the stairs and out the front door before any of the patrons even noticed.

Night had settled upon Naples, grasping the town like a cool hand. He looked at his watch; it had stopped at 3:42. The Brera Quattro was waterproof, but it stopped right about the time the pulse of light occurred. No wonder it rattled her senses. It had to have been more than just light; only some kind of major electrical pulse could disable a sealed battery. He was amazed the flashlight still worked, but it had been turned off at the time of the incident. Why did Fara turn it off?

Although he never used cabs for security reasons, a long line stretched back from the corner stand. Normally, it was an irritation, getting in the way of their reserved parking directly in front of the club; today it was fortuitous. A cabby wearing a Greek fisherman's cap leaned against the door of his car.

Gae pulled Fara along behind him. She seemed reluctant to rush out into the open, so he followed her instincts and looked around to be sure no one was watching.

The cab driver straightened and smiled with recognition, tipping the edge of his cap. "Donna Fara, good to see you again. I see you survived the night at Corte dei Sirena."

Gae stopped short and glanced over his shoulder. Her face was even paler in the yellowish light of the streetlamp. "That's perfect."

"You're as weird about that haunted-" the driver's eyes grew wide. "Oh, Don Caravaggio, beg pardon. I didn't realize it was you until you were-, well you are-" The driver swallowed hard and then bowed. "I am honored to be in your service, anytime, day or night. I am yours." He extended a business card, which Gae snagged quickly just to speed things up, thrusting it into his jeans. "Where can I take you?"

"To the lady's house and then forget you ever brought us there." He stepped out of the puddle forming around his feet.

"Dear God, you're soaking wet."

"I'll make it worth your while." He slipped inside the reeking interior. Their personal aroma of damp decay wasn't much better, but he preferred it over cigarette stench. The plastic upholstery covers were deeply yellowed with nicotine in the paltry glow of the equally stained overhead light. He reached up and flicked the switch off.

Perhaps also offended by the smell, Fara hesitated at the door, but when he tugged on her hand, she followed him into the backseat. Tensely, she grew just about as still and cold as the malevolence in the catacombs.

The cab eased into traffic and headed toward the coast. With each passing mile, she kept inching closer to him until her body nestled against his. He spread his arm across her shoulders, and she leaned into him, securely bonded into his side.

Her profile was exactly as he remembered. Everything about her was strong. She hadn't changed much in four years; her body was just as wiry, honed, and balanced like a good blade. Although she was always reserved, there was a bigger wall, a mightier shield protecting her. Again, he couldn't blame her, not after what had happened.

They turned toward the coast, and a streetlamp cast a beam across her face. Her eyes were wide and edged with fear. All of the rich and vibrant emotions flooded back into him. Dear God, she needed him now more than ever. He didn't know what was going on with her, but his mending things with Fara were looking up.

CHAPTER 16

Although he had thousands of frequent flier miles, tonight was J.C.'s first time to fly business class. Even with the wide leather seat and decent meals, he couldn't get comfortable. As the plane approached Italy, his thumb circled the three-carat emerald hypnotically, and he attempted to make mental contact with Fara. He didn't know what he was doing, but doing nothing was worse.

The set of emerald rings had connected them in Puerto Rico, and he figured the gems connected them now, thoughtform or no thoughtform, whatever the hell that was. The rings had to be the source of the green light Agent Finius was talking about.

He stared absently at the computer screen which had gone into screensaver mode hours earlier. An idea took root, and he located the game-like control mouse on the side of the seat. His wallet wasn't quite as easy to remove undetected, and he arched up as if stretching. His fingers jittered, pulling the credit card out of its slot and swiping it on the right side of the screen.

The United website popped up, and thankfully, it was automatically hooked into the headphones. As soon as the cursor responded, he clicked through to Google. He wasn't sure if thoughtform was one word or two, but he typed it in as one and hit enter. The connection was slow, but for service at 30,000 feet, he wasn't going to be picky.

He glanced across the aisle. Agent Delphae appeared to be asleep with her head balanced on the inside curve of the headrest, facing Agent Finius. The loose flow of blond hair covered her cheek, almost to her chin. Most men would consider the girlish curls and cherubic cheeks appealing, even that sort of girl-next-door innocent. Shit, in her case, looks were deceiving, especially in that clinging spandex bodysuit. She dressed neck to toe, even down to wearing gloves, like some creepy version of a cat burglar. If she had worn a hood, the get up would look like the sensory deprivation suits people wore during kinky sex. This was way over the top of normal. But what else would he expect from some covert spy with psychic abilities?

When he first met Fara, he hadn't expected her to be some super spy either. She propositioned him for sex within two minutes of meeting him. Saying yes to go to her hotel room changed his life; hell, it saved his life.

In the dungeon of San Cristobal, he didn't think Fara created the vortex, or even manipulated it for that matter. She placed herself in harm's way to keep him and their boss safe. Regardless of what the Feds thought, she was a hero, not a villain.

His finger circled the green stone again in the same rotation as the circular cursor on the screen, praying in his own way for her to be fine. Whatever they meant by off-grid couldn't be a good thing, but knowing Fara, she would land on her feet. She was the most capable and resourceful person he knew. Her abilities went beyond any kind of training; it was how she acted upon her instincts that set her apart from everyone, even Special Agent Delphae.

Finally, a list of website links popped up. J.C. went straight to Wikipedia; it always had the strangest assortment of answers. Right now, weird was ideal.

A thoughtform is a manifestation of mental energy, also known as a tulpa in Tibetan mysticism. Its concept is related to the Western philosophy and practice of magic.

"Magic?" J.C. caught himself as the word mumbled off of his lips and shot a quick look at Delphae. The Feds had a paranormal office teaching agents how to do magic? He didn't think they meant parlor tricks or sleight of hand.

An image or images held in the mind of a practitioner which aids in the manifestation of intent.

An agency of psychic effect which exists and takes form on the pre-physical realms of existence, which acts in accord with the intent of its creator(s).

A contemplative hum rumbled deep within his throat. No wonder they thought Fara did something.

Did she create physical things with her mind? Was that how she escaped San Cristobal the first time? Maybe she didn't scale the wall. Maybe she just floated down. He shook that thought from his mind. Her fingers and toes were a bloody mess from pushing them into the minute recesses between the rock slabs fortifying the fort's exterior walls. Those injuries were real, not magic.

A living spiritual being created by humans. It could be a magical person's helper, or a being created by the belief in it from masses of people.

Fara said the Cult of the Dead worshiped the ghost bride. Hundreds of girls throughout the years went to Lucia and prayed. The energy had to go somewhere. Was it possible to manifest a ghost out of collective thought?

That which takes the image of some material object.

A material object? His right hand quickly covered his ring. He and Fara each wore their respective rings on the third finger of their left hands, like a wedding band. Well, that was where they had appeared, and they hadn't removed them. They were bonded in an ethereal sense. That was stronger than any paper contract. But once this ordeal was over, he would formally propose marriage. They had been through too much together for her to say no.

He thought about that again. Fara could always find some way to say no. She was definitely the most stubborn person he knew, the most skilled as well. No one else in the whole world was like her.

She had been a super psychic spy. Perhaps, she was blocking the signal purposefully. Shit, in that case she would be pissed when she discovered he was helping the Feds find her.

Although the whole going undercover, under the radar, well whatever in the hell it was called, was a plausible solution for her disappearance, something else was wrong. He didn't have to be a trained special agent to feel it down within his gut. Out there in an ethereal half-life, Fara was lost.

Shifting toward the window, he slid down the plastic shade, not wanting to see the blinking safety light at the edge of his hair, hitting his bare chest. The cold prick bounced him to his senses.

...er hair was butch short. It didn't need more than a quick ...ith a towel to be dry, yet beads of moisture glittered as if ...idn't even try. She looked around the room and then to the ...ny. The subtle yet exciting scrutiny continued over his ... chest. Her amazing green gaze dropped lower, and his ...on tightened until the stiffness hurt. All he had on were ...ylon jogging shorts. His jeans were trashed. He couldn't ... himself to put them back on, at least not until they dried. ...ached behind him, touching the wet denim as a reality

... smile opened her lips, and as if connected, her fingers ...d with the same ease. The towel puddled around her feet. ...ugged and hard contours of extreme workouts were softer ...ounded into tantalizing curves. Her breasts were just as he ...abered. Now exposed to the night air, her nipples ...ded, drawing into tight circles. With a provocative tilt of ...ad, she laughed softly, and the rippling sound mirrored the ...f the siren's breeze skimming over the sea. That was the ...e remembered, his personal temptress.

...h a flick of one wrist, she opened the bed and crawled ...he mattress, moving a limb at a time with excruciating ...y. One leg remained extended, and she twisted her body ...a inviting pose an artist would have wanted to capture ...anvas. "Gaetano. Come. Let us make love."

... asked him! Now he didn't have to worry about the ...uences of seducing her. The relief only heightened his ... The past was gone, and they had the opportunity for a ...ure, starting in the here and now. That was exactly what ...ed.

...u are so very beautiful." Each word drew him a step ...o the bed.

...arently pleased with the compliment, she stretched into ...ows. Hot pink fingernails skimmed her inner thigh then ...into the tight curls gleaming with moisture from the ... She pressed more firmly, and the frosty pink fingernails ...ared within the enshrouded folds. The movement

peripheral vision. The plane descended through some bumpy cloud cover, and he adjusted his watch to the time on the internet screen, 11:50, almost midnight. The screen reverted back to its default setting, and the iconic depiction of the plane kept steady longitudinal progress along the virtual map. There was one longitudinal line for each hour.

Time was finite yet relative. Was it an example of a shared thoughtform? When maps first recorded longitude why were there twenty-four hours in a day and not ten, with each hour having 100 minutes? It would be easier to add time with a base ten system rather than something set up with random numbers. What did twenty-four hours have to do with rotations of sixty minutes, with sixty seconds? It didn't make sense, but everyone accepted it as fact, all the way around the world.

To his body, it was about 6 p.m., but here it was six hours later. He wasn't six hours older. He was the same J.C., the crazy Puerto Rican who was in love with an ex-spy.

Turbulence rattled the plane, and the ice cubes in the glass shifted drawing him out of his crazy contemplation.

The steward stopped at his shoulder, brushing his left sleeve. The slightly younger man reached for the glass sitting on the armrest tray. A sly smile curled the edge of his mouth. He'd seen that expression before, but he didn't swing that way. For some reason, gay men liked him, a lot. Some even told him he looked like Johnny Depp and refused to believe his name was Juan Carlos Calderon. Now that his hair was wickedly burned in the hellfire, he didn't think the resemblance was as noticeable.

"Would you like anything else, Mr. Calderon?" He tipped his head back and the smile grew into a grin. When J.C. didn't answer, he continued, "Is this your first trip to Naples?"

"Yes," J.C. decided blatantly obvious was best. "I'm meeting my girlfriend."

The statement didn't slack the steward's interest. "Oh, a lover's retreat."

"Not exactly." J.C. saw Delphae shift in her seat and lowered his voice. "Work related. Fara and I produce *Ghost Lovers*."

The man cooed way too loudly. "So, there're going to be more? I love that show, and the last one in Scotland was in-cre-di-ble." He articulated each syllable of the word.

Emails and calls from drooling fans flooded Robert Hartz's office for Trenton Sloan, but J.C. never even thought how some of them would be from men. The Scottish Lord would just love hearing that. "The former producer, Lily Cameron, ended up marrying Lord Sloan a few weeks after the taping. They are doing well. Their third child is on the way. Hoping for a girl."

"Excuse me," Delphae snipped from the other side of the aisle. "Could I get some water before we land?"

The attendant twisted, and with a nod was gone. J.C. had the impression that was the first nice thing Special Agent Chrystal Delphae had ever done, and he doubted she had intended it that way.

He petted the stone once more, willing for something to happen. He closed his eyes and concentrated. The stone remained dark and empty. That void filled him, chilling him to his very soul.

CHAPTER 17

The shower turned off with a rumble, growling pipes. Letting go of the balcony railing, Gae bedroom. The bathroom's door was ajar and ca light across the bed, Fara's bed. Jesus, just look four-poster bed made his need instantly alert. F of her, but what would she think of him if he s her faculties were clouded?

She'd be fucking pissed when she came to came to her senses. What would happen if thi He bit his thumbnail and rubbed the rougher his bottom front teeth, contemplating wheth considered a good thing.

Being around Fara was scary as hell, but t he would rather be. They had been to hell ar once. Today was just another ripple i relationship, but underneath it all, he loved he diminished and was at the heart of his disco never again feel complete without her. Perha of his betrayal, she still felt the same way fo remembered him.

She hadn't mentioned the man she'd been hadn't mentioned much of anything. He kn past few years of her life from his internet se divulged in their few hours together. She wa now she didn't remember any of it, nothin regained her full memory, she would realize before he saved her. They were even. But way?

The bathroom door eased open, and she clutched between her breasts in a single han beauty, he swayed, and a single drop of wate

caught the light, exposing the intimate lips and then instantly obscuring them again in shadow.

Mesmerized, he watched her flesh respond, tinting into a shade of desert rose. Her fingers dipped and twisted, rounding her clitoris and diving into her secret depths. She had learned some new moves while they had been apart, so darkly erotic, so incredibly Fara.

Her center fingers remained inside the hidden valley. The strokes grew in depth and pace. With a desirous moan, her head fell back and knees opened, exposing the glittering moisture on the hot inner folds.

His flesh throbbed. It felt like ages since he made love to a woman. Regardless of the actual frequency, none of those women counted because they weren't Fara. She was the only woman in the world for him. She had returned to him. After four long years, she was finally his again.

He didn't remember moving closer. Suddenly, he was just at the side of the bed and climbed aside her. More so out of habit, he glanced to the bedside table for a condom, so accustomed to taking precautions, but neither of them had anticipated this night. The thought of her carrying his child opened an even deeper need, aligning with his family duty to continue the Caravaggio line. He wanted this night more than anything in the world.

With a gentle caress, his freshly shaven cheek glided toward her lips. The kiss was little more than a sigh, a gentle brushing of silken flesh back and forth until an even gentler moan eased from her. Her arms slipped around his neck.

"Tell me you want me." His breathy words were softer than a whisper.

She made an equally small hum. So close, the murmur breathed across his eager lips. Extending her tongue, she wet the edges of her lips, but didn't quite touch his. Still the moist heat was there, drifting across the molecules separating them.

Thought left his mind. Only instinctual desire remained. Cradling her face, his fingers swept into the damp hair, and the strands curled around his fingers, oh so close and intimate. He stroked the edges of her temples and over her ears. Her chin arched toward him, and his tongue dove inside her mouth. She accepted the invasion, opening for him as he had fantasized.

Beyond control, he kissed her hard, and she replied in kind. Their mouths opened and suckled. Their tongues plunged and stroked. The motion drove him mad with wanton frenzy, and then it happened, their teeth clacked. That happened so rarely, but tonight it befitted the fervor.

His lungs burned for breath, but he didn't pull away. How could he? The tumultuous whirl of furious lust was upon them both. He craved this moment more than life, for without Fara, life didn't exist. The tempo built until they were both gasping. He had to inhale a real breath, so he pulled away just enough, lingering against her lips to savor her taste like a final drop of fine wine. Panting their breath coursed and mingled, relishing its own embrace.

Making an inarticulate sound, she arched her divine body toward him with the grace of the goddess of love, and her mound of Venus brushed his aching erection distending the front of the navy blue shorts. Those hot pink nails slid down his abs and played with the waistband, stretching it and allowing it to snap back playfully. His hands covered hers, helping her lower the elastic carefully over his swollen shaft. As soon as his erection felt the night air, his desire spiked. If he was less experienced, he would have lost his struggling need to the moment. Instead, the heady rush ignited his mind and body, insisting he enter her, yet he first needed to hear her accept him. Nothing regarding their reunion could be left to chance.

"Fara, please," the words rumbled through his dry throat, "I've dreamt of you every night and with every dawn. In those dreams, you tell me something I've longed to hear. Please tell me…" the word drifted, lingering on his lips.

She smiled, and raising up onto her elbows, her lips naturally touched his. "I want you Gaetano. I want you to become as close as a man and woman ever shall be. Join with me."

A low growl escaped from some genetic remnant of primitive man carrying over into this most primal act. He could barely catch his breath beyond the lump it left in his throat.

"First, tell me, Fara. I've waited all these years with that one desire." He brushed his tongue over her lips, licking their fullness. His hand did the same to her breast, so warm and heavy in his palm. "Please just admit this one thing. That's all I'm asking for. At least tell me if you loved me then."

Entrenched pain thinned her visible ecstasy, and the conflicting emotion danced across her features, hidden, yet there none the less. He had hurt her, too deeply for words. That could have never happened if she hadn't loved him.

The growing lump constricted, but he forced out the words. "For the past four years, I survived off the memories of us together. I don't want to go on without you. Even with what I did, do you think, that maybe, one day, you would be able to love me again?"

Sighing, those distant green eyes flared with inner light just as he remembered. "Love isn't something that stops and starts. True love is eternal. Vibrant emotions bind the dead to this world, sometimes through hatred or revenge, but mostly love is the cause of their imprisonment."

"I don't understand." Confused, he stared at her exotic eyes. "Does that mean you still love me?"

She swallowed and then whispered, "I will always love you."

His pulsed raced, and he felt instantly dizzy. Unable to control the raging emotional onslaught those simple words created, his mouth seized hers, stealing her breath. Both hands held her head, and absently his fingers massaged her scalp in tiny circles.

Just as he remembered, her body responded, so hot and sweet, and the scent of her inner readiness mingled with the night air still drifting through the open balcony doors. Over the water, the sirens' sighs grew, and the ocean breeze shivered over his heated flesh. Under him, Fara's sighs added to the bewitching chorus.

He repositioned himself between her thighs and pressed forward, staking his claim in the most elemental way. She arched with the invasion, accepting him in every way a woman was able to accept a man. He pulled back and moved inside in long thrusts. Possessively, he gripped her hips and went deeper still.

She was so very wet yet still perfectly tight. Making room for him, just for him, more than just her channel opened. He felt something inside of her, allowing him to enter her mind and soul just as he entered her body. This was a moment of perfect clarity, a few timeless seconds where their inner Zen met and mingled in perfect harmony. They were meant for each other. The past didn't matter. The other affairs didn't matter, for either of them. Fara was his to have and to hold, forever. As she said, true love was eternal.

In time with the lapping rush of the sea, he worked in and out of her gently, savoring every moment of the indescribable ecstasy. She had a natural ability to grasp at him in rhythm with his thrusts, stroking him as readily as he stroked her. Pushing him out with a rippling wave, she then opened and again tightened around him.

As if this was his first time to make love to a woman, the urgent need for release swelled within him, and on the next stroke, he held himself fully within her allowing time for the sharp sensation to ease. Breathing in long and ragged pants, he looked down to witness her sensual stare and lost touch with the intimate moment. Instead of being wide and unfocused, her eyes were closed. With the prolonged interruption, she opened them, but the look within the green depths just wasn't the same.

She didn't give him time to contemplate that very fundamental change. Her inner calves skimmed along thighs, over his ass, and up along his waist, raising them agilely to his ribs. Leaning back for balance, he hooked his arm around her leg, kissing her calf, down toward those pink toes. Everywhere his lips touched, they suckled with need.

Giggling, she arched her back, squirming under him, encouraging him to begin again. Breaking into a full-fledged laugh, she slid her hands to his ass and pulled him forward sharply, then added a playful spank. Even with him catching himself on his arms, she kept up the rhythm with her inner muscles while lifting her hips in time. She added her lips to the cacophony of sensation and then slid teeth and tongue over his throat and upper chest, biting him just enough to enliven his flesh.

A rush of power flowed from her with each startling thrust of lustful interplay. The rhythm grew along with her inner tightness squeezing around his shaft. He was losing his breath, just as if a giant anaconda was taking his very life, yet he didn't fight. Her eyes were still closed while agonizing pleasure rippled within her distinct features. Those heavenly lips opened, so red and full from his kisses. Within the next breath, her siren's song escaped through them and into the night.

Seeing the pleasure play across her features brought him to the brink. Not able to control himself, he asserted his domination and pumped harder and faster, holding her to him. Every thrust sent that pulse of heat and power deeper and deeper, pounding with need.

Recovering from her orgasm, she writhed under him, arching and bucking toward his rapid thrusts, taking him all the way within her body, accepting him completely while screaming his name. He bumped the blunt end of her vagina, and the extreme pleasure arched his penis to the hardest it had ever been. Her nails clung to his torso, holding onto him for support. He cried out, losing the battle for control. The pressure was building, so very deep and hot, and this time he wasn't able to control it. Sweat beaded, and the wet slapping sounds of sex spilled into the night.

Trying to maximize the time he had remaining, his stokes lengthened. Taking him, all of him, she gripped the mattress, gathering handfuls of the covers into clenched fists while screaming her pleasure. Along with his own climax building, he felt her finding another release, as if it was the last thing she wanted to give him, yet he demanded it of her.

The beast rose within him, consuming his last vestige of will. His words growled with each final thrust. "Oh God ... Fara ... I-"

His lips drew into a tight line, and then they burst open, matching her scream. Upon the moment of the furthest extent of his deepest thrust, he capitulated to the charging need, releasing the lust raging through him that had been unanswered for four long years. Every nerve in his body stood on edge. The heated surge rose, and he thundered inside of her, wave after heated wave. He held himself at the point of their deepest union issuing his seed, filling her, and the hot white light of pure pleasure engulfed him.

Her inner energy shivered with orgasmic spasms, tightening her channel and rocking him into senselessness, compelling him to thrust again. Blinded by the ecstasy, the heated flow continued pulsing from his body, and she accepted him, all of him without hesitation. Behind his closed eyes, great plumes of golden light lit the room, flaring into the night. Spectacular. Magnificent. This was the most satisfying moment of his life, joined with his mate, his one true love.

When his glazed vision refocused, he noticed long red scratches down his sides. Only then did he feel their sting. She trusted him enough not to hurt her, but she hadn't promised the same in return. She had marked him as her own. Dear God, Fara was back.

Slowly his gasping breath eased, and he softened degree by miniscule degree around his still rigid core. Yet, she wasn't going to let it end. She circled her hips as if using him to stir the physical mixture of love and lust mingling within her. A wash of raw nerves escaped him in a gritty moan, and then he felt himself growing once again, hardening and lengthening within her. He wasn't completely hard, not yet, but firm enough for her to slip out from under him. Startled by the unexpected change, she used the perfect amount of leverage and flipped him over, easing him back inside of her in the same continuous motion.

Pinning his shoulders with her hands, she straddled him and started to rise and fall along his shaft. Fara used to lock her feet over his thighs, but not today. She used them as leverage against the bed, and each stroke claimed more of him as he rose to the challenge. She rode him hard and fast, forcing him fully within her depths. His next orgasm grew quickly. It filled him like gunpowder inside a firecracker. Once the fuse lit, there was no holding back. He exploded in a sudden rush, catching them both by surprise.

He dug his hands into the crumpled bed linens and arched, bucking himself out of time with her internal spasms, and she screamed, forcing herself down onto him fully and deeply.

Without a condom, the sensation exploded, so vivid and alive. The rush continued to pulse, strong and steady until he issued every last gram of his essence. Only once he completely waned, she melted around him, collapsing down on top of his heaving chest.

A content yet exhausted smile grew across his face. He wasn't able to stop it, and he didn't want to. This was his moment to make things right. No regrets. No playing games. He had to set the wrongs of the past to order. His hands encircled her waist, holding her to him until their heartbeats slowed in time with each other. "Every single day, I've lived with regrets; the deepest was not asking you to marry me."

"What?" She tried to rise, but he held her too firmly.

One hand slid up from the curve of her butt, and for the first time, he felt the scars, raised welts crossing her back. He didn't need to see them to know what they looked like. The Taliban had lashed her with a whip. If he had been a better man, none of that would have happened. He had more to atone for than any man in history and silently vowed to dedicate himself to her happiness.

Tenderly he cradled her head to his chest, "I was afraid if I asked you to marry me that you'd turn me down, and I've lived with the doubt. Every day wondering whether you would have. Fara, I love you, more than words could ever express. I need you and want you to be part of my life. I want you to be the mother of my children. I wish it had happened years ago, but all we have is the present. And from here on out, our future, together."

His hold relaxed, and she pressed up onto her arms, looking at him with a perplexed stare. "Is this just a passing whim enticed by the frenzied state of elation?" Her old-fashioned pronunciation heightened with her alacrity.

He didn't really know why she was acting to eccentrically, but it was strangely sexy, alluring as if it was a prelude to a new game. He flipped over the top of her and caged her between his muscular arms. "I'm perfectly serious."

Her expression slackened and eyes grew wide. "You are asking me to pledge my troth in marriage?"

His fingertips rotated around her nipples, now soft and broad. "I should have taken you with me. I've regretted that every moment of my life. I'm not complete without you. I want you to marry me and live with me, here in Naples. I'll not take no for an answer."

CHAPTER 18

Just as the cab pulled onto the highway, the waxing gibbous moon rose, illuminating the landscape with brilliant silver glitter. At times, Ted Finius' abnormal sight was a blessing rather than a curse. At night, everything changed. He didn't know why he could see moonlight. None of the hundreds of specialists had figured it out, especially once he described what he saw in the night. Every person had a projection of energy, termed an aura, regardless of its potency.

During the day, he could only see those who were psychically gifted or somehow stained by the paranormal. For most people, auras appeared as an egg-shaped glow. An obese man's aura may appear thin and frail, while a petite woman could emanate an aura of considerable magnitude. The size and shape depended upon the person's inner power. On very rare occasions, he could ascertain the shape of the person, like when he saw Faradahl Trotter's echo of energy in the dungeon of Fort San Cristobal. Her aura was unique, clinging to the outline of her body like a glove, so closely protected no one or nothing could penetrate her personal shield unless she let him.

Right now, Ted knew without a doubt Fara Trotter was no longer on this plane of existence. J.C. had lost their interconnected emerald glow. Although his bodily energy still had a unique resonating pattern, the ring upon his left hand had quit emitting the unusual green light. Ted stared at the ring not understanding how the two stones linked. If he understood that, he might be able to use J.C.'s ring as a homing beacon for Fara's matching gem. He didn't reveal his hypothesis to Chrystal. He'd keep it to himself until he determined how to use it effectively.

Over time and after a few painful lessons, Ted learned to keep many things to himself. All through school, he was a freak, even to the other blind kids. When the light was just right, some of them could see gray shapes as shadowy outlines. No one else saw auras or sparkling moonlight, or worse yet, things creeping through the night. Children had every right to fear the dark.

At first, he thought Joe Daily was making a cruel joke when he asked him to join the FPI, but he had hoped there was more to life than being a freak. Even sideshow oddities were better off than he was. At least they earned a living by being different. To an outsider he appeared blind, but normal. Normal! As if that was the cruelest oddity of them all. No one understood the depth of his specialty until he joined the FPI. Every special agent had some paranormal gift, which most would consider an abnormality. All of the FPI agents considered their talents as putting the "special" in special agent, which was why his partner insisted on being addressed with her full title. Special Agent Chrystal Delphae.

At this late hour, the streets were quiet and empty, so the cab moved swiftly through the city. Although he couldn't see the buildings per se, most of Naples was hot, and not in temperature. More so than any other city, the buildings radiated psychic light. Vibrant colors blossomed, emanating into the sky like earthbound aurora borealis. Most of them were in hues of rich, velvety blue, but about every mile or so, a hot spot split the darkness. He had heard the shape described as a flame, but he had never seen regular fire burn, only psychic fire, and apparently, they were just about the same. A burning flame emitted a plume of energy and heat while psychic flares emitted a plume of energy in a color which represented its relative age and strength.

Now that the cab was entering the suburbs, the newer homes had much less residual energy yet more recent emanations. Over some of the houses, the psychic flares remained close, licking the roof like real flames. Yellow denoted rage. Perhaps one of them gambled away the rent money or slept with the other's best friend. The lighter the yellow, the milder the anger. When rage crossed into violence, orange and red licked the flames, leaving a deeper scar on the radial energy signatures. The darker the color, the longer the signature remained, dark damage, like a bruise upon the very marrow of the world.

Anger and damage weren't the only colors in the night. Long before he even knew the FPI existed, Ted's sister would drive him into the middle of the desert. They sat on the broad hood of her beat up '76 Cougar and leaned against the windshield, staring into the night sky. Grace was the only person who would listen as he pointed out the different types of stars, even the barely noticeable white dwarfs that weren't really white at all.

Intrigued with the luminous heavens, he studied the types of stars. An infant or protostar was a spinning collection of gas, and over time with increasing gravity, the mass collapsed. At the end of that phase, it turned into a T-Tauri star. They had intense x-ray flares and stellar winds, which looked to him like a cosmic spray can propelling light across the heavens. Over 100 million years those condensed, shrinking into a main sequence star, like our sun, which was in a state of hydrostatic equilibrium. Those were the most stable, emitting light from fusion reactions in equal balance to the gravity pulling down upon itself. Once a star consumed the stock of hydrogen in its core, the fusion reaction stopped, igniting the hydrogen in the outer shell and increasing its size exponentially. It turned into a red giant, 100 times larger than it had been. Red giants were spectacular, however rare. When a red giant consumed all it could from its outer chromosphere, it shrank back onto itself and became a white dwarf, which looked like a cosmic cinder in the sky.

Only once had he seen a star burst into a supernova. September 9, 2011. Even Grace saw it with the hand-held telescope Ted had bought her for Christmas, but what she described didn't even begin to compare to what he perceived. Color was everywhere, growing like a cosmic bubble.

The strangest thing about watching the supernova was how they were watching the past. Twenty-one-million years ago, a star exploded, and the light was just now reaching the earth. Just north of Alcor, the star marking the bend in the handle of the constellation called the Big Dipper, was the Pinwheel Galaxy. With just his naked eyes, he perceived the individual pinpoints of swirling light in such detail. On nights like that, he actually regarded his disability as a special ability.

Even with her telescope, Grace never saw what he did, yet she listened to his descriptions and added practical knowledge of similar functions of everyday objects, like the spray can. Ted would have never understood what that item really looked like without his sister's analogy. In many ways, she was his eyes, but for the universe, he was hers. To him the distance of the sky compressed; all of the stars were there, as if the past and the present of the universe overlapped, filling every square inch of the sky in a display of infinite cosmic proportions. The universe existed ad infinitum, changing and morphing from one form into another, epitomized by the lifecycle of the stars, and he saw it all, every segment of light in the full spectrum. Magnificent and foreboding all at the same time, the scope filled his mind with more information than he could ever process or describe. It was as if he could see into the very essence of God at the center of it all.

They would stay out in the Mojave Desert until dawn when his vision would fade once again into obscurity. Grace never commented about his bizarre descriptions. She accepted him just as her brother. He missed those nights with her.

After this assignment concluded, he would go home for a couple of weeks to see Grace. She was out of college now and had a job in L.A. at an advertising firm. Her specialty was marketing items to the disabled. Her most recent commercials for the scoot-around aired during the national news. Every time Ted heard it, he missed her that much more.

The cab turned into a neighborhood dense with narrow houses, blocking out the sky. On the edge of the resulting darkness, a psychic flare grew, shooting out a burst of exploding light, not unlike a star blowing up into a supernova. He held his breath, trying to memorize the sight. This was more than just unique; it was mesmerizing. Magnificent!

That one house resonated with the same wavelengths as the center of the universe, with time itself. And then, a giant plume of golden psychic fire exploded, filling the sky. That had to be where they were going, to the most psychically alert house in all of Italy.

The mansion was suddenly there, in exquisite detail. The fascia was uneven, and high up a few graven symbols glowed, as if the release of the golden power brought them to life. Two stood out, some version of a winged caduceus, the staff carried by Mercury across the heavens. He squinted at the detail. The wings were there, but on top of each staff appeared to be a dragon's head. They were looking at each other across the arch of the window.

Strangely, the blank areas that had to be windows stared like soulless eyes. Something or someone inside the house had to have blocked the glass from emitting psychic light. For the first time in many years, the skin on the back of his neck crawled. Whatever had happened inside of this house had been not only powerful but also purposefully calculating.

The cab slowly approached the curb, and before the car stopped completely, he opened the door. Without needing his cane, he walked into the street, standing in the center of the road on the slight crest of the asphalt. The aural projections were so strong they sprang from the eaves and danced across the pavement like showers of sparks from a fireworks fountain, adding dimension to the texture of the street. He had never seen a pothole, but it was just there before him, lit up by the colorful display, as if the extra energy oozing into the street puddled in the low areas. Never in his entire life was there so much power concentrated in a single place. Then, similar to a real fire exhausting its fuel, the golden flares slackened enough to see the emanation of inner light. This residual signature was intensely powerful and hundreds of years old.

The inner and outer light mixed and mingled, brilliant and mind-boggling. Even with two distinct sources, the glass was still dark, but not empty. As if the dark voids were eyes, the house watched and waited. Whatever had damaged this place anticipated resolution.

Ted rarely received emotional responses to the environment, as if his lack of sight filtered out stimuli others perceived. The initial creep he felt along the back of his neck now slithered down his spine, and then lit his nervous system with an electrical charge. Almost dizzy with it, he felt this place on a multitude of levels, pulsing with ancient power, and his inner awareness sizzled with each emission of psychic light. It reminded him of a distant pulsar star, but the cycle of the light bursts were off kilter, yet familiar. That sense tingled even deeper, and again, he knew something was askew, out of place.

He had only imagined such power truly existed. When he was a boy, Ted's older brother would read stories of super heroes with extraordinary powers. Their mom came in every night and told them to go to sleep, but as soon as her footsteps creaked on the floorboard in front of Grace's bedroom, Gary would pull out his flashlight and continue reading. Of course, most of the stories were in comic books, but he didn't seem to mind describing the pictures.

One of those descriptions came to mind when Ted first met J.C. He was like the Green Lantern. The shimmering green energy field was somehow connected to his ring, which was somehow connected to Faradahl.

The mounting pulses from the house reacted to J.C. being near, and the dark windows sprang to life, flowing with visual streams of power. The tendrils of vibrant color reached toward him, bending and stretching across the blank yard. Ted had never seen anything like it before; however, who was he to say that something like that couldn't exist. He was walking, talking proof that the world didn't come with an instruction manual.

His jaw dropped, and the word "wow" formed on his lips. The swirling patterns flowed and shifted, depositing color within the churning energy fields. Each shade was distinct from the other, and although they swirled in and through, they never mixed. The multiple tendrils writhed like an octopus or a jellyfish propelling itself through the sea, and even through the undulations, they seemed to focus upon the figures waiting at the gate.

"What do you see?" Chrystal stepped closer but didn't touch him. After a few moments, she whispered, "Is it active or residual?"

"Both!" His voice just burst to life. He wasn't able to contain his excitement. "I've never seen anything like it. At first it was huge, a flame of pure golden light reaching up into the sky." He took a breath while trying to find words to describe what was before his eyes. "But now it's different. You've heard of resonant residue, but this place pulses with it, in a color I've never witnessed. It's almost purple. Purple!"

Taking a half-step closer, she stood by his shoulder and stared through the bars of the gate. "Red and blue make purple." Delphae replied, but not sarcastically.

"Yes, and yellow and blue make green. So what?" J.C.'s green aura flared, and like a magnet, the closest plumes of living light stretched toward him, stopping just on their side of the gate, as if the barrier guarded the gap between dimensions.

Reluctantly, Ted broke away from the mesmerizing sight and looked toward J.C. His aura was also pulsing. He looked between him and the house and back again. J.C. was pulsing in time with the emanations. No doubts remained. The man was tied to this location, this disturbance. The tendrils were trying to make contact with his ring. Logically, it would mean Faradahl was in the house, but if she was in the house, why would she be off-grid?

Perhaps she had the first chip malfunction, or the massive aural energy masked her chip's signature. That was plausible.

J.C. reached for the bars, and Ted's mind perked to their current reality. His conscience wouldn't permit him just letting J.C. enter unprepared. He deserved an explanation to know what was out there before they crossed the threshold of the gate. "Red is recent energy, usually caused from something strong, like anger, but not necessarily malevolent. Deep blue is rarer and old, very old. Usually it's just a faint residue, like a tiny gas flame, but this place glows with it, like something from the past has punched a hole into the present."

"Shit, like the movie Poltergeist?" J.C. chuckled to lighten the comment, but it wasn't a happy sound. When they didn't join him, he cleared his throat and continued, "That's both ends of the spectrum of visible light. It ranges from red as lower frequency to blue which resonates at higher frequencies. Over time, shouldn't the frequency deteriorate which would make red older than blue?"

Delphae's mouth gaped open. "How is it that you know so much about light?"

J.C returned a like-duh look. "I was a cameraman for years. You can push or pull colors based upon the light you allow to filter through the camera's lens. When you filter for blue, you actually put in a red filter, which absorbs that spectrum, only allowing the other ranges to go through the filter medium. Most of *Ghost Lovers* is shot with a red filter to make the light temperature look cooler."

"And older." Delphae added.

J.C. shrugged. "It adds to the creepy factor." He looked back at the house. "I don't see anything out of the ordinary. It's just some old seaside mansion that the family didn't want to live in anymore, so they rent it out. Come-on, let's go inside and see if Fara's here."

His hand didn't hesitate and pushed down upon the latch. The gate's spring was old, and the rusty scream lingered as J.C. shouldered against the metal bars. Like a gentleman, he held the gate open for them. Instantly, all of the tendrils turned toward him, but J.C. didn't notice. He stepped upon the property and turned to face the quickly approaching, writhing mass. It didn't look like a jellyfish any longer; these were like the snakes on Medusa's head. She had been a Gorgon, immortalized in classical mythology for centuries. Every myth had some bearing in fact. Perhaps this very spot had been tied to her energy, damaged by some catastrophic event centuries ago.

Lest for my daring Persephone the dread, from Hades should send up an awful monster's grisly head. The quote from Homer's Iliad resonated in Ted's inner voice as the first appendage neared J.C. It was red, recent energy, and as soon as it drew within two feet, the man's aura lit into a green shield. The finger of energy touched that glowing bubble of protective light and jumped away, recoiling quickly back upon itself. As if connected, all of the other undulating ribbons retreated, returning to the house. Intelligence. Whatever was behind the embodiment of light, it was intelligent.   Yet more importantly, J.C. was protected from its effects.

Boldly, he approached the front porch, and Ted maneuvered Chrystal next to him in order to stay in his wake.   He normally didn't touch her, but this was one time to make an exception. She shivered, perhaps sharing his vision for that moment even through the protective fabric.   He would have to ask her later.

J.C. lifted the glowing brass knocker and rapped four times. The knocks resonated, echoing hollowly through the house, and rippled through the colorful bands.

"I can see the sound waves."   Ted exclaimed.   "The protoplasmic residue is so thick that the sounds ripple through the inner mist."   He shoved his hands into the pockets of his overcoat and felt the camera.   Damn, he should have been documenting this from the very beginning.   He pulled it out, and so excited, his fingers fumbled with the lens cap.   Not that he couldn't see every detail with this much light, but his hands were shaking.

"You a photographer?"   J.C. asked a little too sarcastically.

"This is a full-spectrum camera.   Maybe I can document some of this."

With his right fist, J.C. beat on the door, "Hey Fara, it's J.C. Come-on, let me in."

"I detect motion in the red spectrum."   Clicks from the camera fired off in rapid sequence, and Ted took a step back from the door, just before it swung open.

"What the hell do you want at this hour?"   Colored lights flared around the man, like a Christmas tree covered in flashing, blinking lights.

Ted couldn't be sure, but this man appeared to have been in contact with both recent and very old energy with some anger twirled into the mix.   When he looked at J.C., the color of the light emanating from his solar plexus shifted to a deeper yellow with flickers of urgent red.

"Who are you?"   His voice lost the Italian accent, speaking English as if he was native to the U.S.A.   It took training to do that so smoothly, especially while maintaining a neutral tone.

"J.C. Calderon with *Ghost Lovers*." J.C.'s voice tightened. "Is Fara here?" And then he added, "She rented this house for the crew to stay in one place."

"There're only three of you? I expected more." The colorful flare swung toward Chrystal, just as she removed her gloves.

"We are the first group. Didn't she tell you?" She moved in front of them, holding her hands out and then extended her right, ready to shake his hand, but the man backed up a step as if he knew what to expect. "Mind if we come in?"

Chrystal was a somatic psychometrix, a psychic who received visions upon touching an object. The ability wasn't that uncommon, but she could also project emotions through touch, and in some cases just simple proximity, which made her exceptional. She had told him that her efforts to wield her influence over J.C. when they visited his home in Puerto Rico didn't affect him.

Ted closed his eyes, trying to shut off the dazzling palate in order to concentrate. He listened to their breathing patterns. Either the man in the doorway was a highly accomplished practitioner, or he didn't mind them being there. His breathing was slow, steady, and even calculating. J.C.'s was openly hostile and anxious, grating through his throat and through his open mouth. Did he think Fara was having an affair with this man?

The blind man's eyes shot open, looking for that telltale glimmer of Faradahl's green signature. She had touched the man standing in the doorway. Ted stared closer, squinting to make out what would be in the area of the man's mouth. Perhaps, she had kissed him. If so, both were hours old, on top of that signature, the areas glowed with deep blue residual power. Ted blinked, but the vision remained steadfast and true. This man had been in contact with something very old and perhaps even more powerful than Faradahl Trotter.

J.C. followed Chrystal into the house and asked casually, "Who are you?"

The stranger had a certain refined coolness surrounding him, like an aural shield. Under the smooth veneer, Ted saw the flicker of something strange. Lies usually appeared to tint an aura with orange, but this color was more yellow intermingled with the red energy, technically orange yet different.

The man cleared his throat. "Gaetano." It was the truth.

"His name is Gaetano di Casapesenna." A brilliant blue suddenly appeared at the top of the stairs. Power flowed from her, something exotic and deep, rolling off in pulsing waves of midnight blue, tinged with red. Arms of the tangible energy flowed like something suspended without gravity. Oh my God, she was the source of the purple light!

Oddly, out of nowhere, Ted imagined a mermaid. If he was to meet a mermaid, this is how he expected her energy signature to look. The color was so deep and old, yet vibrant enough to see her features. She was beautiful with remarkable dark hair flowing around her shoulders, yet her eyes were two blank voids.

"Fara!" J.C. took two steps and stopped, speaking in English. "You're alright. Why haven't you answered my calls?"

"What? I don't understand." She quickly answered in Spanish and then laughed a heady rolling sound, which visibly drifted down the stairs.

Although he had never met the woman in person, Ted had seen Faradahl Trotter in the repeating remnants of light in the dungeon of San Cristobal. He knew her energy signature. Each person's aura was even more distinctive and individual than the way someone looked or spoke. Faradahl Trotter was off the scale. Her signature was so unique, more than any other, and so was this woman's, however not in the same way.

"What? What in the hell have you been doing?" J.C. answered in Spanish. His voice struggled to stay flat. Even with the effort, it sharpened with nerves. "Why are you wrapped up in a sheet? What the fuck have you been doing?"

Before Ted could reach out to touch J.C.'s shoulder, the Puerto Rican bolted up the stairs. The woman turned on heel and ran down the hall, and Gaetano charged after them both.

"What the hell was that?" Chrystal leaned in to him, and he felt her senses shining with a crystalline pattern. She really lived up to her name. "Apparently, there is such a thing as a chip malfunction or else it's being masked by all of this energy." She held up her fingers and swept them through the air. While rubbing her fingertips together, she sniffed the residue.

Stunned by seeing all of the action transpire as if he had actual sight, Ted had to swallow the lump within his throat. "Did she appear to be Faradahl?"

"Who else would greet guests wrapped up in a bed sheet? Both Fara and her new lover certainly looked as if they culminated one hell of a good time just before we arrived." She let out a snort of derision.

Ted hated her doing that. Just because she didn't have an intimate relationship, she didn't want anyone else to experience intimacy either. He pressed again, "So she looks like Faradahl?"

"What do you mean?" Her tone softened. "What did you see?"

Ted answered softly, even less than a whisper. "That's not the same woman who was in San Cristobal."

"Then who the hell is it?" Chrystal barely whispered, staring up the staircase into the swirling eddy of dark energy.

CHAPTER 19

The blinding burst of light melted into a white blur. Shapes moved closer, darkening the room, yet directly overhead, the blur took shape into pinpoints of flickering light. Candles, there were thousands of candles in circular tiers directly above Fara.

Distinct aromas clung to the warm air. Stale body sweat, roasting meat, flowery perfume, and tobacco smoke each held their own traces, intermingling but not truly mixing in the tangible humidity.

The sound of music grew in time with the pounding beat of her pulse. The lyrical composition was a fusion of strings, and the breathy tones of a flute rose above one other instrument, something strange and with a resonant twang. Abruptly, the music stopped, and a murmur of a thousand voices resonated in its place. From very close by, one deep male voice commanded the others, but she still couldn't quite understand what he was saying through the constant pounding in her ears.

Fighting to clear her head, she purposefully inhaled but couldn't take a deep breath. Panic briefly charged adrenaline through her. During the days of her abduction, the Taliban had restrained her with leather straps, but this was different, binding and pinching her torso. Not even while in training did she hear of trussing someone to limit their ability to breathe. She inhaled again, and the binding allowed only a thin breath, enough to stay alive but not adequate for physical exertion, a most creative technique to limit a captive.

A pair of strong hands held her torso, squeezing the binding's vertical rods against her ribs. Still not able to control her body's movement, her head jostled forwards, and the world flipped right side up.

Her eyes hazily focused on the press of dozens, perhaps even hundreds, of men and women in strange costumes. They were staring at her. Not wanting to meet any direct gazes, she turned her face toward a velvet-clad shoulder with leather bindings. That was perfectly clear. She looked up again, this time squinting. The pinpoints of light were white tapers almost burned to mere stubs. Strings of wax hung like stalactites.

The man lifted her into his arms, and the flames danced and spun with the movement. The motion made her dizzy, lightening her head until she felt the world fading away in a hazy wave. Strange words faded in and out. Nothing seemed real except for the arms, cradling her gently.

In this half-conscious state, her body was some distant and foreign thing, aware yet not aware all at the same time. The man carrying her jostled her more securely into his arms then charged up a flight of stairs. A group of men crowded toward them on the landing. Their murmurs grew into a cacophony of rumbling chatter that made no sense. The group parted reluctantly, and the man carrying her continued down the hall as if he knew the complex layout of the mansion.

A much smaller man held open a door almost to the end of the hall on the left. They passed into a dark room, and those same strong arms lowered her onto a soft surface. Her body sank into the airy down.

Women in white scurried about the room lighting candles and old-fashioned oil lamps. Within seconds, a warm glow suffused the room. As if a common drill, they pulled back the folds of gauzy fabric surrounding the bed and tied them hastily to the bedposts, triggering Fara's memory of the ghost lover. That same face appeared above her, leaning to swipe a lock of hair from her face.

Hair?

In one sudden move, she bolted to a sitting position. If the man hadn't had excellent reflexes, she would have smashed into him. The movement was too rapid, spinning pain inside of her head, splitting it in two behind her eyes. She raised a hand to her temple and felt soft tendrils of curls. Voices swelled around her, shouting for her to lay down, and she melted back into the downy softness.

"Are you fit?" The man's lips moved out of time with the words. She understood the Italian, but at the same time, the dialect was oddly unfamiliar.

Above all of the other chatter, an authoritative voice bellowed in an archaic form of Spanish, reminding her of Capitan General Dufrense, a hideous entity she had encountered in Puerto Rico. She forced her head to loll to the left. The room was crowded, yet the throng parted as the Spaniard approached the bed.

"Mercede! What tragic damage hast befallen you?" Strong hands grabbed her shoulders and shook her none too gently.

The motion made her arms tingle with life, dragging her back to the moment. She never remembered anything like that happening in a dream.

"What reprehensible purpose did you conduct upon my niece?" He snapped at the man who had carried her.

The darkly handsome stranger retained his composure and didn't retreat from the far edge of the bed. "Nothing, your Grace."

Fara stared at him, again squinting, and the man's features gained clarity. He looked like Guy, except his cheeks were thinner and his features darker. Her breath sucked in, and her bleary eyes widened. This was the ghost. The phantom who came to her bed. The ghost she thought was Guy while she still thought Guy was dead. Her head hurt just trying to make sense out of the tangled mess of who was dead, who was a ghost, and who was only pretending to be dead. Now the ghost appeared to be alive.

Shit! Shit! Shit! Literally, she was up shit creek. That was perfectly clear.

"She merely fainted in my arms whilst dancing." He continued.

"He speaks the truth, your Grace." A thin voice replied using the same odd style of Italian. "I witnessed the escapade unfold. Your darling niece fainted during the lift in the Curanto, and Signor di Casapesenna shielded her from collapsing upon the floor. Upon my recommendation, he transported her here," he swallowed, "to her bedchamber."

Fara didn't trust her awareness. Her senses had to be playing tricks upon her mind. A dream, this all had to be just some weird dream. Somehow, rising above all of the weird confusion, she remembered the story J.C. had told her about the ghost dreams the show's former producers experienced. Clearly, this was just a strange and all too vivid dream that felt real. If this continued, she would be able to convince herself she didn't really have sex with the ghost. It too was just a dream, a strangely real and perverted dream, just like this one. She almost smiled at the ghost man.

"Mercede, fix your eyes upon me!" The harsh man demanded in Spanish.

Mercede? Who was Mercede? Perhaps one of the maids?

When Fara didn't respond, he grabbed her chin and turned her to look fully upon his face. Although he sounded like Captain General Dufrense, he looked nothing like the Spanish commander of Fort San Cristobal. This man's clean-shaven face was broader with deep-set eyes, glowing like dark beads in the candlelight.

"Have you taken ill?" His skin was heavily lined, especially around those beady eyes, yet not necessarily with age. He couldn't be over fifty, yet his face bore the signs of stress and lack of sleep. "Mercede?"

Through her foggy mind, reality slowly dawned. He was calling her Mercede.

He shook her again, "Mercede!" Damn, his breath stank like spiced wine. She never remembered smelling anything in a dream. Sights, sounds, even touch, but she never remembered smelling anything.

"I am-" she broke off her reply to say *I am Fara*, deciding to learn more about what in the world was happening before destroying her cover. If he thought Fara looked like Mercede, she might as well play along, for now. "I am better, thank you." She adjusted her Spanish to mirror the man's tone and cadence but still hadn't localized the dialect. Under normal circumstances, she could determine not only the city where the speaker was from but also the undertones of where they lived as a child. Not even his grammatical syntax matched anything she knew.

Geez, her brain had to be fried. That light had done something to her. Focusing, she tried to recall the events leading up to this place. She was in the ancient mausoleum of the Cult of the Dead, with Guy. They were searching for a way out. Something was stalking them, coming closer. Guy went through a broken wall, and she… Ooh, she couldn't remember. It was like a giant void blocked her thoughts. Maybe she really was losing it.

"Leave us!" The man waved toward the door, and the lace around his wrist flounced from under the black velvet sleeve.

Lace? Men only wore lace when they dressed up as pirates on Halloween. The other people were in costumes as well. It had to be some fancy period ball, maybe Baroque. That at least would explain the music. The twang had to be a harpsichord.

"Shall I send a page for the physician, your Grace?" The man who had carried her angled his body toward the door.

"No, I believe the worst of the episode has passed." His tone softened. "My niece simply overexerted." He turned to the man at his left elbow. "Insist the assembly return to the ballroom and then wait for me outside the door. Ensure we are *not* disturbed."

Niece? Fara raised her head to survey the large room. Her sight was still blurred, but she didn't remember hitting her head. She squinted to make out the crowd gathered just outside of the hallway door, pressing forward to catch a glimpse of the scene. Perhaps they were in a play, a weird ultra-realistic play.

Shit! That was a really stupid idea. Her? Playacting? She restrained the scoff. Just the fact she could do that made her feel a little more normal.

While the crowd took its time to disperse, she had an unobstructed view of the man who had carried her upstairs. His clothes weren't really those of a pirate, rather a representation of the late Renaissance, perhaps even the Elizabethan period. Fara had never studied costuming, so all she knew came from the few movies she had seen, and she was no movie aficionado either. She relied on J.C. for that. But this dude's velvet hat, tights, and cape slung over a single shoulder were something right out of the Three Musketeers, except that was France, and this was clearly Italy. At least she knew that much.

"Your Grace," the man servant bowed and as part of the fluid motion removed the plumed hat from his head, swept it to the floor, and replaced it with the same flourish. He stopped alongside her rescuer and motioned for him to leave, closing the door behind them.

The middle-aged man at her bedside waited, watching the door for several seconds. A deep breath expanded his already voluminous torso, and as he exhaled, he faced her with a blossoming expression, brightening his dark eyes with a twinkle.

"That's my goodly girl!" His muted voice couldn't contain the joy. "My veritable genius! The Guzman family be known for our conniving wit. Not only are you quick witted, you played the role to perfection. An ingenious plan to beg a faint in his arms!" He patted her shoulder with four quick taps. "In less than a fortnight, your ingenious efforts to seduce him shall certainly break his will."

Seduce him?

That snapped Fara out the funk, and she mulled over the words, wondering if they could perhaps have a secondary meaning.

"What overcame you, Mercede?"

Fara swallowed, and her throat felt different somehow. "I dare not claim ownership of happenstance, for I truly fainted." Her voice sounded different too.

"Happenstance then is our blessed conspirator." This time he patted her hand, and his triumphant glee faded slightly. "Shall I request your aunt's physician?"

She shook her head and felt the weight of the up-do rock with the motion. "I just need a few moments to regain my composure." Then she noticed, for the first time, the volumes of fabric surrounding her. She moved her leg against the stiff texture of the inner skirt, yet the outer velvet folds didn't even shift.

"Very well, yet do not tarry long. Maintaining the man's attentions effectively shall divert them from your aunt. Gaetano di Casapesenna will quit taking to her bed as soon as you are sharing his."

Her eyes widened. "You want me to seduce him."

His thick black brows furled for only a second before settling back into place to frame those drilling eyes. "You truly must be confounded, for this plan was hatched in that devious mind of yours, the underlying reason for you to leave the familiar comforts of Madrid. You specifically came with the intention to lure away my wife's lover. Anna requires a dose of comeuppance to humble her into submission. The barren bitch has baked me dry."

Baked him dry? Fara wondered about what the phrase regarded. Was he impotent or broke, perhaps both?

Bracing himself with his left arm on the other side of her waist, he skimmed his right hand along her cheek. "Your mother's features flatter you." Leaning in, he laid a gentle kiss upon her lips. "I see her every time I look at you."

The sensitive skin crawled with the lingering sensation. It felt all too real, more real even than the night with the ghost. His breath slid inside her mouth, and a sickening clench tightened in her gut. Fara's mind swam, and dizziness again overcame her. Shit!

She had to devise some way for him to leave her alone. Only then would she be able to determine what was going on. "Would it distress you if I remained in my chambers for the rest of the evening?"

"You think it wise? You hast only just captured his interest, and only peaked his desire."

She smiled. "What would you think if I remained in my chambers and asked you to send him to see me, in order for me to thank him for saving me?"

His face lit once again, forming a much more youthful appearance than the otherwise heavy features allowed. "Rumors of such an interlude would instantly spread. Yet a prudent man would not come, thinking it to be a trap into a marriage offer."

Marriage offer? Her head felt even dizzier than before. If she could only take a deep breath to clear her mind, she would be able to think clearly. Wait, that was redundant. She sighed within herself. "Well then, if it would not be wise-"

He interrupted. "It's a brilliant plan. The ladies' whispers are our allies. Surely, they will reach my wife's ear faster than any other suspicion. Her jealousy will spike instantly and an argument between her and her lover will most surely ensue. She is already seething from your role in the night's Comedias. You played Yeselda, to perfection! That kiss you shared brought silence to the entire room. No one even dared to breathe, fearing your aunt's reprisal."

"Me?" Fara was never one for theatrics. Apparently she kissed someone, but who? Why couldn't she remember?

"Of course. Dimonico falls in love with the slave and shuns the advances of the spoiled princess. I selected the play for such the reason. When you melted into Gaetano's embrace, he desired only you."

"Gaetano?" She rolled onto her side to face him.

"Gaetano di Casapesenna, he played the role of Dimonico." The fine lines returned to the corners of his eyes. "Have you forgotten? The diversion occurred only a few short hours ago."

"Apologies Uncle. The faint has clouded my faculties. I shall be myself again momentarily."

"I know you shall my devious one." He kissed her again, lingering against her lips longer than what she considered appropriate, but she didn't struggle. His rank breath swirled once again. Thankfully, he didn't try to push his tongue inside of her mouth, but she wondered for a split second if he was going to do it. "I shall send in your ladies and wait long enough to have you in your sheerest night rail afore Gaetano arrives."

The door closed, and she slid out of bed, strategically noting her surroundings. The room was large, easily ten meters in length and about eight in width. A single door exited into the hall. A fireplace was opposite the bed, but the grate was empty. The air was sticky and hot, so she couldn't imagine needing a fire. She walked across the highly polished marble floor toward the windows, and the sound of the surf grew.

The window latch was a simple curved hook made from brass. It was old with greenish oxidation around the divot encircling the central bolt where a cleaning cloth couldn't reach. Even an inexperienced burglar would be able to open it without much effort. She slipped a finger under the curve, and lifting the latch, swung open the windows. Immediately, the ocean breeze greeted her. Finally, all remnants of the vile bad breath dissipated.

She inhaled as deeply as possible. The fresh air felt wonderful and invigorated her mind, but it did nothing to aid her hazy sight. She blinked several times, hoping this wasn't permanent damage from that damned blast of light. Yet, she didn't need perfectly clear vision to see the dark expanse extending toward the horizon. She was apparently at the coastline, but which coastline?

Brilliant moonlight shifted on the swells of the waves. The unending beauty was hypnotic, one slipping into the next. Staring at the distant patterns, the scene reminded her of something. Shit! Why couldn't she remember?

A sudden manly guffaw burst from below her feet. Leaning over the narrow ledge, bright paper lanterns dotted the water's edge where dozens of small boats bobbed within the easy waves. They were skinnier than rowboats, with a pointed bow and stern. Each had a short mast, but she didn't see any sails. Certainly, they would be stowed while tied off at the dock; at least something in this tricked out world made sense. In the combined light of the moon and lanterns, she could just make out colorful scenes adorning the sides of the listing boats. The men loitering on the dock had to be the boats' captains.

The man with the booming voice laughed again, gesturing with an uncorked bottle toward the hillside. All of the men were similarly dressed. White shirts were open at the neck, and the loose fabric fluttered in the wind. All wore tight breeches and dark boots. Fara leaned a little further and squinted.

"My lady," in unison, two young voices called from inside the room.

Fara twisted to face them, and again as one single living organism, they curtsied a quick bob.

The taller cocked her head, causing the ribbons on the back of her cap to flutter. "The Duke of Medina said you were faint and requested we prepare you for bed."

The other girl's voice was equal to her stature, small and delicate. "My lady, please move away from the balcony. A light head and steep drop never make a safe match."

Contemplating what would be an appropriate answer, Fara returned to the room. Her stiff skirts rustled with each step. The closer she approached the clearer their faces became. They were wearing identical uniforms all in white. Clearly, these were her chamber maids.

"Are you well, Donna Mercede?"

"As well as can be expected." Taking a breath, the bindings bit into her ribs. "This dress is so restrictive. I can't breathe."

The girls immediately went to work. One retrieved a sheer gown from the upper drawer within the armoire while the other waited next to the vanity. "My lady?"

Fara struggled momentarily within herself, not understanding while understanding at the same time. She approached cautiously, standing within arm's reach. In circular fluffs, the maid motioned upwards with her hands, and Fara lifted her arms, exposing the nearly imperceptible laces down the sides of her body.

An oil lamp burned on the far edge of the vanity, and the circular mirror reflected the lamplight. Fara caught the edge of a reflection. She stared, thinking this could possibly the maid, but then she recognized the hands working down the side of the woman's reflection in the mirror, her reflection.

All of the blood drained from her head. Her knees weakened, melting out from under her, and the two maids drew her onto the tiny stool. One balanced her while the other flipped the skirts over the back, making the seat disappear within the volume of the skirt's folds.

No! This had to be some weird dream, a hallucination from the explosion. Reaching out for the mirror on the vanity, she grasped the carved ivory base and slowly turned the glass. One of the girls handed her a monocle on a thick chain. Fara accepted it, and adjusting the distance, she found the right depth and angle.

Eyes so dark they were nearly black stared back. Intricate curls of ebony flowed down past creamy-white cheeks and draped equally pale shoulders. She was young, probably not much over eighteen with a face which could be a model for angelic frescos. A brilliant pendant laid against the pale flesh on a long and twisted gold chain. The blue of the stone matched the dress, a rare ocean blue.

Shit! The breath caught in Fara's throat before she could give wind to the exclamation. She was wearing the Hope diamond. Okay, she took a breath and pulled it together. This couldn't be the same stone. Fara remembered being at the Smithsonian with Guy and looking at the pendant slowly rotating within its glass case. This stone was larger, easily 60 carats, and it glimmered in the candlelight, emanating an internal power. Research on the Hope diamond demonstrated its phosphorescence power when exposed to ultraviolet radiation. Was she irradiated? Is that what was wrong with her?

While she contemplated the stone, the maids continued working, and the corset released. With an audible gasp, she inhaled a long, cleansing breath, but the residual pain throbbed against her bruised ribs. She had no clue how women tortured themselves like that, putting on a corset day after day. From that single perspective, the short life expectancy would be considered a blessing.

Another long breath eased the residual discomfort, and the added oxygen helped clear her head. She took mental stock of her situation, the real situation. The flash of light transported her into the body of someone named Mercede, whose uncle was the Duke of Medina. Neither of those names meant anything to her. His wife, the Duchess, had a lover, and Mercede was here to seduce him away from her. Fara didn't want to think about that right now. This wasn't her body to utilize in such a personal way. Her breath caught. If she was in the past in Mercede's body, was Mercede in the present in Fara's body?

"Oh shit, shit, shit!" She said out loud in English. If Mercede was with Guy, who looked similar enough to this Gaetano, just what was she doing in Fara's body?

"My lady?" The taller girl asked as she lifted the sheer nightgown and draped it over Fara's head.

She didn't have a chance to reply. A soft knock rapped on the door, and the girls giggled. Just what had Mercede done with Gaetano all of those hundreds of years ago? If she made any change to historic events, the entire timeline of human existence could skew. Fuck! She had to behave just as Mercede or else the future could be completely rewritten.

The knock repeated.

"My lady," the shorter one bowed, "shall I permit your guest entry."

She snapped out of the inter-dimensional conundrum. "Yes, and then you both are excused for the night."

One maid left through the door concealed behind the tapestry while the other opened the hallway door and bowed, scooting around the man who blocked the doorway.

CHAPTER 20

Chrystal remained in the foyer while Ted pursued the threesome upstairs. Her warning not to follow them paused on her lips. If he wanted to get mixed up in Fara's weird affairs, then that was his own business. She'd never seen him move so decisively, taking each step of the staircase as if he actually saw them.

He probably did.

When Ted had touched her, she channeled what he perceived through his abnormal eyes, and the colorful energy array of psychic light brightened the room, revealing every minute detail, just like while they were inside of the old Puerto Rican fort. Through touching Ted, she saw everything. The men. The vortex. The hellfire. The image was in surreal relief of what normal sight would perceive, but it was there nonetheless. That wasn't natural, and neither was this.

The preternatural world and the world everyone claimed as being real held equal shares of the universe. Rules governed both sides, natural rules. The two coexisted in balance, most of the time. When they investigated the Puerto Rican dungeon, it had been collecting residual energy for centuries. This house was exactly the same, and both were connected to Fara Trotter.

That woman was a menace.

Chrystal grimaced, and the all too familiar seething burn rekindled in her chest. The goddess was back in her life, once again, and yet, why didn't she sense her presence? It was as if Fara had fallen off the face of the earth.

So absorbed in her hatred, she absently brushed the newel of the banister with her bare hand. As if singed, she drew away quickly, but already, pieces of the past started flooding her mind. A jumbled mess of overlapping images slammed into her senses. She saw mostly faces; laughing, crying, screaming, all bonded together by the strength of acute emotion. But instead of the dramatic masks of just comedy and tragedy, additional emotions of love and hatred, lust and anger, joy and misery appeared upon the features of the long-forgotten dead. Her variety of psychometrics responded to the most extreme situations, and all of those jumbled feelings became her own for that moment in time.

She hated it, hated all of it.

Her gloves were in her waistband, where she normally tucked them for quick retrieval, but she didn't dare expose her hands to any new impulses until these faded, not even to minute particles in the air. When Ted started acting so strangely, she should have known better than to remove her gloves to feel the floating vibrations, but she didn't want to be outdone, not once again, especially not while Fara Trotter was in the vicinity.

Crossing her arms, she tucked her hands into her armpits while trying to shield against the contrasting sensations, but once they were in, the energy had to run its course. Fighting against the progression only prolonged the connection. The rampaging emotions twisted in her stomach, making her nauseous, but throwing up wouldn't help, not now. She crumpled onto the bottom step and stuck her head between her knees. The extra blood in her brain added internal stability, but the position made her look weak. Even though no one saw her, she knew, and that was enough. The amazing Fara Trotter had trumped her again.

The phantasmal bodies swirled into scenes, and snippets of emotional altercations slammed through her mind. As usually happened, the arguments escalated until the worst of the worst stood out from the rest. Anger flowed between two women, regal in appearance and beautiful in face, yet their attitudes were common, oh so very common.

Chrystal focused. It wasn't as if she could actually hear the words, but rather understand the women's emotions. They were fighting over a man, whom they each loved.

The older blond had a brass candlestick clutched in her hand and pursued the dark-haired beauty up the stairs. Chrystal didn't need to move physically to see the continuation of the scene. The younger woman slammed the door, hiding inside a bedroom overlooking the cliff.

Flickering in afterthought, the blond had someone with her, hidden in unnatural shadows, whom Chrystal hadn't detected while they were in the foyer. The humanoid silhouette followed with little more substance than a figment of the imagination, and yet was there just the same. Masking energy cloaked her figure from the real world, as if she was an avatar or a manifestation of an excessively strong thoughtform linked to her regal mistress. Now that at least was something new.

The shielded figure raised its hands, and a ball of light amassed in front of outstretched palms. With lightning speed, manipulative energy blasted the door. Despite the younger beauty's valiant attempt to brace the door with her body, the burst exploded in cosmic proportions. Nothing in the physical world had the capacity to withstand that amount of psychic energy, as brilliant and forceful as lightning.

The regal blond stood triumphantly in the open doorway, watching her rival recover. The normal reaction to such an assault was fear. Strangely, fear had yet to enter into the beauty's consciousness. Still confident in her physical ability to overcome her adversary, she staggered to her knees and then crawled toward the bed with anger fueling her resolve.

The blond and the shadow figure stepped inside the room and stood shoulder to shoulder, repeating something. The dark beauty had to be injured, for she moved in short and stilted jerks toward the bed. For the first time, panic infused her emotions but not yet fear. In all of Chrystal's existence, only those trained to tune into their psychic power could exact such control, and the first noted experiments were still centuries in the future.

Fortified by the shadow figure's glowing energy, the blond moved toward the bed while the shadowy wraith slithered across the room and twisted the telescope from its tripod. Through the strength of sheer will, the wounded woman reached the bed and searched for something under the pillows. Withdrawing a bejeweled dagger, the girl turned to face the wizened woman, assuming a fighting stance. The woman raised the candlestick, and in a mirror form, the shade leveraged the telescope. Just a split second ahead, the girl blocked with her left forearm, but she was too slow. The larger end of the telescope connected.

Time stopped at the point of impact.

Everything in the room shifted, hanging in a temporal distortion, except for the shadow figure. It turned toward Chrystal and acknowledged her presence in this shared reality!

A violent chill shot up her spine.

That shouldn't happen, couldn't happen. The past was past. Nothing Chrystal did would change the outcome of what she witnessed, but somehow that thing had an active consciousness in both the past and the present.

The figure saluted her with a pleasant nod and then inhaled. The effect was unlike anything Chrystal had ever witnessed. With the breath, the woman absorbed the emotional energy from the room. All of the rage, fear, panic, and pain flowed into her body feeding her corporeal form, providing definition and substance. A woman with dark red hair and robust figure materialized out of the miasmic shadow.

The room was cold, devoid of all energy, and along with it went Chrystal's connection. However, the last image remained in her mind. A thin stream of blood trickled down the girl's pale cheek, curling with the contours of her temple, cheek, and chin. In a macabre way, the blood looked like a wayward piece of hair lying across her face. Even in death, she was beautiful, like a perfect rendition of Snow White. Except for this girl, there wouldn't be a happily ever after.

The channel was gone.

The energy spent.

And yet something remained. Whatever had been in that room was more than a thoughtform. She hadn't believed in angels or demons, but the evidence was too strong to deny. Something evil had made its way into this world and connected itself to this place. She shivered. Whatever it was still remained.

Trying to shake the ominous cold, she focused on the present, forcing her senses to switch channels and used the heat of the quarrel to fill the void within her.

The men's shouts quieted, and then Fara snapped at all of them, sending out a blast of deep energy. Like an old radio requiring fine tuning, Chrystal's mind adjusted, listening to the woman's thoughts, but they weren't similar to Fara's, not at all.

Ted was right. The spirit inhabiting Fara's body wasn't the woman who broke every training record at the FPI.

Chrystal squeezed her eyes closed, but the sensations poured into her anyway. Tears swelled, and that uncomfortable stuffiness filled her sinus. She wasn't going to cry, not for that impersonator or for Fara Trotter, who had been the core problem throughout her entire career. Fara's energy signature had tainted everything she touched, and the residue was so strong. Chrystal wasn't able to get Fara out of her awareness, not ever.

With a definitive tug, the gloves snapped out from her waistband, and she slid her fingers inside, stretching them into the fabric with a contented familiarity. She headed outside for some distance from the argument.

When she first joined the FPI, she was hopeful for the first time in her life. Throughout school, she had been known as "glove girl." Her parents thought they were helping by sending her to Catholic girls' school, but those girls were experts at relational aggression. They knew exactly how to manipulate situations to not get caught, while making Chrystal's life a living hell. Most people think boys made the worst bullies, but girls were far, far worse. And these girls were the best at everything they tried, straight A students, perfectly pressed and dressed, answering every question in class before anyone else had the chance to raise a hand. Even when Chrystal anticipated the question and raised her hand first, the bitch of a teacher never even saw her, having eyes only for her perfectly stellar pets.

Of course, Chrystal took it as her sworn duty to bring the bullies to justice, teachers first.

Instead of using the girls' bathroom, which was one of the most dangerous places in the entire school, she snuck into the teachers' facility. She always used the same stall to minimize receiving new sensations, and although she lined the toilet seat in multiple layers of toilet paper, the intimate contact resonated through the thin barrier. Miss Adams had used that same stall within the hour, and when Chrystal sat down, she immediately knew why the woman had been ill. Not only was she pregnant, she was also HIV positive. Ironically, the bitch taught health and fitness.

After class ended that day, Chrystal remained in the room, again unwelcomed to join the other girls and therefore unseen. The school closely watched internet usage for inappropriate access to websites. She removed her gloves and placed her fingers upon Miss Adams' keyboard; the impression of the password vibrated since those were the most commonly used keys. Her heart beat rapidly, and a smile creased her pale lips. Miss Adams would be able to explain accessing an HIV site for classroom instruction purposes; so Chrystal thought of what would be most damning in the eyes of Sister Marjorie, the head mistress. The nearest Planned Parenthood office was in Boston, and Chrystal made an appointment for an abortion and STD counseling in Miss Adams' name. She was fired within the week.

Building upon that success, Chrystal found unique and creative ways of guiding her revenge, and one by one, the paragons fell. She had dealt with the last on her hit list the day before graduation. The world was now hers.

She thought the CIA would use someone with her skills, and then out of the blue, Joe Daily contacted her. He applauded her initiative and gave her every opportunity to excel. She applied herself as never before and studied for endless hours determined to be the best recruit ever; however, Faradahl "Amazing" Alecto set every record within the agency. She was faster, stronger, smarter, and more intuitive than any other recruit, including Chrystal. That was not acceptable. There had to be something the woman had done to boost her prowess.

She needed to get close to something Fara had prolonged contact with, so she mildly poisoned the recruit who had Faradahl's former bunk. While she was in the infirmary, Chrystal transferred into that bed. She expected by absorbing Fara's residual energy she would receive additional insights into her abilities. Instead, the close contact formed an indelible bond, which was the reason why she and Ted received this assignment. Work was all she had, and she wouldn't let Fara screw this up too.

She stared back at the house and knew she had to go back inside. Just as she reached the curve in the staircase, Ted dealt the trump card, announcing the woman in front of them wasn't really Fara. An emotional cocktail of surprise and disgust mixed with a dash of disbelief blew out of the room with a gale-force emotional wind.

Shielding the frenzied chaos, she stopped in the doorway of the bedroom. Each of the three men held a geographic corner of the room. Fara was in the center, holding onto the post of the bed.

Ted continued, "…She has shoulder-length curls of dark hair and blank, hollow eyes."

J.C.'s back was facing the door. Even though she couldn't see his face, his body was rigid. "Did you say hollow eyes? Are they filled with swirling fog?"

"That's one way to describe it." Ted turned his stare back to the woman. "She's definitely not Faradahl Trotter."

"Okay, you keep saying that," J.C. swung his arms in small backward circles, "but if she's not Fara, who the hell is she?"

"Why does she look like Fara on the outside?" From the far corner, Gaetano faced them. Guilt seethed through the air, and each breath brought another mini vision. She could control the microscopic effect, but too much more and she'd have another meltdown.

"Como te llamas?" *What is your name* was one of the few Spanish phrases she knew. She was never good with languages that didn't translate word for word, and very few did. The Spanish phrase literally meant *how are you called*. Her focus on emotions transcended language. Love was love. Anger was anger, and so on. It didn't matter who, what, or when. Emotions conveyed all essential facets of human existence.

The woman whirled to face her, but no recognition passed over her features. Chrystal was as much a stranger as any of these people in the room; even though, she and Fara had met twice. Both of those situations were damned memorable.

"Fara Trotter" stammered off her lips.

"Que es tu nombre completo?" Gaetano stepped closer.

Chrystal was able to pick out *nombre*, name, and assumed *completo* was complete.

The woman waited, swinging her gaze from man to man, apparently looking for sympathy, or perhaps a champion.

"De donde nació?" He added even more forcefully, but Chrystal didn't know what that meant.

The imposter blinked absently.

"Fara-" J.C. stepped forward.

Gaetano interrupted in English, "No, don't give her any clues. Can't you tell that's not Fara?"

"Couldn't you?" The Puerto Rican snapped back.

Chrystal watched the woman try to determine a course of action. Even if she wasn't Fara, she deserved what she was getting.

Her head tipped, but the short haircut didn't change with the motion. Fara Trotter had been a little too proud of her thick mane of hair. Having it burn in the hellfire was just the first step of her comeuppance. The time was ripe to take her down, whether her soul was home or not.

The brilliant idea lit Chrystal's mind. Actually, this was ideal! Her ties to Fara were broken, gone, deleted. She would never have to worry about Faradahl Alecto Trotter ever again as long as she could maintain the status quo.

Back to Spanish, Gaetano asked something more complex, and she was only able to pick out a single word *espalda* which meant a person's back or maybe it was shovel. She didn't quite remember and winced at her own ineptitude. Sooner or later, she would have to learn Spanish.

Fara blinked and with a full dose of bravado answered something Chrystal didn't understand.

Ted replied quickly. "It's no use. She's not lying. She just doesn't know, so she's making something up that could be plausible. Her aura emits an orange hue over the dark blue base." He motioned to Chrystal, "Would you lay hands upon her?"

Crossing her arms, her entire body tensed. "Absolutely not!"

CHAPTER 21

The candlelight from the sconces in the hall outlined the dark shape with startling clarity, even with Mercede's poor vision. A cape draped a single shoulder, yet the definition of masculine shoulders remained, tapering in a definitive V toward snug hips. The man's britches hugged his muscular contours, and the Hessian boots almost glowed with inner light they were so highly polished.

"Please, come inside. Gaetano, you will, come inside." Although Fara added the special cadence to compel him forward, the light and airy voice wasn't trained in such things.

"No," his response was flat. "Donn'Anna suspected her husband's plot upon your arrival in Napoli. Frankly, I thought she was making much ado about nothing, exaggerating the Duke's interest in our discreet encounters, so why now?"

"That is precisely what we need to discuss. Please come in for just a moment."

"And be caught in your bedchamber? I am no fool. Goodnight, Donna Mercede." He bent at the waist in a stiff bow.

"Wait!" But it was too late; he had spun on his heel, closing the door with a definitive bang.

She stood still, replaying the brief conversation. Anna… Anna… Her mind scrambled to place the name. Duke of Medina. The Duchess of Medina, Anna…

Wandering to the balcony, she flung open both sides of the long windows, leaning precariously over the balcony's metal railing. The coastline edged away from her in both directions. She was on a promontory point.

That was significant.

What was there?

Damn it, she knew the answer. Concentrating on the veil inside her mind, she drilled down upon that one piece of information. The point. The promontory point. P... The letter P was significant. P... P...

Suddenly, Posillipo was just there, and with that single revelation, the rest of her memories flooded back. A gleeful laugh bubbled out of her before she could stop it. The men on the boat dock paused their rowdy banter to glance in her direction. She stepped back just enough to be out of the brilliant moonlight and continued watching the listing boats from the shadows.

This was the old castle on the Posillipo rise where earlier that same day someone had tried to kill her. The past, or rather her future, became clearer. Guy had called it the Syren's Palace, but before her call to J.C., she had asked the waiter at the café. He said it was Palazzo Donn'Anna. Anna Carafa. Jesus, that was it! Mercede's aunt was Anna Carafa. Gaetano's lover was Anna Carafa.

Everything now was so obvious.

All of those books on the table in Guy's house had been about Anna Carafa, and Fara stole the one off from the top of the stack during her hasty retreat. She didn't know why at the time, but this was it. Shit! It was still in her backpack, which was in the 21st century. Why didn't she read even a paragraph of that stupid book? Her fate, or rather that of Donna Mercede, was right there, at her fingertips!

She couldn't be sure Mercede was inhabiting her natural body, but a pretty even assumption was a soul for a soul. She'd studied cases of true possession, of a stronger, usually malevolent spirit overshadowing the will of the host. Verified cases were very rare and required some willing approval of the host. She never heard any documented reports about two individual souls exchanging bodies other than as a fictional story plot, but this happened. This was real. If the body was just a host for the soul, logically souls could switch hosts.

Okay, she accepted that piece as a fact. But if this all centered on the Duchess of Medina, why would Fara switch places with Mercede and not Anna Carafa?

Frustrated, her mind overloaded. Backing away from the balcony, she slowed her thoughts and traced one fact at a time.

She was in the underground crypt when her mental faculties exchanged places with Donna Mercede. But why? How did that benefit the Duchess?

Taking a deep breath, she sat on the low stool in front of the vanity.

Hosts.

Bodies.

The future blended with the past.

The past with the future.

Fara and Mercede switched places.

She was missing some critical linkage.

She ran her fingers through her long hair, and it felt so good she did it again. She had loved her hair, especially the way it looked in the sun. Guy had told her many times that her hair looked like a silken waterfall in how it caught the light.

Guy.

Silken waterfall.

Aleri!

In the catacombs, Guy had asked her what was wrong with Aleri. The girl was experiencing radical mood changes. Uncommon behaviors. Violence. She witnessed her hitting on Guy. She called Fara a harlot and demanded vengeance. The symptoms indicated Aleri was possessed, but by whom? The soul of Anna Carafa?

Focusing, she remembered the bitter hiss of a voice emanating from the girl's delicate body, "Purgatorial wreathed serpents, only their everlasting power shall slake my thirst." Later, they heard Aleri's voice in the crypt. At the time, she thought it was a trick to get Guy out into the open, but his cousin could have been there while under the influence of Anna Carafa.

Perhaps Fara and Mercede weren't the intended beneficiaries of the inter-dimensional burst. Perhaps they were a byproduct, caught in the wrong place at the time.

She was holding a skull, someone who had been hidden deep within the series of mortuary tunnels, in a place no one would find. Could it have been Mercede's skull? If so, how did it get there? She was a high-ranking niece of a Spanish diplomat. When she died, her funeral would have been elaborate.

Her initial impression when she touched the skull of Lucia was watching the raven-haired beauty dancing with... with Gaetano! The surge of hatred and jealousy was from Anna Carafa. Could Anna Carafa's skull be in Lucia's shrine?

The incongruent pieces knit together.

Aleri worshipped Lucia and prayed at her shine almost daily, and not only Aleri. Other young women visited the idol. All of the energy generated through prayer had to go somewhere. The purgatorial souls' power was in the crypt as well. The new and old energy were perfect catalysts for a cross-dimensional transfiguration.

All of that focused energy created a thoughtform, and not just any thoughtform. Someone was controlling it, feeding and guiding it.

But who?

Not Aleri, she was a victim, not the perpetrator.

Not Guy.

Perhaps his aunt? Her energy was strong, but not other-worldly strong.

There had to be someone else. The doctor was too weak. The armed guards too obedient. Someone else was present, controlling everything from a nearby location, out of sight but not out of mind.

Guy described Aleri as sweet but headstrong. Perhaps she was too strong to be possessed completely. The only other option would be to switch souls. Anna would continue living in a modern host body, and not just any body, a lovely young woman with wealth and power.

Fara contemplated how many assumptions were in her line of reasoning, and at the juncture of each assumption, the probability to other tracks exponentially multiplied. Even if her fantastic and nearly unbelievable explanation was true, what could she do about it?

Doing nothing wasn't an option. She couldn't just pretend to be Mercede and live out the woman's life. Timeline or no timeline, she had to take definitive actions to return to the 21st century. Hopefully she wasn't the only one working on it. Would Guy be astute enough to notice the change in Fara's behavior? His actions in the crypt clearly indicated he wanted to seduce her. Would he figure out she wasn't herself before or after he fucked her? Oh shit, what about J.C.?

She had to do something!

The sea air flickered the only lit candle, pulsing the flame until it nearly extinguished. Fara didn't have any flint or tinder, so she carefully closed the balcony's doors. With confident strides, she grabbed the candle and rushed to the armoire. Abundant measures of lace and silk nearly leapt from the cabinet's depths. Everything appeared to be just as frilly and ornate as the dress that had tortured her earlier that evening.

What would she give for a simple pair of dark sweatpants and a hoody?

She rummaged through the dresses, hoping to find something manageable. The last dress on a peg in the back corner looked dark, so dark it blended in with deep shadows of the armoire. She tugged, but the fabric snagged on something.

Setting the candle onto the bedside table, she returned to grasp the dress by both shoulders and eased it out of the tangle of gowns. She held it out in front of her, examining it in the meager light. Back then, women wore black to indicate they were in mourning. Why would Mercede pack a black dress to visit her uncle? Did they expect someone to die? The fine hairs crept up on Fara's arms. Was the Duke's plot more elaborate than she thought?

The soft nightgown was so loose just a shrug of her shoulders had it pooling at her feet. The night air had cooled considerably, and her flesh tingled with the chill. Spreading the dress upon the bed, she wiggled into it from the broad skirt, but it wasn't like a normal dress. The pieces were layered and not quite sewn together. This was a time long before zippers or even buttons apparently. Everything had laces like giant shoestrings.

After struggling and tugging on this cord or that for at least ten minutes, she finally was in the gown. No wonder ladies had maids to help them dress. She could have called the girls to help her, but the fewer people who knew she was out and about the better. She wasn't sure where she was going or what she would investigate, but she had to do something. Clues linking Anna Carafa to the future had to exist somewhere in this house.

Out of the corner of her eye, the tapestry moved. Instinctually, Fara jumped back, landing in a crouched position, and the billowing skirt fanned out in front of her like spilt ink. Although she focused on slowing her pulse, her training again failed. Right mind, wrong body. Fara's seething will surfaced, swirling within her frustration.

A tall figure slipped around the edge of the intricately embroidered scene and stood in relief to the moonlight streaming through the windows. She recognized his silhouette immediately.

"Donna Mercede?" The voice confirmed he was Gaetano di Casapesenna.

Smoothly Fara rose, raising the hem of the dark fabric to ensure she wouldn't trip. "What are you doing here?"

He remained close to the service door, but this time he didn't appear ready to flee. The tilt of his head followed her. "So what of the Duke's plot?"

"Clever of you to publically refuse to see me and then return via the servant's corridor."

"As I said, I am no fool." His voice was crisp and bitter, tangible enough to break.

"Neither am I."

"Great accolades regarding your intellect and clever tongue have circulated throughout court, and are even more compelling than your beauty. Your wit and charm left a lasting impression from the evening's theatrics, enough so that speculation abounds, questioning whether you fainted purposefully to lure me to your chamber. What pray tell is so important to create such a complicated ruse?"

She returned his contemplative stare. "As I relayed to my uncle during our private conversation, there was no trick or subterfuge. The dress was restrictive; I could not breathe."

"And yet, you require my attendance once more?" A single brow arched warily. "Express your plot, and I shall be gone."

Gaetano's ghost was part of the spiritual conundrum; therefore, he had to be part of the solution. She thought for a moment on how to articulate her purpose. She needed him to trust her in order to receive information or his cooperation at the very least, and the best way to earn either was through the truth.

"I valued your assistance, so I asked you here to warn you." She glanced around the room, wondering if they were being observed, and then approached him, taking his arm. She drew him closer to the masking sounds of the ocean and the drunken sailors. "My uncle wants me to lure you out of Anna's bed and into my own."

He didn't react adversely. His voice remained calm and steady. "And why would you be informing me of this plot?"

"To protect us both. Anna Carafa is a dangerous and devious woman. Should there be speculation of an affair, both of our lives would be forfeit."

"Perchance it is too late to avoid her wrath. She is furious after the comedia this night." With a rattling sigh, his tone deepened, and he looked down upon her with softening regard. "Our performance bred suspicion as to our intentions. Mercede, when I kissed you-" He stood perfectly still, and then turned his face toward the sea. A wedge of moonlight highlighted the angular contours of his face, exactly the same as the ghost who made love to her. Internally, her internal sorrow deepened. Clearly, he died very close to this same age. "The Duchess' revenge runs deeply. I fear more from her than the Duke." He sighed.

Impulsively, she asked, "Do you love her?"

Mirth burst in a quick and shuddering laugh. "Donn'Anna is compelling and powerful. She uses and discards people as easily as seasonal gowns. I mean nothing to her."

"Then what do you receive out of the affair?"

"After that blazing kiss, I did not believe you were naïve." His dark brows shot up and eyes narrowed warily. Yet a devious twinkle glimmered in their corners. "She is an amazing lover with clever appetites. At first, I enjoyed her games and the rewards for winning." His voice faded.

"But now you don't?"

He paused, clearly studying her non-reaction. "Her tastes stretch the boundaries of the imagination. As we speak, she presides over another night of exhibitions and expects me to join her down in the foundations to witness the games." His bitter voice deepened to a harsh edge. "Shortly before your arrival, I informed her that I would no longer participate, and so she forces me to watch by her side. Her bitter mood will edge its way to deepen the depravity this night."

"Depravity? What sort of games does she play?"

"Donn'Anna never participates. She likes to watch things that never should beg mention, especially not in a true lady's presence, innocent or experienced alike."

"Sadistic and sexual games that harm the participants?" She pressed. "Has anyone died?"

His expression deepened. "Only one, since I have been at court; however, rumors exist of others."

"What happened?" Fara searched his face and saw the depth of his pain. Either he inflicted the final blow, or he knew the person who died. Regardless, he held the blame within himself.

He shook his head. "She was a simple peasant, who made a living on the street. No one cared whether she lived or died. Donn'Anna considers her participants little better than cattle. She owns all in Napoli; therefore, their lives shall be bent to her will and bidding." He took a step closer, and the drifting breeze carried the spicy scent of cologne and a deeper, masculine musk. His voice deepened to a low whisper. "You are a tender and beautiful lady, far too sweet and naïve for life in this court."

"I am not as I appear." She tipped her head back to gaze up into his eyes. Against her intentional will, her inner heat stirred with him so close, yet not quite touching. The irrational desire arched its way to the surface. It was the one thing she and Mercede shared; they both desired him in an intimate and familiar way. Fara forced herself to pull back and not act upon those instincts. In a husky tone, she regretfully added, "Trust my words in that I have no intention to fulfill my uncle's wishes. You are safe with me, Don Gaetano."

Physically, he took a step back. His expression tightened, and then he performed a stiff bow. "Then, I must take my leave, dear lady. Your confidence is safe."

He silently slipped behind the tapestry.

She didn't protest, and yet her inner need screamed for her to hold him close. After a few seconds, her intentional will won, and she followed him into the dim passage.

CHAPTER 22

The interconnecting service corridors created an elaborate maze, hidden from sight from the owners and guests, yet an integral part of the castle. Sconces burned at intervals, just far enough apart to maintain a dim glow throughout the complex system. The resulting smoke clung to the dense air along with other putrid scents Fara didn't want to identify.

She hurried to keep pace with Gaetano's long-legged stride, and the physical effort made her breathing labored. She pushed this body to its maximum effort, which wasn't enough. Her lungs constricted, and she had to stop.

"Sweet Jesus," she wheezed, not wanting to believe her bad luck, "Mercede has asthma?!" Only one person she knew in high school had asthma attacks, and he collapsed in the library. Frantically he pushed on the end of his inhaler, but nothing came out. After getting him into a chair, she went for the nurse. When they got back to him, he was inhaling through pursed lips, sucking in air as if he was sucking through a straw.

Leaning against the wooden plank wall, she applied the same technique, inhaling a trickle of air. After three whistling breaths, her chest started to loosen. She continued until finally she inhaled a regular breath through her nose, blowing each exhalation out of her mouth.

For over ten years, she relied upon her honed conditioning to see her through a thousand complex assignments. This trans-dimensional body switch just wasn't fair. Mercede had her toned and honed human machine, while she now had a younger but less fit host. The young woman had no real muscle. Her cardiovascular system was a wreck. Now, Fara wondered if the fainting spell had been a real part of history and not just the byproduct of the freaky bilocation. How could she ever manage getting back to her own time when she'd been given the proverbial beaten up loner car from a cheesy garage?

Resuming her progress at a slow yet steady pace, she entered an intersection resembling a peace symbol, with three forks leading off from her entry passage. Not knowing which way Gaetano went, she tried to listen for the scuff of boots, but over her own lumbering breaths, it was impossible.

She'd never been inside the inner workings of a castle, and she doubted Mercede had any cause to use them either. During the day, the corridors would be busy with people carrying and fetching everything from chamber pots to bathwater, according to the wills of their masters and mistresses. The corridors were clean, but not immaculate. The well-worn boards were swept, but not polished, and consequently left no discernible spoor. She knelt and felt the boards, hoping for a vibration, but Gaetano was too far away.

A low moan eased from the passageway angling to the right. She knew better than to charge off in a new direction and not mark this juncture. The last thing she needed was to be lost in the endless system. Even if she tore a piece off from her skirt, someone coming through might just pick it up, or shuffle it out of the way. The sconce nearest her was yellowed with years of continual use, and yet appeared well maintained. Still, the glass had a fine layer of soot from the burning wick. It would remain untouched for a few hours at least.

Raising up onto her tiptoes, she skimmed a finger around the upper edge. The inner glass was hot and smooth. The rim now bore a distinct stripe within its glow, and Fara added a point to indicate the direction to return to Mercede's chamber.

Her breathing had normalized. No reason to rush at this point; conserving Mercede's physical abilities was frustrating, yet wise. She had lost Gaetano, but reason told her she had to be close. The castle wasn't of infinite proportions. He mentioned foundations, which had to be the series of archways at the very bottom of the structure.

Back in her current time, when she crossed into those shifting shadows that very morning, something not of the living world had been down there, waiting and watching. After witnessing Gaetano's reaction to the results of Anna Carafa's games, those were clearly one of the contributing causes. Emotional trauma remained for centuries, collecting in sinister puddles of negativity. Nothing Fara did would change any of that.

Regret again swept through her for not reading some of that damned book. Any clue on how Anna Carafa, Gaetano, and Mercede fit together would help, but she probably had enough clues. She just had to identify the significant pieces and put them together. To do that, she had to find out what Anna Carafa was doing in the cellars, foundations, or whatever her place of inequity was called.

A muffled chortle of masculine laughter drifted, and then a feminine giggle slid into its place. She followed the sound, and just around the next bend was a staircase, right out of a classic piece of gothic literature. The stone steps were smoothly worn, sloping slightly toward the middle from hundreds of years of use. The walls were made of the same rock, and she placed her open palm upon the cooler stone, feeling the residual vibrations. Although she sensed something, she didn't have the refined talent to ascertain specific details.

Fara had met one FPI agent who saw clear images through touch. The woman was gifted, a veritable genius, and yet every time she was around her, something always left Fara with clinging suspicions as to ulterior motives. But who wouldn't be a little off upon seeing fleeting snippets of the past throughout her entire life? Chrystal Delphae was almost a prisoner to her exceptional talent, having to keep her skin covered at all times while in proximity of others.

Even though Fara didn't see any details, deep down she knew this place had its share of troubled times. Logically, she also concluded the stairs headed down, which led to the foundations. Like Fort San Cristobal, certainly some people went down into the hidden areas and never returned to see the light of day. What was it about creepy old places like the palazzo and Fort San Cristobal? Were all old buildings similarly affected or afflicted by the passage of time?

Within the dungeon of San Cristobal, the emerald ring helped clarify the images. She glanced at her hand and wished the ring had come with her, but it was still upon her true body under the controlling will of a different soul.

Step by wary step, she eased closer toward the intermittent sounds. At the bend of the second curling turn, another corridor led off to the left. Only one wall sconce burned with a nearly extinguished flame, adding a hazy darkness to the dim confines. Several doorways arched at regular intervals. The doors were sensibly shut with only a rim of darkness peering around the ill-fitting door jams, except for one.

She approached cautiously, one room at a time. Muted voices drifted from under the door along with escaping remnants of flickering candlelight. She stopped and pressed her body against the wall, leaning closer and listened to natural sounds. Nothing more than a booty call.

With a sigh, she returned to the staircase and followed it lower, and yet now she doubted if this would actually lead to the forbidden party rooms. Her senses and reactions were misplaced and thick. No wonder, she was thinking with someone else's brain.

Education not only taught facts and figures; it allowed the brain to develop through series of cognitive synapses. Although Mercede would have received an education, the limitations of being a girl would also limit the subjects and theories, and she didn't strike her as the type of woman who would have thirsted for knowledge.

At the base of the stairs, only one corridor led off into the darkness. Just like the row of servants' rooms, all of the walls were rock, fashioned with supporting arches. She was clearly under the castle, more than likely at the very bottom. About ten feet from the staircase, a set of double doors blocked the passageway. Grabbing the bars that formed a glassless window, she hoisted herself up and peered through the dark night; however, she doubted this place received any light even during the day.

Concentrating Mercede's untrained senses, she didn't perceive any movement, sound, light source, or any other sign of life. The only scents were an accumulation of damp rot, which trembled uncomfortably within her lungs. The underdeveloped muscles in her arms quivered under even this minor strain, and she eased the frail body back onto her bare feet.

Finding her way back to the marked sconce was easy, but all along the way, she hated making the wrong choice, costing her precious time. The two other choices jutted away, and for a brief moment, she entertained the thought of doing the arcane "eenie, meenie, minee, mo." Instead, she selected the next passage, which would have led straight on from her original direction. She discounted other branches from that main hall which were in a similar configuration to the one she investigated. Clearly, they were servants' quarters. She passed one row after another, seemingly ad infinitum. How many servants were required to run a place like this? More than she thought, that was for damn sure. This place was like a hive of worker bees.

This corridor was significantly longer than the first, traversing the underbelly of the grand palace. She passed the final sconce and continued into the dimness. Her eyes adjusted until there was just nothing left to see. She held her hands out in front of her, and after just a few more steps, the corridor ended abruptly into a wall of rock. Anger lashed out, and she smacked it with the palm of her hand. The texture appeared natural, with defining gouges of a handheld chisel. She reached as far as she could, encountering both side walls. No other corridors, just rock.

With a growling sigh, she returned to her marked light. The wick was low, almost out. A clank of metal pots resounded. The cooks were up, and yet there was another sound, laughter sliding and recoiling. She turned into the final passageway, running past the drifting wood smoke.

A massive door blocked the way, similar to the one she encountered at the base of the other staircase. An old-fashioned torch burned on the other side, casting jumpy shadows through the upper bars. Once again, Fara lifted her body weight and peered through the caged window.

Seemingly endless archways spread toward a distant light source. An ominous chill shivered, and she knew this was it before even hearing a muffled exclamation and echoing laughter.

Easing back to her feet, she worked the chain around, a link at a time, until a giant padlock filled her palm.

A faint wail drifted from within the shifting shadows, and her pulse leapt as irrational fear gripped Mercede. Her hands, weak from the exertion, shook as she felt within her hair for a pin. The back of her hand felt a whoosh of air then blistering pain.

The steady throbbing helped Fara regain consciousness. While in a bewildered half-state, fear drove through her like a blade, cold and chilling, bringing her heart into her throat. She squelched the small internal scream and swallowed past tears she refused to shed. Continuing to focus, she used her own strength to overcome Mercede's innate human instinct.

The combined stench of heavy smoke and something bitter assailed her nose, yet she inhaled deeply, letting the repugnant scent revive her senses. She was facing a rough wall with her wrists bound above her head. Her fingers were numb, but she could move them, estimating she had been in this pose for around ten minutes, no longer than twenty.

Several people milled behind her, shuffling their steps, and then a feminine voice rose above all of the others, "Ah, our guest has decided to join us." Smooth articulation forced each word. "Turn around, my dearly beloved niece. You are just in time to witness round three."

Fara faced the room, and the chain holding the manacles twisted, hoisting her up onto her toes. The area was bright with four torches blazing on each wall of the relatively small room, and something bulbous hung from the ceiling.

A circle of men held hands while facing a central table, blocking it from view. All of them were naked from the neck down. A loose hood draped over each head, masking identity and quite possibly blinding the man; she didn't see any holes cut in the heavy white fabric. The pale skin of their butts glowed in the brilliant light, nearly as white as the hoods.

Another enclave formed a secondary circle around the perimeter of the room, all facing the inner circle. Some of the men wore long robes, not specifically ceremonial robes, more like a 16th century version of a loose bathrobe. Others were still fully dressed in their ballroom attire. The majority of the observers were men; however, a handful of women in fine gowns were interspersed throughout the circle, not in any particular pattern. Unlike the cult in San Cristobal, this outer group didn't appear to have any significant purpose other than watching what was happening in the center of the room.

Nearly hidden from the angle imposed by the handcuffs and chain, Fara saw the glint of a silver and black dress. Heavily jeweled hands clapped, and the strummed notes of a single instrument began. Another sound rose, harsh and tight. It took her a few seconds to recognize it as feminine laughter. She cast a sidelong stare at Anna Carafa who was chortling and clapping with delight.

The inner circle unclasped their hands and started to rotate around the table, keeping a single hand upon whatever was in the middle. Between the moving men, she saw occasional glimpses of a pale body lying face down with the hips lifted at an awkward angle. Mercede's poor vision made it difficult to discern whether the prone figure was a man or a woman. Hands and feet dangled limply off from the edges of the small oval table, and the person's head also extended off the far edge. However, it didn't droop. A strap extended from the shoulders to wrap the forehead, forcing the head to arch up and face the door.

One detail was extremely clear. All of the parading men's genitalia were erect, not only arching but straining in alertness. They hurried around the prone body out of time with the music, circling faster and faster, jockeying for position near the head and feet. Position for what?

The spectators pressed closer, and inarticulate murmurs rose, growing with the fervor.

The men continued to circle, nearing a jogging pace, while always keeping a hand upon the body.

A flash of jewels catching the light preceded a single clap, and the strumming music stopped.

The circling men fell upon the prone body, and a communal row of excitement rose as the crowd pressed closer, blocking the men's actions from Fara's view. Cat-calls filled the room, "Her hands, between her toes, her ass, her ass, her ass!" Another communal cheer rose. "They did it! All twelve found purchase!"

Anna's laughter rose above the cacophony of jeers and taunts. "Stop," she called clearly, and the rowdiness settled. "I want Mercede to witness our artistic triumph."

A wave of bows parted the crowd like the tide upon the sea, rolling back towards the perimeter walls.

The disrobed men were upon the prone figure, but at first Fara didn't make sense of what she was seeing. Each man had penetrated some part of the woman's anatomy, even the spaces between her toes had a penis.

"Hands and feet, off!" Anna waved, and reluctantly six men stepped back.

Someone murmured, "I told you her Grace would not call the same parts twice."

How that was anatomically possible, Fara wasn't quite sure, but the remaining details had those thoughts fading from her mind. Every orifice had been entered.

"Mouth and ears, off!" Anna again commanded.

The two men at the ears pulled away immediately, while the man in front of the arched face had buried himself to the hilt, so just his short hairs were visible around the face like an abnormal beard. With a dramatic flair, he twisted his hands behind his head and then prolonged the slide from the depths of her throat. With a brusque hitch of his hips, his penis slapped wetly against his thigh.

Two men remained, one straddling the back of the other; both were behind the woman.

"Gentlemen, your creativity is commendable. Now, who will win the test of flexibility and stamina."

The man in the very back grabbed the hips of the other man and began to thrust.

"Check to ensure they both have penetration." Leaning to her left, Anna delivered the line like requesting a second cup of tea.

For the first time, she recognized someone, and beyond her will, her heart clenched. He didn't look at her, or even acknowledge she was there in any way. Gaetano just walked straight toward the men and tipped his head to peer at the smacking genitalia from the side. "Yes, they both found purchase."

A cheer arose.

Anna commanded, "Take the torch and such enhance our view."

Without hesitation and showing no emotion, he retrieved the closest torch and angled its light onto the men who were now grunting with each thrust.

Anna's dais was directly opposite the door, and no one obstructed her line of sight. The men on the table were directly in front of her, both of them humping the prone woman. Fara felt the bile in her stomach rise, and she looked away from the sex.

On the advancing edge of middle age, Anna's beauty was still too tangible to deny. A creamy complexion along with a flawlessly powdered coiffure made her appear truly regal, at least until the jeer returned, marring the perfection. Pure evil was at the core of her soul. Without a doubt, Fara could picture her conniving to live forever regardless of the price.

The woman craned her head forward, but too overtly. "Does each hold a separate entry?"

Gaetano didn't need to reply, for the crowd pressed closely once again. "A combination, your Grace. I assume the man in the vagina is Herberto. His length proves an advantage."

Once again, Fara drew her gaze away from the grotesque human display and carefully watched Anna Carafa. The woman perched on the edge of her ornate dais, leaning forward intently. "Gaetano, count the strokes aloud."

His voice started, but soon the swell of the others joined in. The red-headed woman just on the other side of the dais clapped the beat.

"Faster!" Anna commanded.

The counting quickened. Compelled with the same unavoidable intensity like looking at a car wreck, Fara couldn't help herself. Several people blocked her view, but the men's heads and shoulders rose above the gathering crowd. The hoods flapped as they worked. The neck of the man in front started to arch back toward the second, as if he was laying his head on the other man's shoulder.

"You must hold your seed upon my command!" Anna shouted over the communal chaos.

The count was now over eighty.

"Faster! Faster!" She cackled. "You must reach one hundred, or you shall replace my niece upon the wall of shame."

The count continued, "Ninety-four, ninety-five, ninety-six, ooh!" A disappointed murmur rolled, while others continued counting, "Ninety-seven, ninety-eight, ninety-nine, one hundred!"

"Release!" Anna cheered. Similar to a communal shout of *Happy New Year*, others joined her.

The second hooded man arched upon their repeated command, thrusting wildly until he was finally spent and collapsed upon the man in front of him.

A few of the dressed men slipped behind the others, and coins exchanged hands.

"Gentlemen, approach for your rewards." Anna slid back into her chair. "Magdalene," the woman at her side leaned closer and handed her something, which Anna palmed while the two men climbed off from the narrow table.

"Unmask," she lifted a dramatic hand, and they removed their hoods.

Both of their faces were red from exertion. The taller man stood proudly even as his erection waned. The second was flaccid.

"Herberto, you are the winner of our third contest. Approach your princess and claim your prize." Graciously, she extended her hand, and the man collapsed down upon a single knee. "Your manhood is an exceptional example of virility and skill." She placed a gold coin into his palm. Upon issuing his thanks, he immediately backed away. The other man was left all alone in the steadily building silence. "Marius, what happened to my champion of the games?"

"Your Grace," he bent upon a single knee, but didn't approach the dais. "The body of Herberto rubbed my scrotum during each penetration. It proved twice the stimulation, which forced my concentration to fail."

"Marius, you have been victor on many occasions; therefore, you understand the consequences."

He bowed his head, "Yes, your Grace."

Anna motioned toward Fara. "Release her, but she shall remain in this room until the final games of the evening are spent, and I have three more coins!" A wicked crinkling of the edges of the blood red lips preceded a stiff smile. "And so my comely niece, were the games not exceptional? Did we exceed your expectations? Is this what you anticipated discovering when you ventured into areas forbidden?"

Carefully crafting her response, Fara swallowed in order to ensure a clear voice, "My Duchess and dearest Aunt, I knew not what I would find when I explored your magnificent palace, but this display was beyond anything within the bounds of my imagination."

Anna smiled again, but the brightness didn't reach her eyes. Clearly, she expected a different answer. "Well then, you must join me by my side to have a better view." She patted the seat Gaetano had vacated.

A burly and sweaty man in a dark hood, mirroring the expectation of a medieval executioner, approached and unlocked the manacles, one at a time. He stunk like a dead skunk lying in the sun, and when he spoke, his rotting breath burned her eyes. "I didn't hit ya too hard? Yer such a pretty little thing. How's about a turn upon the table? I'd pay a coin or two for that."

That foul beast snuck up on her! Shit! She couldn't trust Mercede's senses for anything!

She held her breath until he stepped away. Rubbing the red marks on her wrists, she met the steely gazes of the enclave, but then quickly joined her gaze to that of Anna Carafa and approached the woman who owned this part of the world and ran it as if it was a perverted toy box.

Nearly as an afterthought, she curtsied deeply and then climbed the three wooden steps. Dramatically with her chin held high, she turned, and upon smoothing her skirts, sat upon the cushion with the utmost grace and dignity. Although the bump on her head hurt like a son of a bitch, she wasn't about to rub it while all of those eyes were judging her every move.

Voluntarily, the loser of the exhibition quickly assumed her place upon the wall. The woman who had handed Anna the winner's token walked past a torch which highlighted her strawberry hair. She raised her bejeweled cup in a jeering salute to the loser and poured the wine down his flaccid penis. Uproarious laughter erupted, reverberating off the thick stone walls. She withdrew a coin from her purse and handed it to the shorter of the two bookies.

During the interlude, two young women tended to the body on the slab. Their loosely-fitting gray shrifts looked like something nuns would wear, but nuns had no business being in this den of Sodom. They unclamped hoses hanging from the udder attached to the ceiling and rinsed the prone woman's bodily cavities. The wet scent of excrement tainted the air, but one woman quickly rinsed the dirty water through a drain in the floor, otherwise hidden by the table. The other applied lubricant with a thin wooden spoon, filling every orifice, even between the fingers and toes.

The woman on display didn't move, and Fara carefully watched for a sign of breathing from the bony ribs. The movement was shallow but there just the same. Perhaps she had been drugged.

Anna clapped her hands, startling Fara, and she caught the pleasure crease the corners of the woman's eyes. "Gaetano," she snapped sharply, "I want you to participate for the express enjoyment of my niece."

The man's face flushed crimson. "My Grace, the preference of my desire is akin to your own. I prefer to watch."

"And it is my desire to watch you." Her voice edged deeper. "Do as I command."

"My dearest lady, my interest wanes and does not embody the robust hardness to compete."

Anna's abrupt chortle rippled off from the rock walls and echoed within the sealed chamber. "A lazy cock is all too familiar, and based upon my intimate knowledge I am keenly aware you do not suffer from the malady so evident in my poor Duke."

His quick breath preceded a brief bow. "The night is late, and my energy drained. I would provide no amusement through such a poor performance."

Anna shot a vile look at Fara, "What if we exchanged the depleted whore for someone of your choosing, someone with youthful vigor?"

Other than tension at his jaw, he didn't adversely react. "Perhaps on another night's festivities, for dawn should surely be approaching and the night's energies spent."

"Come, attend me." She nearly flew off the dais and headed straight for the door but stopped and swung around with a flourish of waving hands. "Commence the final round, and you shall preside over the festivities." She fit a murderous stare upon Fara.

How could she possibly do such a thing?

The woman with the coins stopped at her shoulder. "The bets have been placed. If you do not continue, the Duchess will discover your disobedience." Her tone carried an underlying glee, since she would be the first to tell Donn'Anna.

"Places!" Fara clapped, and the man in the corner started to strum the strangely long instrument, with two sets of strings. The main body appeared to be a lute, and the longer secondary strings he plucked like a bass.

Knowing any sign of weakness would haunt her exponentially, she boldly looked back to the men circling the table.

CHAPTER 23

The soft repetitive hush called to some primitive need upon returning to her bedroom. Fara thought back, remembering closing the balcony doors. Perhaps she hadn't latched the two sides completely. Listening intently, the lyrical ebb and flow contained an additional element, singing an accompaniment within the calm waves. She mused whether the positioning of the palace's structural columns echoed the rolling sound. Regardless of the source, this place had earned its name, the Syren's Palace.

Perched above the undulating currents, the curved wrought iron balcony was more decorative than functional but appeared sturdy enough. She took a hesitant step, testing her weight, and then stood suspended amongst the frothy droplets clinging to the approaching dawn. Moving water released negative ions, leaving the air charged. Inhaling, she drew the power into herself while blanking out her mind, hoping she would be able to locate her inner Zen while inhabiting a different body. Her mind slowed until her thoughts finally ceased. Nothing except calm focus remained.

Using this form of meditation, she encountered inner clarity and felt her body, normally adding focused repair for any physical injuries. However, today was different. The link between mental and physical was imperfect, flawed in the fundamental connection between this body and her soul. Searching even deeper, she discovered cracks between the matrixes of time humming within her. She just needed to unlock the abnormal resonance within herself. Hope filled her for the first time. She needed that right now, however real or imagined.

The late moon shone in the west while the first light of a new day tinged the opposite horizon. The two extremes clashed in the damp air, charging the releasing ionic energy with sparkles of competing color. Visually, the charged dewy particles flowed past her, filling the bedroom with magical light. The sensible part of her underlying cynicism knew this was just a manifestation of Mercede's vision, probably an astigmatism, yet the reason didn't matter. The effect was stunning.

She stepped back over the raised sill and reached behind her left shoulder, feeling for the edge of the long and narrow door, and then changed her mind, deciding to leave them open. Just that minimal motion thrust her over the final threshold of total exhaustion, and she staggered toward the bed. Her legs ached from running through the corridors, and her head hurt where the filthy guard hit her. Deep within Fara's inner resolve, she wanted to force this vessel to do more, but she had exceeded Mercede's physical capacity. This was her new reality.

Holding onto the corner bedpost for stability, she sank against the oiled wood, wanting a shower almost as much as wanting to return to her own time. Just like zippers, the concept of a shower probably hadn't been invented yet. Perverted sexual games, yes. Hot and cold running water, no.

Deep down, her mind was still trying to process the realization of what she had witnessed. Clearly, the world had been twisted for a very long time. The damnedest thing of all was the woman wasn't a hapless victim. Fara didn't quite believe she enjoyed having every body part penetrated with a penis, yet she answered Fara's questions without hesitation upon the culmination of the final game. Apparently, the thirty-something earned more in that single night than entire families earned in a year for manual labor, and Fara ensured she left with all of the coins from the pocket of Anna's deviant lady in waiting.

Fara had never been a prude when it came to women or men using their bodies to earn a living. Everyone did in some form or another; intellectuals used the power of their minds while dock workers used muscles. Each was an incumbent gift. Prostitutes appealed to baser instincts, but too many patrons of the sex trade bought more than just a standard experience. Dangerous work, the real trick was staying alive.

Her thoughts flickered to the look upon Gaetano's face, and again, she wondered what had happened on the night he gave up the body sports. In too many ways, he reminded her of Guy, and she certainly didn't want him to suffer as a ghost for all eternity. In her linear timeline, she already had sex with the man.

Ghost sex. Now that she met him and knew him as a person, the concept of having sex with his ghost wasn't nearly as creepy.

Unlacing every string she could find, she shrugged out of the dress and let it tumble onto the floor. The nightgown was still where it had fallen not a step away, and her head throbbed as she bent to pick it up.

The silky fabric was cool and felt comforting, settling so smoothly upon her back. With both hands, she pulled the gloriously full hair from under the sheer fabric and let it slip through her fingers, aware how every strand settled upon the silk. She rocked from foot to foot allowing the hair to glide but refused to get too accustomed to having flawless skin and hair. Her own body had a few dents, but internally, it hummed like a well-tuned Hemi. She wouldn't trade that for all of the external perfection the world could offer.

Indignantly, she swiped the soles of her bare feet across the crumpled dress until the clinging dirt was gone and crawled into heavenly softness. The old cliché of falling asleep before her head hit the pillow wasn't too far off reality.

Simple exhaustion consumed her body while her mind tried to make sense of the unbelievable events. The room was dark. The few torches filled the air with more smoke than light. Shadowy creatures moved within the smoky haze, taking form and then evaporating again. A clap of hands resounded, and the smoke retreated, brightening the room.

Men and women surrounded a wooden table, the old-fashioned kind with planks and pegs. The surface was bare and splintered from age. From out of nowhere, a body appeared, strapped down with wide leather belts crossing her exposed back.

Fara remembered how the leather wore into her skin. Day after day, the relentless pressure broke through the cellular structure, crushing it beyond recognition. A black-hooded executioner tested the straps pulling them one notch tighter until the captive's flesh curled around the edges. A final tug pulled the flesh of her buttocks, spreading the cheeks higher and wider than could be humanly possible. A collective gasp brought the gathering closer. Hands, more hands than seemed possible, touched the form, pinching and kneading whatever was in their path.

Suddenly floating, Fara peered down from near the ceiling, hidden within the thin wisps of gray smoke. She knew where this was headed, and suddenly an answer to her unspoken question appeared in her hands. She spread her fingers, and pieces of gold showered through them.

While the licentious swarm fought greedily, the executioner approached the body, lying immobile upon the wood. A cat of nine tails appeared in his hand, and tiny silver barbs sprang from the leather straps like claws. The torches exploded with light, and the silver glistened with sinister motion.

The dream jumped. The barbs dug into Fara's skin, and real pain seared, sharp and deliberate. She had to scream. She tried to inhale. The straps were too tight, binding her ribs.

Focusing, she sipped the air, slowly and deliberately. The building force amassed speed. Her will focused, ready to shatter the nightmare with the mighty sound of her own rebel yell. The mass of air propelled through her throat and over her tongue. Forced consciousness rode the wave. She would stop this right now. The mighty force passed her lips, roaring into the silent dawn. For one second, and no more.

The scream met a moistened wad of cloth. Her tongue pushed against the gag. Trying to flatten it, she bit down as hard as she could, catching the side of her cheek in the process. Again, pain flashed through the bizarre dream. The metallic taste of blood puddled against the side of her tongue, tasting it and not tasting it all at the same time.

Her eyes flew open and witnessed a dark hood fall over her head.

"Oh shit!" The words had nowhere to go.

Vibrantly awake, she tried to land an elbow, but the man pinned her with a single knee wedged against the small of her back. His hands made fast work of tying hers together and then her feet, tighter than necessary to make them simply immobile. Her racing pulse gathered within her fingers and toes, swelling against the bonds.

The oppressive weight lifted, and she heard the soft landing of two booted feet.

Her left shoulder felt the edge of the bed. Twisting she headed for the floor, and yet at that same moment, the man hefted her into his arms, binding Mercede's weak limbs.

The breeze blew through the rough hood, and Fara heard the sea. Something thick and rough passed between her bound hands and feet, hoisting them together above her body. Her back tucked, as if she was performing an upside-down, jack-knife dive in perfect form.

The strong arms released, and she swung out, momentarily weightless. Her gown caught the wind, spinning her body while falling like a drop of water. Waves crashed and foamed, roaring around her. The briny mist weighted her nightgown, forcing it to gather around her waist. Suddenly her only thought was whether or not she had worn underwear. The next splash of a wave proved her exposure without a doubt as a rivulet flowed over her most intimate divide.

A set of callused hands grabbed her shoulders, snagging the fabric of her nightgown. His balance wavered, rocking, and then the next wave tilted the vessel again. He set her down and quickly pulled the heavy coil of rope free. The boat once again rocked, knocking Fara onto her side. Her right hip and thigh felt the contoured detail of the interior wooden decking. The curve was steep. The boat couldn't be very large.

Tightening her abs, she made herself ready to use the next jolt to force herself to a seated position, but just as the subsequent wave hit, the rope wiggled and twisted in an absent pattern back and forth over her exposed flesh. The man who gagged her had to be climbing down. Just as the thought landed so did he. The boat banked, sloping against the weight, and the next pulse of salty froth splashed inside the vessel.

A flurry of activity ensued all around her, yet neither man spoke a word. The only sounds were of the sea crashing into the rocks and then hissing as the foam slid through the gaps between the stones.

The snap of a sail taking the wind was clear and sharp, reminding her of the bizarre dream. To clear her mind, she inhaled quickly, and the wet hood sucked against her mouth and nostrils. Mercede's lungs panicked, tightening unnaturally. With a wiggle, she rolled enough to be facedown. Arching her back, the hood gaped, allowing her to take an extended breath. Slowly her lungs relaxed. Just when she tried to move again, a hand spread between her shoulder blades, holding her in place, pushing firmly but not roughly. The warmth from his palm radiated through the soaked nightgown.

Fara's mind actively sought out possibilities of escape, but each scenario ended up with her drowning. Unless she could unbind her hands and feet, she didn't have a decent probability of making it to shore alive. In her own body, she would risk it, but Mercede's capabilities were too iffy. She probably didn't know how to float, let alone swim, and Fara couldn't take that chance.

Ironically, the thought was comforting. Whoever this was wanted her alive or else he would have tossed her in to drown. But, what was his purpose? Why would he create such a dangerous escape plan to kidnap her?

The boat cut across the waves, rising and then slapping down in a regular rhythm. They hadn't traveled far when it bumped into something immobile. The sound of wood rubbing on wood vibrated through the hull on her side of the boat.

Hope surged along with adrenaline. This was her chance. She tucked her legs and hefted her torso, using the natural curve to help her roll. Now upright, she pushed and arched backwards, but Mercede's legs weren't strong enough to launch her into the water.

The boat rocked, throwing her off balance. Two pronounced booted feet landed on the dock, followed by a muffled clank of glass. A steady hand slipped around her torso and drew her upward. The firm planking touched her bare feet for only a brief moment. In one continuous smooth motion, her captor hefted her over his shoulder.

Anger rose vibrantly, heating her internally, almost as much as the warmth of sunlight shining upon her bared ass. At least it was Mercede's body exposed for all the world to see, and the little bitch deserved it. Her weakness and physical ineptitude were unacceptable, and Fara's disdain for her femme fatale host grew. Flawless skin or not, this was going to end. She would find a way!

Her head pounded, and hanging upside down wasn't helping. Her upper body swung with the kidnapper's steps. Each pass loosened the clinging hood, except for one spot against her right cheek. With the next natural sway, she twisted to brush that side of her face against the curve of the man's muscular back, and the hood fell.

Daylight stung, pounding furiously through her head. She welcomed the sensation and used it to focus, squinting until her eyes adjusted. All she could see was a man's backside. She arched, just in time to witness the calloused man hoist the felucca's sail. Based upon the predominant direction of the steady breeze, they had to have traveled from the north, down the coastline. She squinted in that direction but couldn't see the Syren's Palace. The difficulty wasn't just her eyes; heavy morning mist obscured most of the coastline. Even the foaming rocks lost definition from this height, yet she could still hear the churn of the water.

Rocky steps angled up the steep cliff, switching back every ten steps or so. About halfway up the climb, the man's breathing deepened with the labor, but he didn't slow. By the time they arrived at the top, he would be tired and winded, giving her an advantage, and she needed every advantage she could get.

Searching for any distinguishing details, she noticed the man's breeches were some type of soft hide but didn't appear to be leather. Saltwater darkened the natural light fawn color into khaki brown. The tapered pant legs ended in a pair of black boots, not of the popular soft and floppy style. These were tall Hessians with a highly polished surface.

Holy shit! She recognized those boots. Did Gaetano think Anna Carafa would share her power with him by doing her dirty work?

His muscled arm wrapped around her upper thighs, and he released his other hand. A quick look down the edge of the cliff evaporated the thought of squirming out of his grasp. Any wrong move would find them both dead.

He jostled her again, twisting the other arm forward, and the edge of a solid wooden door opened. The inner darkness was cool and comforting, at least until he set her onto the edge of the large wooden table, and the odd dream sprang to mind. No part of her would ever be victimized again!

Fara tensed to bite the hand reaching for the gag, but then she saw his face. Concern deepened the lines at the edges of his eyes and pulled down the corners of his mouth. His chest hefted each breath, spreading the unlaced V on the front of his soggy shirt. Unsteadily, he swayed and caught himself with a quick hand on the table next to her bare thigh. "Do you have any idea how precarious your position has become?"

Quicker than she thought possible in his apparent state of exhaustion, Gaetano thrust his other arm to the far side of her body, leaning until his broad chest was level with hers. His eyes narrowed dangerously. "Now you threaten the Duchess' party games. She more than hates you. She abhors your presence. I overheard plans to poison you this very morn, which forced me to act so boldly." He bounded off the table and stormed across the room. "Donn'Anna's private parties are invitational affairs kept in the strictest confidence. She believes I betrayed her secret."

Her own anger mounted irrationally, pulling her to a fully upright position. "She has no proof of something that didn't happen. I lost track of you long before reaching the lowest tunnels."

"Proof? Her spies are deftly observant, following me even when I thought I had eluded them. Donn'Anna knew of my clandestine visit to your chamber. That be proof enough. She anticipated your arrival, posting guards at each regular entrance and the back corridor." He stormed back toward her, stopping within arm's reach. "Your words were prophetic. Both our lives are forfeit."

"I didn't expect to get caught." The surging adrenaline bolstered her resolve, and she savored the fleeting rush.

"Intention or not, the results are equally damning." Bitterness sank into each word, filling the depth with regret.

How could she argue when he was right? Nothing she could do or say would change their situation. She let out an almost inaudible groan with the inevitability of it all. Had this happened in the true timeline as well?

Gaetano inhaled a shaky breath, watching her with growing intensity. His eyes widened and expression brightened, but he wasn't looking at her face.

The wet fabric of the sheer nightgown clung to her body, like something out of a skin-e-max porn movie. The aureoles of her breasts formed dark circles, peaked with rigid nipples. She didn't need to lean more forward to know her entire torso was exposed in equal detail. Modestly, she closed her haphazardly spread thighs. "Gaetano, I apologize for involving you. I had no intention of risking your life."

"Then what was your intention?" Growling with frustration, he turned his head toward the door as if contemplating leaving but then looked back, quickly adding, "You are the most confounding woman! During the comedia, you nearly stopped my heart with your rousing kiss. I had been warned of the plot your conniving uncle hatched prior to your arrival, which steeled me toward the effects, but then you announce it to me, deflating an ulterior purpose. You formally denounce any desire to seduce me, yet then you boldly follow me toward my chamber and then unwittingly land in your aunt's very grasp. A none of it constructs a formulated purpose." He inhaled deeply and articulated each word, "What be your purpose Mercede?"

She wasn't about to tell him how she needed to return to not only her own time but also her own body. So as the crazy pieces flooded her mind, she just stared up into his face, the proverbial deer in the headlights, yet headlights wouldn't be invented for another three hundred years!

"Donna Mercede," he swallowed, once again glancing over her form, "you are a miraculous beauty, of a form so pleasing I am wanton to contain my baser instincts. Since that first kiss, I have thought of naught else. And now-" The remaining words choked within his throat, but his body spoke the remainder of his thought with action. Those gentle and sure hands parted her knees, moving forward another step to keep her from closing them again. The heat of his body radiated into her damply chilled thighs, and those tender hands skimmed higher, gathering the soggy hem until the veil of fabric lifted from the triangle of dark hair.

His larynx bobbed with a dry swallow. "So tantalizingly feminine and glorious in presentation."

Against her will, the heat within her core ached for him, urging her to spread her legs and provide entrance to her need. Fara focused, refusing to give in to Mercede's physical lust, and yet intimate moisture gathered. And like a male of any species, he inhaled the telltale scent of her readiness.

"Many a maid and matron alike have declared I present a fine manly form, yet I have never encountered anyone equal to your womanly charms, especially one paired with such a robust sensibility. Avarice does not taint your action. Deceit does not cloud your judgment." His face tipped, and something similar to a growl gurgled within his throat. "You are more than a woman. You are a goddess, equal to the legendary Venus herself."

A quick tongue tasted her nipple through the fine fabric, and a frisson of sensual acuity shivered too strong to hide. The glow of physical awareness continued to heat her core and forced a flush upon her skin.

His eyes blatantly roamed over her once again. "You blush like a maid, and yet the kiss we shared was not chaste." He glanced to the bulge distending the front of his pants, and his hands followed, repositioning himself within the snug confines. "Since that moment, I have fantasized whether all of your lips would be as softly inviting."

Her breathing quickened, shallowly fighting for control, and yet this body's desire was strong. Had all this happened historically? Had Gaetano and Mercede become lovers?

Holding onto her will, she fought Mercede's need, but each of the tiny fissures binding Fara to this weak body failed one after another.

He licked his lips and then pressed them to her other breast. Mercede's head fell back limply, her eyes closing. Instead of allowing the waves of pleasure to continue softening her mind, Fara focused on the guilt she felt after the ghost sex.

He groaned again, which turned into another low growl as his mouth pulled away.

Tightening from the sudden change of heat and pressure, her nipple tingled. Her fingers tensed into fists holding onto the frail remnants of her personal resolve. Her nails bit into her palms keeping her in charge of Mercede's faculties.

He leaned in again. Unfurling her fingers, Fara placed a trembling hand against his chest, but that was as far as she could go. "No Gaetano," was poised on her lips, but once again, Mercede's body thwarted her control.

His hand clasped over hers, holding her palm against his beating heart. "There are other provinces, other countries, even the New World where the Duchess holds no sway. I will make the requisite arrangements, and on the morrow, we shall travel to Rome and then discover the quickest egress."

"I cannot ask you to do that. To give up your life just because-" she couldn't bring herself to finish the thought when overpowered by the binds of history. Mercede's love for the man beat so strongly. They were destined to be together. This was the right thing for them both. Who was she to judge the constructs of their love?

The dark hollows of exhaustion under his eyes remained, yet the rest of his expression filled with energy. "Happiness has had no more fiber than a shadow, eluding me for many months, and yet I had no true reason to go, until now. I shall take you somewhere where Donn'Anna cannot harm you." Drawing her forward off from the table, he eased her down until her feet touched the cold stone floor, and disappointment trembled at her core. "The world holds treasures untold, awaiting discovery. We shall flee to the Orient and explore tall mountain peaks or even the dark continent of Afrik to be lost in its steamy jungle clime. Until this moment, I had no idea of the depth of feeling a man could hold for a woman. I swear upon my own life no harm shall befall you."

Taking her hand firmly within his, he drew her through the old kitchen with its open hearth where a black kettle hung over the empty grate. Long handled cooking tools rested on pegs in the masonry, but she didn't have time to discover each implement's intended usage. He led her up the short staircase chiseled out of the incline of natural rock.

He ducked through the doorway and continued along a covered walkway toward the main house. The proximity of the two buildings and the angle of the morning breeze sliced like a wind tunnel. Her wet nightgown conformed to her flesh. She huddled behind him, using his body as a shield, while he unlocked the door. The hinges complained, grating metal to metal, and he braced the weathered door then followed her inside. The wind snapped the door closed, slamming a sharp echo through the house.

A shiver raced through her, only partly from the wind. Crossing her arms tightly to conserve her warmth, she turned toward the bank of multi-paned windows. With a flick of each wrist, she parted the heavy drapes, and golden light filled the room. The mist was lifting to expose the immediate coastline.

Fara recognized where she was. The past and future were linked. The rental house in the 21st century stood on this very spot!

"Mercede?" Gaetano smoothed against her back, wrapping his arms around her torso. "You are wet clean through. A disruption of the humors shall surely ensue if not tended soon."

The foyer was larger in this time and oval in shape with an arching staircase leading to the second floor. A golden cloth, similar to the one in Guy's house, covered the round table in the center of the room, but under a mirror, the side table had a brass candlestick sitting on its dusty surface. The candle had been burned down to a nub, and long waxy tears descended down its tarnished length.

Across from her, the drapes kept the next room in nearly perfect darkness. Around the edges, just enough light filtered to discern a massive table and separate lumps where the chairs stood covered by the same massive sheeting.

He led her by the hand, and the wooden steps were firm and sturdy under her bare feet. As she neared the upstairs' landing, the arrangement of rooms was once again related in both times, and of course, he opened the very bedroom where time held no sway.

"Whose house is this?" She stopped, placing a hand on the doorframe to feel for the otherworldly resonance, and detected nothing. Was nothing there, or were Mercede's senses just not tuned to such things?

"A goodly friend who traveled to Rome for the season, who be the only soul knowing the malady of my discontent. Although the revenge was most nobly born, the arrangement has drained my sensibilities, emptying my very soul. My intent to seducc the Duchess was a way to wrong the Duke of Medina in turn. His highhanded-"

So, he had sex with Anna Carafa to get back at Ramiro Felippo de Guzman! Holy shit, now his comments finally made sense. He hated Anna from the start, and she was too blinded by her own vanity to notice or care.

Fara waited for him to elaborate, and then asked, "What did he do?"

"I beg forgiveness my lady, for I forgot your close attachment to your uncle, the Duke."

"You may speak plainly without fear of reprisal." She touched his sleeve, and his expression once again softened. "You saved my life this very morn and deserve my respect along with my gratitude."

A sparkling glimmer brightened his eyes, making him appear younger than she had estimated, probably a late twenty-something. "Your uncle claimed my friend, Giulio Mergellina, owed him tax for mooring boats upon his dock at Posillipo, and so Ramiro Felippo de Guzman conscripted the last remaining painting touched by the delicate hand of his beloved grandfather, Giulio Pippi, better known as Giulio Romano. He loved to escape to this summer home and paint."

"I love his art and saw it on exhibition in-" abruptly, she stopped, catching her anachronistic blunder in the nick of time. She had seen a collection of his more risqué work at the National Gallery in Washington D.C. with Guy. In 1643, Washington was a village of log homes on the shores of the

Potomac. The Revolutionary War was over a hundred years in the future.

"In the palazzo," he finished for her. "It hangs in the Duke's private drawing room."

Fara just nodded. She had never been in the drawing room and didn't need to make another mistake.

His brow furled in response to her silence. "This is just a simple country house." He motioned once again for her to enter the bedroom. "I know these chambers are not as spacious or grand as those in the palazzo, but I beg you to set aside comforts for a single day. Upon our arrival in Rome, Giulio's ancestral estate will be commensurate with your standards. I plan to enlist his aid to make our escape."

After staring at the threshold for a heartbeat too long, she boldly entered the room and expected some change, some wary feeling akin to what she had experienced in her own time. The air was a little stale, but normal. Nothing otherworldly existed here, at least not yet. Whatever happened to bind this room to the past was yet to come.

She remained close to the doorway and ran her fingers over the defined texture of the wall. It was plaster, not wallpaper. The deeper blue swirls were nearly a pinky-width deep and had silvery blue highlights tipping the raised patterns. Perhaps the erosion of time made the detail less pronounced, or the volcano dust had settled in the ridges, making them less apparent. Either was a travesty to the artistic beauty. Even if Gaetano hadn't told her, she would have known this had been an artist's home.

This room had wonderful light, full-spectrum, yet still soft. The morning's sunshine filtered through white sheers hanging in crisp waves from the broad wooden rod. Through the gauzy fabric, the window frames shone from vibrant maintenance.

What she could see of the vanity, bed, and armoire was an exact match; however, once again sheets draped the furniture. And yet, something was different. It was like one of those Hocus Focus pictures in the newspaper. Things were missing out of this scene that were in the other.

He uncovered the bed first. The canopy and drawn curtains were exactly the same as the night she had ghost sex. She looked from the man who had just uncovered the armoire and then back to the bed. In this very location, Gaetano made love to her. Clearly, that scenario had happened before, right now in her present reality. Fara gasped.

He rushed toward her and encircled her waist with an arm. "You are weak my dearest Mercede. Please sit and rest." He led her toward the vanity, and once she was securely seated on the small stool, he removed the protective drape from the wood. "I collected a few of your possessions and did my best to maintain them dry during the short voyage, yet the precarious mooring under your chamber's balcony caused the boat to pitch and collected the splashing waves. I shall retrieve the bundle from the dock and return hence." He quickly jogged from the room.

Next to the unlit oil lamp, she caught her reflection in the unique mirror shaped like a tree. Mercede's face was even more pallid than her norm, and exhaustion darkened the thin skin under her eyes. Her fingertips gently touched the flesh, just to ensure what she was seeing was real. Dark hair hung in heavy tendrils. She squeezed the cord nearest her face, damp, but not dripping wet. The hood had protected it from the worst of the waves.

No baubles or bottles were on the gleaming surface, so very opposite from the future state. Reaching forward with her left hand, she ran the fleshly point of her fingertips over the surface with the merest touch. Tipping her head to be level with the surface, she couldn't detect any change in the finish.

She thought back to what seemed like ages ago; although in reality, it had been only three days. The message wasn't complete, and she didn't use a forensics kit to uncover additional details. At the time, it didn't seem that important. Closing her eyes, she focused. The first time she read the phrase, she had only the central portion cleared, something like "…me leave…"

Heated blood pulsed quicker through her mind, recharging her faculties. "…elp me leave 1643" was the most complete message. She was sure of it. Why would Mercede write that?

Unless it wasn't Mercede.

A shiver raked through her, shaking her down to the very foundations of reality. Mercede's asthma constricted the air passages. She couldn't breathe. Suddenly, the room spun.

CHAPTER 24

Sleep became a luxury of the past, yet Fara cuddled into the warm bed, not wanting to acknowledge she might never leave this existence. By snooping for clues, she became a fugitive and had no way of returning to the palazzo to discover Anna Carafa's secret. Without knowing how she came to be in 1643, she had no way of going home. Everything in the past was a foregone conclusion, and the outcome of that conclusion was recorded history. Mercede de las Torres lived and had to have died. If Fara didn't find a way-

A man coughed.

Her hand automatically shot under the pillow and wrapped around the hilt of a dagger. She felt the weight in her hand, balancing it within her grip, and absently rocked the knuckle of her index finger against the curved guard. Then surprised, she nearly dropped it. Who owned this dagger?

Heavy velvet draped the bed in a rich shade of indigo, and the bedspread gathered at the foot gave the appearance of waves. The parallel struck her, and to control a gasp, she clutched a hand to her throat. Her silk nightgown had darkened to a pale gray, just like in the perverted dream.

With the tip of the knife, she parted the fabric widely enough to see into the entire room. The window sheers were open, revealing unending darkness pressed against the panes. That was wrong. Moonlight should have been streaming through the windows. The ghost used the moonlight to help gain corporeal form. Instead, the oil lamp burned with a low flame, just enough to add a warm glow. The setting was the same, and yet opposite. Was this how it was able to balance within time?

A man was bent at the waist peering into a brass telescope on a tripod. The broad line of shoulders and narrow hips unmistakably belonged to Gaetano, and just like before, he was intent upon his purpose. He moved to look further down the coast, and a ripple of muscle skimmed under the loose-fitting white shirt. The first time he looked like the god Apollo, but not now, he was too vital to be anything but pure man.

Her inner emotions stirred. Nothing was as sexy as a man with great hair, and his shoulder-length waves of unruly dark curls fanned over his shoulders. "What are you doing?"

His shoulders stiffened, pulling him upright. He was wearing fresh clothes with breeches and a softly ruffled shirt. Only a robust man could pull off that look and not come across as gay.

"The castle is a buzz with your disappearance. Just before the dawn, sailors upon the dock noticed you leaning upon your balcony. The rumor be that you lost balance and tumbled into the sea. Your uncle manned a vigil to find your body. Soon, they will decide the current took you and will expand their search in this direction."

At least the Duke was convinced. "And Anna Carafa?"

"The Duchess considers a myriad of elucidations. One being you received a sudden spiritual calling and pledged your troth to a nunnery." Stopping next to the bed, he untied the small string at the softly ruffled throat of his shirt and loosened the laces, exposing his robust chest.

"A nunnery? Me?"

A wicked smile thinned the edges of his closed lips, and naughty little thoughts played across his features. Pulling the shirt over his head, he then crawled through the gap in the drapes and passed within inches of the drawn blade. "The Duchess will require the discovery of a body to be fully convinced. My agents have located a recent corpse of similar stature and complexion. She will be tossed into the current this night. Once the decoy be discovered, we shall flee to Rome, for Donn'Anna has posted sentries on both land and sea."

Making room, she scooted back until she felt the pillow softly press against the small of her back and leaned to slip the knife into its hidden sheath. Déjà vu shimmered through her and yet was no surprise. The past-future collided within her present existence. The decision to make love with Gaetano was a foregone conclusion.

Balanced upon his knees, he fingered the lacings of the casual britches and slid the cloth away from his body and down his thighs. His erection was exactly as she remembered, standing hard like carved alabaster. The only change was the color of his skin. His complexion was vibrant with life as heated blood pumped through his veins. Not wanting to stare overtly, she raised her gaze, and his eyes nearly shone with fiery vitality.

She slid her hands up his chest, brushing the curves and contours she remembered so well. His skin was hot, and under her fingers, a fine sheen of sweat beaded. Chest hair curled around her fingers, so soft and downy. She just had to run her fingertips the rest of the way down his body. Of course, there was only one place to stop, and she wrapped her grip around his hard shaft.

He inhaled a quick breath, closing his eyes while dropping his head back. Dark curls flowed over his shoulders, and Fara promised herself she would run her fingers through those silken locks before the night was through.

Coming back to the moment, his eyes not only opened, their intensity traced her every curve, and in turn, his fingers roamed up the soft contours of her abdomen, gathering the grayed silk with gentle pulls. In complementary timing, she lifted her shoulders and arms, and he slid the fabric over her head. Now bare beneath him, he surveyed her body once again, gazing upon her form as if this was the first time he had seen her; for him it was.

One in each hand, he cupped her breasts and teased her nipples, rounding the peaks until they stood away from her body. Tingling sensations coursed through her nervous system, bombarding every synapse with physical desire. He was delicate and careful, taking great care with her body, but he was capable of so much more.

With the thought, her face flushed, and a devious smile tugged at the edges of her lips. "Harder," she whispered, and using Mercede's feelings as a guide, added, "take me as you will."

From deep within his body, a resonant hum rumbled an unintelligible response. He balanced his weight upon his arms and lowered his mouth, leaving broad and wet kisses along the sloping curves of her abdomen, and then those soft kisses added playful bites. Mercede's body responded exactly as Fara knew it would; her soft flesh grew rosy and hungered for more.

Roaming higher, he pulled her left breast into his mouth as deeply as it could go. Her back arched, allowing the yearning body the full enjoyment of the act. His teeth skimmed the edges of her areolae and then tested the hardness of the rising points. The sensual electrical charges skittered through their shared forms, highlighting the bonds between times. With the additional impulses edging into feverish pain, Fara made a mental note of the spiritual bonds' exact locations. Her consciousness remained there, buried within the connection, hoping an answer laid within that realm. Her focus allowed Mercede creative reign of the physical act, for this was her first time with her one true love.

The intensity of his hunger grew, suckling upon her other breast with renewed vigor. His mouth opened widely, drawing her inside, and his teeth scraped her skin as he lifted his mouth. The pressure was exquisite agony, the perfect blend of skin and teeth. Over and over again, he licked and tasted, drawing each to the fullest extent of sensation.

Despite her attempts to remain aloof, Fara's own hungers rose, joining the young couple into an otherworldly ménage-a-trois. The divine union shivered across the realms of time and space. The how or why of their situation didn't matter anymore.

With a strangled sound between a moan and a cry, he released her breast, and her own vocal protest joined in the sound. The aching between Mercede's legs bombarded their conjoined senses, demanding fulfillment. One at a time, she lifted a leg, rubbing the soft skin of her inner thigh against his sides.

As if they always had been lovers, the tip of his erection found the soft center of her entrance. He lingered there, and Mercede's need inundated their shared awareness. A sharp throbbing issued from her clitoris, growing with the torment, and her flesh quivered with anticipation.

His wicked smile returned, banking the lit fires within his eyes. He pressed forward but not all of the way. She watched the change play over his features, overrun with emotion sparring with concentration. So well prepared, her body willingly accepted him. Masculine heat radiated into her, prompting even more moisture to soak her channel. She had to have him in her, completely, right now.

Her hands cupped his ass and drew him into her body. With each long inch, the opportunity for satisfaction filled her and teased her in a tantalizing mixture. A low groan of eagerness shuddered from her lips.

Holding himself at the point of deepest union, he leaned forward until they were pressed as closely as two people could be. His lips kissed the contours of her brows and drifted along one temple to the curves of her ear.

The expectancy built within her, requiring him to thrust into her most private need. Instead, he remained entangled as intimately as a man and woman could ever be.

"Mi amore," whispered ever so softly, "I knew not the depth of desire within mine own heart until our lips first met, and now we are joined. I love you, my darling Mercede. I shall spend my life ensuring your happiness."

"As I pledge my love and troth to you." She flicked her tongue along the curve of his ear and bit the upper edge, harshly yet not to break the skin.

With a tug, he pulled away, arching his back until the bulging tip barely remained within her. The movement of his hips started slowly, pressing in and withdrawing with the utmost tenderness. He filled her perfectly; their bodily contours so tuned to each other as if designed expressly for one another.

At each juncture of their deepest union, Mercede grasped with her inner muscles, to feel every contour of his masculine form and then released to allow him unfettered access once again. She matched his pace until the lustful demand consumed her. That same pressure showed upon his features. As if he had enough of his own teasing, the fiery onslaught burst, and he plunged wantonly. The wet smacks of body against body filled the enclosed space, but it still wasn't enough.

Feeling his energy building within her, Mercede's calf muscles graced the curves of his rounded ass while her fingers lowered over his back, sliding along the muscular chords with rhythmic intensity. No longer sharing the tempo, the movements of his hips increased and then slowed. The syncopated rhythm was more essential to her pleasure than she had ever realized. Each sent a tingling rush curling down into her toes. She screamed, playfully twisting underneath him, until she once again dominated the rhythm of their erotic dance. She clawed his chest while her body took what she demanded.

Wanting to experience him to her deepest core, she lifted her calves, and one at a time, he moved his arms to allow her to position them upon his shoulders. As if understanding her on a molecular level, he matched her challenging need, thrusting harder and faster, plunging his hardened shaft to the hilt, and she accepted each invasion openly while encouraging more. Each full contact exploded with that amazing energy, brilliant and luminous. The bursts suffused every living cell with sexual splendor.

He lowered his body toward her, pinning her to the bed until she could barely breathe. While maintaining the nearly impossible rhythm, his teeth sank into her earlobe and then bit her neck. Brilliant pain exploded within the tangible energy.

"Oh God yes!" Basking in the shimmering lust, Mercede was willing to give him anything. He could have her totally and completely, without hesitation. His tongue swept in an arch, and suddenly those teeth sank into her shoulder, hard enough to break the skin and bring Fara back to full awareness. She remembered the vampiric suckling, but this time, he didn't feed upon the pulsing flesh. And yet, when their lips met, the same metallic flavor was there. The thick taste heightened the erotic combination of pleasure and pain, sending her screaming toward the emotional horizon.

"Let me feel your power." A caged growl moaned deep within his throat.

By that command, her orgasm burst. All of the amassed energy alighted every cell with licking flame. She was breathing so hard she couldn't think, only feel wave after glorious wave of her own pleasure, and then he joined her. His strangled shout echoed throughout time itself. The moment hung there, demarking the point of those two bodies joining together for all eternity.

Saturated with churning endorphins, they sank into each other's embrace. Her arms wrapped around his body, holding onto him firmly, so he couldn't fade away. They lay intertwined until the natural course of physical love insisted his body leave hers. He shifted to the side and drew her to him. Her head fit in the notch of his shoulder so perfectly.

His gentle hand brushed the hair off from her forehead and slipped into the heavy locks. "Mercede, upon our arrival in Rome, will you agree to join with me in matrimony?"

A fluttering warmth quivered through Mercede, and she knew exactly what she wanted. "I will."

His hands lifted her face to meet his kiss, but before their lips met, a ship's brass bell rang only twice through the otherwise silent night. Gaetano perked toward the sound.

"That be the signal. They have arrived. Mi amore, we soon shall both be free of the nightmarish deceit and unyielding ambition." He placed a quick kiss upon her forehead and then hopped off the bed. "I must leave you my precious Mercede. Please linger and rest, for our journey begins at dawn. I shall rejoin you in this very bed as soon as this venture ensures our freedom."

She watched him hastily dress and pass through the doorway. Moments later, the exterior door slammed closed with the pressing wind.

A satisfied yawn stretched through her, and curiosity rose. Her bare feet didn't make a sound as they pattered over to the telescope. She adjusted the focus, and for the first time since the bodily transition, Fara was able to see clearly into the distance.

The night sky was still absent the moon, and she couldn't tell if the small boat docked at the base of the cliff was the same one which enabled her escape. The shape of a man stood on the dock, waiting patiently, and then he turned toward the house, arching his head up the cliff. She got the unmistakable feeling he was looking at her but knew that was ridiculous. Although the lamp burned softly, the light would be barely perceptible from that distance. She continued her vigil and watched the man greet Gaetano. They both stepped into the small craft and set sail, heading north.

A chill clung to the night. She shivered but didn't necessarily feel cold. Turning back toward the bed, she noticed items scattered upon the top of the vanity, and draped over the stool was a dress. Grabbing it by the shoulders, she raised it to eye-level and recognized it as the same one she had worn the night they had danced. She smiled, hoping Gaetano had selected it on purpose.

Another pulsing chill sliced through her. She slid the dress over her head, and now familiar with the complicated design, fastened all of the lacings. With a triumphant chuckle, she sat on the vanity's stool. Standing right where Fara had seen it three hundred years hence was the vial of perfume, pristinely beautiful in its golden splendor.

The filigree design was magnificent, much more detailed than she originally noted. Sculpted stems interconnected delicate flowers, which seemed to burst with life and hope. With the added clarity, she recognized the blooms of the Boswellia tree, whose sap made Frankincense.

In her excitement, the crown-like stopper lifted so easily a splash of the liquid fell up on her skirts and coated the rim of the decanter. The scent was significantly lighter, as was the color. On a whim, she dipped her index finger in the vial and inhaled the fragrance, allowing so many associated memories to flitter through her mind, including the last Christmas with Guy.

With everything that had happened, her anger toward his duplicity mellowed. She had loved him, and the feeling remained inside of her heart, which was why the discovery of his deception hurt so badly. But Joe Daily had been right. The key to Guy escaping undetected was her believing he was dead. Both he and Daily knew she could hide her emotions, but she sucked at theatrics and wouldn't have been able to grieve the way she did without experiencing the heartbreak. Their plan made perfect sense, and if the situation had been reversed, she would have done the same.

Guy was alive, which brought a brief spark of hope. He had the best odds of determining a way to get her back into her correct body and correct time, but too many ifs were in the equation. She dropped her head into her hands and groaned.

If Guy discovered her body.

If he discerned the woman wasn't her.

If he discovered what caused the discharge of light.

If he could recreate it.

If she was in the proper place at the proper time during the secondary detonation.

Unless each of those elements happened in the perfect order with unerring precision, she would end up living out Mercede's life in the seventeenth century, however long that may be. She glanced around the room and then stared at the items on the vanity. Whatever happened within this room happened right around this time period. Maybe the discharge of the blast had a residual effect on time. Maybe she was exactly where and when she needed to be.

An unmistakable shiver raced through the house, echoing like a silent scream. She placed her palm on the edge of the vanity and didn't detect any motion. Not even the monocle wavered, which was perched on end next to the jar of powder.

Something was happening.

CHAPTER 25

J.C. tossed the cigarette butt onto the front porch and crushed the empty pack in his fist. As the final puff smoldered, he leaned against the railing and dropped his head back against the column. The nicotine didn't get rid of the full and fuzzy crud stuck inside of his brain.

"Jet lag," he whispered to himself, but underneath it all, he knew he was hiding from the truth. It was as real as the rosy light creeping over the eastern horizon.

As soon as he walked inside the house and saw Fara, he knew, but the moment of certainty happened when he followed them into the bedroom. A bed doesn't get trashed from waking up unexpectedly. The mattress was even a little twisted with the back edge hanging past the footboard. Three pillows were on the floor. Only one was still on the bed, and not even close to where it should have been.

Worse yet, a musky scent clung to the air. The mix of perspiration and passion was distinct and unmistakable. How many times had he come back into their bedroom after having hours of sex with Fara and smelt that same scent?

His headache pounded and seethed with each beat. He hated himself for the bitter fury wrapping around his heart because he wanted to be livid and outraged. He wanted to storm inside and confront them. He wanted to yell and hit something. He wanted to be the crossed lover who took revenge upon them both. But, how could he be furious with Fara when literally she wasn't herself?

He still didn't quite understand how someone else could be inhabiting her body, but possession did happen. Poor Alex Shane, the hombre would never recover, but he was always a weak-willed son of a bitch. But not Fara. She was one of the most self-assured and accomplished persons on the planet. If she was still inside her body, she would have resisted.

That realization didn't help.

Turning to go back inside, the door handle felt cooler than the ambient outdoor temperature, just like the inside of the house. This place was abnormal, one of those shiver places he had sensed too many times while on assignment with *Ghost Lovers*. Every haunted place had at least one, but none of them was ever this large. This whole house was damned.

Over his shoulder, he glanced across the courtyard. Perhaps it was the land. He had witnessed a location near Charleston which had multiple houses demolished, but the paranormal damage remained linked to the soil. The ghost didn't care if the house was colonial, federalist, or modern. Something beyond explanation linked it to that point on the earth.

If Fara never came back, would she become trapped?

Was she one of the ghosts already inside this house?

Shit! He cursed for even thinking the morbid thought, and his anger turned inward, hating himself for not knowing what to do.

Shutting the door with a deliberate thump, he passed into the foyer and stared at the staircase where the Fara impersonator stood just a few hours ago. If Ted said it wasn't Fara inside of the Fara package, then it was the truth. He trusted Ted. J.C. didn't know why, but the hombre had it going on, blind and all. He insisted there was a different spirit inhabiting her body, and more than likely, her soul was inside this other woman. When or where, they didn't know until they could get this bitch to talk, but J.C. wouldn't resort to violence. The outer shell was Fara, and she'd been through enough physical torture for anyone. He had to discover another way.

By Ted's description of the spirit woman's appearance, she was from the seventeenth century. He said her dress was royal blue, which indicated she was wealthy if not royalty. Her accent wasn't Italian, but she spoke Spanish with a rare lisp perfected by the royal court. At least Fara wasn't destitute and on the street, at least probably not. He just wished he knew!

When Chrystal had joined them in the bedroom, Ted asked her to lay hands on Fara, and she refused. It seemed straightforward and easy enough to determine who the woman was and from where, but Chrystal was adamant. This went beyond being a bitch with a capital B. Somewhere, somehow, Fara got on Chrystal's shit list.

While Chrystal and Ted were arguing, the woman in Fara's body had eased her way out of the bedroom, and once in the hallway, made a mad dash toward the door.

At least J.C. saw her take off and tackled her in the main foyer in the nick of time. If she got loose and he lost her, he would never be able to undo whatever in the world had been done. He had to take care of Fara's host body and ensured she stayed safe. Although he hated doing it, he handcuffed her to a dining room chair Gaetano had dragged into the living room.

J.C. paused in the foyer and stared through the arched entryway. Fara's body was sleeping. Her head had fallen forward, leaving a gap in the back of her robe. The very end of one faded scar curved up with an errant curl of damaged flesh. Whoever was inside of her body had no idea how hard she had worked to stay alive, how much she had sacrificed. This entity didn't understand how the lash of a whip would tear more than just flesh. Each strike had made her disciplined and determined. She would be trying to find a way to return to the present. Even if Fara was in hell, she would find a way to get Lucifer to let her out. She would seduce the devil if she had to.

He shivered, both from the thought and from passing through the pronounced cold spot near the base of the stairs. Something bad had happened there, and he had the strangest impression it had something to do with Fara. Maybe there was a portal in this crazy house that would help her escape, like in the movie *Poltergeist*, an area of bilocation. He extended his hand, feeling the air with spread fingers, but no impressions came to him. On a whim, he blew his breath out in a huff, and it condensed into mist right before his eyes.

The scent of coffee drifted from the kitchen along with the final bubbling sound from the automatic drip coffee maker. He thought about taking a detour, and then out of the corner of his eye, he saw the contents of Fara's backpack strewn across the glass table.

Be a man, he prodded himself.

speaks in a form of Spanish no one's used for two to three hundred years."

"I noticed that too."

"But why would she be speaking archaic Spanish in Italy?"

The man rubbed the stubble of at least a two-day growth of beard, and then threaded his fingers into his loose hair.

J.C. felt a stab of envy since his own hair burned to the roots just a few weeks ago. Fara loved men with long hair. Was she attracted to this man even before the incident? Would she have had sex with him anyway?

"Long before Italy was united into a single country, it was a bunch of smaller kingdoms. Naples was fought over throughout the Middle Ages and Renaissance. Both France and Spain controlled it at one time or another." Gaetano nodded to something unspoken. His hair fell back into his eyes, but he didn't seem to care. "Spain mostly. They assumed firmer control with the marriage between the Princess Anna Carafa and Ramiro Felippo de Guzman, Duke of Medina de las Torres." He motioned behind him, "If you look out that back window, you can see her palazzo on the Posillipo rise, the Syren's Palace. Been there for centuries."

The pink hue of dawn had brightened into morning sunshine, but the palazzo appeared dark in spite of it all. J.C. stared, and then his mind lit with the phone conversation he had with Fara. His hand tightened on the skull. "Wait, has that palace gone condo?"

"Yeah, well at least part of it. Why?"

"Fara was checking it out yesterday and then she headed into the underground to shoot some footage on Lucia." The thought sizzled through him, and he twisted toward the table. "Where's the camera?" He skidded to his knees, placing the skull in his lap, and then started rummaging through her stuff.

"What?" Gaetano leaned forward.

"The camera! The mini DV. Fara had been carrying it around with her. It's not here."

Gaetano physically withdrew upon himself, sinking back into the cushions again while rubbing his hands over his face in the same pattern. He took a deep breath and then carefully measured his words. "I interrupted her setting up some shots of candles burning in front of Lucia's altar. When I came in, she set it aside."

"And left it? Why would she do that?"

Gaetano shrugged. "As I said, we were interrupted."

He didn't buy it; this hombre knew more than he was telling. The lead on fresh information filled him with determination. Finally, something tangible was happening. "Why did you go to the crypt in the first place?"

"Aleri." His voice wilted, and the dark circles under his eyes visibly darkened. "My cousin isn't well. We had a séance, and she collapsed. I thought Fara might know what was going on."

"Why would she know what was wrong with your cousin? She wasn't at the séance, was she?"

"No, my aunt has a séance every Friday with the hope of connecting with my father's spirit. I never believed in any of that bullshit, but something tangible happened. I heard my father's voice, and then- I don't even know how to begin to describe it. I got punched in the chest with what felt like a bolt of lightning, and Aleri collapsed."

"I still don't see why you thought Fara would be able to help."

"All hell broke loose the moment I saw Fara in front of my church." He winced, and then closed his eyes trying to cover it.

"Dios mío, you're the ghost?" J.C. shifted backwards and propped his elbow on the cushion. "I was on the phone with her. Wait, she said your name was something else." He closed his eyes, squeezing harder while recalling the memory. The breakthrough made his mind crystal clear; he could hear her voice inside of his head. "Guy, Guy Carver." He said with finality and caught the man in a dead stare. "She thought you were dead. She said she saw you die."

The man's eyes flashed to the both empty doorways, one leading to the foyer and the other toward the kitchen. He dropped his voice to little more than a whisper, but it growled with intensity. "No, that wasn't me."

"No way." The clarity rush through him, energizing every inch of his flesh. "This is significant. You don't have to lie to me. I don't know why, but really I couldn't care less about what you and Fara-" J.C. groaned as the realization hit him squarely between the eyes, and the headache doubled its intensity. "You were CIA agents. Both of you. Were you partners?"

"No." It was spoken a little too quickly to be believable. Gaetano scooted across the cushions until he was next to J.C. His hands balled into tight fists. "You wanted to know about the crypt? Well, Fara and I were arguing. She refused to help me with Aleri saying it was none of her business."

J.C. nodded, letting the other topic go, for now anyway. "Earlier, you said that someone interrupted. They came into the crypt."

"Yeah, even when I ensured the church was locked from the inside. There are only two people who could have gotten the priest to open the door. Aleri or my aunt. But I didn't think of that at the time." He closed his eyes and dropped his head into his hands.

"Then what happened?"

Gaetano grunted. "Fara sensed someone was coming, and then, I noticed the same signs. The abnormal chill was just like during the séance. It felt like something was sucking all of the energy out of the air. I wanted to stay and fight it out, but she said we wouldn't win. We fled into the preparation chamber and didn't get to see who it was. It sounded like Aleri, but Fara indicated there were four people." His body continued to wilt as if the weight of the world was upon his shoulders.

J.C. knew exactly how that felt. "Quite possibly there were there to conduct the ritual and whatever happened either overflowed or backfired into Fara and this skull. Any idea why all of this is happening?"

"I haven't a fucking clue," grated out of his throat.

For the first time, J.C. believed him. He squeezed the skull as if that would help make sense of this new information. "Wait," he hopped to his feet, and the motion made his head reel. "The ghost bride is a skull in a shrine."

"Yeah, so what?"

He held out the skull, articulating his words with the motion. "What if there was a tricked out spell by whatever voodoo psychic you had doing the séance, and Aleri was to take on the soul of Lucia? Anyone know who that skull belonged to originally?"

Gaetano weakly shook his head, but the energy in his eyes intensified. He had thought of something. "Look this is my problem. I will go and get the camera." He rose from the sofa and flipped the black hoody over his head.

"Not without me you're not." J.C. tossed the skull onto the sofa and beat him to the foyer, blocking his passage to the front door. He wanted to see the raw footage before anyone had the opportunity to jack with it.

The Italian's shoulders tensed, but instead of hunching, he rose straighter. "I'm going alone. It's not negotiable." His voice had deepened nearly an octave.

"Like hell!" Adrenaline burst through J.C., and at this moment, he didn't care if it was the Terminator standing in front of him. He grew up in San Juan and learned how to fight by getting his ass kicked. Then, that time in Mira Flores, he earned a reputation for winning. If this Italian dude had been Fara's partner, he would not only know how to fight, he would fight well. Even with the possibly of getting his ass royally kicked, his hands tensed into fists. "No way man. You're not getting rid of me. I'm as much a part of this, actually more. That's my camera down in the crypt, and that's my girlfriend cuffed to the chair. I'm not letting you leave without me."

"You piece of shit!" Like a flash, Gaetano shoved him roughly, yet it still felt like a warning. "I don't know what Fara would see in an asshole like you, but I don't need-"

J.C.'s ears heated with the surge of blood and didn't hear another word. He was ready to get in at least the first punch. Just as his arm was swinging forward, a woman's scream split the air, and yet resonated, echoing through the rift in time as easily as through the house.

That realization didn't help.

Turning to go back inside, the door handle felt cooler than the ambient outdoor temperature, just like the inside of the house. This place was abnormal, one of those shiver places he had sensed too many times while on assignment with *Ghost Lovers*. Every haunted place had at least one, but none of them was ever this large. This whole house was damned.

Over his shoulder, he glanced across the courtyard. Perhaps it was the land. He had witnessed a location near Charleston which had multiple houses demolished, but the paranormal damage remained linked to the soil. The ghost didn't care if the house was colonial, federalist, or modern. Something beyond explanation linked it to that point on the earth.

If Fara never came back, would she become trapped?

Was she one of the ghosts already inside this house?

Shit! He cursed for even thinking the morbid thought, and his anger turned inward, hating himself for not knowing what to do.

Shutting the door with a deliberate thump, he passed into the foyer and stared at the staircase where the Fara impersonator stood just a few hours ago. If Ted said it wasn't Fara inside of the Fara package, then it was the truth. He trusted Ted. J.C. didn't know why, but the hombre had it going on, blind and all. He insisted there was a different spirit inhabiting her body, and more than likely, her soul was inside this other woman. When or where, they didn't know until they could get this bitch to talk, but J.C. wouldn't resort to violence. The outer shell was Fara, and she'd been through enough physical torture for anyone. He had to discover another way.

By Ted's description of the spirit woman's appearance, she was from the seventeenth century. He said her dress was royal blue, which indicated she was wealthy if not royalty. Her accent wasn't Italian, but she spoke Spanish with a rare lisp perfected by the royal court. At least Fara wasn't destitute and on the street, at least probably not. He just wished he knew!

When Chrystal had joined them in the bedroom, Ted asked her to lay hands on Fara, and she refused. It seemed straightforward and easy enough to determine who the woman was and from where, but Chrystal was adamant. This went beyond being a bitch with a capital B. Somewhere, somehow, Fara got on Chrystal's shit list.

While Chrystal and Ted were arguing, the woman in Fara's body had eased her way out of the bedroom, and once in the hallway, made a mad dash toward the door.

At least J.C. saw her take off and tackled her in the main foyer in the nick of time. If she got loose and he lost her, he would never be able to undo whatever in the world had been done. He had to take care of Fara's host body and ensured she stayed safe. Although he hated doing it, he handcuffed her to a dining room chair Gaetano had dragged into the living room.

J.C. paused in the foyer and stared through the arched entryway. Fara's body was sleeping. Her head had fallen forward, leaving a gap in the back of her robe. The very end of one faded scar curved up with an errant curl of damaged flesh. Whoever was inside of her body had no idea how hard she had worked to stay alive, how much she had sacrificed. This entity didn't understand how the lash of a whip would tear more than just flesh. Each strike had made her disciplined and determined. She would be trying to find a way to return to the present. Even if Fara was in hell, she would find a way to get Lucifer to let her out. She would seduce the devil if she had to.

He shivered, both from the thought and from passing through the pronounced cold spot near the base of the stairs. Something bad had happened there, and he had the strangest impression it had something to do with Fara. Maybe there was a portal in this crazy house that would help her escape, like in the movie *Poltergeist*, an area of bilocation. He extended his hand, feeling the air with spread fingers, but no impressions came to him. On a whim, he blew his breath out in a huff, and it condensed into mist right before his eyes.

The scent of coffee drifted from the kitchen along with the final bubbling sound from the automatic drip coffee maker. He thought about taking a detour, and then out of the corner of his eye, he saw the contents of Fara's backpack strewn across the glass table.

Be a man, he prodded himself.

In the process of finding her handcuffs, he hastily dumped the wet contents of her backpack onto the wide coffee table. Since the situation in Puerto Rico, she had beefed up her survival kit. But as soon as every piece of everything fell out onto the table, he couldn't bring himself to touch it, which was why he went outside to smoke.

Be a man.

Shit! He had to suck it up and go through her stuff. Maybe it held a clue. There had to be a fucking clue somewhere to point him in the right direction. He owed Fara his life, and he would spend the rest of his life searching for a way to bring her back, regardless of what he had to do.

The Italian asshole was sitting on the couch, slumped into the nearly colorless overstuffed cushions; some interior designer would describe the color as buff or taupe. To him, the dingy fabric looked like dried dirt.

The hombre looked asleep except he kept turning the skull around and around in his hands. J.C. didn't know the real reason as to why Fara had a skull in her backpack, and at the time, it wasn't as important as securing her body. He wasn't about to buy this asshole's lack of involvement in the incident. He knew more than he was telling. Even without any special psychic power, J.C. knew a line of bullshit.

Biting his inner lip, he knelt next to the table and shuffled through the items. "Wasn't there an old book?" He remembered setting it aside. Fara wasn't in the habit of carrying around reading material, especially not anything old. It was the first thing to strike him as being out of place.

"This is what she was holding right before the burst of light." Opening his eyes, Gaetano gestured the skull toward the sleeping woman, as if this proved his account of the night's encounters. "When I went back for her, I thought it might be useful, so I shoved it into the bag before we escaped into the aqueduct."

J.C. groaned silently, mentally noting the evasion of his question; the book had to be important. He left the table and sat on the opposite arm of the couch, straddling it like a saddle. His foot was on the ugly brown cushion, and he propped his elbow onto that knee. "Okay, so what? From what you've said, there's like a million skulls down there."

"Not like this one. Watch," the man spread his hands, balancing the skull in his open palms. The empty eye sockets were facing him, and then quicker than a flash, they were facing Fara.

"Holy shit!" J.C. bolted upright. "Let me try." Feeling like a kid on a playground, he took the skull out of the man's outstretched hands and stepped back, mimicking the actions. A pulse of power hit his palms, and the skull twisted of its own accord.

His heart skipped a beat and hands felt tingly.

"It doesn't matter how many times you twist it or even turn it upside down. It reacts the same every single time." Gaetano spoke English without any accent, sounding more middle-American than J.C. ever would.

He rubbed his palm over the cranial curve, and the fleshy part of his fingertip snagged in the crack just above where the right ear would have been. The cause of death had to be from this trauma. But what did this have to do with this woman hiding in Fara's body?

Trying to be scientific, he methodically walked around the room, selected different angles, facing toward and then away from Fara. The skull always twisted to face her, like a polarized magnet.

"Dios mío," mumbled off his lips after his experiment within the foyer resulting in the same motion. He walked back into the living room. "What do you think it means?"

Gaetano shrugged, but then added, "I think whoever is inhabiting Fara's body once owned that skull. The blast of light was some specialized discharge of power, like nothing I've ever seen, and it happened while Fara was holding it." He motioned toward the sleeping woman. "Once we get her to talk and tell us who she is, we'll have a better idea on where Fara is."

"When she is." He corrected, not yet willing to share the detail about the woman's dress Ted told him in confidence. Everything pointed to her being transported not only into another woman's body but also into the past. "This muchacha yet she placed a hand on the wall to steady herself. There was something there, something wrong, like a splinter stuck between space and time.

When she and Gaetano arrived a few hours earlier, she didn't feel anything abnormal. Now, the space-time continuum fluxed. She inhaled a quick breath. Maybe this was her ticket home?

Hearing nothing set her other senses on fire. No sounds entered the house. Not the ever-present wind. Not the rolling surf. The house had been separated from the physical world. She didn't know how something like that could happen, but facts were facts. A few minutes ago, the wind and sea created a lonely duet, and now dead silence prevailed.

Her sense of smell heightened, and the spicy odor of frankincense overpowered any other mustiness of the old, closed-up house. Sniffing the air, she followed the strength of the scent and then realized she had splashed the liquid across the skirt of her dress. Great, if someone was inside the house, he would smell her coming.

Easing her way down the outer curve of the staircase, her bare feet respected the silence one step at a time. Other than her rapid pulse, she even kept Mercede's body in check; her breathing was slow and steady with the intense scent of the spilt frankincense still permeating her lungs, like an overdose of vapor-rub.

Upon reaching the final step, she hadn't seen anyone. The presence of a boat meant someone was on the property. The door slamming indicated he was in the house. But why? Who? No one knew where she was, unless someone was here to rob the house. Boy, did he choose the wrong time and place.

She scanned the oval foyer, and that same overwhelming feeling filled her as two distinct pictures formed in her mind. Something was missing, but she hadn't committed the room to purposeful memory. The round table still consumed the center of the foyer with the chandelier directly overhead. Other than that, she didn't remember. When she walked through with Gaetano, she was more concerned about him leading her upstairs rather than noting her surroundings.

A smile crept along the edges of her mouth. He was a responsive lover and deserved happiness with Mercede. In Puerto Rico, all Fara could manage was to reunite the ghosts postmortem, but in this reality, she would be able to give Gaetano and Mercede a real life, filled with love and even possibly a family. That had to be why she had come here. She was a fixer, always had been. She'd break the chain of events, and once the couple was on track, she would focus on finding a way back to her time. If there was a way in, logically there had to be a way out.

Startled by her own mental distraction, she focused on the present. Now was not the time for wandering contemplations.

Reverting to military precision, she surveyed the three exits from the oval foyer. The front door was closed and appeared locked. Even if it was, the old-style lock wasn't that secure, but for the seventeenth century, it was the best they had. If she remained much longer, she would definitely invent a better lock. It wouldn't change history, at least not that much. A simple modification to a multiple tumbler-

Shit, her mind had wandered again! She bit the inside edge of her lip and forced her focus.

Whoever had entered the house didn't come inside through the front door. The floor exhibited no evidence; not an errant leaf or scuff. Definitely clear.

On her left, the arched doorway led to the dining room. She had just a glimpse of the table and chairs when they arrived, but now no light drifted through the creases around the draperies. The room was dark and properly still. She extended her awareness on an interpersonal level, expecting to connect with another consciousness, but the room felt vacant.

The third exit led to the spacious living room, but in the rental house, there was a concealed door under the staircase leading to the encased back patio. More than likely, something like that existed in this time as well. Placing a hand onto the banister, she leaned over the railing and ensured nothing lurked under the stairs. The darkness extended, draping the space in obscurity, but once again, she didn't sense anything.

All that remained was the living room, or in this time, it would have been called a parlor. Regardless, this room was the most direct point of entry from the cliff-side mooring. She studied the enclosed darkness, just as obscure as the depths under the stairs.

The drapes were closed, and she distinctly remembered opening the draperies to examine the coastline. It was a moonless night, and yet nothing was pure darkness. Even at night, an open window cast a broader feeling into a room, but not now. Not here.

Had Gaetano closed the drapes on his way out? A man wouldn't have cared if the drapes were open, and even if he did prefer them closed, the boat was waiting. He wouldn't have taken time to fuss with the drapes.

Her grip on the newel of the bannister tightened, and the curved wood slipped away from her fingers as she took the final step. The marble floor was unnaturally cold. Marble was a metamorphic rock, compressed under intense pressure until its molecules were so tightly packed thermal convection was limited. It felt colder than wood because it was colder, but this felt refrigerated, as if a layer of frost covered the surface.

She took a single step. The natural dusty grime instantly clung to the bottom of her feet. This too was normal for a house neglected for a span of weeks if not for a few months, and yet, somehow, it oddly felt a little too real. Her inner sense kicked in, and the hairs rose on her arms warily, as if static filled the gap in the juncture of time and space.

Supreme darkness reigned, and just when she thought she had to be mistaken, a minute glow framed a shadow at the window. A long inhalation filled Fara's lungs while her forefinger pointed toward the figure. "I know you are there. Show yourself!"

"As I too knew of your presence. Magdalene's divinations be once confirmed." A haughty voice sliced through the heavy expectancy, deep like a feline growl, yet richly feminine. Fara knew who she was before Anna Carafa turned. A small flame highlighted her features, casting elongated shadows up her face, edging darkness into the sharp hollows under cheekbones and chin, making her face look more like a skull than flesh. "Through deceit and treachery, you lay siege to what be mine! I shall not stand for it."

Something else moved in the artificial obscurity, just a few steps behind the Duchess, as if there was a two second delay. Fara knew those all too well while reporting the news, but although similar in principle, this was something entirely different. She couldn't see anyone, but knew nonetheless someone or something was there. Of course, this shade would ply Anna's bidding; the Duchess would never do her own dirty work.

Fara's instinct for survival ignited. A quick plan flashed to mind, make it back to the bedroom and retrieve the dagger hidden within the bed. At that point, she would determine the next course of action. Logic fueled her tenacity and allowed her training to supersede any distractions inside Mercede's panicked brain.

Knowing better than to turn her back upon an assailant, she backed up slowly while keeping the two figures in view. The bump of the first step behind her heel brought a sense of accomplishment, and she continued up the stairs backwards, watching the pale light approach. Normally a flame would flicker with movement or even the passing of breath, but this unnatural emanation floated along with the woman, highlighting Anna's corporeal body with what some would describe as a heavenly glow. Fara sensed nothing about the disdainful Duchess was divine.

The woman didn't seem concerned about the passage of time. Unhurried, she paused at the base of the stairs while holding the single candle. One hand balanced the base of the candlestick while the long, bejeweled fingers of the other stroked the brass, lingering semi-erotic caresses at the juncture of each rounded curve. That was what was missing from the foyer. Just to be sure, Fara's eyes swept to the thin table under the mirror.

As if waiting for that distraction, Anna's lips started moving, forming strange words. Just a few steps behind her, the paranormal shadow joined in the chant, slightly echoing within the relay. "Basiliske Galeōte meta Kōktō Podōn kai Kakoin Ommatoin-"

Fara tried to locate the root language, definitely wasn't Latin, perhaps ancient Greek. In and of themselves, she didn't believe words carried innate power. Magic spells were sensationalized mumbo jumbo. Belief in the words is what made them powerful.

"-to Phōs Emēi Cheiri Kathias tōi Kakōi Dergmati Toxeusatō! Kakon Omma Petrōseōs!" The shadow behind the woman gained physical presence with the passage of each mystical syllable.

Fara stopped her ascent next to the upstairs landing. She was about fifteen strides away from the open doorway, yet she waited, not sure if Anna was actually going to follow her up the stairs. Maybe the woman wanted her to barricade herself inside of the room.

Anna's funky lady in waiting stepped out of the swirling darkness. Shit! She was the red-headed woman with the coins. How could a living person change into shadow? Not even the strongest practitioners were able to modify physical forms, only influence others in the perception of their form.

Who was she?

What was she?

Possibilities swept through her mind. Not human. Not spirit. Not demon. Definitely not angel. For the first time, an icy thread of uncertainty shivered up her spine.

A combined thoughtform was exponentially stronger than a single belief. Drawing upon her inner strength, Fara challenged the power. "I will not succumb. Whether only the two of you chant or if you call upon the power of twenty, your vocal persuasions will not work on me."

The shadow added a shrill cackle to Anna's throaty chuckle, creating a purposeful disharmonic rolling through the words. "I be all-powerful, drawing upon the strengths of this plane as ardently as from the next." Anna stepped upon the first step. The cadence was well-trained and precisely timed to achieve maximum control.

Fara had never encountered anyone so adept at audio hypnotic induction.

Overtly dramatic, Anna's fingers spread, fanning away from the candlestick, and then stroked the circular newel of the banister. Each circular passage was slow, and yet deliberate, scratching her pointed nail audibly, until the wood resonated with the movement. The scratchy echo vibrated within the enclosed space, adding depth to the unnatural bubble engulfing the house, resonating into its foundations.

"Oh, dearest niece. No hope abides your willful soul. Nothing shall save you now. No one shall rally to your aid." Anna inhaled through pursed lips, drawing in the longest breath Fara had ever witnessed. A tangible current flowed toward the woman from every point in the open foyer, leaving the atmosphere empty and hollow in its wake. Silvery frost tipped the edges of the steps, creeping the crystalline patterns toward her.

Mercede's skin prickled, reacting to the sudden change. The chill went deeper, penetrating her pores. The next hissing intake lingered inside of her ears, mocking Mercede's brain. Setting her jaw, Fara pushed against it, focusing on heat and the power of truth. "I am not what you think me to be."

Anna's skin glowed brighter with the absorbed vitality. "Nay, Magdalene Lucedio foretold your coming. It was she who called you here, not your uncle, nor his inverted ruse." Some superhuman power compelled Anna, who nearly flew up to the second level, and Magdalene followed, pulled within the shadowy wake.

Mercede's instinct was to panic, but not Fara's. Breaking the freezing stiffness, she sprinted through the open bedroom door and slammed it, throwing the metal bolt into the bored out hole in the doorframe, but it didn't make her feel secure. The keyhole was empty, not that it would do much good.

The only item of furniture that could possibly brace the door was the armoire. She ran to the far side of the broad cabinet and threw her weight forward. It had to weigh over 500 pounds! Setting her feet, she lowered her center of gravity and then shouldered into the heavy chest, scraping it forward a fraction of an inch. Mercede's heart pounded, thrashing from the sudden exertion. This body didn't have the kind of strength or stamina the task required. There was no way she would ever move it in time.

Just as she turned to survey the room, chanting words resonated within the solid wood door. She stared in disbelief as each syllable visibly seeped into the curving wood grain. With the same syrupy consistency of natural sap, the enchanted words oozed through the porous membrane. Like long golden fingers, the droplets eased along the curves toward the latch.

The two distinct voices became one, growing in intensity. The rivulets joined, and the power coalesced, gathering in a bowl-like swirl within the grain. The sap filled the oval pool and then extended into five buds, forming the shape of a human hand. A forefinger of amber light extended from the wood grain three dimensionally. Fara's mind struggled with the physics, knowing that wasn't possible. And yet, a hand glowing like that of the proverbial Midas reached into her reality in front of her cynical eyes.

The hand extended, and its fingers rounded the latch. Visibly, the bolt started to move, sliding out from the door jam. The physical rules of existence no longer applied, leaving only one option. Fara threw her shoulder against the wooden door and braced the heels of her hands against the ball affixed to the head of the latch. All of her internal and external strength focused on that single point. The metal bit into her flesh. Exhaling sharply, she doubled her physical efforts.

"I am protected inside this room from anyone who seeks to harm me." Although Mercede's voice wasn't trained, Fara had to try. She visualized her own protective bubble surrounding the room. "Protected inside this room. Protected inside this room." She envisioned a force field of pure white light sealing the door. "Protected inside this room."

Another unnatural inhalation hissed, and the force of Fara's light dwindled. Using her core being, she added strength to her visualized barrier, and each time, they absorbed it in equal measure. Their chanting increased in volume, using Fara's own strength against her.

Suppressing Mercede's panic, Fara collected her thoughts and ran through potential scenarios. Immediately she discounted any more attempts at mental manipulation. She had to switch to a full-on physical assault.

With a quick scan, the only real weapon in the room was the dagger. Her gaze shot to the rumpled bed at least five strides away. But if she left the door unprotected, they would enter the room. She had to avoid that at all costs.

The bolt was relentless. Weary pain collected in her palm, and a ribbon of blood gathered at the lowest part of her thumb on her right hand. Her palm burned, and a drop of blood fell, slapping the bare floor with a wet thud. Anna's next perverted inhalation sucked it under the door. Fara pictured the sadistic woman savoring the taste with vampiric delight.

The pressure upon the bolt stopped.

For a fleeting second, Fara's mind flickered to the opportunity of achieving the knife, but this had to be a trick. She held her hands, one cupped over the over, bracing for the next push. Her torn flesh released another drop of heavy blood and then another until they flowed with every beat of her pulse. Still she retained the intense pressure on the bolt, not willing to allow physical pain dominion over her actions. Mere seconds felt like minutes. Still no reaction. Her eyes flicked again to the bed. The knife had to be there, perhaps under a pillow or clinging to a fold in the sheets.

Her gaze returned to the door in time to see an oily finger of sap drip off from the wood grain. Smooth as honey, the golden liquid pulsed forward with each disharmonic syllable. The weight touched her hand with frigid cold, so opposite its appearance. The glow emoted harrowed agony from the lowest bowel of hell, and still, she refused to release her grip. The frigid syrup continued until it covered both hands. Mental agony overshadowed the physical pain. Still she refused to relinquish her hold.

The sap once again took the form of a hand. The pronounced and yet delicate fingers squeezed, as real and vibrantly strong as a jungle snake, tightening until the very marrow of her bones felt like snapping.

The continuous chant increased in volume, glowing brilliantly, curling along the grain, and like a megaphone, the curves magnified the volume. The vibrations resonated in Fara's ears and absorbed into her hands. Each word crept inside her flesh and became a physical part of her, and yet the pain was all she could think of, so brilliant and sharp. Her hands were being crushed.

The temperature plummeted, frosting the metal while encasing her hands in the growing floe. Carried by the rapid beating of Mercede's pulse, the glacial chill invaded her body, cooling the anger which had fueled her strength. An unnatural gust of power blasted the door, splintering the compromised metal. The blow knocked her halfway to the bank of windows.

She couldn't feel her hands. For a fleeting second, she wondered if they too had shattered. Her eyes landed upon the bloody pulp of her palm. Agony exploded, bright and blinding. Forcing herself to accept the pain, she looked up.

Anna Carafa stood in the open doorway. The shade stood in her physical form by her side. Both smiled an identical diabolic smirk as if once again linked. Anna's bejeweled fingers stroked the candlestick, and the glow returned. Yet, the tip of the candle had no true flame.

Their lips recited the unknown words, articulating each syllable with added emphasis. "Basiliske Galeōte meta Kōktō Podōn kai Kakoin Ommatoin to Phōs Emēi Cheiri Kathias tōi Kakōi Dergmati Toxeusatō! Kakon Omma Petrōseōs!"

Fara didn't listen. Summoning every ounce of will, she pushed to her knees. Not able to gain her footing, she crawled toward the bed. A quick glance over her shoulder told her they weren't pursing her. She thrust her right hand under the pillow and found nothing. Her stomach did a flip-flop.

"Shit!" The knife wasn't there, or perhaps she just couldn't feel it.

With her forearm, she flung the pillow across the bed and then saw a ruby glimmer from the circular butt of the dagger. The motion from their love making had wedged the sheath between the massive wooden headboard and the mattress. Glancing back, the women were still chanting, standing patiently by the door, again nonplussed, as if the outcome of the day was a foregone conclusion.

Fara launched Mercede's shoulder into the post, hoping to dislodge the blade, but the bed had to weigh even more than the armoire and wouldn't budge. She reached toward the hilt, but her damaged fingers were numb, not able to grasp it. Like a bird pecking for a seed, she tucked her head and grabbed the hilt with her teeth, inching the blade from the sheath. Nearly collapsing on the floor from the effort, she stared at the fingers on her left hand and willed them to open one at a time. With equal concentration, she wrapped them around the dagger.

Now, more than in tandem, the two voices spoke as one, gaining in volume while they approached the bed. They each held a crimson drop of Fara's blood smeared upon their extended palms. "Basiliske Galeōte meta Kōktō Podōn kai Kakoin Ommatoin to Phōs Emēi Cheiri Kathias tōi Kakōi Dergmati Toxeusatō! Kakon Omma Petrōseōs!"

Magdalene Lucedio clapped her hands together, and the sharp resonance connected within Fara's mind. She understood part of the recitation. They were calling upon the evil eye. Shit, the cabby was right.

Her heart thudded with adrenaline, and its heat battled against the consuming chill in her veins, pushing the force back with equal measure. "I will not succumb."

Now within five feet, they chanted the phrase again, "Basilisk, Lizard with Eight Legs and Evil Eyes! Life Placed into My Hand, Shoot Forth the Evil Look! Evil Eye of Petrification!" Anna and Magdalene clapped their hands.

Mercede's flesh crawled and grew so very cold. It was just a glorified thoughtform, and like any thoughtform, the effect had to be transitory, which was why they kept saying it over and over. Yet these words carried power, more than a thoughtform. It was a spell. They were witches, real fucking witches!

Fara refused to listen and concentrated on squeezing the hilt of the dagger in her left hand, and even though she couldn't feel, she forced her hand forward until it had to have encountered the blade guard. Her instinctive will grew, overcoming the spell and any of Mercede's inherent weaknesses. She would not give up.

She was adept at knife fighting and had practiced left-handed more times than she could remember against Guy.

I will succeed. I am strong, rounded through her head, countering the swirling curse until it gained enough forceful clarity to spill from her lips, "I will succeed. I am strong. I will succeed."

The women repeated the verse yet again, and Fara countered, shouting her reply. Her arms and legs felt five times their normal weight. Forcing her limbs to move, she crouched into a fighting stance. The golden sap still visibly glowed within her and consumed her flesh inch by inch, stiffening her veins. Her will alone was not enough. Each pulse brought it closer to her heart.

Having to take the offensive, Fara squinted, and arching back, flung her arm forward, throwing the knife. Pride soared along with the blade; it was right on target. Magdalene Lucedio's hand thrust forward. A foot away from Anna's heart, the blade hit an invisible barrier and clattered harmlessly to the floor.

Mercede's body grew colder, too cold to even shiver, but Fara refused to relent. Her will was stronger than the weak body. She would not succumb. She would fight her way free! A jerk of her forearm brought a powerful smile to her lips.

Anna smiled a reply, but worry edged those thin lips. "Mercede, do not fear. You shall not die. Your life essence will seal the tomb of pending souls, and in the future, when the world is primed for my greatness, I will embody a new vessel and live again. You are honored to be the vehicle of mine ultimate salvation."

Fara opened her mouth and forced out a shrill keep, using the break in their power to push to her knees. "I will succeed. I am strong. I will succeed."

Underneath the echoes, Fara heard Anna whisper toward her accomplice, "The spell is too transitory."

"There is another way." Magdalene replied.

Fara straightened, wavering, yet growing stronger. "I am strong. I will succeed. I am strong." Feeling returned to her shoulders and upper arms.

The Duchess of Medina approached. Each sharply articulated step snapped against the wooden floor. Behind her, the lamplight glittered on her jewel laden fingers. "There be other ways to take thy soul." She raised the candlestick.

Fara's instinctual training commanded Mercede's body, and her left arm jerked forward and up, blocking Anna's forward sweeping blow with enough force to surprise them both. She held the braced stance. "I will succeed. I am strong."

A scrape of metal resounded from behind her.

Shit! Where was the red-headed Magdalene?

Using her deepest core muscles, Fara twisted toward the window. The polished telescope blurred with motion. She keoped while throwing another block. Her scream lingered in the resonant air while the crack of Mercede's skull was quick.

The world turned white.

"Strip her. Nothing physical shall bind-" Anna Carafa's words drifted into the oblivion.

CHAPTER 27

Gae's reflexes were fast, but not quite fast enough to miss the blow to his chin. The Puerto Rican was more adroit than he anticipated, but that didn't sit well with him.

More likely, the distraction of the feminine scream edged him off his game. The shrill sound still resonated, sliding under his skin. Having sparred with Fara more times than he could count, he felt her character in the quality of the tone, so like her keop. Following the bend in the reverberation had the potential to lead him to her. He listened carefully, trying to locate the source, tuning his inner sensitivity. The core within his chest tingled, connecting to the fragile manifestation above him. He had to go upstairs.

"J.C.!" Ted's panic sliced through the lingering resonance, cutting off the otherworldly connection. The threads of lingering vibration scattered like blowing into a puff of smoke. The blind asshole ruined it.

Fuck! The situation sucked on numerous levels. Yet the deepest insult was Ted wanting J.C.'s help more than his, and that slight was just enough to send Gae over the edge. That scruffy Puerto Rican had nothing on him, not physically, intellectually, or economically. There was no comparison, yet Fara replaced him with this good for nothing ass-wipe.

The idiot even turned toward the stairs at the sound, leaving his back exposed. If Gae hadn't been analyzing the connection to Fara, he would have taken the easy shot. Just a single jab to his left kidney would double him over. Nothing too severe. The mark would never show, but the pain would linger. Gae would be out the door and on his way to Purgatorio ad Arco to recover the evidence. He would find the camera Fara had hidden near Lucia's shrine and erase their argument. He didn't know which part was the worst, when she accused him of planning to kill her or describing him as the new Godfather.

Worse yet, if that camera fell into Ted or Chrystal's hands, they would discover who he was, and then he'd be dead for real. He'd have to bunker down. It would be impossible to leave his home. That stopped him. It was impossible to go home. His home, his personal fortress was compromised, infiltrated by the real criminals, the ones who orchestrated this entire mess.

Shit! He was fucked either way.

His only chance at a future was to resolve all of the issues. He thought back to the beginning when he saw Fara at the church. *The obvious is rarely the truth.* Her voice resonated inside of his head.

Fara being there could have been coincidence, just like she said. The real plan may have been ongoing for quite some time, infiltrating, gaining trust. Week after week, Aleri visited Lucia's shrine. That started long before his father's murder, under the advisement of his aunt.

No! Under the guidance of Magdalene Lucedio. That red-headed bitch was the key!

The how or why she was part of this still eluded him. Perhaps the tape would reveal that as well. She controlled his aunt and cousin, and possibly Luigi, but he may have joined her of his own volition. Regardless, he had adversaries on every front and no true allies. He needed Fara as his partner now more than ever!

"Gae. J.C. Where are you guys?" Ted's voice was shrill, near a full octave higher. "I think Chrystal connected with Fara."

Just the mention of her name instantly changed Gae's plans of immediately charging to the crypt. If Fara was still connected to this house, as her keep implied, he would be able to save her. She'd be so grateful that she'd return to him, forever by his side. This was his chance to make everything right.

J.C. was already on his way up the stairs. Gae couldn't let him get there first, so he bounded up three steps at a time until they were shoulder to shoulder, arriving on the second floor landing together.

The third door on the left stood ajar. When Gae arrived with the woman whom he thought was Fara, he assumed she had checked the house. At the time, he was focused on mending the rift between them, and she was so receptive.

The vision of Fara's naked body filled his mind. The way she felt. The way she smelt. All of that was her, but on the inside, she wasn't Fara. He should have known, but he wanted it to be true so badly he had been blind to all of the clues.

The only wash of daylight came from that doorway and folded oddly over Chrystal, adding to the strangeness of her position. She was doubled over towards them, like a backwards head of an arrow. He had seen bodies like that on the sidewalk after taking a leap out of a fifth story window. Not by merely fainting. What in the hell had happened?

Ted hunched over her but raised his head toward them; his eyes were filled with tears. "I can't see anything. There's so much energy emanating from this room, it's like staring into the sun."

Morning light filtered through grimy windows, but it wasn't even close to blinding. The sky was starting to cloud up. He inhaled a quick breath to-

"What happened?" Damn, J.C. beat him to the question.

"We were checking every room. All I did was open this door, and the psychic light was glorious, brighter than anything I've ever seen. Pure white energy. It was amazing. Chrystal came to look. She didn't even touch anything, just stepped up to the threshold, and something like static discharge sparked, blinding me. She screamed, and I heard her hit the floor. Is she okay?"

J.C. squatted to check her pulse while Gae stepped up to the threshold.

Ted held his hands out in front of him, touching Gae's chest and then shoulder. "Can you see inside? What's in there? What's making that light?"

An invisible barrier covered the doorway, clinging to the door jamb like electric plastic wrap. The energy signature was barely perceptible. He held up his left hand, and the hairs on his arms stood on end, drawing toward the static field. Extending his fingertips, he was surprised when there wasn't a shock. The energy encased his fingers, emitting a hum perceptible only to his inner senses. Again, it reminded him of Fara. He didn't know why, but it did.

Closing his eyes, he tuned himself to the internal frequency, willing himself to encounter her. The tonal vibration grew within his head. He listened carefully. It sounded like an E. The tone was constant, no variation of an encryption or code. Not taking nothing as an answer, he tried again, and then his eyes flew open. Fara had sealed the room! Only certain people were allowed inside. People Fara trusted. A clue had to be in there.

Hastily, he removed Ted's hand from his shoulder. With one quick look at J.C. who was still bent over Chrystal, Gae broke the plane, and instantly his skin exploded in gooseflesh. Even his nostril hair stood on end, prickling the inside of his nose, and setting his senses ablaze with wariness. Now he was getting somewhere.

"What's in there?" Ted asked from right behind him. "Can I enter?"

Now inside, he heard a secondary signature, much lower in tone and abnormal. The sub-vibration climbed under the gooseflesh, chilling him to the marrow of his bones. "No, this place isn't right."

"What do you mean?" Ted's voice sounded distorted, each word echoing with a prolonged resonance, as if he kept getting further and further away.

"I'm not sure," he was going to discover what was happening. Just him, and that filled him with confidence. He had to be the one to save Fara. "Stay with Chrystal."

Out of professional habit, he scanned the large bedroom filled with endless layers of undisturbed dust. No other exits. Nothing lurking in the corners. Nothing hovering near the high ceiling. Nothing clinging to the interior or exterior of the multi-paned windows. But something was there, prodding his subconscious.

A bulky armoire and vanity stood on the closest interior walls. A four-poster bed was in the far corner where decaying drapery hung in moss-like cords. The furniture was old, real vintage work. Craftsmen hadn't made furniture like this for centuries, and the room was at least that old. The temporal distortion had to be three or four centuries old, and yet the contents hadn't been completely preserved. Had Fara been interrupted? Maybe, counteracted?

Gae swept his fingers through the air, feeling for any lingering remnants of the past. Like a war zone, the very atmosphere of this place was injured, caught in the middle of an epic battle of opposing forces. All that remained was the faint frequency guarding the door and the growling sub-frequency trying to counteract it. Over time, the vitality of both had diminished; however, that much energy took ages to dissipate and would charge the interior atmosphere with ionic particles. They would attract other ambient units, hence the dust. He smiled at his superior deduction. The Puerto Rican wouldn't know those things; this type of knowledge was definitely above his pay grade.

The decaying shreds of the white drapery shifted, releasing motes to dance in the infiltrating light.

"Fara?" He whispered into the heady air. "Fara, are you here?" He took two more steps toward the windows and glanced back at his tracks.

She would have checked every room in this house before sleeping in it, but there weren't any other footprints. It was like this place was an ancient tomb undisturbed for a thousand years, but she would have come inside. He was sure of it. Her curiosity would have gotten the better of her. So why weren't there any prints?

Walking a few more feet, he checked his tracks again and squatted to test the depth with his fingertip. Consistently at the first knuckle, about five centimeters deep. Each footfall was equally pronounced. Distinct edges. He rubbed the grainy texture between his forefinger and thumb while calculating the possibilities. Perhaps at a certain time of day the room reset back to the default moment when the damage occurred. If a room could reset back through the centuries to a particular point in time, so could their lives.

Hope swelled. Fara would have left a clue, and it would still remain.

The armoire was huge, easily seven feet tall and four feet wide. The upper two-thirds had elaborately inlaid starburst patterns, and the contrasting colors of wood were still visible through the obscuring gray layer. Three narrow drawers started at knee level and extended to the floor. Dust clung to all of the brass knobs, now tarnished green with oxidation. He touched the hanging teardrop on the left door and smeared a sample of the heavy soot once again in between his thumb and index finger. Just like the floor, the consistency was heavy, granular. It wasn't dust.

His gaze shot to the ruined window panes, adding credence to his theory. Even through the gathering clouds, he could still make out the lower slopes of Mount Vesuvius.

Ash. This place had layers of ash.

Carefully, he opened the door of the armoire. Even with the minimal stir, the current of air wiggled through the lonely dress hanging on the central peg. The fabric sagged, unraveling on a cellular level until it hung by a single thread.

Ted shouted, "I see a flame of blue fire. What's in there?"

Gae answered over his shoulder. "Just an old dress." He examined the fabric, careful not to breathe too hard, or it too would turn to ash.

Stomping like a primate through the open doorway, J.C. shouldered next to him for a look.

"Be careful." Gae snapped.

"Looks like mid-seventeenth century."

Gae didn't budge, holding his position squarely in front of the open armoire door. "And how would you know that?"

"I'd been researching Italian costuming for this episode of *Ghost Lovers*. This style of gown," he pointed to the heavier braid clinging to the decomposing fabric, "specifically the scooped-box neckline was popular in the 1650's, give or take a few years. Look at that," he squatted down to sift his hands through the pile of dissolved fabric on the floor of the cabinet and pulled out one intact piece, "looks like something spilt or splashed the gown, preserving this one sample." Standing, he examined it between forefinger and thumb, touching it gingerly. "It was blue velvet."

Gaetano shouldered against him to get a better view. Shit, he was probably right. How had he missed that? "Back then, indigo was the only dye to turn something blue. Expensive stuff. Whoever owned this dress was rich."

"Royalty. All clothing embodied code in the type of fabric and color. At a glance, anyone would immediately know their station. Blue was coveted by the royals, and they didn't let anyone else wear it." J.C. pulled a flashlight from his pocket and shone it around the inner cavity. "So why is there a single dress in an otherwise empty closet? Rich women would have dozens."

Fara was hiding out. Gae wasn't about to share his theory, and his shrug started a cold-shoulder turn. "This whole place is from that same time period. No one's made a lady's vanity like that for hundreds of years. The wood is sculpted, not milled." He swiped a finger along the rounded edge and continued to examine several bottles and small jars scattered haphazardly. Other than the basic shape, it was hard to tell what the different items were under all the layers of sediment. None of it screamed Fara.

Dawn eased through a break in the clouds, casting a beam through one of the cleaner panes of glass. The long finger of light reflected off of the tarnished mirror and onto the flat surface at a canted angle. J.C. followed the light and leaned closer. "Holy shit!" He squatted in order for the surface to be at eye level.

"No fucking way. I see it too." Gae mirrored his actions. "Those are words."

The Puerto Rican clicked on the flashlight. The swirling effect hiding under the dust became in descript until he reflected the beam off the mirror. The angled light highlight three, no four words. "Looks like modern English."

"No way. This is old." Gae blew along the lower edge of the imprint. It looked like a curlicue number three. "There's at least three hundred years of layers on top of all of this-"

J.C. blew across the grime from the other angle, clearing it better than Gae had done. "It is English, 'Help me leave 1643'." He swiveled, and their eyes met. They both said, "Fara" at exactly the same time.

"By writing it in English, she didn't have to sign it." J.C. blew another breath across the top of the letters. "She knew that we would know it was her."

"What did you find?" Ted called from the hallway.

"Not sure yet-" Gae answered.

J.C. talked over him. "We found a message from Fara."

"We don't know it was Fara." But deep down, Gae knew she had been here and sent a message. He just didn't want the asshole to know. "1643. What's significant about 1643? Why would she be transported back then and not any other year?"

"What happened in 1643 to Anna Carafa?"

Just the mention of the woman's name added strength to the underlying growl. "Why do you think she's connected to this?"

"That book you took out of Fara's stuff was entitled *The Court of Anna Carafa*.' The palace down the coast was her home, and things went strange after Fara checked it out. Whatever is going on here has something to do with her." His eyes narrowed suspiciously. "Why'd you take the book?"

The man was observant. Gae would give him that. He turned back to the vanity, inspecting the baubles, and withdrew a gold chain from the dust until the monocle dangled from the end. No impressions came to mind. While watching it swing, he answered as nonchalantly as possible. "I don't know what you're talking about."

"Look," J.C. punched his shoulder, none too lightly. "Pull out whatever is up your ass. We have to work together to resolve what's happened to Fara and have to set aside personal issues until we find her. Two heads are better than one. I know you took the book, so tell me why."

"It's mine." Fresh anger swelled, but he held it in check, vowing to wait for vengeance. "Fara took it from my house, and I-"

"What?! Your house? When did that happen?" J.C.'s questions fired in rapid succession.

Gae shrugged and set the monocle back into its divot, knowing that it too would revert to its former state. Maybe the exact time was important. "It's complicated. We ran into each other at Palazzo Donn'Anna, and I asked for her help with Aleri.

While she was at home, my cousin started screaming about purgatorial wreathed serpents." He interrupted J.C.'s unspoken comment with a wave of his hand. "When I was taking Aleri back to her room, Fara skipped out on my Ducati, after taking this." Gae reached into his coat and withdrew the book. "I had no idea it was in her backpack until it landed on the table. I took it back because it was part of my father's collection. He had several books about the Carafas along with many other historical Italian families." A drop of water fell from the frayed spine, and he was glad his father wasn't alive to see it. "It's ruined. At least it wasn't the rarest. I'll be able to replace it."

J.C.'s eyes narrowed again. "That was yesterday morning."

"Mostly. I caught up with her in Purgatorio ad Arco in the early afternoon."

"And then she translocated with … with..." J.C. shrugged. "Anna Carafa?"

"I don't think so. Anna was born a princess and then became the Duchess of Medina. She lived for unyielding ambition, and in the end her empire came crashing down. She died in October 1645 after her husband left her to return to Spain earlier that same year."

"That's two years after Fara's note."

"Exactly the point. Anna died alone, broke, and friendless at the end of her life."

J.C. interjected, "Or maybe that's what she wanted people to think."

"Possible, not probable."

"Fara always said the obvious is rarely the truth."

Gae cringed but didn't let it show. She'd shared that with the asshole too. "When you arrived, the woman inhabiting Fara's body introduced me as Gaetano di Casapesenna."

"That's not your full name?"

"No." Gae scoffed while putting the book back inside his inner jacket pocket. "He was Anna's lover. In this particular book, Matilde Serao describes how Anna Carafa competed with her niece, Mercede de la Torres, for Casapesenna's attention. Mercede arrived for a visit from Madrid in 1643 and played opposite Gaetano in a play in which they kissed and that sparked Anna's jealousy."

"The gentry put on theatrical productions during parties, placing themselves into the starring roles during that era. It was really popular. I thought about adding that as a scene in the *Ghost Lovers* script."

Ghost Lovers, Gae silently scoffed. "The crowning feature of the palazzo is a massive amphitheater. When the Duke invited his niece to stay with them, he made sure she played opposite Casapesenna."

"So he knew Anna was having an affair?"

"According to the books, it was common knowledge. After the play that night, the two women had a fight, and Mercede was never seen again. Anna spread a rumor that her niece had a sudden religious calling and went to a nunnery."

"Really? A nunnery. People actually bought that story?"

"Casapesenna didn't. He searched for Mercede, and when he couldn't find her, went off to war and was killed in battle. All of that happened in 1643."

"A renaissance version of suicide by cop." J.C. picked up a tall decorative bottle and balanced the weight in his hand. "So you think the woman downstairs could be who, Mercede?"

"She speaks Italian with a Spanish accent."

J.C. nodded while removing the stopper, and the spicy scent tangibly rolled from the vial, filling the immediate space. "The archaic form of Spanish would fit the seventeenth century timeline as well." Continuing his focus, he pulled the strip of cloth out of his pocket and sniffed it. "This is what splashed on the dress. A little woodsy to be a lady's perfume."

Gae took the extended vial. It was heavier than it looked. "Frankincense." His last Christmas with Fara filled his mind, and his hand slipped into his pocket to feel for the cellphone. With a quick beat of panic, he pulled it out. Nothing. The water in the aqueduct had ruined it. Now, all he had left were memories. A lump grew in his throat. Everything had gone to shit. "We need to confirm her identity, and maybe she remembers something."

"How do you propose we get her to talk?" His body tensed. "I won't let you hurt Fara."

"I'd never do anything to hurt her." Gae snapped back. "I was thinking about giving her a few stiff drinks, vodka's Fara's favorite, and get her talking about anything, nothing in particular. Once she's relaxed, I'll call her Mercede and see what happens."

J.C. squinted again, and Gae realized it was his innate signal of distrust. "But what will that get us?"

"Knowledge and potential leverage." His stomach tightened at the thought of having to trust this man, at least for a short while. This was getting more complicated than he originally assessed. It was better to have someone at his back. Even an oaf had some skills. "I need to know who she is." He inhaled deeply and decided to release more details. "I think my cousin, Aleri, is involved. Hell, I think she's possessed, but not completely, at least not the last time I saw her. She's the sweetest and kindest girl on the planet. Now she's arrogant and demanding. From everything that I've observed, she's acting like Anna Carafa. I think the ceremony in the catacombs was to translocate Anna with Aleri."

"But Fara got in the way."

"If she wasn't holding onto the skull, it probably wouldn't have been an issue."

"If we bring Fara and Aleri together, what might happen?"

"I don't think that's a good idea, at least not at this point. Anna and Mercede were spiteful enemies, and they still may be at counter-purposes." Gae glanced at his watch. It was almost seven-thirty. The priests would be unlocking Purgatorio ad Arco. "I need to determine potential consequences."

"Fuck the consequences. I'll do anything to get Fara back. We've got to go to the crypt." J.C. rose and glanced around the room once more, absently sliding both the cloth strip and the bottle into his pocket.

Gae almost called him on it but realized he didn't care if the dude was clepto. This wasn't his house.

"We need to see what's on the mini DV. The maximum running time is an hour. I don't know how much footage Fara already recorded before leaving the camera running, but if we're lucky, it caught the entire ritual. All we would need is recreate it, and we would get her back ... and your cousin."

He stopped his train of thought and really contemplated what the Puerto Rican had said. The man surprised him again. "Sounds like a plan." The wind whistled across the windows, rattling the loose panes. "Looks like a storm's brewing."

"It can be to our advantage." J.C. stood and wiped his hands on the thighs of his threadbare jeans. "Psychic activity increases during storms. Spirits use the additional energy in the atmosphere to manifest."

This was the popular shit he expected a *Ghost Lovers* producer to say, and a scoffing snort escaped before he could stop it. "Who says that?"

Immediately after the words left his mouth, he remembered the storm when the ghosts appeared outside of the conservatory's windows. That night, he had seen enough to change his mind on a lot of things. He'd have to expand his thinking beyond what seemed rational.

"Psychic experts, and *I* saw it happen in Scotland." J.C. faced the empty doorway. "Hey Ted, does a storm provide ambient energy for spiritual activity?" There was no answer. "Ted?"

J.C. started for the door, and Gae followed him out of the bedroom. The instant they stepped into the hall the air changed. It was a different type of musty, heavy with an abundance of ozone, and clear of the ambient hum. Still, something else was in the air, something unnatural.

"Ted. Chrystal?" J.C. hustled to the staircase. "Where are you guys?"

Gae remained just outside of the door and let his senses adjust. The hallway was abnormally dark, blacker than black. Blinking a couple of times, he made out shapes of the half-moon table and a chair outside of Fara's bedroom door. Something else extended across the runner. Looked like legs. In the shadows behind the door, Ted was slumped against the wall, unconscious.

"Shit," Gae muttered and then called out, "Turn on the lights."

In a series of two rapid clicks, J.C. flicked on the light switch by the stairs and the flashlight, and both hazy yellow and bluish-white light extended down the hall.

"Oh shit! Ted!" J.C. skidded down onto his knees as if he was sliding into base and his pants let out a rip, but he didn't notice. Immediately, his fingers touched the carotid artery in Ted's neck. "He has a pulse." He examined the rest of his face and neck, arms and legs with the beam of glaring light. "I don't see anything physically wrong. No wounds, at least nothing rising up yet."

When J.C. shifted Ted's head to the other side, his body slumped over with the momentum. A syringe was shoved needle deep into the back of his shoulder.

"No don't touch it!" Gae shouted, and J.C.'s hand stopped just inches away from the plastic. "It contains evidence. Finger prints. Residue." He tapped his pockets while thinking. "Did Fara have an evidence bag in her stuff?"

"No."

"What about gloves?"

"Usually, but they were gone too."

Gloves made him think of Chrystal. The hairs on Gae's neck rose. Something new was wrong. Warily, he checked both directions. Where would the bitch go? With her sudden departure, clearly she did this to Ted. But why? To shut him up? To slow him down? To keep him from following her?

Pushing to his feet, he ran into Fara's bedroom. He stripped the one pillow still on the bed of its case and headed back into the hall. Seeing the tousled bed flooded him with physical memories of how it felt to hold her once again, but he didn't let his mind go there.

J.C. was slapping Ted's cheeks each in turn. "Talk to me! What the fuck happened?"

A low groan was his only reply. The man's eyes lolled up until the whites showed, and he passed out again.

Gae shoved his hand into the pillowcase and barely touched the two plastic handles on the syringe, easing the needle out. After sniffing the contents and not smelling anything, he flipped the case over and tied a knot into the open end. "Chrystal did this." He growled the name and took off running, charging down the staircase, and stopped short at the entrance to the living room.

Fara's body was gone.

"Shit! J.C., get down here!"

A rumble of footfalls stormed downstairs. "No fucking way! There's no way she could get out of those cuffs."

"Not without help." His inner state grew cold.

J.C. rushed past him, stopping next to the empty coffee table. "Fara took all of her stuff."

"Fara didn't do this. Chrystal did."

"But why? Where would they go? How will we find them?" With each question, the loudness of J.C.'s voice increased until his shouts echoed across the room.

Gae shook his head, not able to find words. All of his rage focused on strangling Chrystal Delphae.

"The skull!" J.C. nearly dove into the sofa, searching within the soft cushions. "Shit! Where is it? Chrystal didn't know its significance, so why would she take it?" He threw each cushion off the sofa until only the barren frame remained. "Fuck! What else can go wrong?"

Gae's fingers gripped the back of the empty straight-backed chair while he focused on possibilities. "They had no transportation, so either they are on foot, or made other arrangements, which would mean accomplices."

"Who else would be involved? Who knew we were even here?"

"Hell, I don't know. You know more about the woman than I do. You're the one who brought her here. Had she ever been to Italy before?"

"She didn't say much of anything other than bitch about shit."

Gae believed that. "An agent doesn't act on a whim. Chrystal drugged her partner and stole a key witness. There had to be a reason. It doesn't add up."

"We have to go after her. She couldn't have gotten that far."

"My bike's still midtown." He couldn't call Mario; his free will might be compromised. They'd need a cab. The cabby.

Thrusting his hand inside his jean's pocket, he pulled out the business card, Renzo Dionetti. "Do you have a phone that works?"

CHAPTER 28

A wickedly satisfied smile tingled the edges of Chrystal's lips. Revenge was so sweet and this time profitable. Upon receiving the bounty, Chrystal would live the rest of her life independent from the agency and everyone else for that matter. Her smile broadened into a grin, and her facial muscles ached from the unaccustomed movement.

A quick look at her watch told her she was right on schedule. The woman said to meet at the second intersection east of the rental house. Chrystal didn't ask questions. Frankly, she didn't care how the mysterious benefactor knew where they were. As soon as she got her money, she'd head to Rome, assume the secret identity she established over three years ago, and disappear. Her long-term goal was on the cusp of fulfillment.

The barefoot woman stumbled, over what, Chrystal had no clue. This part of the sidewalk was new and smooth. More than likely it was a muscle spasm. Her hands and feet had been bound for hours. Like an injured child, she just sat there, staring at her scuffed palms. Glossy tears brimmed in her eyes.

"Oh no, no, no. No tears." Chrystal couldn't afford any delays. She grabbed the hybrid's arm and hefted her to her feet, letting go as soon as the woman regained her footing. Even through the black polyester gloves, Chrystal felt the emanating vibrations, all twisted and misaligned. The main signature was that of Mercede de las Torres, but a shadow of Fara was underneath it all. Chrystal knew her vibration better than anyone on the planet. The bitch was going down today!

A large black limo approached, as out of place in the cracker box suburb as she was. "Thank God."

The hybrid looked down the road then faced Chrystal with those perfectly sculpted brows drawn together into a deep furrow. "God." She repeated while pointing at the limo.

"No, that's a car. A ride. My ticket to get you back." Chuckling at her clever double entendre, she raised her arms and waved them frantically. In black, she couldn't be seen easily. The limo had slowed to little more than a crawl, still a ways away. Just when she went to step into the road, the cellphone buzzed inside of her sleek hip pouch. Unlike her counterparts, she didn't use a high-tech phone with a touch-activated screen. Well, she could, but she'd run the risk of touching something else. Anyway, the older push button phone worked just fine with gloves. Opening the flip phone, satisfaction filled her when she noted the number. She pressed the green button and smiled again, "Hello."

"Ciao Miss Delphae, you are in Italy after all." The syrupy, cultured voice eased over the line.

Chrystal corrected, "Ms. Delphae, and ciao." She'd never get used to the same word meaning hello and good-bye. Why would anyone want their language to be so confusing? "I have what you want, right here." She flagged the limo again, wondering why the driver wasn't approaching. Surely, he saw them.

"Sì, I know. *Prendere due piccioni con una fava.*"

"I don't speak Italian. What did that mean?"

"What a shame. Italian is a beautiful language, so lyrical and full of nuance."

Chrystal contained her snort of derision, forgetting to ask why she evaded the translation. "That is open to interpretation."

"As is everything." A prolonged pause grew as if she really expected Chrystal to comment. Finally, the woman continued, "My driver says he sees you and our special guest on the side of the road. You may stop waving your arms. Dressed in black, you give off the appearance of a giant bat."

A bat?! She'd been called lots of things while in her sensory deprivation suit, mostly a sadist or dominatrix, but never a bat. Her inner anger rose, but she kept it in check. She'd put up with a few insults as long as she received her reward.

The limo eased forward, stopping directly alongside the two women, and the backdoor opened so smoothly it had to be motorized. The interior was dark except for a luminous glow emanating from the roof. Inside, a red-headed woman waited in an equally bright red Italian-styled business suit, which meant the skirt barely covered her twat. Her legs were pale and extended forward to slim ankles with impossibly high sandals in a matching shade of crimson. "Get in."

"That's not what I negotiated. I get a million euros upon delivery." Chrystal motioned her special guest toward the door. "Here she is, and I want my money."

"You will receive your reward upon delivery." The woman's legs folded with the practiced grace of a supermodel, and she leaned forward to look through the door. A smile grew, pulling the corners of her eyes. She had to have had some work done because she wasn't nearly as young as Chrystal first thought.

"What of the stolen skull?" The bright red lips formed the words, but something was off. Like a badly translated movie, there was a miniscule delay.

Chrystal blinked while contemplating calling her out on it, but reminded herself this was all about the million euros. "It's in the bag along with her other personal effects." She tossed the backpack onto the floor. "I've completed my side of the bargain."

The woman's long red nails released the drawstring and only removed the skull, which appeared grayer and older in the strange interior light. The bizarre smile once again pulled the corners of scarlet lips. The knife job had to have deadened some of the nerves in her face, either that or too much Botox. That had to be why her lips seemed just slightly ahead of her words. "Perfection."

Holding the skull in the open palm of her left hand, a pale white forefinger stroked the sloping forehead tenderly. She wore a gaudy ring on each finger, except for her right pinky. The different color stones represented the transitional colors of a rainbow, from violet, indigo, blue, green, yellow, orange, and red. She cupped the cranium, and then, very lightly rubbed the crack on the left side.

"It was like that when I found it."

"Sì," her eyes sparkled but not with light. The dark shimmer spread from the black pupils, consuming the irises. "That is how I know you are legitimate."

"Of course I'm legitimate!" The dead and empty air within the limousine filled her lungs and nearly made her cough. She had sensed that same calculated nothingness during her vision in the rental house. It ended with the young woman's head getting hit with the telescope, just above her left ear. Shit! She glanced from the skull and back to the woman.

"Oh Ms. Delphae I meant no disrespect."

Was she the avatar who materialized out of the miasmic shadow?

How was that possible?

For the first time, Chrystal doubted her senses. Her memory of the event had to be askew. "Then take her and give me my money."

"I am just an emissary." The shapely legs shifted further to the side. The motion released a disruption within the immediate space, and something tightened deep within Chrystal's body. "My name is Magdalene Lucedio. I'm Signorita Caravaggio's personal secretary. She wanted to reward you herself. The delivery is not complete until she receives Mrs. Trotter in person."

"Where is Miss Caravaggio?"

"At the moment, Purgatorio ad Arco. She's the matron of the Incontri Napolitano. Today is a very special day, and she's finalizing the preparations. In fact, it's the event of a lifetime. You don't want to miss it."

While prepping for the trip, Chrystal read about Incontri Napolitano, a historical preservation society associated with an ancient church. The last thing she wanted was to be in an enclosed space with a bunch of strangers, especially in a culture who hugged and kissed cheeks at a drop of a hat. "I'm not prepared for a party."

"Then you won't remain for long. Luigi, help our guests into the vehicle."

So intent upon their conversation, Chrystal hadn't noticed the driver. In his tight black t-shirt, he looked more like a bouncer at a girlie club than a chauffeur. He was standing next to Fara's body and motioned to the limo while saying something in Italian. She approached without issue, but once she looked inside, she totally freaked. Mere size or even strength wouldn't have made a difference to Fara, but Mercede apparently didn't have access to her training and skills.

"Get in." His deep voice accented the English with a rumble. English? Mercede didn't understand English. He repeated the phrase while looking Chrystal straight in the eyes and pointed to the door.

Without any visible muscular motion, Magdalene Lucedio slid across the seat, making room for her guests, but Chrystal had no intention of getting inside that enclosed space, especially not with that woman.

Tucking, she evaded the man's slow lunge and gained a better view of the interior. The light she initially thought was a standard fixture dropped into Magdalene's hands. She rolled the ball along her palms, hard and firm as a marble. Absorbing the warmth of her hands, the shiny surface became malleable, melting and oozing around her fingers.

Now the size of a softball, she stretched and prodded the swirling energy like a piece of dough. Each time the mass connected to a jeweled ring, it took on the appearance of that color, like a drop of dye. The twirling shifted and flowed, spinning webs of color within an inner gyroscope. Layers upon layers of colors, twisted and connected, intertwining with a kaleidoscopic effect.

The patterns were stunning ... beautiful ... electric.

Brilliant light swirled, and her eyes remained fixated, anticipating the next starburst, and the next. All of those vibrant fibers of color glowed, puffing up with energy.

The woman's hands continued to knead the glorious glow, stretching the mass even larger and larger again.

The twists knit and then slipped apart, never knotting, always slipping, one over another.

A part of her drifted, and she didn't care so mesmerized by the colors ... beauty ... power ... light.

With the dexterity of a slight of hand magician, the redhead twisted one hand over the other, and the pattern encased within the orb followed. In a continuum of motion, the entire globe twisted, coiling into a short, bulky rope. The threads of distinct color broke, mixing into a brackish green. Purple veins pulsed over the otherwise smooth, glass-like surface, glowing and twisting, hideous and beautiful, all at the same time.

The orb was alive!

Chrystal's instinct sensed the threat, and she shook herself out of the hypnotic stupor. She was almost inside of the car!

She backed two half-steps toward the curb. The burly man didn't lay a hand upon her, having also fallen victim to the mesmerizing vision. She backed up a full step, and with the next beat of her heart, confidence surged. All she needed was about a ten foot head start. She'd outrun the fools. Her foot lifted, extending back-

Without warning, the wound cord struck like a snake, springing through the open car door and into the light of day. The feeling of sharply pointed teeth punctured the black protective fabric, sinking into Chrystal's forearm. A yelp stalled in her throat.

The instant psychic connection was more intense than anything she had ever encountered. Rough and dark images swirled, squeezing intelligent thought from her mind.

With a yank, it pulled her toward the open door. Her basic instinct of self-preservation threw out her right elbow, bracing against the outside of the doorjamb. The momentum carried her lower body forward, and using it to her advantage, she kicked both legs, angling them to knock the ball of light to hell. She encountered nothing. That wasn't possible!

She tucked her legs back under her and glanced inside. The woman hadn't moved, and the space wasn't that vast. Her kick had been on target and should have knocked the red bitch across the backseat.

Magdalene's glowing fingers squeezed the ball of light, and the fangs sank to the bone, pulling her arm out of socket.

Pain screamed through Chrystal's body, heightening with each pulse. She braced, hooking her practical two-inch heels over the lower edge of the doorframe. "You will let me go, let me go, let me go."

She focused on the stupid backpack and calmed her inner panic. She had to have clarity of mind to evoke the audio hypnotic induction. Her vision grew hazy. The scent of ozone tingled the fine hairs inside of her nose. "You will let me go." The venomous grip slackened enough to give Chrystal hope.

Through the brackish mist, the woman grimaced with deep concentration. Her face sucked in, the lines visibly aging her at least twenty years. Her jeweled fingers struck the orb, and the colorful stones sparked, adding fresh power to the glowing form. The purplish veins pulsed, and like a poisonous snake, the dark venom flowed through the fangs.

"Let me go, let me go, let me go," Chrystal repeated, slightly faster than before. The venom continued to pump, consuming her now translucent flesh.

The evil bitch's eyes turned black, and pointed fangs tipped her incisors under the horrid grimace. The muscles and even the flesh shrank, giving her arms the appearance of spindly crab legs. What was she?

"Let me-" A strangling grip encircled Chrystal's throat, squeezing with infinite strength. Not even a whisper of air left her lungs. The chords of muscles instinctively tightened, trying to protect her fragile windpipe, but it did no good. The lack of circulation gathered unbearable pressure inside of her head, pounding with the beat of native drums, and her eyes wanted to explode.

The Italian woman flicked her wrists. Like a lasso, the grips pulled Chrystal headfirst into the limo.

The bonds immediately vanished.

She wanted to scream, but only a weak whisper managed to flow through her damaged throat. Her watery eyes weren't able to focus. She blinked rapidly and stared at her left forearm, that was stinging from the fangs. She expected long gashes in the fabric and lots of blood, but her suit bore no evidence, none at all. Was it all inside of her head?

Several slaps to the outer surface of the limo and vehement curses punctuated the stale air. Chrystal didn't know if it was Italian or Spanish since the two languages sounded so alike. But even without understanding the words, she knew what they meant. An instant later, the body of Fara Trotter landed on top of her.

The door slammed. With the same sucking sound as a pneumatic pump, the interior of the limousine became frigid, but Chrystal couldn't focus on that. There was too much physical contact.

Shit! The vision started instantly, without any time to prepare.

The physical space was pure dark and still, yet filled with expectancy. Despite the absence of light, Chrystal knew two women faced each other. Their lips moved in perfect synchronization. One complete cycle later, their hands joined, and a ball of light formed, small as a marble. Just like in the limo, the swirling light tucked and flowed, tumbling into and over itself, but this one was exponentially more powerful. Suspended within its own power, it rose from their hands and provided illumination of their faces. One was a middle-aged Magdalene Lucedio, and the other was the blond noblewoman from Chrystal's other visions. They both wore white ceremonial robes and matching rings, sequenced to parallel the other. Violet to violet. Blue to blue, and so forth. Thin beams of those same pure colors arced from one to another. The gyrating sphere neared the arching rainbows. Similar to a celestial object, the mass of the orb attracted the arching rainbow, bending the light to its will.

Their bejeweled fingers spread. The rainbow filaments formed an outer sphere, like electrons encircling an atom. Those new filaments were less dense, swirling in thin threads that looked like spun angel hair. The colors collided, forming the brackish mix.

Instead of continuing to rise, the ball of light descended to illuminate a prone body on a stone floor, as gray and cold as the orb. Even though dark hair obscured some of the woman's naked body, Chrystal recognized the embodiment of Snow White. Rarely did she have multiple visions of the same individuals, and yet underneath it all, she knew this would be the final one.

The radiant definition of the human soul surfaced, outlining the body, so much brighter and clearer than any she had ever encountered.

As the women's mouths continued the repetitive chant, they raised their hands and then lowered them again. The rhythm was familiar, pulsing in time to a standard heartbeat, and they gestured for the pulse of life to connect with the soul and rise.

It did not.

Their concentration deepened, their faces aging from the strain. Still, the life force remained a protective coating over Snow White.

With a signal felt more than seen, they surrendered the vitality from their own souls, and the ball of light greedily fed, growing brighter than a star, yet it wasn't white light. The taint of evil deepened it into blood red. A visible pulse throbbed, and purple spidery veins strained to break the surface.

In direct response, the soul attached to the body glowed more brightly and took on the appearance of ... of ...

Chrystal couldn't believe what she was seeing. She had recognized the body of Snow White who had to be Mercede de las Torres, but rising above it was Fara Trotter, the real Faradahl Alecto Trotter. Her soul was magnificent, sparkling with power.

Something had changed within Fara since Chrystal had slept unprotected in her former bunk. A new potency fueled her, operating on a level that was beyond human capacity. At some point, she had been touched with divine privilege. That had to be how she had created the vortex at Fort San Cristobal, and not only survived, but also cleansed her soul of the unavoidable stains caused by intense violence. Her soul now had the authority, perhaps even the prerogative to fight malevolence. That force now shielded this helpless body from their damning influence.

Again, the women tried to feed upon her, and again, Fara resisted in equal measure, glimmering like a golden warrior.

Still growing from the energy it was consuming from the two women, the glowing orb now illuminated the entire room. They were in a tomb with neatly stacked slabs for the dead. Each slot was narrow, just large enough for a body to slide within the excavated depths. All of the slabs bore decomposing skeletal remains, save one. The wedge on the upper right was vacant.

The battle raged. Within the stalemate, the room swirled with a maelstrom of rising force, electrifying the atmosphere. Requiring still more power, the two sadistic agents called forth souls, challenging them to rise from their fusty remains. Men, women, and children, oh so many children, reacted to the summons. Perhaps they thought the divine light of heaven finally found them, which was why they came so willingly, but just as their energy connected with the consuming orb, expressions changed from elation to terror. Soul by soul engorged the glowing ball, making it denser and larger, expanding to fill the confines of this tomb and then the entire underground labyrinth of crypts. Upon seeing this consummation, the remaining souls tried to flee, and yet the gravity of the hellacious orb had them.

As with all of her visions, Chrystal was an outside observer, powerless to change the outcome of the scene, but this time, she knew a change was warranted within herself. She had thought Fara Trotter epitomized the evils of the world, but now, her rival wore the golden glow of a righteous soul. Chrystal's heart ached at the thought of her own soul, tainted with enmity and plotted revenge. If Fara could find salvation from her sins, perhaps she could-

She broke with the mushy thought when the air chilled, going stale and lifeless. Evil smut rose into the women's auras, encasing them in a tarry fog. They drew their hands together once again, and the amassed filth flowed into their creation. The ball contracted, shrinking, while turning so black the surrounding light had to flow into it, bending with unrelenting force. Throwing their faces upward with matching screams, they raised the ball of dense matter, and then with that added momentum, threw it down onto Mercede's chest.

The explosion blinded Chrystal's every sense. Even her ears rang from the intensity of the concussion and then everything sucked in.

Nothing.

The world was as vacant and dead as deep space.

Slowly, as if it took the condensation of primordial ages to recover, awareness finally eased back into Chrystal's surroundings. It was cold, and she shivered. All of the warmth in the world was gone.

She waited, expecting to awaken back in the limousine, but the vision wasn't over. She was still in the crypt, but not alone. The embodiment of darkness was with her.

In the center of the small stone room, Mercede's body lay on the dusty floor.

She didn't move.

She didn't breathe.

Mercede was more than dead. Her body had withered. Every ounce of life and energy had been sucked out of her to leave a desiccated corpse. Chrystal had seen Egyptian mummies with more mass.

Her awareness continued to expand, and she saw the two women, collapsed alongside the dead body, equally naked, as if the negative force demanded even the fabric of their gowns as it had consumed the fabric of time and space. In front of Chrystal's eyes, the decomposition continued. Magdalene shriveled, losing her physical form as if her skin was less vital than a fancy balloon. It shrank into and upon itself until it turned into a deep red orb, no larger than a jewel. The bloody light continued to decay, seeping into the cracks and pores of the stones.

Anna's chest moved, struggling to inhale vital breath. Her hair had lost its golden glow, and large clumps had fallen out of her scalp. Deep lines of wrinkles covered the once smooth and vital complexion. She stirred, and in stilted movements, staggered to her feet, her bones almost too fragile to hold her upright.

Her withered hands rose, summoning another dark connection to the black energy. The noxious substance slithered toward the remnants of Mercede's body. Spreading into bands, it lifted the corpse and slipped it onto the available slab.

Staggering backwards, Anna doubled over, bracing her jeweled fingers on the archway. The gems were drab, barely holding a trace of their former color. She sipped in long breaths, inhaling the very essence of life. The temperature chilled again. The air became vacant and still. Not even a spider would have enough energy to live in that accursed place. Anna absorbed every bond to the living world, leaving a negative vacuum in her wake.

With the last vestige of her energy, she recited the final incantation and metaphysically sealed the tomb.

The attachment to the vision faded, yet darkness still surrounded her. There was no sense of motion, no sense of others near. She definitely wasn't in the limousine. After listening to the quiet for several minutes, her normal human senses grew acute. The singular sound of running water meandered in the distance, and the scent of forgotten decay sweetened the stale air.

No, not the hypogeum under Purgatorio ad Arco!

She tried to move, but her hands and feet were bound. All she could do was turn her head. Both directions were dark and damp, almost vacant of the elements that composed the physical world. She sniffed the air, and it too was empty. And yet, she sniffed again. There was another scent, of ozone and something smoky, like a piney forest recently burned.

Pulling at her bonds, they wouldn't loosen. She wiggled hoping to bump a wall or table, something she could use to help gain her feet.

In immediate response to her movement, chanting words started slowly, filling the air with resonant sound. Immediately Chrystal froze, and although she tried not to listen, she had to. She had no choice. Her ears were starved for input, and the words swirled into her mind. The darkness seeped into every thought, stealing it from her mind until nothing was left, not even the wherewithal to know how to breathe or how her heart should beat. The tarry substance oozed through her veins, absorbing every ounce of energy her body contained, and only then did it start to eat at her soul.

The negativity became tangible, embodying thoughts and giving voice to the darkness, slipping into every fiber where blood had once traveled. All of the other voices and impressions faded, leaving only this dark passenger. A shiver ran up her spine, and it felt strangely good.

CHAPTER 29

"Keep driving." Gae leaned an elbow on the back of Renzo's seat, motioning the direction with a quick nod. "Make a left."

J.C. understood Italian, but he didn't understand why they passed the church with pillars crowned with skulls, especially when the doors stood wide open and a couple of regular-looking tourists were in the courtyard. "That was it. Purgatorio ad Arco. Wasn't it?" He twisted with each phrase, trying to keep the church in sight.

Gae didn't answer and just kept giving Renzo directions. The vehicle stopped at the curb four blocks and two turns away. "We're going in the back way, through the aqueduct."

"What?" J.C.'s patience was shot, and every frayed nerve screamed for action. "Fara's somewhere in that underground mausoleum. Why would you waste time? Right now every minute counts."

"Which is why we have to be smarter than our adversaries. It's a trap. It has to be. That's why it's so, so, open. It's better to come through the back of the crypt and surprise them." He punctuated each syllable with cutting sharpness, while the stress etched into the lines creasing his face.

J.C. didn't care how high-strung the hombre was; they had to take the offensive. Whenever 007's femme fatale was in trouble, Bond would take the direct route and rescue her in the nick of time. Strangely, he was really more of the James Bond out of the two of them, even if he had never been a secret agent. That upped his confidence a notch. "Fara's life's at stake. We don't have hours to play it safe."

The Italian ignored him, checking the supplies in her backpack one more time. His long and spindly fingers squeezed the rounds of rope.

Anger heated J.C.'s gut, burning away the underlying fear. "Fine, do whatever you want. I'm walking back and going through the front doors. Nobody knows me. Or what I look like. They won't give a damn if I come walking through."

The man's face turned crimson, but he didn't try to stop J.C. who opened the door and stepped out onto the curb in front of a club. A neon sign in the blacked out window flickered on to read "Karaoke" and shut off again.

"That's the signal." Silently, Gae had left the cab and sneaked up on J.C., giving him a shove toward the metal door.

"For you maybe." He used the momentum to his advantage and twisted to the side. Returning, he leaned through the driver's window and shot a look at Ted in the passenger's seat. His sightless eyes fluttered open, and he said something so slurred it was impossible to understand. Still, drugged ineptitude was better than being out cold.

If it had been up to the asshole, he would have left him behind. The hombre had no sense of right and wrong. Anyway, once Ted regained his snap, he would be able to help them read the energy, or at the very least, keep Chrystal occupied once they found her.

J.C. nodded to the driver and practiced the Italian pronunciation once more in his head, then said, "You'll stay here with him, right?" He pointed at Ted.

"I stay here." The driver responded in heavy English and smiled, showing crooked, yellow teeth so long they looked like ancient ivory piano keys. "I stay here and smoke." He pulled a pack of American Marlboro reds out of his pocket.

The twang of addiction twisted inside J.C. He hadn't had a smoke for hours. He held out his hand. "Can I have a cig?"

The need for nicotine transcended any language, and the driver did an expert flick of his wrist. A single cigarette popped up from the foil corner of the pack. J.C. pulled it out and nodded his thanks. Just knowing he had a cigarette in his hand made him feel better.

Purposefully not looking at Gae, he headed down the block. The wind was blowing in his face. He had to be walking west since the breeze had been coming off from the coast. The sky was overcast, but it hadn't started raining, at least not yet. The air had that feeling to it though; the expectancy of the first raindrop hung inside the heavy clouds.

He turned the corner and leaned behind the next stone building in a calm eddy away from the steady wind. Only once he pulled the lighter out of his jeans did he notice how tattered and dirty he was. He had wanted to blend in, and now he looked like a vagrant. Hell, maybe that was good. Most of society purposely didn't see the indigent.

With a sigh, he lit the cigarette. The first inhale was always the best, especially after going several hours without a smoke. It was almost pure satisfaction, relieving that tight ache inside of his gut.

Relief.

Pleasure.

Fulfillment.

He could come up with a dozen justifications and just as many descriptions of satisfaction. Best of all, it felt normal.

Inside his mind, it calmed his challenging fear. Okay, maybe the church was a trap. Maybe it wasn't. Regardless, he had to do it. He had to do it for Fara.

In long and deliberate strides, he continued down the narrow sidewalk. He glanced at his watch, a little after 9:00 a.m. It would be midafternoon back home. He didn't want to think about how many hours he had gone without sleep. God, he wished he had slept on the plane like Chrystal.

Although she was twitchy and bitchy, he never thought she would betray them. Something else had to have happened. Someone came into the house, drugged Ted, picked up her unconscious body, found the skull, and took Fara. They would have had them under surveillance, waiting for the right moment to strike after she fainted and they entered the room.

His stomach tumbled, feeling sick. Put that way, it didn't seem likely. He took another long drag to steady his nerves. He hated to admit how Gae's scenario was more probable, especially within the tight time frame. This all happened in less than ten minutes. Fifteen tops. He knew better than anyone how the world could change in a matter of minutes. But that didn't necessarily mean the asshole was right about the church.

Another prolonged drag sizzled through the paper, and he let it slowly slide out through his nose. In the morning air, he probably looked like a Chinese dragon. He glanced at the other people hurrying down the street. No one except a young girl noticed, and her mother tugged on her hand a second later.

J.C. turned the corner and saw the open space in front of the church about mid-block. On the edge of the sidewalk, a public trashcan with an arched top had a basin filled with sand for cigarette disposal. He then looked at his hand. About two drags were left on his borrowed cig. Inhaling, he chuckled to himself at the ironic phrase. No one gave back a burnt cigarette. After all of this was said and done, he'd buy a carton for the driver. The man was Johnny on the spot and did exactly want Gae requested. Cab drivers usually did what their fares told them, but this went beyond that, like something out of a made for TV miniseries or even a comic book movie. The Phantom or the Shadow each had a driver as their accomplice. The way Renzo revered Gae was more like that, like the Italian owned him blood allegiance.

Nonchalantly, J.C. studied the street. The people looked normal, going about their business. The parked cars appeared empty. Really, no one other than him was loitering suspiciously. Taking the final puff, he fortified his courage. Fara came back for him in Fort San Cristobal. He had to do the same or else he could never be her equal. If he wasn't her equal, she wouldn't want him. This shit sucked, but she was worth it. He didn't want to live without her.

His fingers twisted the butt into the sand next to a discarded Camel filter. One thing about Italians, they loved their American cigarettes. Taking a definitive step toward the church, J.C. felt better. Instead of playing it safe, he was now a man of action, controlling his destiny, which definitely included Fara.

He heard a soft, squeaky rub of a step behind him.

J.C. stretched his stride and adjusted the cadence of his steps to favor his right leg. The footfalls behind him continued perfectly timed to his own. If his hearing hadn't been so jacked up, he might not have even noticed. Shit! He was being followed.

His pulse jumped and breathing lurched. The flowing adrenaline told him to take off into a run, but he stalled that urge. He had to stay cool, like 007. What would Bond do?

The corner of the hip-high metal pole and sloping chain fence delineating the edge of the church's property was getting closer. In five strides he would be there. When he turned the corner, he'd take it sharply and would be able to see who was following him. But then what?

He'd be tackled and shoved inside a waiting car.

The double doors to the sanctuary were open, and from this angle, he saw about a dozen or so parishioners sitting in the back of the church. He'd go inside, and if the person was still following him, at least there would be witnesses. Someone might even intervene, or at least call the cops.

Stretching his stride, he headed toward the doors between two skull-encrusted columns. The following footsteps rang out on the stones of the courtyard. Whoever was following him was wearing boots or dress shoes with hard soles.

A priest in dark robes appeared in the doorway and held up his hands shaking them gently toward the sky, as if thanking God for a response to an unuttered prayer.

"Ciao," J.C. forced a pleasant smile and called out from about ten feet away, still a little too far to be nonchalant, but he didn't care. "I'm with *Ghost*-"

The priest gave him a startled glance and then looked past him, gesturing to the person who was following him. "Greatness to God you are alive. Signor Caravaggio, I'm so glad you have arrived. Capitan Abercia waited for you. Unfortunately, he left about twenty minutes ago."

J.C. stopped and turned.

Gae's chiseled stress lines were even darker, sucking in his hollow cheeks and making the relief of his cheekbones devilish even in the soft morning mist.

"What happened?" The cropped words struck with the deliberate quickness of a venomous snake.

The priest visibly wilted.

A wave of Gae's hand told J.C. to go ahead, but he didn't want to. He lurked just inside the doorway to hear what the priest had to say. Gae's dark stare narrowed, communicating he would deal with him later, and then he addressed the priest again without any polite decorum. "What happened?"

The phrase, *shaking in his boots*, came to mind, but it wasn't the right metaphor. The priest was wearing traditional leather sandals, similar to his own pair, except for the soles. His were made of rubber, nearly soundproof, which made them perfect to wear while taping *Ghost Lovers*.

The priest cleared his throat. "Vandals destroyed Lucia's crypt. Sometime last night. I know you specifically told me not to let anyone in, but Signorita Caravaggio was insistent."

Gae's face turned a chalky white, and his voice deepened. "Who accompanied my cousin?"

"Her mother, of course, your bodyguard, and Signora Lucedio."

Bodyguard?

J.C. shot a stare at Gae, who returned a motion with his head for J.C. to leave. Like hell! He crossed his arms in response. Gae's narrowed eyes glared, but the priest must have thought the intense expression was intended for him.

Now visibly shaking, the priest continued. "There was an explosion. So violent it shook the church on its foundations. When I went to investigate, the bodyguard was carrying Signorita Caravaggio up the stairs, but he claimed she was unhurt. Your aunt and Signora Lucedio confirmed she had just fainted."

"And the police came." The words formed deep within his throat, growling out intently.

"Later. I tried contacting you first, Don Gaetano." He bowed his head and nodded toward his hands, clasped so tightly his knuckles were white. "I called throughout the night. I had to do something, so I phoned Capitan Abercia before morning mass. I feared you had died in the blast."

Don Gaetano closed his eyes and looked as if he was asking a silent prayer. "Are there any bodies?"

"None were found during the initial investigation, but Father Dominic did not arrive for morning prayers. We checked his room, and it appeared as if he never returned last night."

"What of my cousin, Aleri? How is she?"

"She responded to Capitan Abercia's call since he couldn't locate you." The priest looked him up and down. "Are you alright, my Don?"

"I will be." He glanced past J.C. toward the front of the church. "Is anyone in the underground?"

"No, but an officer is posted at the entrance."

"I want to see what happened."

"Of course, Don Caravaggio." The priest walked past J.C. without a glance.

"Father Rugo," Gae stopped when his shoulders were in line with J.C.'s, and with a huff added, "This is Signor Calderon, with *Ghost Lovers*." Blankly, as if an afterthought, he added, "He will be accompanying me."

The father reverently nodded his head toward him. "I'm afraid the hypogeum is destroyed. You will need to find another location for your television program."

"*Ghost Lovers* can wait. Did you see Fara Trotter this morning?" J.C. knew he was speaking Italian with a Spanish accent, but the embarrassment over his pronunciation had faded.

"Signora Trotter was with Father Dominic yesterday afternoon. I didn't see either of them leave, and then Don Caravaggio joined them, but the good Capitan said there were no bodies, at least no recent human remains, found near the site of the explosion."

"Did Abercia's men search the remainder of the crypt?"

"They found nothing." The words were empty, rote, as if memorized.

On most occasions, J.C. liked old churches. They contained manicured feelings of consistency from the ritualistic ceremonies, but this one was different. Purgatorio ad Arco was disturbed, as if this part above ground was the rattling top to a pressure cooker. God, he wished Ted was with them to describe what the psychic light looked like because something otherworldly had happened here. Anyone with any sensitivity was able to feel it.

Parishioners were everywhere, hundreds more than his original estimation. Why they were here, in this church, rather than any of the hundreds of other churches in the area? Some knelt and fingered rosary beads. Others sat on the wooden chairs with heads bent in prayer. In the alcove to the left of the main altar, a line of at least twenty waited to light candles. The entire wrought iron rack was ablaze, and the golden light illuminated a statue of the Virgin Mary with Baby Jesus in her arms. The magnificent effect added a golden glow to their cheeks, making them look alive.

J.C. had grown up with Catholic friends. Lighting a vigil candle was a way of extending one's prayer and showing solidarity with the person on whose behalf the prayer was offered, but the vast majority of these candles were votives, which indicated seeking some favor from the saint.

"...And the benediction of God came to show us this sign..."

"...Your miracles shine upon the souls lost and long forgotten..."

"...Resurrection of those in purgatory..."

Apparently, all of these parishioners came today thinking the explosion was divine.

"...Affirming the power of goodness over the darkness of evil..."

In some ways, J.C. regretted not having a traditional upbringing in the church. At the time, his friends thought he was the lucky one who had Sunday as a play day. If they had only known about his grandfather's true religion, none of them would have ever set foot into his house.

"...In the one light of Christ, our prayers rise up to Heaven..."

J.C. shivered at the power of their combined belief, rolling off in tangible waves.

They were the generator.

He turned, looking for Gae and saw the curl of the priest's dark robe disappear behind the golden altar. Jostling through the waiting crowd, J.C. round the corner to a small marble room. The sentry had a hand on a trap door. Gae and the priest were gone.

"Wait, I'm with them." J.C. panted while skidding to a stop.

"Who are-?" The man's deep voice rumbled.

"Gae, Gaetano!" J.C. shouted and heard his voice echo across the chamber and probably into the sanctuary. "Tell him who I am."

A hand braced the inside of the door, and a dark head poked up through the narrow opening. "He's with me." He said none too enthusiastically.

The uniformed guard leveraged the door and allowed J.C. to pass onto a steep staircase. With each step, the air grew still and dark. His senses sent shocks of warning throughout his system, but he refused to falter now that he was so close. With a quick inhalation, he charged down the staircase and through the metal gate into an underground cavern.

Instead of sensations pouring into him, blank nothing prevailed. That in and of itself was abnormal. In his three-year stint with *Ghost Lovers*, he had been to dozens of haunted locations. None of them felt like this. The tomb was overtly dead and unnaturally cold. Underground locations were usually a few degrees cooler than the surface temperature, but not this cold. It felt like the place was on top of a glacier rather than hundreds of feet of volcanic sediment.

He let the held breath out slowly and inhaled even more calculatedly. The charred scent of burnt paper seasoned the space, along with something else. Something he had smelt recently.

The two men continued through the dimly lit vestibule at least thirty feet below him. "Hey, wait." J.C. clicked on his flashlight and ran down the steps and across the large room where low poles and chains delineated dirt graves.

He followed the sound of their footsteps and caught up as they entered a side chamber. Gae walked inside first, and J.C. was right behind him, edging out the aging priest. The explosion took out just the lights and then he remembered the flashlight hanging limply in his hand. Everything had been blown against the walls from the exact center of the room, as if a real bomb had exploded and the concussion of the blast shattered everything in its expanding path. The central circle of bare gray floor was perfectly round except for the narrow walkway which had been cleared in order to enter the room.

"Will you give me that?" It was a cross between an ask and an order, but J.C. didn't argue and handed him the flashlight. Gae shone it on the wall to their left. "That was Lucia's shrine."

Nothing remained intact. Even the crazy neon sign Fara had described was little more than a limp transformer hanging by a cord. Below that were the remnants of a shelf-like structure. Sitting neatly on top of the pile of wood scraps and bone fragments was the upper half of the little cherub Fara had described. He picked it up. It was a piece of plastic dollar-store crap.

Gae stepped closer and spoke over J.C.'s shoulder. "The skulls are gone."

"Skulls?" He glanced back, putting their faces a little too close for comfort. "There was more than just Lucia?"

"The other represented her husband."

Father Rugo clasped his hands, "Although the two souls only had weeks of wedded bliss, their true love was everlasting."

Gae scoffed at the priest. "Those old skulls wouldn't have withstood that blast. They are just bone and dust as is the legend."

An unspoken comment flowed into J.C.'s mind; *someone just wants you to think they were destroyed.* His eyes darted to the shadowy corners and then studied the other two men. They hadn't reacted to the feminine voice.

"That's the crypt," Gaetano swallowed heavily while pointing to his right, "where Fara set down the camera. Nothing's left on top, so you take the right, and I'll take the left. Sift through everything. It's probably blown to bits, but we've got to try. Let's find it and get out of here." He knelt next to the battered grave and swiped a finger down an intact piece of tile, sniffing the sooty residue. "This wasn't gunpowder based, and yet it doesn't have the appearance of plastic explosives either."

"The police said something to the same effect." Father Rugo stated, but J.C. didn't think Gae was expecting a response. Like a bloodhound, he was intent on the moment, emotions switched off.

J.C. mimicked his action and rubbed the soot between his fingers before sniffing it. There was that same scent, deep and woodsy, too pungent to be perfume! His hand flew to his pocket, but he delayed sharing his discovery. Father Rugo was too close to the situation.

Redoubling his effort, clanks of debris being cast aside echoed in the small chamber adding to his anticipation. They were getting close; he felt it in his bones.

Just as Fara had said, this was a historian's nightmare, mixed across the ages. His fingers sifted through dozens of partial paper notes, asking Lucia and the Holy Virgin for assistance. No wonder the Vatican wanted this place closed. Most of the notes were dated, but his curiosity wasn't stronger than his determination. Bits and pieces of dried flowers, wax from candles, singed corners of photographs, and shards of tiny statues were all mixed into a hodgepodge of timeless confusion.

With the next sweep of his hand, a piece of broken glass struck his finger, and a dark bead of shiny blood started rolling. A drop landed a top of the still massive pile of debris. The blood disappeared, instantly absorbed, and the feeling in the crypt changed. He definitely wasn't a psychic, but he had moments of recognition. And right now, his internal perception was humming.

He held out his hand and waited for another drop to fall. A smooth and cool hand slid within his, touching palm to palm. His pulse skipped as the invisible fingers squeezed. Fara filled his mind and soul.

Closing his eyes, he allowed the inner force to guide his other hand. He slid it into the pile, flowing through the pieces without disruption. His forearm was hidden under mementos of the ages, and yet he continued leaning deeper until his arm was buried up to his shoulder. His fingers encountered something hard and flat. Hope surged, and the hand holding his vanished.

With both arms, he skidded the junk off to the side. At the corner of the freestanding crypt and the stone wall, he found the palm-sized mini DV. In the dim light, he couldn't tell if the casing was cracked, but he didn't really give a damn about the camera. All he needed was the tape. J.C. waited, listening to the careful progress Gae was making. He didn't know. He didn't know he had found it!

Worried that he might even hear the rapid thud of his pulse, J.C. hunched down, and just as he had done a thousand times before, switched on the camera with his thumb. A full second ticked by with no result. He twisted it back to off and then clicked it again.

While absently shifting through the pile as a diversion, J.C. used his other hand to pull a battery out of his shirt pocket. Releasing the latch, he exchanged the batteries with practiced swiftness.

His heart was beating at least twice as fast as normal, which made the tape compartment appear to open in slow motion. Again, he rummaged to cover the sound and exchanged the recorded tape with a blank one, snapping the compartment closed.

"What did you find?" Father Rugo bent over him, just as he palmed the recorded tape.

His shout of elation even startled himself. "I found it."

Gae sprang to his feet and leaned over the upper edge of the boxy tomb. "Is it intact? Does it turn on?"

"Surprisingly yes," he held it up and swiveled the screen toward him to show nothing but static. "Either the screen is fried or the tape is. I'll need cables to plug it into a TV to be sure."

"And," the sarcastic tone returned, "You left those back at the house I presume."

"No," J.C. bristled, "I expected the worst and left my bag in the car with Ted."

The dark shadow crept again into Gae's features and etched his scratchy voice. "Give me the camera!"

"No!" J.C. angled his shoulders away from the man and slid the recorded tape into his pocket.

"No? You give it to me, or I'll take it from you."

"Look, this is my equipment." He flipped it over to display the *Property of Ghost Lovers* just above the serial number. "You will be right by my side, and we'll see whatever is on this tape." He tucked the small camera to his side protectively, watching and waiting for Gae's next move.

A growl issued into the cramped space. "I'll give you one more chance. Give me the camera."

If he just gave it to him, it would look suspicious, so J.C. wrapped his other hand around it.

With the swiftness of a professional boxer, Gae placed a jab right on the inside curve of J.C.'s shoulder. His arm went limp, and the momentum made him fall backwards, landing hard on the floor in the center of the room. Gae snatched the camera and stormed out. The priest followed, like a dog that had suffered one too many beatings.

"Mother fucker!" J.C. yelled for good measure, but then his askew grin faded with wonder. On the ceiling was a perfect circle, exactly the same size and shape as the one on the floor. Whatever explosion happened here, it went up, into the church.

Go after them. The voice whispered, once again filling the chamber with hope.

"Hey, you're not leaving me here." With angelic swiftness, he gained his feet and sprinted after the men, climbed the stairs, and caught up to them in the sanctuary. Gauging the approximate distance, he looked across the church. "What's in that direction?" He pointed past the mass of burning candles.

"The seminary." Father Rugo muttered.

J.C. wanted to ask about Father Dominic's room, but already knew the answer. The missing priest had to sleep directly over Lucia's shrine.

CHAPTER 30

Gae gazed up the steep hillside knowing his home was there, as were his ghosts waiting for him in the foggy clouds. Whatever was happening was tied to his world, his home, his personal sanctuary. Whatever was there waited for him, and him alone.

This insanity would end here, today, one way or the other.

But the closer the cab approached, he felt the distance continue to grow. Aleri might already be lost to him, and his stomach twisted, souring at the thought. He leaned back into the seat and rubbed his face. God, he was tired.

Outside the rain fell dark and slow. The steady drops on the roof of the cab weren't helping the throb of a headache. The asynchronous pattern fed the disorder. Normally, a long and slow breath would clear his mind, but not now. The thoughts continued ending in places he refused to accept.

The vitriol anticipation ate his stomach from the inside out. Whatever happened to Aleri would be on the tape, along with his damning conversation with Fara, when she accused him of wanting to murder her. That was always in the back of his mind, rotating like a carnival's carousel, coming back around to the same conclusion. She was an articulate person, so her words weren't misplaced. In her mind, he was the Godfather who extorted money from the innocent. Nothing she said could have cut him deeper, except perhaps for her to say she had never loved him.

"Shit," he muttered to himself. He had to erase that tape before Boy Blunder discovered what it contained. If J.C. knew any of that information, he would be too dangerous to remain alive.

Just the thought of killing edged adrenaline into his blood, finally easing his headache. Taking all of the tomorrows from someone was a unique high. All of that potential energy fled at the moment of death, and in some macabre way, fed his soul.

Or tainted it. His victims appeared once again within his mind. Perhaps they tethered their fallen existence to him. J.C.'s death would just add another in the purgatorial chain of his own construction, just like Phillip Marley, Charles Dickens' legendary ghost.

Ghosts? Jesus, he pressed his left fist to his temple. He had to step out of the Twilight Zone and focus on finding Fara. But what then? If they did find her and bring her back into the world of the living, just who would she choose?

While still appearing to be watching the road, he cast a sideways glance. The Puerto Rican did have a way about him, not sophistication, rather wholesome sincerity. Normal human behavior indicated people seek out an opposite extreme after a deep pain. He didn't blame Fara for being angry, but once he saved her, she would realize he was the right man for her, not that Puerto Rican.

J.C. described the way the energy, or lack of it, felt in Lucia's vault, while the church brimmed with potency, and Ted nodded in response. The blind man was astute, and not really blind. He pointed to the road and described the shape crossing back and forth. Then, almost as an afterthought, he added, "But this is the first time I've ever seen a zigzag."

"What?" Gae blurted out, startling everyone.

"A residual trail leads up the hillside switching back and forth like a zigzag, my sister said-."

Gae cut him off. "That's the shape of the road. Are you saying they came this way?"

"Most definitely, but this residue isn't normal. A regular physic line emanates in either red-."

"Or blue, yeah, we got that part. What's going on here?" In a few minutes, they'd be home. He had to learn what he was up against. What was waiting for him within his infiltrated fortress?

Ted started again, just as slowly and methodically. "The color of this psychic singularity is either damaged or cloaked. Perhaps, this is something else entirely." He shrugged and then ducked toward the dash to look up the remainder of the hill. "The line looks like the description of pollution or sludge."

"Are you sure it's not just oil on the surface of the road?"

"I've never seen oil, but I can see this. The psychic residue is clinging to the surface, too heavy in its degradation to float midair, but regardless, it's there."

Gae's heart doubled its pace. "How long ago? Can you tell?"

"There's no way to know, except it's strong." He leaned an elbow on the back of the front seat and turned. "Whatever we're hunting has scratched its way into this world, leaving smut in its path."

Hunting? Dear God! He was hunting Aleri or whatever it was she had become. Just what happened to her?

The cab was almost at the gate, and his pulsed raced. "Describe it to me again. Just what is it?"

"I told you. I don't know, but I can tell you why it's different. Psychic light draws upon the luminosity of the human chakras, depending on the type and intensity of the emotion. An aura is the emanation of that colorful light. Right now you are turning a deeper orange, which means you're frustrated and getting angry. Whatever came this way didn't contain any human light."

"So it's not human."

Ted shrugged. "There is no chakra color to the trail. This is the first time that I've ever seen something like this."

J.C. asked, "What about in San Cristobal?"

"Even there, the light contained color. This is absent of that. Like," his face turned up in thought, "like it's being formed from the antithesis of life."

Gae felt his anger ripen. "Isn't that death?"

"Not at all. Death is part of the natural cycle of life. That's why this is so rare. I wish that I had my full spectrum camera to document the find. This is the stuff of a bestselling book."

"Great," Gae wheezed more than said the word. He was going to end up on the next episode of *Fact or Fiction*. How in the hell was he going to keep his identity secret?

"Okay boss, road's blocked," the driver stopped the cab with a squeaky rub of wet brakes just before a broad metal gate. "Where to now?"

His skin prickled from being called boss, but the sensation didn't last for long. Tucking the hood over his head, he stepped into the rain. Using his back as a shield to maintain his privacy, he punched in the security code on the device next to the driveway. Oddly, the rainwater felt good, pure and natural. Instead of getting back into the cab, he started walking toward the house up the slant of the curve and waved the cab toward the wide area in front of the house. Just a day earlier, he stood here with Fara, and now his life was shattered, just that fast. He snapped his fingers, but they were too wet to make a sound.

Anyone who was inside would know he was here. A chime, similar to a doorbell, rang whenever the gate opened. At any moment, he expected his guards to rush out of the house. To be on the safe side, he held up an open palm to his rag-tag allies, signaling to wait in the cab.

Above him, the outcropping of the hill kept silent vigil. It knew what had happened here. Once again, he sensed the same feeling of movement he had experienced at the Siren's Palace, as if the hill leaned just a little closer to his home in an unspoken reply.

"This is wrong." He flipped back the dripping hood to stare at the house full on. The windows were dark, bearing no sign of life, yet they seemed to watch him, anticipating the moment when he would step inside, as if daring him to do so.

While protecting the camera clutched under his hoody, he swallowed his irrational fear and ran for the front door. The raindrops intensified, pushing him away. Summoning his moral strength, he succeeded ascending the steps and faced the closed door. Absently, he felt for his gun, and the motion brought an empty pang, hitting him in the gut.

Flinging the door open, he crouched low and pounced inside the foyer. His muscles were fast and ready, anticipating an attack.

Nothing moved.

The hall was dark, darker than just dark. Technically, it was around midday, but the inside of his house was as dim as the lightless crypt and felt equally empty.

Except hidden within the obscurity, something was there. The embodiment of evil clung to every corner, fitting against the lines and angles of the home he had known his entire life. Every nerve within his body told him so. Systematically, his gaze swung to every point of entry. He studied each steady shadow.

Nothing moved.

Nothing changed.

No one was at their posts. At all times, day and night, someone was on duty.

None of this made sense.

He glanced up to the second and then the third-floor landing. No one was there. Normally the palm trees obscured the view, at least partially. Even they were out of place. His father planted those tree with his own hands. If someone had fucked with them-

He stalled the need to call out for Aleri, and in two determined strides, was at the wall and hit the light switch. His hands turn instantly cold, and the precious camera tumbled out, clattering onto the floor. Nothing in all of his combat training prepared him for what he saw.

The guards were at their posts, at least what remained of them. At every position around the room, the men were little more than desiccated lumps, looking more like a pile of shit than the remnants of a man.

Gae looked to the lines of the gabled glass roof, expecting to see the vile perpetrator waiting to pounce down and suck the life out of him. The foul air, deeply encased with the unnatural fog, blocked out all detail.

He knelt next to the closest body and recognized the silk shirt, which appeared undamaged and pristinely clean. He extended a shaking hand toward the shriveled flesh but couldn't bring himself to touch Eduin. With a finger and thumb, he gingerly pulled back the overly loose garments. The man's 357 was holstered.

While vigilant for the malevolent countenance that had committed this inhuman act, Gae noted each guard, one at a time, going from station to station. All of their guns were holstered. Whatever had done this caught eight trained men unaware. The last body was his friend, Mario.

Gae's wet clothes seemed to shrink, sticking to his skin. The resulting chill went down into his bones.

Aleri!

In a swooping arc, he drew the man's Glock 22 and charged up the staircase, but he stopped midway. The palm trees were more than wilted. Just like the men, their shriveled forms had been stripped of vitality.

"Holy shit!" J.C. shouted.

Startled, Gae swiveled toward the front doors, pointing the barrel of the gun while flicking off the safety with instinctual precision.

J.C. and Ted stood shoulder to shoulder in the entryway, not reacting to the loaded gun. Gae lowered the barrel and clicked on the safety.

"What happened to them?" J.C.'s voice shook.

Gae didn't even know if he could talk; a giant lump had formed in his throat. Even if he could speak, what would he say? He didn't have any answers. Right now, he had to find Aleri.

Turning his back on the men, he ran the rest of the way to the second floor. Trying not to look at the house, he focused forward. Yet, motion came around him in a rush, the hallway growing longer within his despair. At a full run, he traversed the distorted distance.

He wasn't prepared for what he might find, but still he didn't hesitate, throwing Aleri's bedroom door open. Just like the rest of the house, darkness enshrouded her room so thickly it was impossible to see. He hit the light switch, holding his breath, afraid to see what might await him. The curtains hung limply around the antique bed providing thin glimpses of rumpled sheets.

Suddenly out of nowhere, the similarity between Aleri's bed to the one in the room that time forgot made his head reel. Maybe this was what happened there. Maybe this was what made it get stuck in time.

The chill in his bones went even deeper, hardening his arteries until his blood didn't even want to pulse. Holding his breath, he extended one foot, and then the other, step after step, moving stealthily except for the steady squeak of his ruined boots. Near the footboard was another body. The clothing belonged to Aunt Elena. Normally, he would detach his personal self, but there was just too much. He felt sick.

His fingers grasped the light fabric hanging around the bed, one hand on each side. Slowly, he let out his breath. *Steady. Steady.* Both wrists flicked back each side of the curtains.

Aleri wasn't here! Relief immediately charged his system, but then fear superseded its place. If not here or the crypt, then where?

CHAPTER 31

Nothing in this house was like anything Ted had ever encountered. Rather than the blankness he normally saw during the day, a smutty fog filled this house, akin the oily residue on the road, equally foul and heavy. He sniffed the air, expecting the acrid scent of smoke, but there was nothing.

He stared at the now almost imperceptible line where Gaetano's blazing aura charged up the staircase. The smutty fog had parted and then folded back upon itself, sealing the rift where he had gone in lumpy puffs. Ted held his hand out in front of him, trying to feel the texture. Hollow. Empty. Void. And yet, something tangible filled this place, a clashing disharmony.

"Dios mio." J.C.'s words sank in the heavy air, adding to the clogging despair.

"What's wrong?" Ted turned, trying to see what he was examining, but other than J.C.'s aura, nothing was there except the thick darkness. And then, from an indeterminable depth behind him, a golden beacon cut through the dense fog. Not believing his eyes, he closed them tightly and then reopened to the same effect.

"Oh my God! It's beautiful." He rushed toward the shining light and tripped on steps, falling onto his knees. His normal embarrassment didn't rise, not worried about anything except finding the source of the glorious splendor. Like an infant, he crawled on all fours until the floor leveled.

"Dude, it's just a library." J.C.'s voice was close, but not right behind him.

In the center of the room, a round item glowed with flames, adding light and dimension to the entire room. Within that golden flame, red psychic fire lifted from the circular surface but specifically from something long and narrow, just like how his sister described the wick of the lantern she'd bring with them into the desert.

Curiosity drew him forward, like a moth to a flame, and Ted extended his hands over the surface. He twisted his fingers, watching how the flames slipped and realigned, while willing himself to feel what he was seeing. With a sigh, he stopped.

Only Chrystal had that ability. No matter how much he wished he would be able to sense through touch, his talent just didn't work that way. Chrystal was difficult at times, but underneath the hardened exterior, he knew she meant well. He couldn't, wouldn't believe she had tried to kill him. His partner was missing, and he had no way to know where she had gone. Once he fully awakened, he called the agency. At least they confirmed her beacon was still active, which meant she was alive. A replacement agent was on his way, but it would be another twelve hours until he arrived. Ted was now in charge and had to investigate the anomalies.

One was right in front of him, and he had no way of documenting it. He so wished they'd go back for his camera, but Gaetano had squashed that idea. Without documentation, all of this paranormal activity would be a personal report, which were a dime a dozen.

Lowering his hands into the brilliant glow, Ted's fingertips encountered fabric with a deeply textured, woven grain. The cloth was heavy, and as he lifted the edge, it glowed with its own presence, as if saturated with the emanating force. A deep and woodsy scent drifted. He tugged the edge up to his nose, enjoying the rich aroma. Closing his eyes, he concentrated on the fragrance and remembered. Frankincense. He sniffed again. Yes! Definitely frankincense. This relic held some religious purpose.

Opening his eyes, a fissure of radiance beamed from the exposed edge. Ted had heard of giant searchlights, so bright they could be seen for miles. This round emanation had to be a searchlight, but why would it be inside the house? No wonder they kept it covered with metallic fabric. He tugged harder, pulling with both arms, and as soon as he drew off the cover, the item embedded in the surface ignited.

Ted outlined the shape about the width of his hand. It had a pointed end, a shaft about twenty-four inches long, and the far end narrowed like a handle. It was too long to be a knife and too short to be a traditional sword. Deep crimson clung to its sides, indicating it had seen violence, and the very tips of the edges were highlighted with white vortices. It had released many souls from their earthly bonds, so it had to be a weapon, a close, hand-to-hand short sword.

His fingertips drifted over the table's surface, round and smooth. The sword was under a layer of glass. He traced the edge, feeling for the seam, but it had been inlaid so perfectly the edge of where glass met wood was almost imperceptible, even to his sensitive fingertips. He felt foolish for thinking it was a searchlight. Realistically, this had to be a table with the blade displayed under the surface.

Ted heard someone step into the room and looked up. Two figures stood near the entrance, one had to be J.C. He emerged from Lucia's crypt with his ring regenerated. Its green glow clearly indicated his identity, but his aura was seething with anger. The other was opposite, ocean blue, cool and patient. Whatever Gaetano had found upstairs had quickly settled his aura.

He nodded to the shapes. "Would you tell me what's in this?"

"My God, look at that!" J.C. hurried toward him.

Ted tried to touch the outline again. "What is it?"

"A gladius, a gladiator's sword. It looks authentic."

"Of course it's authentic." Gaetano's churl slid across the room, drawing Ted's attention. His aura wasn't blue or calm. He was confused with flickers of heated anger rising in intensity. That was impossible. No one's aura could shift that quickly.

"Did you find your cousin?" J.C.'s anger visibly projected with each word. Ted didn't know J.C. for very long, and yet he thought he knew him well. He was furious.

"No. No one else is in the house." Gae said it a little too quickly to sound certain. "How's the camera?"

"Fried." J.C.'s voice lifted sharply, almost adding a syllable, while his anger embedded deeper into his core. "There's no

314

hope of recovering the information. Whatever happened in the crypt released electromagnetic energy."

Ted watched the lie twist around him, and it fueled another flow of anger rolling in heated waves.

Silence descended, filling the room with dueling expectancy, and then thunder rolled. The sky gathered clouds and assembled a storm, one that Ted could actually see! Outside of the windows, long fingers reached out from the heavens. Spikes of sizzling light branched ever closer, as if a sentient entity was taking long strides towards them. After each burst, thunder crackled, exploding within the wet air, only to be followed by another bolt striking even closer. The next struck the glass. Ted's heart raced, pounding in his ears, which suddenly filled with the thunderous roar. As if riding the sound waves, dozens of humanoid forms appeared, their auras bright and brilliant.

"What the fuck!" J.C. dropped something that clattered to the floor. "Who are they?"

"You can see them?" Gaetano staggered backwards, bumping into the table.

"I do too." Ted added. Arms developed from the aural mass, reaching to touch the glass, and then he saw the blade respond to their summons, resonating within the same wavelength.

The volume of the storm increased, adding woeful moans of condemnation to the cacophonous roar of rain and wind. Then, a heavier drumming created rhythm out of the chaos. The ghosts' hands beat upon the exterior glass along with the rain.

"What do you want from me?" Gaetano screamed over the noise.

Ted understood their need. "They want the blade; it's a catalyst, a rallying point. They are drawn to its light. Can you get it out of the glass?"

Gaetano didn't even turn to look. "It's sealed, and the glass is over an inch thick."

J.C. set his hand firmly on the top of the table. The glow was at least twice as bright, lighting the flesh of his hand until his bones showed. "Do you think exposing it is a good idea?"

"Just because we get it out doesn't mean we give it to them." Gaetano's fear flared and then determination rose. "I know it's tied up into this mess. It's my aunt's séance table. She got it from Magdalene Lucedio. Every Friday night, they tried to commune with the dead. That woman is at the heart of the problem."

"Shit!" J.C. rushed to the other side, "Looks like they succeeded in gathering quite a following." He touched Ted's shoulder. "Are you sure this is a good idea?"

Ted nodded his reply, while watching the forms writhe against the glass. It formed a barrier, one they couldn't cross.

The two men leveraged the massive table on end and flung the edge down onto the floor. The thud was nearly unintelligible within the noise of the furious storm.

Ted joined Gaetano who was examining the surface. "Nothing."

J.C. was on the other side. "Let's take apart the base, and we can come up under the blade." He twisted the life-size lion's face, and the circular top just turned with it like a wheel.

"Brace it." J.C. sat on the floor and kicked out with both legs against the protruding maw.

The seal broke, and the old bolt roared its complaint each time he twisted the pedestal. After five kicks, it was loose enough to turn hand over hand. J.C.'s green ring cast circular green cones. He wrestled the base free, and a pungent aroma exploded.

Out from under the main bolt, J.C. lifted chunks of hardened golden sap. "Frankincense! This shit is everywhere."

"It's been used for centuries within religious rites. Every Western religion has a use for the resin." To Ted, they looked like nuggets of gold. "In ancient Egypt, even the resulting ash was used as eyeliner."

"The bitch burned it during every séance. She said it created the right atmosphere for the dead."

"Then, we may need it later." J.C. started filling his pocket with the glowing stones.

A warbling call resonated, humming from the gladius. Ted perked, "Do you hear that?"

Next to him, Gaetano extended his hand through the opening, feeling for a way to disassemble the underside of the table. Absently, he brushed the bottom flat plane of the blade.

"Look!" J.C. pointed to the windows, "They're gone."

"No, they're not." Ted edged past him toward the foyer. "The glass sealed the gladius inside the table, just as the window glass sealed them out of the house. When you broke the seal, they came inside!"

Life forms drifted through the psychic fog, sweeping and soaring while absorbing the negative energy clogging the air, consuming it like a swarm of locusts. Immediately, Ted felt the change. The atmosphere grew lighter, and the presence of daylight returned. "They are cleansing the house."

The blue form appeared directly in front of him, in the center of the cleansing whirlwind. Its arms extended and lifted toward the skylight. More souls fell from the skies, and the cool spirit drew them in, adding their number while exponentially increasing their collective power.

"What's happening Ted?" J.C.'s voice warbled.

"There's a manipulator spirit controlling the others, drawing them toward him. Hundreds if not thousands of souls are joining him." The core psyche drew his hands together, and the spinning vortex grew smaller and denser. Just like the motion of the massive electrical storm, the burdened soul approached, lumbering step after step, while still balancing the spiritual whirlwind in its outstretched hands. "Oh my God."

"Talk to us Ted!"

"He's walking this way." He backed out of the doorway, providing them room. "The controlling spirit is powerful but not malevolent. Let's see what they are going to do."

"As if we have a choice?" Gaetano muttered.

Like a swarming hive, the collective swept across the conservatory, drawing all of the lingering smut from the air, while making a beeline for the table.

"They're heading your way, toward the sword." Ted saw Gaetano back away, leaving the table untended. The buzzing current narrowed into the long and gangly shape of a cyclone, twisting its end this way and that. Sweeping up and over the edge of the table, the funnel's point finally penetrated the vulnerable opening. The blade ignited. "They're entering the sword."

One by one, the horde slipped through the narrow gap and infused the blade with their enjoined power until only the large blue spirit remained.

"Did you hear that?" Gaetano's voice shook, but not with fear.

"No." Ted's heart was racing. "What did you hear?"

"My father just told me to kill the witch."

Immediately, the seal upon the glass released, and the thick surface covering the table fell forward, landing with a startling crash against the floor. The blue soul then entered the gladius.

All was suddenly silent.

The three men stood, waiting and listening for what would happen next.

Natural daylight flooded the room, as if filling the vacuum left from the negative void, and Ted's vision faded back into his customary blindness. His cane was inside the cab, so he extended his fingertips, knowing he was just a few steps away from the glass wall. His hand rose to touch the glass. "This is the same material that covered the table."

Images once again flooded his mind. He closed his eyes and concentrated. Receding thunder rolled, and his eyes flew open. He could still see the storm, a little further south. It hadn't dissipated; it was moving. The swarm was moving to another locale!

"You okay?" J.C. touched his shoulder.

Startled at the contact he jumped. "Yeah," he noticed Gaetano's aural image heading toward the foyer. "Where are you going?"

"My office."

"Why?"

With a grunt, the man stopped, "I have trackers on all of the vehicles. We need to learn where they went in order to find them."

"You don't need to do that." Ted calmly stated as if it was the most obvious concept in the entire world.

With three hurried steps, Gaetano joined them. "What are you looking at?"

"That." He pointed toward the south. "Can you see it?"

The thunderous clouds had moved down the coast. The roiling darkness hung over the point on the Posillipo rise, stirring the uneasy mass. "What is that place?"

"Anna Carafa's palace." Gaetano nearly whispered. But then, turning on heel with a burst of speed and intent, he bent to retrieve the blade still perched within its hollow. He pulled it out, and the blade sank to the floor with a clatter. "Damn!"

"What's wrong? Is it hot?" J.C. took a step, but Ted's hand flew to his shoulder.

"No, it's heavy. The sword has to weigh at least fifty pounds."

"No way. A gladius weighed only a couple of pounds."

"You calling me a weakling?" The sneer leveled the words with a slight hiss, "Or a liar."

"Come off it." J.C. left Ted standing alone and reached for the glowing blade. With effort, he hefted it off from the floor. "That's not possible. There's no way."

"It isn't the steel that's heavy." Ted saw them both turn toward him, and behind them, the blue light leaked out of the blade in an aural emanation. "It's the weight of purgatorial souls."

CHAPTER 32

The streets were wet, and psychic sludge coated the pavement. Unsuspecting motorists crept over the abnormally dark roads toward the Posillipo coastline, ignorant of the danger amassing over Anna Carafa's palace. The steady creep stopped, and the cab stalled. They were close enough to the curve for Gae to see down the highway. At the end of the long line of vehicles, the Siren's Palace loomed pale against the black velvet squall.

"I don't know boss." Renzo shrugged. "Motor's dead." He leaned toward the windshield. "Looks like everybody's in the same boat. If it rains any harder, we'll need a boat."

"Don't call me boss," Gae hissed. "Don Caravaggio will do."

J.C. motioned outside his window, "The entire electrical grid's failed. Look, the signals are out. There aren't any lights on the street or shops."

"No brake lights from the other cars." Renzo meekly added.

An uncomfortable shiver surrounded the cab, and the atmospheric pressure increased. The cold pressed closer, hugging the close confines.

"Holy shit!" Ted wheezed.

Gae hadn't heard Ted swear, not once, and that suddenly made everything go from bad to worse. "What do you see?"

"A black cloud is rolling in like a fog bank, but it's not fog. It's absorbing all of the energy it comes in contact with."

"Shit, look!" J.C. pointed at a shivering terrier huddled in a concave doorway with its tail tucked between spindly legs. "It can tell what's going on."

"A blind man would too!" Gae winced the instant the words left his mouth, but he didn't apologize. "I'm going on, by foot." The handle of the door clicked.

"No!" Ted's scream echoed within the enclosed space.

Gae slammed the door shut just as the main force of the squall hit with a physical concussion. Dark matter engulfed the old sedan, and another blistering chill expanded, creeping frost across the glass, as if searching for a way inside. Sealed within the small car, the interior temperature remained strangely warm, even without the heater running. With the side of his hand, he rubbed the window. He couldn't see far. Then, the black mist shifted, and the dog was dead, shriveled like his men, half its original size.

From the opposite direction, the dark wave ebbed back, surrounding them once again, and the coldness pressed in. No evidence of the world existed behind the great wall of foaming blackness. The auto body physically groaned, contracting from both the sudden pressure and falling temperature. The pressure within Gae's head pounded with that same unfathomable weight he had felt while at Anna Carafa's palace. He had met this dark malevolence there. Someone or something unleashed the beast.

All around them the mass swarmed in small eddies of movement, stirring and congregating, as if whatever lived in the caustic mist was sentient, studying them. Almost below the range of human hearing, whispers rippled, and at the center of that maligned consciousness was the small space where the four of them sat waiting.

Ted whispered, "There are creatures navigating the density."

"I can see them too." J.C. kept his voice low, but still it wavered with a quick flurry of nerves. "They are swimming in it as easily as a fish would swim in a river."

The pressure relaxed within Gae's inner ears a full minute before the tide withdrew toward the palace. He imagined it slipping back, under and through the support columns, where the malevolent residue collected the shadowy remains of bygone sins. These creatures were the same as what he had encountered, controlled by the cross-dimensional tide under the palace.

Some of the legends predated the glory of the Roman Empire. The Posillipo rise was warped, as was the brick and mortar standing upon it. Aidao domos, the house of Hades, was a legend bereft of details, and yet he could picture it where Palazzo Donn'Anna stood. That promontory point was evil. The rationale was beyond science or religion, but it was true.

Aleri and Fara had to be there.

Thinking of them pushed back the creeping fear. "I'm going now." Gae shoved open his door, boldly stepping onto the street. The abject silence said more than anything else ever could. The bustle of the city, the constant flow of cars and people, was more than still; it was nonexistent.

Taking a step, his boot skidded. The rain had made the street slick, floating on top of the coating of that other substance. Oil that wasn't oil.

He heard another car door open, and J.C. stepped out.

"Get back in the car! Another one is coming." Ted screeched.

Gae returned, not so much out of fear for self-preservation. He had left the gladius lying on the floorboard of the backseat. Both back doors thudded shut one after the other just in time. The wave of ill will slammed into the cab, as if the malevolence purposefully focused on breaking into their tiny fortress. The resulting shudder rattled the windows and rocked the suspension in long and shrill squeaks. Pressure continued to build, pounding inside his head. The tires blew, and the car sank down onto its rims, weary and beaten.

Dark figures approached once again, slithering through the turgid waste. When he had first encountered the woman under the palazzo, he thought her movements were snake-like. Now the manifestations were more compact and plentiful. Jesus, there were thousands of them lurking in the shadows like how leeches hide in dark water.

All four of them stared, each out of their respective windows. The forms slipped up and seemed to watch them just as curiously, placing their sucker-like mouths upon the glass. The sound was unlike anything Gae had ever heard, wet and forceful, extracting whatever living force it encountered.

A soft humming rose.

At first, he thought the creatures were trying to communicate, until the sound steadily grew within the confines of the car, matching and then exceeding the volume of the sucking smacks. Turning in tandem, each of the men stared at the gladius. The glow was radiant, challenging the darkness with its light, in a full-on battle of wits, as if this was just a game.

Using both hands Gae lifted it, and the creatures released the glass. The ebb caught them, and they flowed back toward the palace. "This is it. They can't get us as long as we have it."

Renzo sank down just a little into his seat. "Palazzo Donn'Anna is a kilometer or more. You will never make it."

"Then stay here. Someone should survive to tell the tale." J.C. slung his bag over his shoulder and grabbed the door handle. "Ready."

"Ted, I want you with us. Think you can keep up?" Gae hated the way it sounded, but the time for polite niceties was long gone.

"I'm blind, not lame. Just give me something to hold onto. I can run."

The three men emerged synchronously, each scanning the area in his own way. The thunderous squall visibly moved away from them, tumbling back toward the roiling darkness surrounding the palace.

Instead of allowing Ted the dignity to hold onto his shoulder, J.C. grabbed the man's hand and started running, and Gae realized he would have done the same thing. He flipped the sword onto his shoulder and fell into step. Now exposed to the foul air, the blade glowed even more brightly. He tried focusing straight ahead and not look at anything, but the carnage layering the streets was impossible not to notice. Desiccated corpses blocked doorways and fell out of cars. Just like bodies in Pompeii, laying where they had fallen.

While evading the bulky remains of a man and woman huddled as one, he bumped into the next car. The Fiat was small, and the motion was enough to jostle the suspension. A body with a bright yellow ribbon still clinging to its hair fell against the interior of the window. He cast a quick look to the densely packed apartment buildings and wondered if anyone remained alive.

Ted and J.C. were ahead, and he doubled his speed, catching up to them at the gate. It stood open, which sent up an internal red flag. He paused but had to keep going. The other men ran through without hesitation, and the black mass was directly ahead of them.

"Wait!" He caught up just as the blistering artic wave foamed from the pillared foundations. In a mighty swing, he leveraged the soul-laden sword over his head. J.C. spun Ted around, lifting their clasped hands to connect with the glowing metal.

"Oh my God!" Elation flooded Ted's features.

"What?" Ted and J.C. spoke over each other. "What do you see?"

"We're inside of a golden bubble. It's glorious." With the one hand still clasped upon the sword, Ted extended the other. "It's made out of tinier spheres. At first I thought they were scales, but they are golden bubbles of iridescent light."

Gae didn't see the protective sphere, only the obsidian wave. He braced for the banding pressure to attack his head, but their cocoon protected them from every ill effect.

Distantly, he heard voices, calling from somewhere below them. He looked down and nearly lost his grip on the sword. They were floating on the turgid ooze. No sense of motion attacked his senses. A stranger sense overcame him, and he wondered if that was how it felt to float prenatally in his mother's womb, secure and protected. But that peaceful serenity was short lived.

Now completely surrounded, little sticky sounds probed the exterior of their opaque cushion, and he imagined the leech-like mouths suckling against the barrier, trying to eat their way through. The sphere shimmered in response, and he finally saw what Ted had described. Millions of golden bubbles formed the radiant barrier. Then ever so slowly, silence descended, covering them like a thick blanket, and the shimmering sphere dissolved. Once again, they stood upon the gravel path, exactly where they had been.

He pointed at the flowerbed, but couldn't find the breath to explain. Even the long irises had fallen, dying in their attempt to shield their smaller brethren. Once again, the similarity to Pompeii struck him. This was a disaster of equitable proportion.

Lifting his chin, he could see all of the way to the palazzo. The shifting pitch dissolved and reformed, churning under the structure while waiting to ride the next release of the hellish tide.

Moving as one, they reach the end of the path. The ankle-deep pool was frozen, hard as rock. In another few steps, they reached the rocky escarpment.

"Wait," Ted extended his arm to block their way. "I see a woman. No, not a woman, she's something else. Dear God," his voice quavered, "it can't be."

Gae's heart thudded hard in his chest. "What is she? What do you see?"

"It has to be a trick. She looks like a mythical gorgon, a Medusa with writhing hair. She doesn't have a human body. It's about thirty feet long and slithers in sweeps."

"She's a snake?" J.C. asked a little too loudly.

"Where is she?" He whispered, elbowing J.C. in the ribs.

Ted raised a shaky hand and pointed right in front of them. His arm rose higher, and the similarities to Gae's visit just a day ago were too strong to deny.

The smallest whisper of a laugh warbled from the churning depths, and his skin stood on edge. The intelligence was calculating, biding its time while determining how to defeat them. A breath of air, not associated with the obscurity, floated past, brushing Gae's cheek.

"She just touched you." Ted uttered with wide-eyed amazement. That part Gae would have liked to have kept unspoken.

The hissing grew into prolonged words, "Come, come play with me." The sound transformed into a mad, rising laugh.

A swish encircled them, drawing the three men over the edge of the rational world. Prickles of ice crawled down Gae's spine. Another gloating laugh rippled, rising into a maniacal scream. The band of sensation crept between his legs and expanded, cupping him once again. Little pats of motion felt the edges of his penis, urging it to rise.

Gae held up the sword preemptively, explaining "The pressure of the next wave is building."

Ted looked at him steadily with those insightful blind eyes. He had to have seen everything and knew how and where the creature had touched Gae, even down to the erection he tried to avoid. Alert against the terror, he motioned toward the shifting darkness with the tip of the glowing sword. "Do we go now or wait for the next wave?"

Ted's eyes narrowed. "The mass appears to be impenetrable. If we wait until it is at the apex of its next flow, there will be less of it under there."

"But more people in town will die." J.C. looked over his shoulder back toward the patch.

Gae shivered internally knowing both men were right.

There was no warning. The wave was instantaneous, as was their shield. The shining bubble covered them. Inside his head, he started counting 1, 2, 3...

"What are you waiting for?" J.C. growled, "Fara's in there. I can feel it."

He gritted his teeth, knowing Aleri was in there as well. "Each wave's coming at expanding intervals. We have to wait at least two minutes."

Ted set a hand on J.C.'s shoulder. "He's right. We have to wait for our best chance. We'll only get one."

Closing his eyes, Gae focused on the count, using it to calm his racing mind and heart. 59, 60, 61...

Contrary sounds warbled past, screaming unearthly battle cries. Again, the flow passed under their feet, lifting them while obscuring everything. "118, 119, 120. Let's move forward, slowly. The rocks will be uneven."

As one, the three men walked forward, allowing time for the bubble to shift with them. The ground was smooth and level, apparently filled with the tarry substance. His sensible side was puzzled and suddenly doubted whether they were heading the right way when he heard voices.

Aleri's sweet soprano was recognizable, and yet not her own. Her voice carried an edge of sharp embitterment. Blistering terror and hellish rage ebbed and flowed with her chants.

Gae refused to believe his cousin might already be beyond salvation. Having to see what was happening, he lowered the sword, and the bubble thinned to a glossy veil.

Two women clad in sheer ceremonial robes faced each other with their arms outstretched. Immediately, he identified Magdalene Lucedio even with her being at least ten years younger than during their last encounter in Aleri's bedroom. The other woman had her back to him, but more than just the long blond hair gave away her identity. He would recognize his cousin at any time, in any form. Fara was nowhere in sight.

He motioned for the men to follow him to the right, and moving more quietly than he thought possible, they pressed behind the next arched column. Leaning around the stone base, he crouched lower to get a better view of what was below the women's arms. Two objects were both about the same size, not quite round, smoothly domed. Something large and dark separated them.

He leaned a little further.

Between the women's hands, a meager light spun and fluxed, glowing like a miniature star. Its pulsing light added definition to the shape of brow bones over shadowy hollows where eyes had once been. Those were the skulls from Lucia's crypt! They hadn't been destroyed. Whoever caused the explosion took care to keep them safe. They had to be integral to the resurrection spell.

The two skulls, representing Lucia and her lover, faced away from each other, one on each side of the central bulky mass. He had never believed those were their actual skulls; the stories were just too preposterous to be true. How would anyone have known their significance over four hundred years ago?

His eyes flashed to Magdalene. Had she been stealing life all that time? Was she over four hundred years old?

In about four minutes, the massive wave would contract completely, so time was of the essence. He crab-stepped forward. Accidentally, the heavy sword scraped against the stones, and his muscles contracted, preparing to fight.

The women continued chanting in ancient Latin, seemingly unaware of his presence. He picked out enough words to understand them calling forth the power of the cross tides, the power which linked birth and death to tangible life. Their voices carried lyrically, beautiful in a strange way.

Their arms suddenly swept forward, and he felt the supernatural wave contract. Their fisted hands didn't touch, except for the bulky rings. They each wore bright stones. The colors complimented each other, yellow aligned with yellow, blue with blue, and so on. He wasn't sure what kinds of stones could be so dazzling, radiating their own light.

The women's chanting rhythm remained unbroken. The low, steady sound went on and on, lifting sometimes for emphasis, falling at others to little more than a breath. On and on. Over and over. Lyrical and mesmerizing. And then without warning, a little laugh, small and gurgling, broke through the babbling. The black mass between the skulls moved.

The lump hadn't looked human until two arms lifted, twisting in motion similar to butterfly wings swimming through the air. With the next punctuated chant, a feminine chest rose, arching off from the floor.

It was Chrystal!

Her signature black on black spandex melded with the floor, adding no physical descriptors until she moved. Now in vigorous motion, she writhed, arms and legs twisting and releasing. Her back arched and knees rose.

The women's hands clapped, and the pressure increased.

CHAPTER 33

J.C. shifted to the next column. Gae was transfixed, watching two women chanting some tricked out spell, and Chrystal was getting off on it lying between them. Fara wasn't anywhere to be seen. Shit! Where was she?

"It's coming back!" Ted screamed.

J.C. sprinted to the blind man. Grabbing his hand, they rounded the column and raced to where the Italian crouched. They got their hands onto the sword just as the negative force surged under the palace.

"What in the hell are you doing?" He yelled at man, who seemed to come to his senses now they were inside the protective bubble. "Or don't you care whether we get killed or not?"

"I ... I," Gae stammered. "I wasn't thinking about that."

"That jacked up voodoo shit got to you." His chest tightened. That was about as close to total annihilation as he ever wanted to get. "Who are those women?"

"My cousin, Aleri." Gaetano motioned to the left. "That is Magdalene Lucedio."

"Lucedio! Like Lucedio Abbey? Holy shit! No wonder she's one witchy bitch. It's one of the most haunted places in the world."

Gae's available hand cradled the side of his head. "I didn't make that connection."

"That's Chrystal down there, in the middle?" Panic sharpened Ted's voice.

Gae inhaled deeply then huffed out the breath. He just stood there, staring blankly.

A Dios! Both hombres were losing it. "Did you see Fara?"

Neither answered his question.

"Let's lower the sword just enough to see what's happening." Ted relaxed his muscles, and the weight of the steel sank until the hilt was about even with J.C.'s chin.

He still couldn't see shit. "Do you see anything, Ted?"

"Oh yeah, but I don't understand. Two women are overlapping inside of one body. She's young, maybe twenty max. The spirit who's trying to possess her is royal blue, old, old power, and yet there're other colors. All of the human chakra colors are bending around her like a rainbow that's been tied into a pretzel." He swallowed, and then added, "Chrystal is on the floor between them. She's fighting the power. The leading edge of the power-" He just stopped talking.

"What? Ted come-on." J.C. steeled himself for the answer.

"It's penetrating her body," he dropped his eyes, "into every orifice. Packing the negative force inside of her."

Now, he saw it, too. Unrelenting dark tendrils whipped around the gravity of the miniature star and thrust into Chrystal's body. Just as Ted described, black matter poured into every opening. Agony filled him as he watched her writhe against the force. No one deserved that treatment, not even Chrystal.

The levitating coils twisted around her, covering her body from head to toe like some perverted mummy. The vines kinked and spiraled, gaining form and mass. The embodiment of the gorgon grew out of the gnarled curls and curves. Like a giant python, she was squeezing the very life from Chrystal. As if it was some type of machine, the pressure transformed Chrystal's life force into a glittering mist emanating from the snakes' mouths writhing on the Gorgon's head.

J.C. had expected for the women to drag on the serpent's heads like a hookah, but instead, the radiant force rose, feeding the miniscule star. The ball spun and grew, just like what he saw on the video tape. That time, Father Dominic's soul fed the spell. That was where the tape ended. He didn't know what happened next, but whatever it was hadn't been good.

The snake-woman slithered back from whence she came, leaving Chrystal naked and exposed. Even with her life force so depleted, she still tried to struggle.

"What's left of the tide is out." Ted's voice brought him back.

In a startling burst of speed, Gae sprinted forward, brandishing the sword. In a move classic to a gladiatorial contest, he slashed the blade from the base of Magdalene's neck down to the other side of her waist. The angle and depth had to have sliced her through the heart.

She didn't fall. She didn't even turn. The ceremony continued uninterrupted.

Jumping back into a battle stance, he aimed and slashed again, this time to sever her head. Again, the blade passed cleanly through her. No blood. Nothing. Magdalene Lucedio had no physical form.

The realization flickered over Gaetano's face. He took a step toward his cousin and faltered. And yet, she didn't hesitate. Aleri's hand was pale yet luminous. The one finger without a ring pointed, and a slash of power hit him straight in the chest. He flew backwards, crashing into an adjacent pillar, crumpling at its base.

Perhaps there was an alternate plan, but J.C. took the one rolling out ahead of him. In a burst, he ran forward, seizing the blade. His hand flew into his pocket and pulled out the golden perfume bottle. With a flick of his thumb, the lid rattled off into the distance, but he didn't care about the gold. The contents were much more precious. Carefully, as to not spill a drop, he poured the condensed frankincense onto the ancient metal.

Directly in front of him, Chrystal's body gave up its battle and fell, a desiccated lump, just like the countless others across the city. The last of her life force joined the glowing sphere, which was now huge, like a bloated tick, nearly filling the space between the two women. The blackness churned overhead, spinning into a funnel.

Holy shit! J.C. had witnessed that before. They were all going straight to hell because Fara wasn't here to save them. It meant only one thing. That icy thought took root in his chest and tightened around his heart. They had killed Fara before Chrystal. That would be the only reason she wasn't here.

Not wanting to live without her, his fist tightened around the grip of the gladius. Reacting to the deepest love for his woman lost, the sword blazed with life, humming like a Jedi's light saber.

Ahead of him, the women thrust their hands into the spinning ball, and their rings discharged the accumulated luminosity. At the polar top of the sphere, the tip of the funnel connected. Instead of funneling the souls out of the glowing ball, the opposite happened. All of the harvested energy sank into the globe. Agonized screeches echoed between the structural supports, filling it with the wails of thousands as the sphere consumed their eternal souls.

The women's heads fell back. Arms spread. The whirling ball stretched, darkening with the black putrescence, sagging heavier and heavier. They strained against the force, leaning ever further until their backs would break.

The gladius in J.C.'s hand grew hot. It glowed like the sun while the orb started to shrink, condensing back upon itself. Caught in its gravitational flow, the blade drew him forward, flying toward the putrid black ball of its own accord. His feet left the ground, and he braced his grip upon the gladius, hand over hand. For being such a short distance, he felt each and every inch, as inevitable as if he was flying through deep space toward a black hole.

Knowing his life was soon to be over, he wanted his last rational thought to be of Fara. He remembered the first time he saw her, leaning against the outer wall of Fort San Cristobal. The way the light struck her hair was glorious. The slight sheen of perspiration glazed her caramel skin. One knee twisted open, and the flap in her wrapped dress caught the breeze, exposing her thighs. And yet, even with all of that feminine perfection, her emerald eyes were her most dazzling feature. They absolutely glistened with inner power. Those eyes were his salvation.

The sword punctured the orb, and the world exploded.

CHAPTER 34

Picking himself up, Ted wiped his gritty palms on his trousers and then rubbed his eyes. Impossible. This was beyond the natural laws of mankind.

The very essence of life flowed, suffusing the environment that had only known darkness with light, heavenly light. Tens of thousands of souls poured out of the hole the gladius created in the unholy sphere, along with the countless souls now freed from the sword. Their ethereal forms intermingled, glowing with a power beyond comprehension. The force was so bright, he had to look away.

A flicker of green aural light flashed beyond the next pillar.

Shielding his eyes with a forearm, Ted squinted, as if that would help him see what was beyond the range of human comprehension. The green glow was fading.

He bolted toward the column. Crumpled behind its base was the physical body of Faradahl Alecto Trotter. The hilt of a bejeweled dagger extended from her chest. Other than being dead, the body was normal, not desiccated like Chrystal or the countless others. But the corpse wasn't the source of the aural light. Fara's unique soul hovered, still protecting her remains from the effects of the black scourge.

"J.C., Gaetano!" Ted screamed over the maelstrom of swirling light and screaming sound. Through the resulting chaos, he didn't see their aural signatures. Realistically, that meant both men had to be dead.

He knelt next to the corpse. Throughout the past several days, he'd gained a deep appreciation for the woman whom he had never met, at least not in her complete form. Fara Trotter was an anomaly, a woman of legend, and he was the only one left alive to tell the story of her amazing life.

Holding out his hand toward the failing green shimmer, he slowly extended his arm. The glow wrapped around his hand in the way his sister had described cotton candy spinning around a paper cone. The emerald light twisted and collected, creeping inside of his senses with a warm contentment. His mind filled with a single smooth thought, the texture of a silken thread. "Take my body to the collector of souls."

Ted gathered her physical form into his arms. The great Faradahl was delicate, so much smaller than her incredible deeds, but he knew how the strength of spirit had nothing to do with the limitations of the body. She was and would always be the Amazing Alecto.

Tears crested his eyes, blurring his psychic vision in a way he had never experienced. He continued walking, carrying her dead body toward the light, now glowing more brightly than any star within the heavens.

At the edge of the immense radiance, a large man stood, the blue spirit whom Ted had seen in the library of Gaetano's home. He waved his arms, resulting in a gentle wind, and with the current, the entity guided all of the confused souls to divine freedom.

Adrenaline coursed through Ted's body, and his heart pounded rapidly as if ready to burst through his ribs. No one alive had ever witnessed this transformation of the spirit unto the divine. He might even survive to tell the tale, but no one would believe him fully without evidence. A moan almost left his lips, but the situation was unavoidable. He knew the truth, and that would have to be enough.

The collector nodded toward him and waved his other arm in a broad sweep. Light flowed like a whip from his fingertips, and the resulting blue cord curled around Ted's legs then drew him forward to the edge of the mass of light that he could best describe as a white star, for it contained the entire spectrum of light.

The blue cord released him, and Fara's body eased out of his grip. She began to float toward the stream of souls. Instead of joining the flow, the blue man's enveloping force set her under the churning sphere where Chrystal had once been.

The man knelt and picked up the skulls from Lucia's crypt, one in each hand. A thoughtful look crossed his features as he weighed the skulls, then he placed one directly under the flowing mass next to Fara's prone body. The other he dropped to the ground and stomped on it until he reduced it to a blanket of ash.

With a twisting sweep of his hand, the green soul unwrapped from Ted's hand, but instead of flowing toward the light, the power drifted away from the central activity. It illuminated a backpack, whose contents had haphazardly spilt across the stone floor. Fara's life force snaked inside the inner fold and retrieved another skull. The green luminescence highlighted the smooth curves of the cranium and delicately stroked the apparent crack on the left side.

Effortlessly, the wisp of green returned to the blue man and placed the skull into his outstretched hands. Once again, Ted expected Fara's soul to join the others, and once again, he was surprised. Her radiant form avoided the gravitational pull and slipped under the mass, coating her body. The collector set the skull on the opposite side. The two now flanked her, facing her in the same way as the original skulls had faced Chrystal.

The blue man recovered the gladius and pointed its tip at the hilt of the dagger still protruding from Fara's heart. Power connected in a brilliant flash. Like a live wire exposed to water, the entire atmosphere sizzled until all of the remaining force from the gladius transferred into the dagger.

Ted had seen the combined luminosity of binary systems in the night sky. Their energy signatures looked like a puffy figure eight. The symbol for the power of infinity was the figure eight, and he now understood why. In that same pattern, the arc of power once again flowed, but now from the dagger and into the two ancient skulls.

Building from the very basic blocks of life, bones elongated. First, the spine added vertebra by vertebra. From seemingly nothing, ribs budded and curved while the shoulders and hips fanned into place. Spindly limbs extended, pale and fragile. The complete skeleton was only a flash before white tendons and red muscles formed, wrapping around the bones and joining them to another. Spun from unseen silken webs, skin covered the finalized infrastructure. For a moment, both looked to be little more than a male and female depiction of department store mannequins, at least until features developed and hair lengthened. Within a span of maybe a minute, no longer than two, Mercede de las Torres and Gaetano di Casapesenna had materialized.

Recognizing each other, smiles lit their faces. Not even glancing at their surroundings, their fingers embraced over Fara's still and prone body. As if knowing exactly what to do, they grabbed the dagger together and withdrew the blade. Long drops of Fara's blood flew upward into the writhing electrical mass, and the pure light exploded upon contact.

Ted flew backwards and landed hard against a pillar, hitting the back of his head, but he remained conscious. Harsh pain pushed everything from his mind except for that excruciating sensation. His eyes burned, and fast tears flowed down his face, dripping from his chin.

Slowly as if in a dream, his sight returned. From the angle of his body and the layers of pillars, he was able to see the blue man, but his soul had lost his blue glow. Now he appeared as a man, who was gazing down upon Gaetano's prone body. Kneeling, he straightened the younger man's limbs then gently swept the hair from his face. The similarities between the two were uncanny. He had to be Don Lazarus, Gaetano's father. With a contented smile, he patted his son's cheek and returned to the circle.

The ball of light had collapsed smaller still, yet it remained hovering in the center of a clean circle in the perfect center of the palace's supports. Don Lazarus stepped inside the circle and slid upon a single knee, extending his hand to the woman who laid directly under the undulating orb. She stretched out her arm and delicate fingers, and he touched his forehead to the back of her hand then helped her to her feet. She was nude but didn't try to cover herself.

Together they stood over the place where the ghost of Anna Carafa still clung to the body of Aleri, refusing to release the girl. Lazarus removed the rings from her fingers, and Fara put them on one at a time, in the order of the highest to the basest chakras. Each time, the ring blazed as it connected with Fara's green aura, and with each emanation, Anna Carafa huddled even more desperately within Aleri.

Lazarus and Fara joined hands, chanting the resurrection spell, but in reverse. The moments of high intensity became nearly silent, and they punctuated the low moments. When they released their joined hands, the synchronous clap drew Anna's soul out of Aleri's body.

Don Lazarus lunged, encircling his arms around the aged soul in a shade of such a dark blue it almost looked black. Squeezing with a strength akin her gorgon beast, he compressed her form. With one more thrust of his powerful arms, the purgatorial serpent popped through the top of her embittered soul. A strange feeling of contentment filled Ted while watching her struggle against the inevitable current that she had avoided for at least four hundred years, but something told him the beast had been ravaging this spot since the beginning of time. She had just learned how to tap into its power and control it.

"What happened?" The gravelly voice wasn't discernible.

Ted struggled to his feet. His body was sluggish, and he had to concentrate on moving his legs one at a time. Once he neared the man who was struggling to rise, Ted realized he was seeing flesh, not spirit. He blinked several times and refocused. For the first time in his life, he saw what had to be the physical world.

The man on the floor rolled onto his stomach and pushed up onto all fours. "Ted? Gae?" A groan of pain accompanied pushing his way to his knees.

The tight green aura still coated his body, yet Ted saw the physical man at the same time. J.C. Calderon had tanned skin and cropped black hair. His brown eyes landed on Ted, and his face twisted. "Ted! You're alive."

A smile twisted his lips. "I'm not the only one." He motioned toward Fara, who was holding the marble-sized ball of deep red light in her palm.

CHAPTER 35

Cogito ergo sum. I think; therefore, I am. Fara had pondered Rene Descartes' philosophical concept while trapped within Purgatorio ad Arco. She doubted the philosopher ever thought about applying the statement to the dead. But dead wasn't really dead. The soul still lived. Sentience continued. While without a body, she did think. Therefore, she existed. She was and would always be, for the soul was eternal.

Another revelation was that ghosts were much more common than she previously thought, yet most of them were unable to hold onto their personal reality. Over time, details faded until only the most vibrant memories remained, which they repeated over and over again. Don Lazarus Caravaggio was one of the lucky ones, but in truth, he had been dead a scant four years, which was nothing in comparison to the souls who had been corralled like spiritual cattle since 1643.

Everything Guy had said about his father being a benefactor of the city had been accurate. Fara's soul had been there during the bombings of World War II. Don Lazarus led the city's residents to safety underground. He was the one who discovered the hole in the wall and used it to siphon water out of the aqueduct. Also, the discovery of the secret handholds scaling the walls allowed him to scavenge food and medicine. Lazarus was a decent man who lived during troubled times and rebuilt the city out of the ashes of war using whatever means were necessary. Now Guy was doing the same, only in a different, modernized way. Lazarus understood that; at least she thought he did. But she wasn't able to ask. His was the final spirit to cross through the open portal.

Although Fara knew the soul continued after death, she still didn't understand where the souls went once they crossed over. One thing was for certain, it had to be better than subsisting in earthbound purgatory filled with endless darkness.

The flashing lights of emergency vehicles lit the night sky over the Posillipo rise; a sight she had never expected to see ever again. She touched the window. This is where she had stood in two separate times, within two different bodies. But now, she was exactly where she needed to be. She was back in her present, in her body. It was a little worse for wear, but there wasn't any other body where she'd rather be, scars and all. She fingered the newest addition on the upper side of her left breast. The jeweled dagger had killed her, and in some weird way, played a part in her physical resurrection. She didn't understand exactly what had happened, and maybe she didn't want to. Some details were better left undiscovered, just like the details of the disaster.

On the other side of the living room, the television news kept repeating the same announcements, calling the black cloud an environmental disaster, because no one had ever seen anything like what had happened. The only real updates were for the mounting death toll. "1,643 residents and counting-"

The number tumbled in her mind. 1643 in itself was significant, but the why still evaded her. What had the year, the number, and recent events in common?

She turned away from the window. 1643 had nearly doubled the previous figure. Had all of those souls been consumed or freed? Now, she had a very different perspective on that question. Each held distinct implications.

"This is the worst disaster to hit the Italian coast, rivaling the historic eruption of Mount Vesuvius in 79 AD. Government officials have declared the Posillipo rise a disaster area. All of the inhabitants within a two kilometer radius are presumed dead. No survivors have yet been discovered. It is as if the promontory point was incinerated, but there are no remnants of radiation or other known contaminates. So far, the cause remains a mystery. Tonight, joining us on the scene is Target News reporter Marcela Baroque." The TV news cut from the studio to a live feed.

A slender reporter rounded the front end of a police car and grabbed Guy's left arm, sticking a microphone in his face in the same smooth motion; the intense expression would have set any other woman running, except for a reporter.

Fara chuckled in spite of the seriousness of the situation. She knew exactly how it felt to be in Marcela's shoes, and she would have done the same thing. With a quick breath, she dropped her head back, and it bumped into the window with a hollow thud. Thank God, she wasn't the one out there tonight. She was right where she needed to be, when she needed to be. A shaky hand gripped the window sill, just to keep a hold on reality, reminding herself the nightmare was over. This was real, not one of her myriad fantasies of being able to return to the world of the living. All of those years of preparation had finally come to fruition. For a time, it never seemed as if today would never come, and when it did, she returned to find her body murdered.

If she hadn't sabotaged Magdalene Lucedio's plans from within the crypt-?

She stopped herself. Second guessing her actions would not affect current circumstances. There was no way to change historic events. She knew that all too well. This was no indelible part of history.

Guy's face filled the screen, and his eyes narrowed into his most intimidating steely gaze.

The reporter's eyes widened then glanced over her shoulder, as if expecting someone or something else to be there. "Don Caravaggio, these emergency crews had never seen anything like this. They have described it as a fire that only burned the living-human, plant, and animal alike. The first speculation of the cloud being nuclear has already been dismissed. Any ideas on what could have caused such a catastrophic disaster?"

His lips were pressed into a thin line, nearly devoid of color. The intensity of his expression darkened the hollows under his cheekbones and eyes. With his right hand, he absently pushed the hair out of his face and looked straight into the camera's lens. Fara felt as if he was looking straight at her, as if he was blaming this all on her. "At this time, the best theory is that Mount Vesuvius vented poisonous gas through an underground channel somewhere off the coast. The prevailing winds blew it toward Naples. At least it dissipated rather quickly. The destruction seems to have affected a radius limited to the Posillipo rise."

"How would poisonous gas cause such desiccation of the bodies in a matter of seconds?"

"I don't know. I'm not a scientist. Like I said, it's just a theory. Experts are assessing the details and will reach some determination soon." Guy perked his head and nodded to someone in the distance, as if one of those experts had just called his name. Even though he looked exhausted, he hadn't lost his flair for dramatics. "Excuse me, Marcie, and don't follow me again." He ducked behind the caution tape and walked into a yellow nest of emergency workers in hazardous waste suits.

"Marcie?" Fara mumbled the name aloud. Apparently, Guy knew that woman on a personal level. The thought tightened her stomach, but just as she had other lovers, so had Guy. After all, fair was fair.

The woman stopped abruptly next to the flapping yellow plastic and turned back to the cameraman, who abruptly halted, as if expecting her to continue. The camera fought to focus, and just as it did, her eyes grew a little too wide. "You just heard from Don Gaetano Caravaggio of Caravaggio Security Systems who is assisting with the coordination of emergency crews. The most recent theory is a cloud of acidic vapor released from Mount Vesuvius through an underground vent and blew over the Posillipo rise. All roads are closed to non-emergency vehicles. Stay in your homes and pray this nightmare is over. This is Marcela Baroque reporting on what's being called the worst natural disaster on Italian soil since the eruption that eradicated Pompeii."

Fara growled at the TV. "Any reporter worth being on camera would have followed him."

"You would have, even if you were told not to." The feminine voice resonated with a familiarity few ever truly appreciated. Mercede knew Fara more intimately than anyone. Just as Fara knew Mercede. They took the phrase *walking in another's shoes* to a whole new level.

"A reporter's job is to be a nuisance and go places where she doesn't belong."

"You must have been an excellent … reporter." Mercede grinned, but then turned back toward the television. "This century is filled with amazing inventions. I don't know how Gaetano and I ended up here."

Fara shrugged. "You deserve a life together."

"It comes with a price." Mercede looked squarely in Fara's eyes, and something within them connected.

"Which we both have agreed to fulfill." She shrugged and turned her attention back to the swirling lights wondering where Guy was in the sea of emergency personnel. "It's my destiny after all. It's what I was put on this earth to do. Perhaps when the day of my death comes, my karmic debt will be paid for using my talents," she paused, "for contrary purposes."

"Of that I have no doubt. The scales of just and unjust are tipped in your favor, my dear Fara, but that is not what I meant. I still feel you within me and know of your indecision." Mercede motioned to the television. "You love them both."

Swiveling, Fara looked carefully at the woman, yet knew there was nothing she could ever hide from her. They had shared too much to conceal even the slightest detail. "There is no decision that I can make without hurting them."

"You love your Gaetano."

"Yes."

"You love Juan Carlos."

"You know I do, which adds to my responsibility. I can't ask either of them to follow me down this path."

"Of course not. This be a responsibility we share. Anytime, anywhere. I shall know when you require assistance, and I will be there. It is our price, not theirs. So, it should not influence your decision."

"The very nature of the promise is the decision." Fara nodded. "I didn't mean-"

Her perfect princess profile turned toward the door and smiled at her Gaetano and J.C. as they walked into the room. "One I will gladly pay for even one more night with the man I love." She dropped her voice, "And one I would suggest you heed as well." Mercede leaned in closer and whispered, "Why can't a woman love two men?" She slowly approached her one true love and drew him without a word toward the staircase.

J.C. remained in his classic pose of leaning one shoulder in the door frame. "You should come to bed, if only to sleep in my arms."

"I'm not ready to close my eyes. I'm not sure if I will ever be able to sleep again."

"'To die, to sleep-no more-and by a sleep to say we end. The heartache, and the thousand natural shocks that flesh is heir to. 'Tis a consummation devoutly to be wish'd. To die, to sleep-to sleep-perchance to dream.'"

She nodded slowly as her heart warmed. J.C. always did something to surprise her. He was a complex man of many layers and talents. "When did you learn to quote Shakespeare?"

"We had a shoot in Denmark, and our actor kept missing his line. We all had it memorized by the twentieth take." His lopsided grin warmed that part of her still cold from the unyielding darkness. "Come to bed, Fara. I'll stay awake and watch over you. Make sure you stay safe."

Her head shook a little too fast, making the edge of the headache return.

"I promise to wake you if the Gorgon returns or soul-sucking leeches appear in the skies."

"That's not funny."

"It wasn't intended to be." He nodded slowly. "I made a promise as well."

"How much did you hear?"

"Most, but I only understood a fraction." As if approaching some injured wild animal, he stepped closer very slowly and cautiously. Perhaps that was exactly what she was. "I love you Fara. That's not something that will just go away, and because of it, I won't go away. Although I don't like thinking about you loving another man, I hate the idea of losing you even more. I'm patient. We will get through this together." He extended his hand, and the emerald ring glimmered in the swirling lights.

The ring on her own finger heated, drawing her forward, and she placed her hand within his.

EPILOGUE

The microphone was live. Fara angled her body just enough to limit the hiss of the wind; even though, J.C. had covered the mic with a foam muffler. The warm touch of the sun caressed her cheek, and she took just a moment to appreciate the sensation. The warmth entered her words along with her compelling intonation. "Just behind the Mediterranean breeze, or perhaps carried in the very fingers of its gusts, an unmistakable murmur drifts over the surface of the blue water. Even a practical man could construe the sound as the lyricism of a siren." She extended her hand in a practiced sweep, and just as they rehearsed, the cameraman followed to shoot the small island just off the shore. "Off the coast of Naples Italy is where the legendary Odysseus ordered his men to tie him to the mast of his ship, for him to hear the siren's song without consequence."

Fara walked into frame. "Every sailor's tale has some anchor in the truth, and this legend has persisted across millennia. That was how Palazzo Donn'Anna gained its traditional name of the Syren's Palace.

"It's most infamous owner, Anna Carafa, lived for unyielding ambition which gave her everything but happiness. She died on a dark and stormy night in October 1645, shortly after her husband abandoned her and returned to Spain. The infamous princess was alone, poor, and friendless at the end of her life. Still, she wanted more.

"Our story begins there. In an unhealthy isolation, the soul is without incentive, and the mind without ideals. Anna haunted her palace in unrelenting pursuit of two lovers, ghost lovers. Rumors still exist of Gaetano di Casapesenna and Mercede de las Torres continuing the romantic plot first initiated in the theatrical "comedia" play, which sealed true love's first kiss. Yet after that innocent consummation at the heart of the Siren's Palace, they forever seek each other's embrace. But the palace has many hearts, and most beat with the pulse of iniquity. And the ravaging legend grows.

"Since beginning this episode of *Ghost Lovers*, a devastating acidic cloud descended upon Anna Carafa's ancestral home, along with the more modern developments built nearby upon the Posillipo rise. We salute those who have gone before us and dedicate this program to them.

"Yet though sadness trims the stage, today's story brings hope of love everlasting. *Ghost Lovers* takes you to witness Mercede and Gaetano's lines of undying love. No truer words have ever been spoken." Fara smiled, but not quite at the camera.

J.C. stood to the side and returned her acknowledgement with a nod.

"Love is the most precious resource that mankind has. It is the one aspect of our existence that continues long after the physical body has died, not gold or fame. Just love lives on, into the next realm, for true love is eternal." She turned full on to the camera lens and watched it constrict for the extreme close-up, "The love bonding Gaetano and Mercede is fraught with churlish lies and deceptions, of murder and vengeance. Anna Carafa wanted, no, she demanded those basic threads binding the lovers to one another, and in doing do, caught her own selfish enmity in the web of her construction. Watch and be wary, and learn from her mistakes, for the story you are about to see reveals truths that live within everyone's own selfish needs. Selfish and love do not, cannot resonate, for the foundation of true love is giving total trust to another. The foundations of the infamous palace harbored the antithesis of the basic pulse of lifelong love, and therefore embodied the opposite. Death, destruction, murder, and vice accumulated under those very pillars. *Ghost Lovers* takes you to that dark world where love provides the only light of salvation."

The red light on top of the camera winked out, and she lowered the microphone, inhaling a glorious deep breath of the fresh Mediterranean air. Her lungs expanded fully and easily, enjoying the simple pleasure. Life pulsed through her veins with the steady beat of her heart. But she wasn't the only one feeling the full-bodied intensity of glorious life.

Behind the set on the back roof of the rental house, Mercede and Gaetano stood with one arm wrapped around the other, pointing with a childlike excitement at the monitor. "May we see that again?"

J.C. waved them forward. "Sure, as many times as you want. But remember, this isn't the final product. At the end of taping the segment, I send this raw footage to the studio for editing, where they take the best bits and pieces to recombine them into a finished product."

"Finished product," Mercede repeated.

"That product is your story. Over a million viewers will know how much you and Gaetano love each other." Fara eased toward the group, yet stopped in advance of reaching them. "It may take some time, but I'm sure you will adjust to the 21st century?"

Mercede met her glance and knowingly nodded. "Of course we will."

"They'll have a place with me and Aleri for as long as they wish." Guy patted Gaetano on the back of his shoulder, but his eyes remained on Fara. "After today's shooting concludes, why don't you join us for dinner?"

Fara shook her head and took a step back, distancing herself. "I haven't found my appetite." She inflected the words to hold a dual meaning, hoping both Guy and J.C. would understand. She loved two men, of course in different ways, but both held pieces of her heart. True love was where you dared to love someone more than you love yourself, and both men proved their love by laying down their lives to save hers.

Facing the sea, she beheld the beauty and serenity, but those feelings didn't enter her heart. Four hundred years as a ghost locked within a magical crypt aged her. Both experiences lived inside of her mind, those she discovered as Mercede and those Mercede lived as Fara. She needed time to sort through all of the encounters. Her hand slipped into her pocket and felt the gold decanter. The red orb containing the quintessence of psychic power heated the confines of its perfect prison. She was now its keeper and would be for the rest of her days.

THE END

A Special Preview of *Ghost Spell* – *Ghost Lovers* Book 4

Regardless of wealth or piety, the ensnared ghosts are all damned until someone shows them the way. They don't realize salvation is possible until Fara Trotter's misplaced soul provides the only light within the imposed darkness. Princess Anna Carafa contrives the purgatorial prison with her mystical accomplice, Magdalene Lucedio. Their spell seals the Cult of the Dead, and Anna guards her spiritual fortress, coveting the day when the enslaved energy reaches critical mass for her to live again. Yet, every prison has a weakness.

Ghost Spell coming in 2013.